Faith-Filled Fiction™

www.faith-filledfiction.com | www.vikkikestell.com

A Prairie Heritage, Book 9

Books by Vikki Kestell

A Prairie Heritage
Book 1: *A Rose Blooms Twice*
Book 2: *Wild Heart on the Prairie*
Book 3: *Joy on This Mountain*
Book 4: *The Captive Within*
Book 5: *Stolen*
Book 6: *Lost Are Found*
Book 7: *All God's Promises*
Book 8: *The Heart of Joy—A Short Story*
Book 9: *Rose of RiverBend*

Girls from the Mountain
Book 1: *Tabitha*
Book 2: *Tory*
Book 3: *Sarah Redeemed*

Laynie Portland
Book 1: *Laynie Portland, Spy Rising—The Prequel*
Book 2: *Laynie Portland, Retired Spy*
Book 3: *Laynie Portland, Renegade Spy*
Book 4: *Laynie Portland, Spy Resurrected*

Nanostealth
Book 1: *Stealthy Steps*
Book 2: *Stealth Power*
Book 3: *Stealth Retribution*
Book 4: *Deep State Stealth*, 2019 Selah Award Winner
Book 5: *Stealth Insurgence*, December 2, 2021

Rose of RiverBend

ISBN-13: 978-1-970120-27-1

A Prairie Heritage, Book 9
by Vikki Kestell

Fall 1923

After a thirteen-year absence, Rose Thoresen is returning to her beloved RiverBend. It may well be her final visit.

Edmund O'Dell, Rose's son-in-law, has accepted the job as head of the Chicago Pinkerton office. As he prepares to move his family from Denver to Chicago, Rose faces a difficult decision: Will she continue at Palmer House where she has led many fallen women to Christ and mentored them in their faith, or will she give up this ministry and follow her daughter and grandchildren to their new home?

I am seventy-four years old, Lord, and I believe that the work you entrusted to me when we founded Palmer House should now pass to Sarah and Olive. By your grace, Lord God, they are ready to assume this great and wonderful responsibility. I pray you make them fruitful branches in your kingdom, always abiding in the vine, Christ Jesus.

As for me? I will go with Joy and her family to Chicago and pour what love, strength, and time I have left into Joy, Edmund, and their children.

Rose asks only one thing of her son-in-law. "Edmund, when we take the train east, I would like to stop in RiverBend and spend several days there. I have not seen my friends and Jan's family in many years."

Not since Jan left us and entered heaven.

O'Dell readily agrees to Rose's request, and as they prepare to leave Denver, they must say goodbye to many friends.

As the train chugs into RiverBend's little station, Rose knows the time she spends here will be filled with cherished memories, the sweet entwined with the bittersweet.

Father, thank you for the precious days before me. In them all, please help me to love without measure and bring glory to your name.

Hymns

Trust and Obey
John H. Sammis and
Daniel B. Towner, 1887.
Public Domain

What a Friend We Have in Jesus
Joseph Medlicott Scriven, 1855.
Public Domain

I Surrender All
Judson W. Van DeVenter and
Winfield S. Weeden, 1896.
Public Domain

Scripture Quotations

The King James Version (KJV)
Public Domain

Dedication

To those in the Body of Christ
who have given their all.
All to thee, my Blessed Savior,
I surrender all.

Acknowledgements

My ongoing thanks to my wonderful team,
Cheryl Adkins and Greg McCann.
We have been together since 2013, eight years now.
Greg and Cheryl have dedicated themselves
to helping me produce the very best
Christ-centered books I can offer,
all to the glory of Christ.
Much love to you both.

To My Readers

This book is a work of fiction,
what I term Faith-Filled Fiction™.
While the characters and events are fictional,
they are situated within the historical record.
To God be the glory.

Cover Design

Vikki Kestell

The Descendants of Jan and Rose Thoresen

As followed in the series, *A Prairie Heritage*

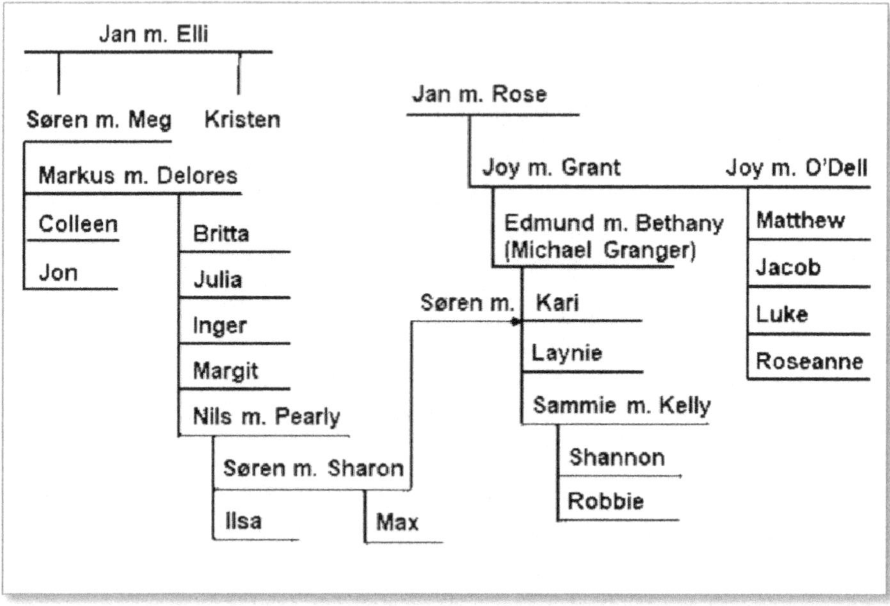

CHAPTER 1

DENVER,
EARLY OCTOBER 1923

Palmer House's dining room was overfilled that Monday evening—not that dining at Palmer House ever boasted much in the way of surplus elbow room. With seventeen in residence, the evening meal was always a sizable affair. Two long tables, set end-to-end to form a single extended table, was the customary arrangement.

However, for this special occasion, Palmer House's cook, Marit, had requested that her husband, Billy, and Sarah's husband, Bryan Croft, fetch a third table from storage to accommodate the overflow.

Overflow? Twenty-six individuals crowded around the usual dining configuration. In addition to the everyday household adults—Rose Thoresen, Billy and Marit, Bryan and Sarah, and ten young women—the dinner also hosted dear friends Pastor Isaac and Breona Carmichael, Minister Yaochuan Min and Mei-Xing Liáng, Mason and Tabitha Carpenter, and frail Mr. Wheatley, who now lived with the Carpenter family where they could offer him the loving care he required.

Edmund and Joy O'Dell were the last couple at the lengthy but crowded table. Their newborn daughter, Roseanne, slumbered in the crook of Joy's left arm, oblivious to the world around her. Joy was seated to the right of her mother, an arrangement that allowed Rose to peer down upon the four-week-old infant's peak of dark hair and occasionally stroke her velvety cheeks.

The adult diners were joined by Will, the older of Billy and Marit's two boys, and Shan-Rose, Yaochuan Min and Mei-Xing Liáng's daughter, who, at the ages of nearly fifteen and thirteen respectively, insisted they were "too mature to dine at the children's table."

Children's table? Indeed! A dozen children, ranging in age from three through eleven years, occupied the third table. Billy had, some years earlier, reduced the table's height to accommodate the shorter stature of the "little nippers." Billy and Bryan had set the table near the dining room's bay window, several feet from the adult table, where the youngsters' antics, if not too boisterous, might escape their parents' attention.

The young ones assigned to the children's table grinned in delight, surreptitiously kicked one another under the table, and wriggled with barely restrained excitement.

Even though their families dined at Palmer House on a regular basis, the invitations generally alternated between the other families so that the numbers never exceeded the dining room's capacity. Only on high holidays such as Thanksgiving and Christmas were their families all together and the youngsters seated at their own separate table—to their immense delight.

The present gathering was not a holiday, however, and although the children sensed that the gathering marked a special occasion, it was likely that they did not yet comprehend how momentous an event it was.

Bryan Croft prayed a blessing over the food, Marit's helpers served the platters, bowls, and dishes that had been kept hot in the oven, and thirty-eight hungry diners tucked in to the feast set before them.

Happy chatter accompanied the meal as the several families present caught up with their friends' busy lives and shared their hearts with one another. Their conversation, often laced with humor and joyous laughter, was designed to include and draw out the young ladies of Palmer House.

A few of this number were too newly arrived to feel truly welcome—*yet*. It generally took time and the development of trust for them to grow into a sense of "belonging" to Palmer House's family.

Such an occasion was never complete, however, without one of Mr. Wheatley's tall (and quite memorable) tales. His whispery recitations left the newer young ladies goggle-eyed and the more familiar girls giggling and chortling behind their napkins. Indeed, it was Mr. Wheatley's great pleasure to charm Palmer House's girls and tease them into shy, dimpling smiles.

Only minutes in Mr. Wheatley's company assured the young ladies that they had nothing to fear from this kindly—and somewhat eccentric—old gent, whose sparse tufts of white hair waved like a display of miniature flags atop and around his head.

The diners within earshot gave patient and loving attention to Mr. Wheatley's oration. Most understood that their dear old friend, whose age was approaching ninety years, had few such opportunities ahead of him. They honored him with their thoughtful consideration.

As the empty plates were taken away, Marit excused herself, then reappeared bearing a large three-layered chocolate cake. The diners—particularly the children—clapped their hands with enthusiasm.

Marit sliced the cake, and her helpers served portions to all. When everyone had their dessert before them, a profound hush fell. Forks clinked on mismatched china plates. Appreciative sighs followed the first bite. The children smacked their chocolate-smeared lips and grinned. And the adults praised Marit's creation from first taste to last speck.

Over coffee and cake and as the dessert plates emptied, the adults spoke of anything but the reason for this evening's celebration . . . until it could be put off no longer.

Dinner conversation wound down, and a stillness crept over the adults. The quiet was pronounced enough to catch the attention of the children at the other table. They noticed the shift in the atmosphere and lapsed into watchful silence.

Pastor Carmichael spoke into the general malaise. "Marit, we thank you, and we thank your helpers, Gracie and Liza, for a marvelous meal. What can compare to sitting down to wonderful food accompanied by the love and good fellowship of close friends?"

He sighed. "However, I suppose we must now address this evening's purpose, as loath as we all are to do so."

Most eyes were downcast, but a few solemn nods answered him.

Carmichael swallowed down the lump in his throat. "Speaking of the love and good fellowship of close friends . . . Ed, Joy, and Miss Rose? You must surely know how sorely you will be missed. We . . . we can scarcely bear that you are leaving us and that it may be . . . years before we see all of you again."

Heads around the table bobbed in agreement, and all pretense that this evening could compare to any other vanished. Eyes glistened with tears. The men at the table, the effort to master their emotions too great, shifted in their seats and cleared their throats.

The children stared at their parents as they weighed Pastor Carmichael's words and tried to understand why emotions were running high among the adults. Red-haired Sally Carpenter, a forthright child of ten years, could abide the tension no longer. "Mum? *Mum!* Where's Grandma Rose a-goin'?"

Tabitha softly answered, "We have talked about this, Sally, remember? Grandma Rose is moving to Chicago with Uncle Ed and Aunt Joy. They will leave on the train tomorrow."

"Wot? Leave on the train? *Tomorrer?*" Sally's objection, already expressed at an unacceptable volume for drawing or dining room, pitched higher and louder. "And Matthew, too? Jacob and Luke? Even baby Roseanne?"

"Sally, lower your voice, please," her father interjected.

"But, Da, Mum said—"

"Shhh, Sally."

Sally may have been shushed, but she was not done. She jumped to her feet and ran to Rose's side. "Grandma Rose! Is Chicago far away? You ain't a-goin' far, are ya? You'll come home soon?"

Rose opened her arms to Sally and hugged her tight. Sally's hold on Rose's neck was as fierce as it was afraid, and Rose's throat was so tight that it squeezed her words until she could scarcely get them out. "I will always love you, Sally. Please remember that, all right? Remember: *Grandma Rose loves you.* I always will, even while I am away."

"But . . . but won't you be here no more?"

"No, child. I am going with your Uncle Ed and Aunt Joy. We won't be back for . . . a long time."

The unspoken words "if ever" hung in the room like black crepe draping hung from the windows at a funeral.

Sally pulled back from Rose, stomped her foot, shook her head of red curls, and shouted, "No! No, Grandma Rose! I don' want you to leave on no stupid, *stupid* train to *stupid* Chicago!"

Mason left his seat, came around, and lifted Sally into his arms. She was a big girl now, but it did not matter.

"It will be all right, Sally," he whispered, holding her, comforting her as she shuddered with tears. "It will be all right."

But it wasn't all right, and the children understood that now. Wailing and sobbing, they rushed to Rose's side. "Don't go, Grandma Rose! We love you! Please don't go!"

Matthew and Jacob, ages six and four, had known that their grandmother would be coming with them on this grand adventure called "moving" and had not worried or fretted on that account. Only now did they realize they would be leaving behind their many honorary aunts and uncles and all their beloved cousins. They scurried to their father and buried their faces in his arms, howling their dismay. Luke, at two years old, only needed to see and hear the room's universal sorrow before he, too, crawled from his chair to climb up into his papa's lap and hide his sad little face in another part of O'Dell's suitcoat.

The parents around the table were undone. Whatever control they had tried to exert over their emotions melted. They wept with their children, and they were joined by Mr. Wheatley and the girls of Palmer House.

They were, all of them, saying goodbye to loved ones they might never see again. But those who lived at Palmer House sorrowed the most acutely over Rose's imminent departure.

Never again would they hear Rose's gentle voice reading Scripture during morning devotions.

Never again would they hear her explain so clearly and with such deep, personal relevance what the passages meant.

Never again would she lead them in heartfelt prayer.

Never again would they lean their wet cheeks on her shoulder while she loved them into God's healing and wholeness.

Only Sarah remained dry-eyed, for she had already shed the bulk of her tears. Tomorrow she would face the greatest challenge of her life, and she wondered—as she had for weeks, *Father, how can I possibly replace Rose? Neither Olive nor I will ever fill her shoes. Oh, we need you, Lord God!*

It was the end of an era.

CHAPTER 2

Morning was far off, and the house was still abed, but Rose had been awake for some time. She had, over the previous days, sorted her belongings, packed her trunk and two suit-cases, and gone through the items she would carry in her valise. In the pre-dawn hours, unable to sleep, she had done it all again.

She reached for her worn Bible and clutched it. "Lord, please calm my heart," she whispered, "for it is galloping about in my chest like a runaway horse." Opening her Bible to the book of Psalms, her finger traced the words she sought.

The heavens declare the glory of God;
and the firmament sheweth his handywork.
Day unto day uttereth speech,
and night unto night sheweth knowledge.
There is no speech nor language,
where their voice is not heard.

"The heavens and the earth declare your glory, Lord, and all of creation hears them! I am part of your creation, and I know you hear me, too, even when I fumble my words and my heart cannot find an outlet for its anxious thoughts." Her finger slid down the page to the last line in the psalm.

Let the words of my mouth,
and the meditation of my heart,
be acceptable in thy sight,
O Lord, my strength, and my redeemer.

She sighed and the knots in her stomach loosened. Untangled. "You, Lord, are my strength and my redeemer. I will not fear what is ahead. May all my thoughts and words this day be acceptable in your sight. Amen." She picked up a smaller book, one with a padded blue cover. She opened it to a clean page and took up her pen.

JOURNAL ENTRY, OCTOBER 9, 1923

GOOD MORNING, dear Lord. Today I will depart this house where I have lived these many years, and I will leave the young women whom I love so dearly. I must entrust them to you, my God, believing that you will care for them—

A soft tap sounded on Rose's door. She set her journal aside and padded to the door. When she opened it, she found Olive on the other side, her face damp with fresh tears.

Olive had been a sad, bedraggled slip of a girl when she arrived at Palmer House. She was thin from too little to eat and nearly unresponsive from having been beaten down in every part of her being. Pastor Carmichael and a small evangelism team from his church had found the orphaned child on the streets of Denver's notorious red-light district. She had survived half a year by selling herself daily for a few coins, but it was obvious to those who saw her that she would not last another month "out there." It was Pastor Carmichael who had brought the gawky and withdrawn girl to Palmer House and given her into Rose's care.

After living more than a decade at Palmer House, Olive was no longer a girl. Indeed, fine lines creased the corners of her eyes and mouth, and her auburn hair glistened prematurely with strands of silver, lending to the overall impression of an age far north of her twenty-six years. But in the decade of her residence at Palmer House, although she had found steady work to support herself, she had never expressed an interest in leaving, in finding a husband, or in raising a family.

She had once professed to Rose, "Why would I depart Palmer House? This is my home and my only family. I wish to remain here, if I may. I would prefer to continue working, adding what I earn to the house's coffers, and helping out in every other means that I can."

So, in addition to defraying the house's many expenses, Olive made herself indispensable to Marit in the kitchen and to Breona in her housekeeping duties. After Breona married and was expecting her first child, she took Olive aside and trained her. When Breona gave up her position as housekeeper, Olive was prepared to step into that role. And it was Olive, when Rose announced she would be moving to Chicago with the O'Dells, who came alongside Sarah and, by her words and actions, pledged to support her.

Rose asked, "Yes, dear Olive?"

Olive bit her quivering bottom lip and forced herself to speak. "I-I apologize for disturbing you this early, Miss Rose, but I saw the light under your door and believed you to be awake, and I was afraid I would not have another opportunity . . ."

"You are not disturbing me, Olive. I have been up for a while. How can I help?"

"Help? Yes, thank you. Well, the other evening, we . . . that is, Marit and Sarah, were remembering when Tabitha went off to nursing school, and I was listening to them. They reminisced how everyone in the house gave Tabitha a little gift to see her on her way."

Olive pressed a small package into Rose's hands. "I hope these will please you and I-I hope you will remember me when you use them."

Rose drew Olive into her room, leaving the door slightly ajar, and undid the package. The fragrance of rose petals wafted from within it. Nestled in the folds of glossy tissue paper, she found three small pink soaps, each one the shape of a rosebud.

"Oh, Olive, thank you. They are beautiful and such a pleasant fragrance. I will enjoy them, and they will most certainly remind me of you and your loving heart. I will pray for you each time I use them."

Olive gulped, "I-I am s-so glad!" and broke down, sobbing.

Rose set the package aside. She sat on the edge of her bed, tugged Olive down next to her, and held her as she wept.

Eventually, Olive sniffed, "I am sorry, Miss Rose."

"What precisely are you sorry for, my dear? Are you sorry for loving me, sweet Olive? Are you sorry that you will miss me when I am gone?"

"No!"

"Then there is nothing to be sorry for, is there?"

"But I . . . I am . . ."

"You are, perhaps, a little anxious about the future? Afraid, even?"

"Y-yes. How did you know?"

"Dear Olive, I have carried the burden of this ministry for thirteen years. I have an intimate acquaintance with fear. I have faced it daily."

"Y-you have been afraid? No! You are the most serene person I know. I have never seen you fearful."

"I, not fearful? Ah, but I have been. I have been afraid of failing our girls, of stumbling in my walk with the Lord and thus injuring them, of setting them a poor example of Christian maturity by not managing my own emotions when I am stressed or overtired. I have even been afraid I might inadvertently teach something contrary to Scripture or give ungodly advice."

Rose's fingertips touched Olive's chin and turned Olive's gaze to her own. "You and Sarah must be terrified, Olive."

"I-I am. We are. Oh, dear. What are we to do, Miss Rose?"

Rose sighed and offered a tired smile. "Why, you must do exactly as I have done: pray well, pray diligently, and pray without ceasing. Then you must speak to your fear, 'Oh, yes, Fear. I see you, you repugnant little liar. I know what you are and the black pit out of which you have crawled. Listen, Fear. My God has given me the courage and strength to do what he asks of me despite your threats and schemes.'"

"And then?"

"And then, Olive, you will do what frightens you, and you will do it with peace and dignity. Whatever the situation, our God will guide you through it. His word declares, *Draw nigh to God and he will draw nigh to you.* And Jesus promised, *I will never leave thee, nor forsake thee.* Jesus does not break his promises, you know. If you surrender daily to the Lord Jesus, he will see you safely through each day and its many obstacles."

Someone whispered through the partly open doorway. "Miss Rose? May I join you?"

"Come in, Sarah. Yes, this is for you also."

Sarah came and knelt by Rose. "I heard what you said. I also confess to being afraid. Will you pray for us, Miss Rose?"

Rose hugged her. "Certainly. But, if you do not mind, I will do so when we gather for breakfast and today's devotions. We shall require a bit more time this morning, I think. Would you ask Marit to serve breakfast a quarter of an hour earlier and let the girls know to be on time?"

"Yes, Miss Rose."

Sarah stood, and Olive joined her. When the girls closed Rose's door behind them, she returned to her journal entry and finished it.

I entrust all of them to you, my God, even though my heart already misses and longs for them. Father, I ask you to lead and guide me this morning by your Holy Spirit. Please fill my mouth with your words to confirm Sarah as your chosen leader for this house, Olive as her strong right arm, and whoever else you add to them. I trust in you, Lord. Amen.

WHEN THE HOUSE assembled for breakfast that morning, Rose seated Sarah on her right and Olive on her left. The meal was quieter than usual, the conversation stilted, the girls watchful. Sarah's husband, Bryan, had not joined them today either. He had left before breakfast to prepare for the early surgeries scheduled in his clinic. Billy, Marit, and their boys generally took breakfast in their cottage.

When the meal was over and the dishes cleared away, Rose opened her Bible. The young women did the same.

"Our study this morning will be in Joshua 1, beginning in verse 1." She read aloud,

"Now after the death of Moses, the servant of the Lord,
it came to pass, that the Lord spake unto
Joshua the son of Nun, Moses' minister,
saying, Moses my servant is dead;
now therefore arise, go over this Jordan, thou,
and all this people, unto the land which I
do give to them, even to the children of Israel."

Rose smiled and looked around the table. Her gaze rested on each one long enough to receive a smile or a nod in return.

"What I believe God's word conveys to us this morning is this: When the Lord calls a leader away, he always has a plan for carrying on. No, I am neither Moses nor am I dead. Nevertheless, let us look into how the Lord handles the transition from one leader to the next. We recommence in verse 5 where the Lord continues speaking to Joshua.

"There shall not any man
be able to stand before thee all the days of thy life:
as I was with Moses, so I will be with thee:
I will not fail thee, nor forsake thee."

She stopped reading and waited until she again had everyone's attention. "This is the Lord's pattern. When he calls one leader away, he raises up another. From this day forward, Sarah is the leader of this house, and as the Lord has been with me, he will be with her. He will not fail Sarah; he will not fail you. He will not forsake Sarah nor will he forsake Palmer House. Do you see?"

Around the table, heads nodded, and eyes shifted to Sarah in acknowledgement.

"Good. Now, let me say this: Change is not easy nor is it always pleasant. Sarah may do things differently than I have done them, but as the leader of this house, it is her prerogative, her choice. I would ask that you give her time and grace as she settles into this role. I would also ask you to pray for her daily. May I have your assurance that you will do those things?"

She looked to the young woman to the right of Sarah. "Hannah, dear, will you tell Sarah that you will pray for her, and will you give her your assurance that you will respect and support her?"

Hannah blushed at being singled out first, but she cleared her throat and replied, "Yes, Miss Rose." She turned to Sarah. "Miss Sarah, I will pray for you and give you my respect and support. I . . . I will also give you my love and appreciation." She choked a little. "I don't know where I would be if it weren't for Jesus, if Palmer House hadn't been here . . ."

Sarah took Hannah's hand. "Thank you, Hannah. We are so grateful the Lord brought you to us. I promise you my love and care in return."

Around the table, each young woman pledged her prayers and support to Sarah, until they reached Olive on Rose's left.

Olive smiled at Sarah. "You well know that I have seen this day coming from a long way off. I realized then that the Lord was grooming you for this moment, Miss Sarah. I will be honored to pray for you, support you, and assist you in any capacity you require."

"Thank you, Olive. I shall lean upon you often."

Rose again spoke. "Very good, ladies. Now, let us return to our study. In the chapter we are reading, the Lord had several more things to say to Joshua when he appointed him leader. Some were specific to the situation they were in and perhaps do not apply to Palmer House. I believe his ending injunctions, however, are essential to every Christian, whether an acknowledged leader or not. Let us read verse 8.

"This book of the law
shall not depart out of thy mouth;
but thou shalt meditate therein day and night,
that thou mayest observe to do according
to all that is written therein:
for then thou shalt make thy way prosperous,
and then thou shalt have good success.

Rose then addressed Sarah. "Sarah, the success of Palmer House and your success as Palmer House's leader will stand or fall on your diligence to both study and obey God's word. This house is a sanctuary for lost souls. We have seen our great and mighty God work in marvelous and miraculous ways here. Why? Because we placed the Lord's word first in all we do."

Her remarks shifted to everyone at the table. "We declare that Palmer House is not a program, a social experiment, or a reformatory. It is none of those things, for programs and human efforts cannot remake and restore a broken life. Rather, this house is the footstool of Jesus Christ, the Savior of the world.

"When we kneel before him and surrender our *everything*—he, in response to our contrition, forgives our sins, heals our hearts, and makes us brand new. As Scripture proclaims,

"Therefore, if any man be in Christ,
he is a new creature:
old things are passed away;
behold, all things are become new.

"This is the very essence of the gospel and the message we preach: If any woman be in Christ, she is a new creation. What she *was*, is gone—utterly washed away by the blood of Christ. Through the redemption of the cross, the power of Christ's resurrection, and the sanctifying work of the Holy Spirit, *we are changed*."

Rose took Sarah's hand and stared into her eyes. "You must never stray from the miraculous, transforming message of the gospel, Sarah. I charge you, therefore, with the words of Joshua 1:9:

"Be strong and of a good courage;
be not afraid, neither be thou dismayed:
for the Lord thy God is with thee
whithersoever thou goest.

"Surrender all doubts to the Father and give no place or foothold to fear, Sarah. Will you do these things? Will you cling steadfastly to God's word? Will you preach the unadulterated Good News and walk in courage, refusing fear an entry to your life?"

Sarah lifted her chin. With tears coursing down her cheeks, she declared, "I will. With the Lord's help, I will."

"Olive, you have pledged yourself to be Sarah's assistant. Will you also promise to do these things?"

"I will, Miss Rose."

"Thank you, Olive." Rose stood. "Will all of you please stand and pray with me?"

The women at the table stood to join Rose.

Rose placed her hands on Sarah's shoulders. "O Lord God, we believe that you have called Sarah to this position. We ask that you now instill in Sarah the confidence of this calling and that you pour your Holy Spirit upon and through her as she takes up her duties this day. We ask that you fill her with grace, love, kindness, faith, and patience, as you set her apart for service to you. Please grant her your wisdom and discretion, O Lord, to meet every difficult situation."

Rose turned and placed her hands on Olive's shoulders. "Father, Olive has committed herself to be Sarah's assistant, her Caleb to Sarah's Joshua. We ask that you give Olive eyes to see Sarah's needs so that she might undergird Sarah's leadership. We ask that you give her wisdom to counsel Sarah when she is faced with difficult choices. We ask that you give her the courage to speak truth to Sarah when she falters—for she is human and will surely have her struggles, too."

Rose then took Olive's hand on her left and Sarah's hand on her right. Around the table, the others joined hands until the circle was complete.

"Father, today I leave this house, this home I love so dearly. You have called me away, and I must obey you.

"I am seventy-four years old, and I believe that the work you entrusted to me thirteen years ago should now pass to Sarah and Olive. By your grace, Lord God, *they are ready* to assume this great and wonderful responsibility. I pray you make them fruitful branches in your kingdom, always abiding in the vine, Christ Jesus. As for me, this part of my life is done. Now, I will go with Joy and her family to Chicago. I will pour what love, strength, and time I have left into Joy, Edmund, and their children.

"I thank you, Lord, for every heart gathered around this table. May our fellowship in Christ never be broken—for I cherish each one."

Rose's voice quivered. "In the name of Jesus we pray. Amen."

The heartfelt replies that echoed through Palmer House's dining room were "Amen" and "Yes, Lord."

ISAAC AND BREONA had asked if they might drive Rose to the train and see her off. So had Mei-Xing and her husband. The last offer had come from Mason and Tabitha following dinner the night before. Rose had declined them all, but Tabitha's request had been the most difficult to refuse.

"It will be easier this way," Rose murmured, watching Tabitha's hope crumble. "Let us say our goodbyes now, so that if I weep, I weep here, and will not embarrass us both in public."

Tabitha nodded, but she had not been able to hide the sadness that crept over her face and into her voice. "I understand."

She blinked hard. "But it is an agony to let you go. I owe so much to you, Rose. I-I will never forget you."

"Nor I, you."

Tabitha sniffed. Her voice wavered. "Until we meet again?"

With Tabitha, Rose felt she could be completely candid. "On that great and glorious day, when we meet before the throne of grace. Until then, Tabitha."

THE GIRLS OF THE house were gone. They had readied themselves to leave for their respective places of employment following breakfast, and Rose had stood at the door enfolding each one in her arms a last time before they departed.

The driver of the hired car that would convey Rose to Union Station climbed the steps to Palmer House's front door and dropped the heavy knocker to announce his arrival. Rose's trunk and suitcases waited in the foyer. Her valise rested next to it. Her coat and handbag hung nearby.

It was time to go.

While Billy and the driver carried her luggage to the car, Rose said her last farewells. She embraced Sarah. She turned to Olive and hugged her.

That left only Marit.

"Dear Marit," Rose whispered into her ear, determined not to break down, but on the verge of losing that battle.

"*Ach*, I know, Miss Rose. Vit all these changes are many goodbyes—and yet I am remembering so clearly the day ven I first met you, ven you and Joy stepped off the train in Corinth. It vas cold and vindy that day. Breona and I ver on the siding, selling coffee, cakes, and *pepparkakor* to passengers."

Rose grew still as she pictured the scene Marit described.

"And I remember, too, vat you said to us the next morn ven you opened your Bible, *ja?* You asked of Joy, 'Haf you studied the new birth yet, Joy?' Vas the first time I hear you talk of being born again—and *oh!* How my heart opened like a flower that day. I vill never forget."

"You came to Jesus not long after, didn't you?"

"*Ja*, not long, and I vill be forever grateful to him."

"We had no idea then what adventures in faith were before us, did we?"

"No, and I vould not trade a moment of them, Miss Rose."

"Nor I, dear Marit."

Marit kissed Rose's cheek. "God go vit you, Miss Rose."

With a last hug, Rose sniffed back her tears, picked up her valise and coat, and marched out the front door of Palmer House.

As she closed the door behind her, she paused and turned to the sign mounted next to the door. She touched her fingertips to the letters embossed there: *Lost Are Found.*

She bowed her head and whispered, "Lord, I trust you to bring our lost lamb home to us, just as I trust you to guide him to faith in you. In all things, I trust you."

Rose turned away and trod on leaden legs down the long walkway to where Billy and the car waited by the curb.

Billy tugged off his cap and fiddled with it. "Me and Marit and the boys are gonna miss you somethin' fierce, Miss Rose."

Rose cupped his cheek in her hand. "I shall miss all of you also. You are a faithful man of God, dear Billy, and I treasure your friendship."

The driver opened the rear door of the car for her. As she turned to step into the car, something pulled her gaze back to the house. Sarah, Olive, and Marit stood on the front porch. They waved to her, and she lifted her hand to them.

It is unlikely that I shall ever return to this place, Lord God, but I am certain that your Holy Spirit shall abide in this house for generations to come. By your Spirit, O God, you will, in accordance with your divine purposes, fulfill all your promises.

For that assurance, I am most grateful.

CHAPTER 3

The hired car pulled to a curb near a line of porters waiting to check luggage and trunks for departing passengers. Rose's driver helped her from the rear seat. Her legs seemed a bit shaky, so she steadied herself against the car's fender as he retrieved her valise and handed it to her.

A porter towing a large cart approached, and Rose showed him her ticket. He offered Rose a scribbled claim check and took charge of her trunk and suitcases. After tipping the driver and the porter, Rose began moving toward the station's main entrance.

Union Station, always a busy place, was no different today. Inside the terminal, tumult reigned. The sheer chaos of its traffic and commerce assaulted Rose's senses—raised voices echoed and bounced off the cavernous ceiling, hundreds of passengers rushed this way and that, long lines queued up to the ticket booths, and passengers pushed and shoved to reach the boards that announced the scheduled arrivals and departures.

Rose took several deep breaths before plunging into the melee. She sought a place before the big board on the wall that listed departing trains, their departure times, and their boarding platforms. As those nearest the board found the information they sought, they peeled away, and those behind them jostled forward. After several attempts, Rose was close enough to peruse the board. She checked her ticket against the listings and, having ascertained and double-checked the correct platform for her train, eased her way out of the knotted crowd.

Safely away from pushing, shoving bodies, and with the number of her departure gate in mind, Rose searched the signs pointing passengers to the station's several railways and many boarding platforms. At the same time, she glanced at the large clock at the center of the terminal.

Just then, a young man pushed by her. His movement jostled her arm and spun her partway around. As Rose sought to keep her balance, she stretched out one arm, and her handbag dropped to the dirty terminal floor.

The man did not slow. "Beg your pardon," the man tossed over his shoulder.

Rose regained her balance and stooped to recover her handbag.

The time!

As her eyes again sought the clock, a flush of anxiety bloomed in her chest. She pushed it down. *I have plenty of time. I need not worry.* She again located the arrows that pointed toward her platform.

"Ah, yes. I should go that way, I believe." She spoke aloud yet could scarcely hear her words over the echoing station noise.

And as she set off in what she hoped was the right direction, her footsteps stuttered. She stopped abruptly, and tried to blink away the sudden, odd sensation that came over her, the awareness of how *alone*, amid so many rushing, bustling people, she was.

I have felt this way before, have I not? She frowned. *But it was long ago, when I boarded another train. By myself.*

A dusty, frayed recollection flickered in the back of her mind. The haze over it fluttered as if tossed by a breeze, then dissipated. The scene in her memory came slowly into focus. It was timeworn, but oddly vivid.

"I HAVE BEEN thinking about a trip, Tom—as you suggested—but I do not wish to trouble you and Abby to accompany me right now. You are busy at the office, and Abby is expecting and, well, you do not need to come. I will just go by myself."

"By yourself? Where do you have in mind? The seashore? That might be all right, but why don't we come along? You know, just for company, hey? I can get away—hang the office anyway."

"Tom, dear, you do not fool me, you know. You have worked too hard building your clientele to take a leave of absence at present. Besides, I want to go alone. No, listen, please. I have quite made up my mind. I have my reasons, too. All I can say is that it is a kind of pilgrimage."

"Pilgrimage? Like a religious trip?"

"Well, yes, something like that."

"Can you not tell me where you're going? I am sorry, Rose; I don't wish to see you do anything dangerous . . . or foolish."

"Thank you, dearest of brothers. I won't be foolish, I promise."

"Sis, I know this change of scenery will be good for you . . . only don't be gone too long, Rosie. What I mean is . . . you will be coming back, won't you?"

"I promise I will do what I believe is best for me. My trip is on a train . . . west."

ROSE MURMURED ALOUD, "Oh, Tom."

Her younger brother, his "little brother" grin, his curling brown hair, his manly concern for her welfare. He had passed away five years back at the age of sixty-five, but in her mind, he would always be her little brother, young, teasing, mischievous, full of life.

"I was thirty-three years old," Rose whispered. "Newly a widow, raw with mourning my husband and children. Seeking solace . . . seeking you, Lord God. And you found me. You healed my broken heart. Restored my soul."

A sigh from the deepest part of her being found its way to her mouth. "How faithful you have been to me since that day, my God."

She stood there a little longer, amazed and grateful. Taking a deep breath, she continued on her way.

The signs and arrows led her first across the breadth of the great terminal. As she walked, Rose took in shoeshine stands, flower stalls, coffee vendors, and the boys shouting headlines as they hawked newspapers. When she reached the far side of the terminals, the signs directed her down an immense, domed hallway. A tunnel. Far ahead, she spied daylight.

Rose emerged from semidarkness onto a roofed but open-sided platform that extended many yards to her left and right. Directly ahead, across the breadth of the platform, her train waited, its engines idling and belching black smoke. Coalmen, engineers, conductors, and porters raced up and down the platform. Rose stared down the length of the train, trying to count the number of cars following the engines, but the track curved away, preventing her from seeing the rest of the train.

She turned her eyes to the platform and the crowd assembling there. Everywhere she looked, Rose noted a thin patina of coal dust. It coated the platform's planks and the lines of benches where passengers might sit. When she glanced down to her boots, a light dust swirled around them.

"Goodness. Wouldn't Breona fuss."

Not many minutes after she reached her platform, the O'Dells arrived. From behind her, she heard the delighted crows of two young children: "Grandma Rose! Grandma Rose!" A little late to the party, but not willing to be left out, their younger brother, Luke, age two, screeched his greeting. "Grama Ro! Grama Ro!"

In a matter of seconds, the three boys threw their arms—and all their momentum—about her legs while trampling on her toes. Her son-in-law reached Rose and grabbed her arm just in time to save her from being toppled.

Rose laughed. "Thank you, Edmund. For a moment, I was quite certain we would all end up in a heap."

Edmund O'Dell chuckled. "I confess, I feared the same."

Without releasing his steadying hold on her arm, he marshalled his troop of boys. "Matthew, Jacob, Luke? Please give Grandma Rose some room. You may hug her when we are on the train, sitting down. Yes, stand beside me. That is better."

He nodded toward Rose. "May I carry your valise, Mother?"

"You have already checked your things through to RiverBend?" Rose asked.

O'Dell laughed again. "You mean our five trunks and four suit-cases? Yes, we safely relinquished them to an army of porters. I declare, shifting a family across the country is no mean feat."

He released Rose, hoisted up little Luke, took Rose's valise in his other hand, and called to Matthew and Jacob. "Come, boys. Let us help Mama."

Joy stood waiting where the boys had abandoned her for Rose. She carried Roseanne in her arms; a sizeable valise waited at her feet.

"Good morning, Mama."

Rose kissed Joy's cheek and peered at the baby. "How is our darling girl?"

"She appears to be sleeping through all the noise and commotion. I pray she will not wail all night while other passengers on the train are trying to sleep."

Joy lifted her chin as a loud voice shouted, "Aaaaall aboard! Aaaaall aboard!"

O'Dell turned. "That is for us." He led the way, Luke in one arm. Matthew and Jacob, each holding to one of their father's trouser pockets, hopped along beside him like excited little crickets. Joy and Rose followed close behind them.

A conductor glanced at their tickets and pointed them to their car. Another helped them climb the steps. The two older boys, wide-eyed and silent, glued themselves to the back of O'Dell's legs as he navigated the aisle toward their assigned seats. When he located them, he directed Jacob to sit on one seat and deposited Luke opposite him, then turned to assist Rose and Joy. Their large party took up three bench seats. Joy and Jacob sat facing O'Dell and Luke. Matthew joined Rose to take the third bench, back to back with O'Dell.

Matthew and Jacob pressed their faces to the windows. They jabbered across the seats to each other and pointed out the many strange sights parading beneath their scrutiny, while Luke huddled against his father's side, quite overwhelmed.

When the train began to move, Matthew and Jacob stilled, captivated by the wonders gliding by. Even Luke, when O'Dell held him up to the window, knelt on the seat, his face pressed to the glass, utterly absorbed.

Rose glanced behind her. Joy smiled back.

They were on their way.

THE TUMULT OF departure eased, and the novelty of the moving train eventually wore off. Rose took the baby from Joy, and Matthew joined his parents. The three boys, after watching with rapt fascination out the windows for hours, yawned and leaned their heads against their mother or laid themselves on the knees of their father and nodded off to the rhythmic clatter of the train's wheels on the tracks. Joy, too, dozed.

Rose, with baby Roseanne in her arms, watched the scenery pass by, yet her thoughts ranged far beyond what her eyes took in.

I am glad Uli, David, and their children came down from Corinth last week to say goodbye. We had a good visit, unrushed by so many other goodbyes. I hope our stay in RiverBend will allow for ample personal time with those whom I hold dear.

O'Dell turned in his seat and said softly, "A penny for your thoughts, Mother."

Rose met his gaze and smiled. "I am thinking of RiverBend. Thank you again, Edmund, for agreeing to the detour and for your generosity. I asked for a few days, but you have granted me closer to two weeks."

His dark eyes danced. "How could I do otherwise? I would have risked marital mayhem had I denied your request. Joy's heart longs to see her brother, his family, her cousins, and the family's many friends again, too. Does your heart long for this any less than hers?"

"No, nor could it. I thank you, nonetheless. If I am to uproot myself to a strange place one last time, this hiatus in RiverBend will lessen the sting."

"There is another reason I extended our stay in RiverBend."

"Oh?"

"Yes. You have labored under a great burden of responsibility for a long time, Mother. In all those years, did you ever take a single extended holiday? I think not."

She chuckled. "Farmers do not take vacations, Edmund—or rarely do, in any case. At heart, I am still a farmer's wife. Besides, I could hardly leave the girls of Palmer House without adequate leadership, could I? Their healing and growth depended on spiritual stability."

"And now?"

"I am confident that they will find the leadership they require in Sarah."

"Good, because when we arrive in RiverBend, it is my hope and wish that you relax, that you begin to take life easier. That you enjoy yourself among your family and friends. I wish you to be happy, Mother. Happy and content."

She smiled. "You are a good son to me, Edmund. Thank you. I love you dearly."

Rose saw the welling moisture he tried to blink away. She was quick to apologize. "I am sorry, dear Edmund. I did not mean to—"

"No, please; I'm fine." He shrugged. "I'm just wondering how in the world I won the greatest lottery in history—a wife and children I adore—and a mother-in-law who loves me as her own."

"Not luck. The blessings of God himself."

He nodded. "Don't I know it? How could I forget how lost I was, how hard my heart was not many years ago? I thank the Lord for his mercy every morning."

THE TRAIN CHUGGED slowly down the mountains and onto the plains. Normally, a journey by train from Denver to Chicago would have taken less than two days.

They called such a train a "through" express because it stopped only at significant cities along its route and roared on past lesser municipalities. RiverBend, as only a sleepy prairie township, no longer rated daily train service.

Travel time on this "milk run," as it was termed, was elongated as the train diverted from the main route and paused at lesser destinations along the way—taking on a few passengers and minor freight, livestock, or produce—at each juncture.

The weekly "special" was now the only train that served RiverBend. This first leg of Rose and the O'Dells' journey would last until early afternoon the following day, and it boasted no sleeping compartments for the night ahead.

Joy fed her family lunch and dinner with sandwiches and fruit from the large valise she carried. When evening fell, she and O'Dell bedded down the boys for the night. Joy gave up her seat for Matthew and Jacob and joined Rose. Luke slept curled beside O'Dell. The three adults passed a miserable night nodding and catching what sleep they could manage.

CHAPTER 4

In a hail of cinders and to the grating screech of protesting metal against metal, the engine braked repeatedly until the cars it pulled slowed and, in jarring fits, the train came to a stop at RiverBend's small "station."

It was no more than a simple siding with a small freight office where passengers could also buy tickets.

Joy and O'Dell were ready. Joy had washed the boys' faces and dampened their hair. Then she tended to her own hair and clothes and repacked her valise. O'Dell took each boy in turn and ran a comb through his hair. Then he tidied them up, pulling up socks and retying shoes where needed.

Rose, too, was ready. She had washed her face and brushed out her hair, braiding it, then twisting and pinning it as she did each morning at the base of her neck. She felt the lack of sleep from the night before in her aching neck and shoulders, but nothing could curb the excitement she felt as she peered from the window, hoping to catch sight of someone dear.

At last, the conductor opened the doors and shouted, "RiverBend! RiverBend! Thirty minute stop only. Thirty minutes!"

O'Dell gestured for Rose to go first. She picked up her handbag and valise and, on legs unsteady from too much sitting, staggered down the aisle to the end of the car. The conductor standing at the bottom of the steps reached out his hand to help her down.

"Have a good day, ma'am," he said.

"Thank you," Rose murmured as her feet reached the siding. "Most appreciated." She moved away from the train, looking, searching for a familiar face.

O'Dell and the boys disembarked next. O'Dell set Luke at Rose's side and said to his three sons, "Boys, you are to stay and guard Grandma Rose while I help your mama. Do you understand?" He intentionally framed his orders to give his sons some responsibility.

The answer came in three versions of "Yes, Papa."

Luke gripped Rose's skirt, and Matthew and Jacob stood close to Rose while O'Dell took baby Roseanne from Joy and the conductor helped her down the steep steps.

Rose was barely conscious of her grandsons' nearness. She was still turning her head about, scanning the small platform and the few people on it for anyone she knew.

A figure rounded the corner, and she was shocked into immobility. A tall man strode toward her. He was dressed in trousers, clean twill shirt, and suspenders. His broad shoulders spoke of hard work and strong genes. His hair, a natural blond, was bleached white from hours in the sun; his face was bronzed from the same.

He lifted a hand and called to her. "Rose!"

Rose's heart stuttered and nearly stopped. "*Jan?*"

She stared. *No, surely not Jan.*

The man's features resolved, and Rose gasped. "Søren!"

He swept her into a fierce hug—scattering the three little men who were gathered around Rose like chicks around a mother hen. When he set her down on the station's platform, he whispered, "You have made me glad today, Rose. I cannot tell you how much we have looked forward to your and Joy's visit. We have missed you both so much."

He straightened and examined the three boys who grasped so protectively at Rose's skirt. "And these young men taking such good care of you—could they be my nephews?"

"Yes, indeed," Rose chuckled. "Søren, these are Matthew, Jacob, and little Luke. Boys, this is your Uncle Søren. He is your mama's brother. Please shake his hand."

Matthew and Jacob, with eyes wide, managed to offer limp fingers to the man who stood half a head taller than their father and whose hand swallowed up theirs whole. Luke, though, hid his face in Rose's skirt and could not be coaxed into saying hello.

"You have a niece, too, brother," Joy laughed from behind Søren. She had taken Roseanne back from her husband. When Søren saw Joy, he wrapped his arms around both her and the baby.

"We are so glad you have come home, Joy," Søren said.

He then noticed O'Dell standing near Joy and offered him his hand. "Søren Thoresen, Joy's brother. You must be her husband, Edmund."

"That I am," O'Dell answered, smiling, "and glad to meet Joy and Rose's family at last."

Joy asked Søren what Rose was wondering. "Why, Søren, where is Meg? Did she not come to meet us?"

Søren scratched the back of his neck. "Weeell, you see, it was this way. We have only two vehicles and couldn't carry all of you and your luggage if she came with us.

"Believe me, she was madder than a wet hen when we realized we couldn't bring her along. So, she's at home, baking and cooking up a storm. But don't worry—we'll have you there soon."

"Speaking of our things, where should we collect our luggage?" O'Dell asked.

Søren pointed with a jut of his chin. "I'd wager Jeremy has all your trunks and cases unloaded and waiting yonder by the freight office. He's been as excited as we are for your visit."

Søren led the way down the siding. As he had said, Rose spied stacks of trunks and suitcases waiting on the siding's creosote-washed planks, watched over by a lean, somewhat stooped man with hair trending toward gray. He walked to meet them, a slow smile creasing his face.

"Is that you, Miss Rose?"

Rose laughed with genuine pleasure. "Why, Jeremy Bailey. I believe I would like to hug you."

His smile widened. "Be m' guest, ma'am."

They embraced, and then Rose turned to Matthew. "Matthew, this is Mr. Bailey. I first met him when he was a boy only a few years older than you."

"Yep," Jeremy added, shaking Matthew's hand. "Reckon I'm getting' on in years now."

Rose feigned a huff. "And what does that imply about me? We will have no talk of age while I am here," she teased.

"Well, now, Miss Rose, I kin agree t' that."

"Tell me, Jeremy, what have you done since I have been gone?"

"Well, biggest and bestest thing is I got me a family now. Beautiful wife and two girls jest as pretty as their mother."

Rose beamed. "Oh, Jeremy, I am so happy for you."

"Thank you, ma'am. I am blessed fer sure. Say, you-all have a passel of trunks and what-not. I'd be happy t' help you load them."

"There's our automobile." Søren pointed out a small vehicle parked in the little station's dirt lot. "And that's our hay-hauling truck."

A brawny man Rose did not immediately recognize waved to them from beside a dusty flatbed truck with tall side panels.

"You have a car *and* a truck?" Rose exclaimed. "Oh, my. How I would have loved for your father to see them."

Søren grinned. "Yup. Both car and truck had previous owners, but I think Papa would have approved and enjoyed tinkering with them.

"We brought the farm's truck to carry your trunks and luggage; however, our little auto seats only four adults comfortably. We'll be a mite crowded unless some of you ride in the cab of the truck."

"Matthew and I can ride up in the truck," O'Dell offered.

"Perhaps the littlest boy might sit on your lap instead," Søren suggested. "That truck hasn't much leg room, what with the gear shift between the two seats."

"Luke it is," O'Dell agreed.

"Well then," Jeremy said, "Seein' as how we have four able-bodied men to help, should only take a few minutes to shift ever'thing to that truck."

"I'll have Jon back the truck up to the siding." Søren signaled to the truck's driver to bring his vehicle over.

Rose stared at the grown man with reddish-blond hair, her mouth agape. *Is that Jon, Søren's youngest? He was barely nineteen when I saw him last, but he must be beyond thirty now.*

It had been Jon who married not long after Jan passed away, Jon whom Rose had allowed to live in her house when she left RiverBend.

His family grew quickly, Rose reminded herself, *and he asked if he might add on to my little house. However, I could not bear the thought of him tearing into it, altering it. Instead, I asked that my house be left intact and gave him permission to build his own house farther up the hollow between the bluff and the creek, closer to the road.*

The notion of a second house standing on her land was, surprisingly, disconcerting.

I suppose I have put it out of mind, being so fully preoccupied with caring for our girls. Whenever I reminisce on the little home Jan and I shared, I never picture another house close by.

That the house she and Jan had lived in was still standing, unchanged, comforted her. *I will see you soon*, she promised.

While Rose was caught up in her thoughts, Jon had backed the truck up to the landing. He climbed down and nodded to her. "Hey, Grandma Rose. We're sure glad you're here. You, too, Aunt Joy."

Rose laughed. "Jon, I would not have recognized you. Please, come give me a hug."

After introductions all around again, the men set to work, transferring Rose and the O'Dells' considerable number of trunks and suitcases from the siding to the back of the truck. Within minutes, the men had finished stacking them in the truck and were tying them down.

"All done. Shall we get going?" Søren asked.

O'Dell took Luke and climbed into the truck's cab. That left Joy, Rose, Roseanne, and the two older boys to ride in Søren's narrow automobile. Matthew scampered into the back seat. Søren helped Jacob climb up after him. Joy handed Roseanne to Rose while Søren held the door for her. After Joy had arranged her skirts, Rose handed the baby back to her, and Søren helped Rose into the front passenger seat next to his.

"Everyone all set?" Søren asked.

"Yes," Joy laughed.

"Well, although the weather is pleasant enough today, it *is* fall. We had some rain night before last and then a freeze. Our dirt roads have lots of puddles and bumpy ruts, so I will take it slow and easy. I wouldn't want to jar you too badly or pelt any of you with muddy water on the way. And Rose, you are particularly vulnerable to splashes where you are seated. I will do my best to avoid the deepest ruts."

"Thank you, Brother," Joy answered. "We cannot wait to see everyone and everything."

Rose nodded her agreement. She was secretly delighted to have an unobstructed view during their drive—and she cared little how uncomfortable the ride might be. She had to restrain herself and not ask Søren to hurry.

I want to see the prairie and my house. Why, I believe I would mount a camel and ride it across the wheat fields if it would get me there any sooner.

She gawked this way and that as Søren motored down RiverBend's main street. He surprised his passengers by slowing and tapping the horn once. Immediately on the left side of the street, two women, their faces flushed and happy, emerged from a dress shop and waved to them. Two little girls were with them.

"Who is that waving to us, Søren?" Rose asked.

Søren grinned again. "I believe they are old acquaintances of yours, Rose. Esther and Ava? That is their dress and what-not shop behind them. By the way, that beautiful wife Jeremy spoke of? That's her, Ava, and those girls are their daughters. Esther is married also—to Brian and Fiona's eldest grandson, Connor. He is the son of Meg's brother, Darra."

"What? Truly? Bless the Lord, O my soul! Søren, can we not stop a moment?"

"Don't you worry, Rose; you will get to visit with them soon enough, I promise. Pastor and Mrs. Medford are hosting some fancy affair for you and Joy at the church the day after tomorrow. I hear everyone within a twenty-mile radius is coming."

"Oh, how lovely that will be," Rose replied, waving at the women. Joy leaned over the boys and waved, too, as Søren drove on.

Soon after, they reached what used to be the end of RiverBend's single paved road. *Used* to be. The town had extended the paved road a half mile farther. Off to the right, seated in what had once been prairie but was now a large patch of well-tended grass surrounded by meadow, was RiverBend's community church. The parsonage stood not many steps from the church's side entrance.

"Why, they have built a wing onto the church."

"Yep. A nice, large fellowship hall."

Søren again tapped his horn. A face appeared in the parsonage window, then the front door was thrown open. Rose recognized the woman who ran from the door, waving her hand to them.

Rose thought her heart would burst. "Søren, you *will* stop this car, please."

"Yes, ma'am," Søren said, laughing. He was already pulling to the side of the road.

Rose clambered down and ran to meet her friend. "Vera!"

"Oh, Rose. Rose! You have come home at last."

The two old friends wept. They relinquished their embrace only to study each other's face, both finding the other's a little more worn but just as dear.

"Oh, Vera, I am so happy to see you."

"And I, you, Rose. I confess, you took part of my heart with you when you moved to Denver so soon after Jan passed. I was bereft of my dear friend and Bible study partner. Managing our women's studies without you was difficult and painful for a time."

"Those many years of gathering women to study God's word prepared me for a greater work, Vera. I could not have handled that work without the experience of leading that women's study with you."

They hugged again, and Rose finally noticed Vera's husband. "Jacob. Pastor Medford."

Her next thought was, *Pastor, you have lost all your hair!* But she managed not to blurt it out.

He came near and took her hand in both of his. "Rose. How grateful to God we are that you have come home for a visit."

Then he chuckled. "You cannot fool me, Rose. I saw you eye my balding pate. How I envy those men in our congregation whom God has blessed with an abundance of hair in their old age."

He spied Joy standing by the car. "Ah, Joy! And you have a family now. How good God has been to you."

The Medfords did not keep them. After another round of hugs, Rose and Joy returned to Søren's automobile.

As they drove on, Rose grew quiet. Leaving Denver had been difficult and emotional. Visiting RiverBend was already more of the same . . . and, she admitted to herself, she was weary.

Lord, I love all my friends here. I long to see them, Lord God, but I could also use some peace and quiet, many hours to sit, alone and unhurried, and just remember . . .

She realized they were passing the turnoff to the McKennies' farm. *No time to stop and hug your neck, Fiona, but I promise to see you soon, dear friend.*

Finally, they approached the rise in the road so familiar to her. Near the top, the road wound left, then took a sharp right and meandered down the slope toward an old bridge spanning the creek.

Farther to their left lay Rose's property.

She craned her neck to see past Søren, but Jon's house, the one he had built on her land, blocked her view. It wasn't until the car's wheels neared the bridge that Rose, her heart thrumming in her chest, was able to glimpse the sight her eyes most longed for . . . the little house she had lived in with Jan, set so perfectly in the hollow with the surrounding bluff not far behind it.

There it was.

It is just as I remember it, she thought. *Oh, and I remember Jan . . .*

She felt the cold spreading through her bones and shivered against its icy grip. She heard his dear voice. Pleading. Urgent.

"*Rose! Li'l Rose!*"

"*Help me! Do not let me fall in the river. Please . . .*"

"Nei, *Rose, I not let you fall.*"

She felt the strength of his arms around and beneath her, his closeness and warmth comforting her.

Oh, Jan! I long for you . . . Without her permission, a sob jumped into her throat.

Joy leaned forward. Her gentle hand touched Rose's shoulder. "Are you all right, Mama?"

Rose sniffed. "Yes, dearest. I am happy is all."

And already overcome by precious memories.

Jan. How I miss you.

Rose was still trembling when Søren helped her down from the front seat and Meg ran down the back steps to welcome her.

AFTER THE FLURRY of happy greetings had calmed, Meg showed Joy, O'Dell, and Roseanne to one of the four upstairs bedrooms and the three boys to the room next to their parents.

Søren and Meg were concerned, however, that walking up and down the steep stairs to the second floor would prove a burden to Rose. They gave her their bedroom, which opened off the living room, and had already moved their things to another upstairs bedroom for the duration of her stay.

Søren and Meg do not realize that I climbed the stairs at Palmer House several times daily for more than a decade—nor do we know yet what accommodations Edmund will choose when we arrive in Chicago. Even so, Lord, it is a blessing not to have stairs to climb while we are here.

O'Dell and his boys changed into old clothes and went out to the barn with Søren to help with chores. When the boys returned later, they were filled with awe and wonder, and talked nonstop about all their new sights and experiences.

For the adults, the remainder of the day into the evening was spent catching up. They stuffed themselves on Meg's fine cooking and baking, then retired to the living room, where Joy and Søren told stories on each other, Meg held Roseanne to her heart's content, and Søren regaled his young nephews with tall tales.

Rose joined in the merriment, but within her heart, she was waiting.

Waiting for morning.

CHAPTER 5

A good night's sleep refreshed Rose. Following breakfast and devotions and after she helped Meg clean and tidy the kitchen, she went to her bedroom and changed her shoes for an old pair of walking boots. She returned to the kitchen and wrapped a thick shawl around her shoulders, tucking its ends under her arms.

The fall morning was chilly, but she cared not a whit.

I am about to make my escape.

"Mama, where are you going?"

Foiled.

"For a walk, Joy." Rose's feet twitched about in her boots. They had a life of their own, and she did not know how much longer she could keep them from jumping out the door—taking her with them.

Joy looked uncertain. "Would you like me to go with you? The boys are with Edmund and Søren in the barn. I could bundle up Roseanne and bring her with us. I am certain the fresh air would do us all some good."

"Thank you but no, my dear. I would like to go alone. And I may be gone a few hours."

She heard again from her feet: *twitch, twitch.*

Rose watched Joy glance at Meg for help, and she chuckled. "I will be fine, Joy. I managed Union Station, after all, and I am quite familiar with this farm—and the one across the creek."

Meg nodded. "Aye, that you are, Mama Rose."

Rose raised one eyebrow in her daughter's direction, and Joy closed her mouth on any further objections. Rose stepped through the back door and closed it behind her.

ROSE STOOD ON the back steps for a long moment. Looking. Tasting. Feeling. She closed her eyes and inhaled deeply. The fall air carried the warm scent of burning cornstalks and the tang of fermenting silage. Rose felt the coolness of the breeze as it caressed her cheeks and recalled days long gone when a similar breeze had riffled her hair or tugged at her skirts. She inhaled again, as if trying to swallow whole every memory it evoked.

She glanced left across the farmyard, passing over Meg's green garden, to the gentle slope where grass and apple trees grew.

Jan planted those trees.

The apples had been picked, and the trees' leaves were turning now as nighttime temperatures dipped below freezing. She knew, too, that the leaves obscured the family graveyard just beyond the trees, where the slope leveled out.

Not now. Not yet. I won't go there today.

Holding to the railing, she stepped down from the porch. She walked straight on, past the water pump, and onto the dirt drive leading away from the house. In a matter of minutes, her footsteps led her to the turn in the dusty road that wended toward the creek. Soon she saw the bridge. It was still a distance ahead, and she felt the urge to walk faster, to rush, but she restrained herself.

I am in no hurry. This day is all mine. I will savor every bit of it.

She walked on, taking her time. Meadowlarks called from the fields. She shielded her eyes and looked up. A red-tailed hawk circled high above her, scouting for mice or rabbits below. Six Canadian geese flew away south in formation.

The cows in Søren's field eyed her. Rose walked over to the fence, and two of the "bossies" trotted toward her.

"Oh, dear. I should have thought to bring you a treat," she murmured. "I am rather rusty at this, it seems."

At the sound of her unfamiliar voice, the cows flinched and skittered away.

Rose chuckled and moved back to the road. Kept walking.

When her boots resounded on the planks of the bridge, something old and deep but intimately familiar rang in her heart, keeping tempo with the tap of her boots. Halfway across the bridge, she stopped and rested her arms on the railing.

She took her leisure and watched the water flow away beneath her as it rushed on toward the river. She studied the mossy rocks in the creek bed, some flashing gold in the sunlight, others the emerald green of ancient treasure. Then her eyes traced the creekbank away from the bridge, walked her gaze steadily upstream, followed the grassy slope up to her house.

Our home, she thought. Its shape and form were as she remembered, although it was no longer the pristine white it had once been.

You are as gray and weathered as I am, old friend.

Rose left the bridge and walked on, eager to visit the house. As she passed the new house Jon had built, she saw his wife, Camille.

Camille was hanging wet clothes on the line. Her three children played not far from her. Camille waved to Rose. Rose lifted a hand in acknowledgement, but she did not turn aside.

She had but one destination.

Finally, she was near enough to run her eyes over the little house, to take in its sad condition. The roof was buckled in places, and the paint on its siding had peeled away. One window was boarded over, the glass gone. The porch Jan had built her when they first met, however, stood strong and defiant against the years.

Rose leaned against the porch's nearest post. Paused to catch the breath that hitched in her chest and throat. Her expectant eyes sought the front door under the porch's eaves. She imagined the door opening and a joyous, loving voice greeting her, "*My li'l Rose!*"

But no dear figure appeared there.

"Silly woman," she whispered to herself. "Not yet. *Be patient therefore*, Rose, *unto the coming of the Lord.*"

After resting a moment, she climbed the steps and reached for the door handle. It turned under her hand, and she walked inside. She made a slow tour of the three rooms—two bedrooms and the open living room-kitchen. Not surprisingly, few items of furniture remained in the house.

Well, I gave most everything away before I left. So many in our community were in need. And besides, I believe the Lord showed me that I would never live here again and would have no need of them.

Besides a pair of rickety kitchen chairs, a dented washtub on the kitchen floor, and their old rocking chair gathering dust in a corner of the living room, only one object caught her eye. She blinked at it several moments, knowing it did not belong in her house, that it was out of place.

Her own wood-burning cookstove, battered and worn, was gone. It had been replaced by a stove equally battered and worn but which, with its graceful lines, had at one time been quite exquisite. Early in its use, the small stove and its handles had been enameled in white and its doors inset with colorful patterned tiles. Many of the tiles were cracked or missing now, the enamel chipped and yellowed by age.

Still, the stove spoke to her and reminded her that she knew it well.

Why, this is Amalie's stove, Rose realized, *the stove Elli brought from Norway, a gift from her parents. Jan built their kitchen around this little gem. Meg and Søren may have given it to Jon and Camille when they married.*

She calculated the stove's age: *Fifty-seven years, at least.*

"You should not have been neglected and abandoned, you know," she commiserated with the stove. "You are part of this family's story, its heritage."

Rose again wandered the empty rooms. With a last look around, she closed the front door behind her with the same care as the memories she tucked away. But she was not ready to leave, not at all. No, she wanted to sit and look across the creek and take in the vastness of the panorama before her.

As I did so many times that first summer when my heart fell in love with the prairie. When I would watch Jan splash across the creek with Søren and their tools. Or when Jan would ride his horse across the bridge. When he and Uli would come to take me sleighing across the snowy fields, the three of us singing and laughing. And later . . . when I began to love Jan and yearn for him to come to me.

She lowered herself to sit on the porch's edge with her feet resting on the step below. She sighed and leaned against one of the posts holding up the roof. Midmorning sunlight warming the steps also warmed Rose. She closed her eyes and let the warmth comfort her. As she nodded in the sun's embrace, she gave herself over to precious memories, all clamoring for her attention.

"Jan," she whispered, "and our baby, the daughter we named Joy Again Thoresen."

Once upon a time, I was raising three children with the conveniences of a nanny and other domestic servants. But after three years on the prairie, I was still inexperienced in its ways and the demands on a farmer's wife. I had never had to juggle a baby, a home, farm chores, and the prairie itself.

All on my own.

SPRING 1884

JAN AND ROSE'S precious nine-month-old daughter was teething. Baby Joy was in pain, yet they were all suffering. Joy had awakened Rose twice during the previous night and kept her on her feet, pacing back and forth in the kitchen, cuddling her infant, praying that her fussing wouldn't ruin Jan's sleep.

Rose had tried to get Joy to chew or suck on a cool, damp cloth, but nothing consoled their baby. Joy alternately sobbed with heartbreak and screamed in agony. It was an hour both times before Rose was able to soothe Joy back to sleep.

In the morning, Joy's wails again pulled Rose from sleep. She crawled from beneath the covers and sat on the edge of the bed, trying to untangle her thoughts.

Jan's side of the bed was empty.

Lord, bless him. He must have slipped out quietly, so that I might rest a while longer.

Last night had not been the first interruption to Rose's slumber in the past week. Joy had gotten her mother up four nights running, and Rose was exhausted. Her eyelids drooped, and she swayed, half asleep, on the edge of the bed until more screaming roused her from her stupor.

"My poor baby. I am coming, my darling."

She peered into Joy's crib to find that her adorable baby girl had soiled herself and most of her bedding.

"Teething, I despise thee," Rose growled.

The morning did not improve as it went along. Rose had prepared a pot for coffee the night before. Jan had apparently perked it, poured himself a cup or two, set the pot to the back of the stove, and left the fire to die down.

Rose built up the embers in the stove, poured the last of a bucket of fresh water into the kettle, set it on the stove to heat for Joy's bath, and moved the coffee pot forward. When the water in the kettle was warm enough, Rose dipped some into an enameled wash basin. After adding cool water to the hot, she washed and diapered Joy. She was about to slip the baby into a warm gown when the forgotten coffee pot overflowed onto the hot stove. As the liquid hit the stovetop, some of it boiled off, but much of it flew as spatters in all directions.

"Oh, no!" Rose grabbed up Joy with one hand and a towel with the other. Using the towel as a potholder, she moved the coffee far back on the stove.

"Thank goodness there's a bit left in the pot. I will enjoy that cup as soon as I have a moment—oh, bother. My goats! No coffee until I have milked my poor goats."

After dressing Joy, she picked her up, grabbed one of the baby's worn blankets and a clean bucket, and headed for the small barn Jan and Søren had built. Inside, their three pygmy goats hopped about, fussing at her. It was past time for them to be milked. Rose added fresh straw to one of the goats' feeding troughs, spread Joy's blanket across the straw, and plunked Joy's padded bottom on the blanket.

"Mama has to milk our goats now, Joy."

Joy loved the goats, and they loved her in return—to a point. When they danced about with happy abandon, Joy chortled and clapped her fat little hands. When they nuzzled her, she cooed and leaned her face into them, nuzzling them back. But when she tugged their long, silky ears, they bleated and jumped away.

One by one, Rose led the goats to the stanchion where she milked them. She began with Star Bright, moved on to Moonbeam, and finished with Snowfoot. She had become a quick and deft hand at milking since Jan had given her Snowfoot almost three years ago. In less than five minutes, she had stripped the last of Snowfoot's milk and released her.

Rose caught Joy and her blanket up in her arms, grabbed a hammer and three stakes with their attached ropes, and led the goats from the barn. She found Prince already staked out and cropping fresh grass. Baron lounged nearby. He cracked open one eye. Assured that all was as it should be, he returned to his nap.

Joy spread the blanket on the ground close to Baron, sat Joy down, and staked out the goats for the morning. When she was finished, she gathered up Joy and her blanket and returned the hammer to its place in the barn before picking up the bucket of fresh milk.

Finally, carrying Joy under one arm like she might carry a fat sausage, and with the nearly-filled bucket hanging from the opposite hand, she returned to the house. Rose set the bucket of milk on the table and placed Joy in the tall chair Jan had made especially for her. Rose slipped a tea towel across Joy's chest and under her chubby little arms, then tied the towel's ends behind the chair's spindles. She scooted Joy's chair up to the table and placed her little tin cup and spoon before her.

"Play with those while Mama strains the milk—oh, dear. I forgot about the mess in Joy's crib."

Taking the tin wash tub from the nail outside the back door, Rose stripped Joy's bedding, piled it into the washtub, and ran it outside to the pump where she covered the soiled sheets with icy water.

"I'll scrub you later. Once I've had my cup of coffee," Rose promised. The vision of that first sip beckoned to her. But not yet.

She flew through her next chores: Peeling and cutting up potatoes for breakfast. Setting them on the stove to parboil. Skimming the fat off last evening's milking and ladling the fat into clean jars for making cheese later. Setting half a jar of the milk aside for Baron and Joy—

Joy pounded her cup on the table and screeched.

"Yes, yes, I know. Be patient, my little tyrant."

Rose grabbed up Baron's bowl and Joy's cup. Poured milk into both. Set Joy's cup before her on the table. Joy was just learning to manage her cup well. Rose opened the back door where Baron was waiting and placed his bowl on the back stoop. He did not immediately lap up the milk. Rather, he lifted one droopy eye at her and huffed.

"I know I am late, Baron, but I do not require your recriminations atop my own. Now, drink it up or I will throw it out."

She didn't wait to see whether Baron bent to his bowl, for a metallic *clank* followed by an angry howl issued from the house. With a sigh, she rushed inside.

Joy had thrown her cup against the wall. She may have swallowed a sip or two first, but the majority of the milk Rose had poured into the cup now adorned the wall and window curtains—besides which, Joy was pitching a screaming fit, throwing herself this way and that against her chair and the table.

Rose hung her head. Sighed. Dug in the dirty clothes for a rag that wasn't already too soiled and proceeded to mop the drips and streaks of milk from her curtains. The forgotten potatoes caught her attention when they boiled over.

"*Wonderful*. Now the potatoes are overcooked and will be mushy when I fry them."

Just then, Rose heard the stamp of Jan's boots on the back steps.

Jan walked into the kitchen and halted. His slow perusal took in the scene: potatoes overflowing on the stove, spatters of coffee on the wall, milk streaking the table, walls, and floor, Joy shrieking while slamming her little body against the back of her chair over and over.

And his disheveled bride.

Joy stopped screaming when she spied Jan. She bounced up and down and reached her grabby little fingers toward him.

"PaPaPaPa!" she babbled.

Jan only had eyes for Rose. Wide eyes. Eyes that dropped from her face to her clothes.

Rose blinked and looked down at herself. Saw what Jan saw. "What? Oh, no. *Oh, no!*"

She was wearing a filthy apron *over her nightgown*. Furthermore, her hair, uncombed or pinned since she got out of bed, hung down her back in a tangled mess.

Her chest contracted, then heaved. "I-I-I am sorry, Jan. I . . . I have tried, truly I have. But I am not a good farmer's wife." She shuddered, and her voice cracked. "I-I try, but I cannot s-seem to do everything. I-I know you are disappointed in me. I-I-I know I am a failure."

Jan fixed his gaze on Rose's crumbling face. "Rose," he murmured. "Come, my Rose."

She walked into his embrace. As his arms closed about her, she sobbed. And sobbed. And sobbed. Finally, she wailed, "E-everything has g-gone wrong this m-morning!"

"*Ja*, I see dat," he whispered. "Go. Take care of Rose, *ja?* I vill vatch Joy. Ve vill eat ven is ready, ven *you* ready. Is not vorry."

"Th-thank you, Jan. I-I will hurry."

"*Nei*, all is gud. Is okay not hurry."

With a grateful bob of her head, Rose shuffled to their room.

It, too, was a disaster. Joy's soiled nightgown on the floor—instead of soaking with the baby's bed linens—Jan and Rose's bedding rumpled and awry, and the trunk at the end of the bed open, its disheveled contents half in and half out.

Rose's spirit sank further. "I didn't even pull up the blankets and quilt and straighten our bed."

After she had tidied the bedroom, she yanked off her dirty apron and nightgown, donned a clean dress, and sat on the side of their bed. She closed her eyes, and with only her sense of touch to guide her, combed out her hair, plaited it into a long braid down her back, wound it tightly at her neck, and pinned it in place.

Sighed.

"Thank you, Lord, for a few minutes of respite. Thank you for a kind, considerate husband."

She brightened. "And thank you for coffee." Rose hurried back to the kitchen.

A sweet domestic scene greeted her. Joy sat on Jan's lap, reclined against his chest, while Jan helped her drink her morning milk. Joy's chubby fingers were wrapped about her tin cup; Jan's palm held the cup steady. Rose could hear Joy's greedy gulps.

"Slow please, li'l *datter*," Jan chuckled.

Joy plunked the empty cup on the table with a satisfied belch followed by a great belly laugh. Jan chuckled. Rose laughed with him. Jan lifted the mug at his elbow and drained it.

Rose blinked. *My coffee . . .*

THE SCENE WAS incredibly vivid! She heard Joy's deep chortle and Jan's deeper, rumbling laughter, and Rose laughed with them. She was still giggling under her breath when she came to herself.

Oh, what a morning that was. It seemed like everything that could go wrong did *go wrong. Yet a moment in Jan's arms had made everything wrong fade away, and he had been patient. Kind.*

JAN READ ALOUD from their family Bible while Rose fixed breakfast. He kept Joy on his lap as he read. She was at that age where she grabbed for everything—and shoved it into her mouth as quickly as she could.

The only thing within her reach was the family Bible, so she scrabbled to reach it until Jan murmured, "*Nei*, Joy."

She twisted her little body around to study his face. He gently repeated himself. "*Nei*, Joy." With a sigh, she leaned back against his broad chest and waited.

Minutes later, Rose placed their late breakfast on the table, secured Joy in her tall chair, and breathed her own sigh of relief. Joy devoured the scrambled egg Rose fed her and banged the table for more. The crust of bread Rose placed in Joy's fist quieted her, and they finished breakfast in peace.

Alas, that had not been the end of her disastrous day . . . and Jan had not been as quick to forgive her next mistake.

I WAS GREEN in the ways of a farm, and I was often distracted and less watchful than I should have been. Particularly when it came to the unforgiving nature of life on the prairie with a growing infant . . .

Rose shook herself. *I need not think on that today. Today is for happy memories.*

She got up, stretched her arms over her head, and set off toward Søren and Meg's house. At the bridge she paused and turned toward her house.

"I will be back," she promised.

CHAPTER 6

That evening, Søren and Meg hosted a potluck dinner for immediate family only, meaning Sigrün, Karl, and Kjell would be joining them—as well as their children and grandchildren.

For Joy, it was the happy chaos of introducing her husband and children to her dear cousins, their grown children, and even their grandchildren, many of whom she was meeting for the first time. In addition to Rose and the O'Dells, close to fifty Thoresens crowded into Søren and Meg's kitchen and living room.

With so many bodies in a confined space, the air grew too warm. Rose, still weary from the farewells in Denver and their train journey, found herself becoming overwhelmed, for it seemed that everyone wanted to speak to her—all at once—even while she tried to snatch a quick bite to eat.

O'Dell observed Rose's dilemma first. He sidled up to Søren and, after a quick consultation, they escorted Rose to a large, overstuffed chair in the living room and appointed Søren and Meg's daughter, Colleen, the task of fending off the well-meaning family members until Rose had finished her dinner.

Afterward, Colleen had two of her three daughters fetch two kitchen chairs and place them beside Rose. Colleen, with her oldest daughters' assistance, then regulated the flow of visitors by inviting Søren and Meg's cousins and their spouses to sit beside Rose's chair, one couple at a time, for a short personal visit and then to reacquaint Rose with their families.

Sigrün and Harold claimed the first spot. They sat down beside Rose, and Sigrün took Rose's hand between her own and held it.

"How happy we are to see you again, Aunt Rose. Everyone in the family has been counting the days until you and Joy would arrive."

"As have I, Sigrün. As have I. Hello again, Harold. I am delighted to see you both looking fit and healthy." Smiling her pleasure, Rose turned to examine Sigrün's grown children as they queued up to greet her. "Let me see. I recognize Jarl, Ola, Liv, and Rolf—but, my! How they and their broods have grown. You must be so proud of them all."

Jarl and his wife, Bette, came forward to reintroduce their adult children and their spouses. It was apparent that Jarl and Bette's oldest daughter and her husband were expecting a child.

"Congratulations, Jarl," Rose said, "I see you will be a grandfather before long."

"Yes, Aunt Rose. We are looking forward to meeting our first grandchild."

"And we will have a great-grandson or great-granddaughter," Harold chimed in.

"Wonderful. A blessing. I am happy for you all," Rose murmured.

In succession, Sigrün and Harold's other children, Ola, Liv, and Rolf, presented themselves, their spouses, and their children, and Rose expressed her delight with each one. Then Sigrün and Harold embraced Rose and gave up their seats to Kjell and his wife, Lily.

One branch of the family tree down, Rose told herself. *Three to go—and that is not even counting Arnie and Uli's spouses and families who could not be here.*

Kjell bent next to Rose's chair and kissed her cheek before sitting down with his wife. "Do you remember Lily, Aunt Rose?"

"Certainly," Rose answered. "I am pleased to see you both looking so well and happy. It has been too long since we have met."

Kjell went on. "Well, we have certainly missed you, Aunt Rose. Seeing you again brings back loads of happy memories."

"I am recalling those happy times myself," Rose murmured. "It is good to be here with all of you." She glanced toward Colleen, who had Kjell and Lily's family queued up. "My, but your family has certainly increased."

"Yes. Our sons, Stephan, Kristoffer, and Jørn, and our daughters, Lisa and Letta are married now.

Kjell, with a teasing grin, asked Rose, "You remember our five children, don't you, Aunt Rose?"

Rose's mind was already reeling. "But of course, I—oh. No. I am sorry, Kjell. Please forgive me."

He cut up, slapping his thigh, and his sons joined his laughter. "We are funning with you, Aunt Rose. We don't expect *you* to remember everyone after being away so long, but you should see what we do to the young men who hope to marry into our family. We show no mercy."

A roar of good-natured laughter agreed with him.

Through narrowed eyes, Rose watched them laugh. *Ah, but I pity the poor suitors.*

Kjell came back to Rose. "I will let each of them introduce themselves, their spouse, and our two grandchildren." He added, "Only two grandkids so far. We are hoping for many more."

Exerting no pressure on the parents, of course, Rose chuckled to herself.

When Kjell and Lily's five children and two grandchildren had passed under Rose's approving inspection, Søren and Meg sat down.

"How are you doing, Rose?" Søren asked, a mischievous twinkle in his eye.

"My smile has a flat tire."

He snickered.

"And if I go missing, you may find me in my room with the door locked and barred."

Søren grinned. "That's our Rose. More spunk than the lot of us put together."

Rose snorted—and grinned back. "I was thinking that I have not had this much fun in some considerable time. I just may grow accustomed to it."

Colleen interrupted. "Aunt Rose, may I present my husband, Feor? You remember him, don't you?"

Rose smothered her laughter and nodded slowly. Thoughtfully. "Of *course*."

"And our three daughters, Mari, Sissle, and Treya?"

"Why, *yes*."

Meg raised her eyes to heaven; Søren had to turn away lest Colleen catch him snickering.

Colleen's family was followed by Søren and Meg's younger son Jon, his wife, Camille, and their four children, Arvid, Eva, Kirsten, and Leif.

"I saw you walking to your house this morning," Camille said. "The weather was cool, and I thought to bring you a cup of hot tea, but I reconsidered, thinking perhaps you wanted to be alone." It was as much a question as a statement.

"Jon, you have married a lovely, insightful woman," Rose replied. "Thank you for your kind sensitivity, Camille. I did crave some time alone to think and remember."

Camille glowed at Rose's compliment, then she and Jon took their leave.

Lastly, Søren motioned to their eldest son, Markus, and his wife, Delores. After Markus and Delores had spent a few minutes greeting Rose, Markus lined up their five children to shake her hand.

Their first three daughters, Brita, Inger, and Julia, had been born before Rose left RiverBend and were now teenagers. Their fourth daughter, born since Rose left, looked to be roughly age nine, followed by a boy seven or eight years of age.

They kept trying. Finally got their boy, Rose remarked to herself.

Markus and Delores' only son, Nils, seemed quite taken with Rose. He jumped ahead of his next-older sister, walked directly to Rose, and put out his hand, grinning the gap-toothed grin of a boy in the process of losing baby teeth and replacing them with adult ones faster than the tooth fairy could cope.

Markus moved up to stand beside Nils.

It appears Markus is not quite trustful of the boy's behavior, Rose thought.

"Never met no famous person, before," Nils announced. "Pleased t' meetcha."

Behind him, Rose heard a handful of titters, quickly covered up, the effort largely ineffective.

"Me? Famous?" Rose pretended to consider Nils' accolade.

"Yes'm. Why, this here party is all for you, and it ain't even your birthday. You must be pretty famous, I'm thinkin'."

"Nils, introduce yourself," his father prompted him.

"Yes, Papa." Nils turned back to Rose. "Begging your pardon, ma'am. I'm Nils Thoresen. What's your name?"

Rose was charmed. "My name is Rose. Rose Thoresen. Thank you for asking."

He squinted at her. "Don't reckon I ever seed you before, and I know all the Thoresens, even Cousin Arnie in Omaha, our cousins, Willem and Petter, even Aunt Uli in Colorado. A'course, she ain't Uli Thoresen no more, 'cause she married Pastor Kalbørg. I jest can't rightly figure how *you* got to be a Thoresen 'thout me hearin' 'bout it."

"And you would like to know?"

"Yes'm, I would. Never been any famous Thoresens *I* know about."

The titters were less restrained now, and Rose experienced her own difficulties keeping a straight face.

"Well, let me see. You know Søren Thoresen, do you not? He is sitting right there."

"Sure I do. He's my grandpa." Nils leaned around his father and waved at Søren. Søren grinned and waved back. "He's my favorite person in the whole world—'ceptin Mama and Papa, a'course."

He hooked his thumbs in his suspenders in a very credible imitation of Søren. "Love my grandpa, I do."

"I can see why you would," Rose drawled.

The audience surrounding Rose and Nils inched in, intent on catching the exchange, but the boy seemed unaware. He was, in fact, so serious and transparent that Rose had to hold her handkerchief in front of her lips to keep from joining in the general mirth.

Nils needed no encouragement to continue the conversation—or to confide important plans to Rose. "See, when I grow up, I'm gonna marry the prettiest girl in the neighborhood."

Rose coughed. "Pardon me. *Ahem.*" She cleared her throat. "And have you any prospects at this time, Nils?"

"Sure, but I can't decide 'tween Pearly Bruntrüllsen and Grace Miller. Thinkin' I should wait and see how they fill out before I make m' choice."

Rose grabbed the water glass by her chair and downed it, half choking as she did.

Nils kept going. "After I'm married, I will live with Grandpa Søren and help him farm his land."

"So. You have it all planned out, I suppose?"

"Yes'm. The farmin' part for certain. Grandpa and I have already 'cussed it."

"Er, you . . . you have *cussed* it?"

"Yup. 'Cussed it a couple times over, fer a fact."

"*Dis*cussed it, Nils," Markus corrected him.

"Yes sir. *Dis*cussed it. And after I'm married, I will name my first boy after my Grandpa."

"I think he would like that very much, Nils."

"Yup. Me, too. Hopin' I don't have no four girls first, though."

Rose stuffed down a snicker and, instead, hiccupped behind her hankie. "Er, pardon me." She hiccupped a second time.

"Sure. Need me t' thump yer back fer ya?"

Out of the corner of her eye, Rose caught Søren pounding his thigh, one fist jammed in his mouth.

"Thank you, kindly, Nils, but perhaps not at this time."

He edged in closer. "So's how *did* you get to be a Thoresen?"

Nils' demand brought Rose back to her promised explanation. She nodded. "Well, it was like this, Nils. Your Grandpa Søren's mama went to heaven when he was just a young man. Quite a while later, Søren's papa, Jan Thoresen, your *great*-grandpa, married me."

Nils' eyes bulged. "Does that make you Grandpa Søren's mama—*and you're still alive?*"

"Um. Erm. Oh, dear." Rose was losing the battle of decorum whereas their audience had surrendered *en masse*. Finally, she managed, "Well, young man, you might say that I am your grandpa's 'second mama.'"

Søren spoke up before Nils could raise another havoc-rousing follow-on question. "And let me tell you, Nils, Rose is the best 'second mama' money could buy."

Every feature on Nils' face lifted in astonishment. "Ya mean ya *bought* her? Why, how much—"

"And that will be enough, Nils," Markus said, rolling his eyes. "Please thank our guest for her time."

Nils bobbed his head at Rose. "'Twas a pleasure t' meet you, Rose Thoresen."

"I believe the pleasure was all mine, Nils Thoresen. Truly."

Markus shepherded him away with, "Let your sister have her turn now."

Rose's conversation with Nils had been the highlight of her evening thus far. She chuckled aloud and nodded to Meg and Søren who were holding their sides and rocking silently forward and back. Rose brought her attention back and found the last of Nils' longsuffering older sisters extending her hand to Rose.

"I'm Margit, ma'am. I'm nine years old, and I 'pologize for our Nils. We're used to him, you see, and you ain't. Told Mama we needed t' put a leash on him or sumpthin', but she said it weren't fittin'. Don't know why we couldn't make a leash that fits him, but Mama didn't want to talk about it anymore."

All Rose could manage was to cover her mouth with her hankie and nod. With that, Margit curtsied and scooted away, her duty done.

When Rose could speak again, she murmured to Markus and Delores, "I promise to make you a daily fixture in my prayers."

"The Lord bless you," Delores breathed. "Oh, how we need those prayers."

Søren and Meg, still holding their sides, gave up their seats to "little" Karl, now in his mid-fifties, and his wife Sonja. Karl engulfed Rose in a bone-crunching hug before he sat down. "Dear Aunt Rose. What a blessing to see you again. You remember . . . " and he recited the names of his and Sonja's five children, their spouses, and their children's children as they stepped forward when called.

While Rose murmured greeting after greeting, a poignant yet amusing observation popped into her thoughts. *Why, this must be what drowning in love feels like, Lord. And if I must go tonight, this can hardly be the worst way.* Cheered, she produced a smile, a kind word, and a hug or handshake for every one of them.

She was mildly surprised when not all of them returned her regard.

Karl was saying, "And, finally, this is our eldest granddaughter, Lucia. She is Einar and Norrie's girl. We call her Lucy."

"But of course. Lucy was learning to walk when I last saw her. You must be, what, fourteen now?" Rose addressed the last to Lucy herself.

Karl answered instead. "Just turned fourteen, she did." Something in Karl's reply seemed a hair too bright.

Rose glanced at him before offering her hand to the girl before her. "Hello, Lucy. My, what a lovely young woman you are becoming. How are you?"

Lucy's hand in Rose's had the responsiveness of a dead fish. "I am fine, thank you." Her words were all politeness. Her blue Thoresen eyes declared something else.

Rose's welcoming smile slipped. *What is this I see? Is it anger?* She delayed releasing the limp trout from her grip. "If I recall correctly, you are also named after your great-grandmother. Your middle name is Amalie, isn't it?"

"Yes." The word dripped from her mouth with cool scorn.

So it is *anger*, Rose realized. *But why?*

Karl's wife, Sonja, spoke into the awkward silence. "Quite right. Lucia Amalie Thoresen." Sonja pointed with her chin at one of the couples in line. "Einar and his wife bought a farm just west of McKennies'. Lucy is their first, the eldest of our grandchildren. She has been staying with us and is . . . such a joy to have in our home."

Staying with her grandparents when her own family lives within walking distance?

Rose focused her attention on Lucy. "Thank you for coming to greet me, Lucy. Amalie was one of my dearest friends. Perhaps we'll find a moment to talk while I am here. I would enjoy sharing with you some of the memories I have of your great-grandmother."

Lucy cast her eyes down. When she did not answer, Sonja sent Rose a brief look of apology. After a moment, she and Karl excused themselves, and Sonja tugged Lucy away.

Rose was left with concern. *Something is wrong here, but what?*

LATER, AFTER THE crowd of family visitors had taken their leave and after Joy had gotten her exhausted boys off to bed, Meg, Rose, and Joy sat down in the kitchen to a calming cup of chamomile tea while Joy nursed Roseanne.

"Thank you for an entirely wonderful evening," Rose murmured, "but, goodness, I am worn out—and all I did was sit in a chair."

"Hardly all you did, Mama. Edmund told me you were besieged and nearly knocked off your feet by a tide of well-wishers—what with everyone in the family wanting to have a word with you at the same time."

"It was quite thoughtful of Edmund and Søren to arrange things so I could have a personal moment with each of them in an orderly manner. Still, it was a bit difficult . . ."

Joy placed her hand on Rose's. "I am sorry, Mama. I see Papa everywhere, too."

"Oh, no, you mistake me, Joy. It wasn't sorrow that made it difficult. It was simply the chore of reconciling so many dear ones with their older faces."

"Ah. I understand now."

Rose's eyes roamed about the kitchen. "That, and other changes."

The kitchen had changed some since it had been Amalie's. The long table they sat at was the same, the beautiful cupboards and counters were the same. Her gaze passed by the door to the cellar and rested on the shelves stocked with colorful crockery. The original rosemåling Jan's first wife, Elli, had done sparkled against the shelves' bright white paint.

But the windows had different curtains, a telephone hung on the wall near the stairs, and the wonderful little stove Elli had brought with her from Norway was no longer the focal point of the room. It was, instead, languishing in her old house, across the creek, replaced by a larger and more efficient propane stove.

"You were saying, Mama?"

"I was remembering this kitchen, a bit more than forty years ago now. It was midday, dinner time. Jan came for me in his buggy, pulled by his magnificent bays. I put on my prettiest dress for Jan, the deep, dusty-pink one he said he loved to see me in. He was wearing his best suit—and *oh!* How fine and handsome he was."

Rose stared far away, smiling. Seeing him clearly enough that she longed to touch him. "When we drove up here, Søren came out to meet us. Such a sweet young man he was. I already loved him dearly. When he said, 'I wanted to welcome you to the family' and kissed me on my cheek, I was nearly undone.

"Then we were seated around this very table. Søren knew what was coming. Karl, Kjell, and Arnie were mere boys, more interested in the food. And Amalie—I will never forget her. She suspected something was about to happen. Uli, too."

Rose blinked back the moisture that blurred her vision, and she realized Meg and Joy were hanging on her every word.

"Then what, Mama?" Joy whispered.

"Then your father stood up and made an announcement." Here Rose deepened her voice and took on an accent familiar to them all. "'Fam'ly,' he said, 'haf happy news today. Soon Mrs. Brünlee and I marry. She be mine vife. She be Aunt Rose for you.'"

She sighed and smiled. "Amidst the whooping and shouting, I was welcomed into the Thoresen family with open arms and open hearts—it was one of the happiest moments of my life."

Meg and Joy sighed and smiled with her.

Rose murmured, "These shelves and the rosemåling are just as striking as the first time I saw them."

Meg nodded. "Søren repainted the shelves last year, and Sigrün refreshed the rosemåling. I am knowin' what an act of love 'twas on Sigrün's part to be preservin' her Aunt Elli's artistry."

Rose put her head to one side. "And you have a new stove."

"Yes'm. T'other was being a wee bit too small for our growing family. Gave it to Jon and Cam when they married."

"I saw it this morning when I visited my house."

Meg nodded. "Aye, Jon bought Cam a propane stove when they were building their house."

"You know, Meg, Jan and Amalie told me that Elli's parents gave her that little stove to bring with her to America. When I saw it languishing in my house, I had a thought."

Meg nodded for her to go on.

"I wondered if Elli's stove, like her rosemåling, wasn't an important piece of Thoresen history. Søren's mother's history."

Understanding bloomed in Meg's expression. "Ah."

"Perhaps someone in the family would like to preserve it?"

"Yes, you are right, Mama Rose. I thank you for bringing it to my attention—I will make certain 'tis cared for."

Rose placed her hand on Meg's. "Thank you, Meg. I am glad of it." Then she asked, "What is planned for the remainder of our visit?"

"Nothing of import afore Saturday's luncheon at the church. The women's auxiliary is hostin' it, so I must be there an hour ahead. Søren will be takin' me, then comin' back to fetch you and Joy."

She chuckled. "I'm believin' my Søren rates attendin' sech an event just shy of a tooth extraction."

Rose's brows arched in amusement. "What makes you say that?"

"Why, think on it: He is volunteerin' to be keepin' six young'uns—Jon and Camille's and Edmund and Joy's—'ceptin' the babe—here at our house so we ladies might be havin' a day w' out cares."

Rose and Joy laughed with Meg, and Joy replied, "Well, I cannot deny it. He is rendering us a great service."

When their laughter ebbed, Meg added, "Only the luncheon be planned whilst you be here, Mama Rose. After? You are free to be visitin' wi' family and wi' friends and naught else."

"'Naught else' meaning you should relax, Mama," Joy echoed. "Use this time to refresh yourself."

Rose looked over her cup at Joy. "Hmm. And where might I have heard those same sentiments recently?"

"Weeell, perhaps Edmund and I—only in passing, I assure you—may have remarked on how hard you worked at Palmer House, especially at the end. We, um, feel that you truly deserve a rest. We wish for you to have that rest. And a bit of fun, Mama."

"You and Edmund. But not Meg and Søren?"

Meg ducked her head sheepishly. "Aye, you have caught us out."

Rose replied demurely, "With appreciation, I shall take your combined sentiments under advisement. I shall endeavor to both rest and relax during our visit."

Meg and Joy beamed at her. "And have some fun," Joy repeated.

"I should have a bit of fun, eh? Seems to me we drank a bucket of jocularity this evening—courtesy of young Master Nils."

The three women laughed into their cups and saucers. Meg's shoulders shook so hard, she had to put her cup down and hold her hand over her mouth. When she could catch her breath, she said, "Faith! The imagination of that one. Naught one thing 'bout our grandson Nils is bein' thick in the head—and nary a moment's rest from his mouth has Delores, his saint of a mother. Another cup?"

"No, not for me," Rose replied, but she asked about her close friend, Fiona McKennie. "How is your mother, Meg?"

"Are you meanin' since Da passed?"

"Yes, I suppose that is what I mean."

"'Twas a blow to us all, I confess, but struck her hardest, of course." Meg looked at her hands. "She was rallyin' well fer a time."

"For a time?"

Meg's eyes glimmered. "She's a-wastin', Mama Rose. Doctor says 'tis a cancer. She has a wee bit of pain, but no' so much she din't get 'round 'till lately. M' sister Martha, her husband, and her little clan be livin' with Mam these days. They will be takin' care of her needs."

Rose turned inward. *Another passing, Lord? Another loss?*

"Will I see her Saturday at the luncheon?"

"*Nay*. She wouldna miss it for the world, boot Martha says she is no' able to be leavin' the house. And you should know aforehand how altered to your eyes she will appear when you see her. Thin. Weak." Meg lifted her honest eyes to Rose. "Loik searchin' through murky water to find the real Mam these days."

"It is likely I would have little time at the luncheon for just her anyway. I shall plan to visit her tomorrow."

"'Twould please her to no end, Mama Rose."

When Meg got up to pour them fresh cups of tea, Joy asked, "Mama, what will you wear to the luncheon Saturday?"

"Wear? Goodness. I have not given it a single thought. How formal will the luncheon be?"

"Aye," Meg said from the stove. "Have heard 'twill be a grand occasion. Mrs. Medford has invited the whole of the county, both men and women. An occasion fer all the ladies to be wearin' their best."

Rose set her elbows on the table and rested her forehead on her hands. "Oh, dear. I suppose I will wear what I have on now even though the entire family has already seen me in it. I have so little to choose from these days."

Joy touched Rose's arm. "I could lend you my silk ivory shirtwaist, Mama. With your good black skirt or perhaps the brown pinstriped one, you will look fine enough."

"Thank you, Joy. I will take you up on your offer."

CHAPTER 7

Rose poured her first cup of coffee of the day and took it to the kitchen window where she had a view of the yard. It had rained overnight, and then the temperature had dropped. She peered through the trailing remnants of night shadows.

Is that frost on the ground?

"Good morn, Mama Rose. I'm seein' you still rise afore the dawn like a good farmer's wife."

"Good morning, Meg. I was always first to rise at Palmer House, too. It is the habit of a lifetime, I suppose, and cannot be broken now. I hope you do not mind that I made a pot of coffee and turned on the oven to ward off the chill?"

"Mind? *Nay*. The kitchen 'tis nice and warm, and since the pot is already perked, I shall set a moment and have a cup meself."

"I see we have a touch of frost this morning."

"Aye. Should melt away by midmorning, but I do not relish the coming of winter."

"Nor I." Rose sat down at the table across from Meg. The years had been kind to her daughter-in-law, but her hair was no longer the beautiful auburn Rose had admired when Meg was a girl of sixteen. Meg had braided and piled her long, thick tresses on her head, but the vivid red had faded, overrun by steely gray.

"I thought I might visit Fiona this afternoon."

"I shall let Martha know to be expectin' you."

They sat sipping their coffee in harmonious silence until Rose spoke. "What can you tell me about Karl's granddaughter, Lucy?"

"Aye, Einar and Norrie's bairn. Lovely girl. Quite clever. Always a book w' that one. All her teachers be sayin' she should go to college."

"Why is she living with Karl and Sonja?"

The space between Meg's brows creased. "Bit of a concern there. Some problems at home, Sonja is tellin' the family, but she does not say what. Truth, 'tis hard to draw a bead on the child, she says little enow."

Rose lifted her eyes to Meg. "I believe she is angry . . . and afraid."

The furrow between Meg's brows deepened. "Whist?"

"Has no one asked her why?"

Meg's shoulders lifted. "I canna say."

Søren clomped down the stairs into the kitchen. He nodded to Meg and Rose, filled a tin cup from the pot on the stove, pulled on his coat and gloves, and headed for the barn.

"'Tis time to be 'bout m' chores." Meg tied on an apron and pulled out the ingredients to start a batch of bread.

AS MEG HAD forecast, the frost melted off by midmorning under a warming sun. Rose donned her old boots, buttoned them up, and pulled a shawl about her shoulders. When she stepped outside, she again stopped and closed her eyes.

Amid the familiar scents that spoke to her heart, she heard the laughter of Joy's sons. They and their father were outside the pig pens. The sows had dropped their second litters of the year, and Søren had plucked a piglet from one of the older litters for the boys to handle.

I am glad my grandsons are getting to experience some of this life, Rose thought, *the life their grandfather lived, the life in which their mother grew up.*

A memory tickled her mind. *What was that? Ah yes.* She laughed low in her throat. *We were sitting on this very stoop, Amalie and I, warming ourselves in the spring sun. Amalie had made tea, and we were sipping it, chuckling together over Amalie's description of Sigrün's toddler—Amalie's first grandchild—and his newest antics, when we heard Joy's squeals of delighted laughter . . .*

"MAMA, LOOK!" Her precocious five-year-old daughter raced toward her. "Look, Mama! Papa is letting me hold a baby pig."

Joy's jubilant announcement was momentarily lost on Rose as she ran her eyes over her daughter. Sticks of hay protruded from Joy's long braids. One plait had lost its ribbon and was half undone. Then she saw the slick mud that spattered her daughter's cheeks . . . and what had been a clean dress.

With no warning, Joy dumped the piglet in Rose's lap. "See, Mama! Isn't he sweet? And he's so clever, too!"

"Is he?" Rose replied, dumbfounded, as her own clean skirt suddenly proclaimed a wealth of mud droplets. Worse yet, the piglet, perhaps only ten inches long, rooted and squealed, seeking warmth and security—smearing mud into the fabric of Rose's skirt with every thrust of his tiny snout.

Jan trailed behind Joy, sheepish guilt competing with the merriment curving his lips.

Amalie's gaze slid from Jan to Joy to Rose. "I take," Amalie deadpanned, removing Rose's teacup from her fingers. "You play vit clever pig, eh?"

Rose scowled at her, but Amalie started up the steps, snickering as she went.

"The baby piggy misses his mama," Joy explained, without a thought to *her* having separated the poor, frantic piglet from his mother. "You have to hold him tight, Mama, so he ain't afraid."

"So he *is not* afraid, Joy."

Rose placed her hands around the piglet, meaning to remove him, but the chubby thing, although breathing hard, calmed under her warm fingers. Then he looked up at Rose. She was stunned by the intelligence she glimpsed in his eyes.

"Oh, my. You *are* a clever piggy, aren't you?" Rose whispered.

"*Ja*, pig ver smart," Jan murmured. "Is husband not so smart."

Rose side-eyed him. "You have created an hour or more of extra washing for me, my beloved."

"I vill set in cold vater ven home. I scrub. Maybe husband li'l more smart next time."

But the truth was that Rose had eyes only for their daughter's wonder as she scooped the piglet from Rose's lap into her arms and cuddled it.

"Pretty piggy! Oh, look at its tiny curly tail, Mama. Isn't it cunning? Why do you think God gave him a curly tail?"

Then Joy peered up at Rose from under her long lashes. "I am sorry I got your dress dirty, Mama. I will help Papa wash it. We will get all the mud out of it, I promise."

"*Ja*," Jan agreed. "*All* clean. Joy and me."

And he held out Joy's missing and bedraggled hair ribbon to Rose.

WHAT A GOOD life we had, Jan. How grateful I am for these precious recollections.

Rose opened her eyes and climbed carefully down the porch steps. Once on level ground, she set off, skirting Meg's vegetable garden, its soil plowed under to await the spring. She turned toward the orchard and began the climb up the slope to the family graveyard.

She was gasping for breath when she reached the top, and her heart hammered in her chest. She leaned upon the wrought iron gate until the thundering of her heart eased, then opened the gate and ventured inside.

Someone had placed a little bench in front of Jan and Elli's graves. Rose assumed Søren had built it, and sank down upon the seat, grateful for its presence.

The graves were freshly tended, the prairie grass that grew so thick upon the mounded graves trimmed, the gravestones wiped clean. A single long-stemmed rose, its petals and leaves dry and crumbling from the recent freeze, lay across Jan's gravestone above his name. Rose saw that the stem was partly green, the cut still fresh.

Joy must have come here late yesterday. She has laid the last of Meg's roses on her papa's grave.

Rose made herself read the inscription on Jan's gravestone.

Jan Arvid Thoresen
1828–1909
Beloved Husband and Father

"I have been away a long time, my love, more than thirteen years, but I know you would have approved of the work Joy and I put our hands to in Denver. I recall your kind heart toward those whom the world has wounded. Had you been with us at Palmer House, you would have given yourself to the same labor."

She sighed. "I miss you, Jan, but I will see you soon. We will worship the Lord together again."

She shifted her gaze to the stone to the left of Jan's grave.

Elli Katrin Thoresen
(Mostrom)
1839–1872
Kjærlig Kone og Mor

Søren had told her years ago what the words in Riksmål meant: *Loving Wife and Mother*. To the right of Jan's grave was the resting place of their young daughter, lost in the same plague that took Elli and Jan's brother, Karl.

Kristen Siljie Thoresen
1860–1872
Kjære datter

"Beloved Daughter." *I wonder how many times Søren comes here to sit with his father, mother, and sister. And his baby brother.* The baby boy's stone was just above Elli's.

Vår Spedbarns Sønn
Født i Himmelen
1871

Rose knew the meaning of those words, too. "Our Infant Son, Born in Heaven." She imagined Elli's loss and grief and wept a little for her, wiping her eyes on her sleeve. She wept, too, for her daughter who had also lost a son . . . a son who was not dead but, they believed, was out there somewhere in the wide, wide world, a boy who would turn thirteen shortly after the New Year.

Rose pinched the bridge of her nose to stem her tears. *Oh, my precious Lord, if we did not cry at times, our griefs would overwhelm us. I am grateful that on That Day, you will wipe away all our tears in heaven.*

She stood and moved back toward the gate, to the first grave. Karl, Amalie's husband.

Karl Magnus Thoresen
1826-1872
Kjære Mann og Far

"'Beloved Husband and Father.' I did not know you, Karl, but I loved your wife dearly. She was both sister and mother to me and a loving aunt to Joy."

Amalie, teaching me to make candles, cheese, butter, jams and jellies. Patiently correcting my canning mistakes—patient even after I turned an entire batch of peaches to mush.

Amalie, worrying I would break Jan's heart while at the same time worrying Jan would break mine. Tearfully kissing my cheek when Jan announced our engagement.

Amalie, encouraging me through the long hours I labored to deliver Joy. Washing my body afterward and washing my bedding.

Amalie, including Joy in every bit of fun with her own children. Loving Joy as her own because Joy had no siblings at home—knowing I sometimes sorrowed over that.

Amalie, reassuring me when my confidence flagged. Quoting Scripture to me when I felt sorry for myself. Praying for me often.

Amalie, suffering a stroke that left her unable to move except to briefly squeeze her right hand.

Me, telling Amalie how much she was loved. Caring for her with the same devotion and longsuffering she had lavished on me and on so many others. Afterward, with Sonja, Meg, Uli, and Sigrün, preparing her body for burial . . .

"I rejoice that you are with Jesus, dear Amalie," Rose whispered, "but I still miss you."

Amalie Lisbeth Thoresen
(Haugen)
1835-1897
Sov i Herrens Armer

"'Asleep in the Arms of the Lord.' Yes, amen."

Rose wandered around the inside perimeter of the fencing to the other side and studied three tiny graves: Søren and Meg's daughter who died in her first year. Two infants Karl and Sonja had lost in childbirth. No other plots as yet.

Room to grow, she thought. *Room for me. My bones will rest here one day.*

She stood a last time before Karl and Amalie's graves, and remembered her concern for Lucy. "I suppose I ought to mind my own business, Amalie, but this is your great-granddaughter. For you, I would hazard getting my head bitten off—that is, if the Lord leads me."

She huffed out a chuckle. "Lucy doesn't know it, but I have crossed swords with young women far more daunting than she."

AFTER LUNCH, Meg offered to drive Rose over to visit Fiona.

"What? You know how to drive an automobile?"

Meg laughed. "Aye, certainly. Many a farmer's wife does. 'Tis drivin' tractors and trucks during harvest we must. But on occasion, when of our husbands we haven't been seein' enough, when they have forgotten they are married to *us* and not their farm, aye, then we are declarin' how we 'need' them to be drivin' us to town."

"Why that is downright manipulative," Rose answered. She tried to keep her expression serious—but the laughter that percolated in her heart and tugged at the corners of her mouth had a mind of its own, and she could not *quite* keep a straight face.

Meg tossed her head, grinning like the young girl Rose had met years before. "Aye, but a long, leisurely drive in the country 'tis great medicine for a listless marriage. Livens many an inattentive husband."

Rose's wide smile stretched muscles in her face that had been less used for years. "Meg, I believe I do like your way of thinking."

MEG AND ROSE'S arrival in Brian and Fiona's yard was heralded by the baying of a small pack of dogs. Rose recalled how frightened she had been the first time she set foot on McKennie land. She had been accosted by Brian's hound, Connie, and two of her gangly pups.

The Baron had been one of those ugly, half-breed pups.

Baron, Rose sighed. *Oh, how I resented you when Jan brought you to me—and how I resented* him *for foisting you on me. Yet you proved your value soon enough, didn't you? And you were a good and faithful friend to us for many years. I mourned right along with Joy the day we buried you.*

Martha emerged from the house. Flapping her apron at the dogs, she shooed them away.

"Miss Rose, what a sight fer sore eyes you're bein'! Mam has been that excited for your visit t'day."

"No more than I," Rose replied. "I came as soon as was possible."

Martha paused at the threshold. "Sure, and Meg has told you of Mam's condition?"

Rose nodded. "I am grieved to hear it."

"She is havin' good days wi' the' bad. T'day she is alert but 'tis likely she will nod off whilst you are here. If she does and you wait a bit, she will wake again and be better for the wee nap."

"I understand. Thank you, Martha."

Martha led Rose and Meg through the kitchen, but Rose halted midway across that familiar room. Around her the shadows of many years danced, and she was momentarily dazed.

"Mama Rose?" Meg whispered.

Rose's eyes roamed the shelves around the room. She knew every piece of china and silver on display and its particular place in Fiona's kitchen. Not one was missing.

"Just my memories rising up, Meg," Rose said, "beginning with the Sunday you introduced me to your family and Fiona invited me here for dinner."

"I remember it well," Meg murmured.

"And I," Martha added softly, "me but a wee girl then and Sean a babe. I must have stared holes through you during our supper. Why, you were bein' the most beautiful lady I had ever seen."

Rose chuckled, and she mimicked Martha's brogue, "Ah, m' sweet Martha. Your memories be slanted by love, I'm thinkin'."

Meg and Martha laughed with her, but Martha answered, "Aye, love indeed, and I can still see you in m' mind's eye, I can, your dress bein' the fresh green of the prairie in spring, as fine as a lamb's fleece when I stroked it. And you? Why, your eyes sparkled like clouds after the rain. Soft gray, a-swirlin' wi' the sun a-shinin' through them, they were."

"Bless you, Martha. I was falling in love with this land, and I wore my heart on my sleeve that day," Rose admitted. "More than that, I was searching for the Savior—that is what you saw. Oh, how I wanted to know him! What you saw was hope, Martha, hope that I might find a place to begin again . . . and I did. Our God planted the Lord Jesus in my soul and rooted me here on the prairie."

"And 'tis right glad we were that you were findin' the Lord Jesus here and stayin' on."

Rose's eyes twinkled. "Oh, but your parents were not happy with me initially, do you recall? Brian was beside himself when I told him I had bought a homestead. Fiona thought I had lost my mind."

Meg and Martha both laughed. "And don' we be knowin' it?" Martha said. "Da and Mam worried o'er you s' many times, that you were bein' in our prayers regular-like for an entire year."

They heard distant coughing and turned toward it.

"Come," Martha said. "Mam is a-waitin'. She was askin' that we set her in a chair, but I'm not knowin' how long she can bear it."

Martha led Rose to the bedroom Fiona had shared with her husband for close to fifty years. The window curtains were pulled back, the room flooded with cheerful light. Fiona sat in an upholstered chair at the foot of her bed. Another chair was near hers.

Rose had to exert all of her self-control to hide her shock and dismay. Fiona's body was a shell holding body and soul together by God's grace and her family's prayers. The once plump apples of her cheeks were shrunken and sickly, like the russets that remained in the bottom of a cellar basket when the next harvest was near.

But Fiona's happiness glistened in her black eyes. "You hev come at last."

"That I have," Rose replied through her tears.

She forgot Meg and Martha as they excused themselves. She sat down in the waiting chair and picked up Fiona's hand. Held it between her own. Fiona's fingers were cool to the touch, her hand as thin and weak as the stalks of grass waving in Søren's pasture.

"My dear friend!"

"Aye, and a sight t' see, am I," Fiona whispered.

"A precious sight to me."

"As are ye t' me, Rose." Fiona attempted to shift her position and pain sketched lines across her face.

"May I adjust you?" Rose asked.

"If ye please. I am slipping t' port and canna hoist m' own anchor these days."

Rose reached under Fiona's arms and lifted, pulling her up into a more upright position. She was astounded that Fiona seemed no heavier than a feather comforter. "Better?"

Fiona coughed and slowly raised a handkerchief to her mouth. "Aye. Thank ye."

Meg appeared, carrying a small side table that she arranged beside Rose's chair. As she left, Martha entered, bearing a tray. She placed it on the table.

"Ring if you be needing anything, Miss Rose."

"Thank you, Martha."

Rose let the tea steep and took Fiona's hand again. She could tell the effort to sit in the chair was costing her friend. "We need not talk, Fiona. So long as I have your hand in mine and our hearts can commune through our eyes, everything is as it was the last time we met."

Fiona's eyes sought Rose's. "Not the same, though, eh?"

Rose sighed and tipped her chin.

"Jesus is a-callin' t' me, Rose."

"I . . . know."

"'Twill be glorious . . . on thet day."

"And I will rejoice for you."

"Will ye promise me thet? Will ye, Rose?"

Rose spoke through clenched teeth. "Yes, Fiona. I promise."

"Thank ye, m' dearest friend."

After a minute, Fiona's eyes closed. Her breathing told Rose that Fiona was sleeping.

They remained that way, hand in hand, the tray untouched.

CHAPTER 8

Rose studied her reflection in the mirror and sighed. Joy's fitted silk blouse was beautiful but hardly abreast with present-day fashions.

"It has lovely classic lines and styling," she told herself, "and the classics are always in vogue." She put her head to one side. "Hmm. Did I not have a blouse similar to this one when I settled in RiverBend?" Then she chuckled. "Ivory silk? Hardly suitable daily wear for a farmer's wife."

Rose looked down and noticed that her black skirt—her *best* skirt—had worn to a shine in two places. Moreover, the toes of the shoes peeping from beneath the skirt's hem were distinctly *brown.*

"Oh, bother." She already knew that her black shoes were run down in the heels. They would not be presentable again until she gave them over to a shoemaker to replace the heels. Shaking her head, she admitted aloud, "I shall need to dip into my savings and refresh my wardrobe when we reach Chicago."

She fingered her other good skirt, a dark brown merino wool with a high waist and narrow pinstripes running down its length.

"Brown it must be, I suppose, although it is a far cry from the wealthy, stylish attire of which I once boasted." She reached for a small cedar box. "This may help."

She chose the purple amethyst brooch set in gold filigree that had belonged to her mother and fastened it to the blouse at her throat. After she had combed and pinned up her hair, she drew a hat box from her trunk and opened it.

Cushioned within the box were her two hats. One was a wide brimmed creation made of straw and suitable for spring and summer. The other was of tan felt with a wide grosgrain band about it terminating in a modest bow on the hat's side. She placed the felt hat on her head and gave it a slight slant to complete her ensemble.

"Better. Presentable, at least."

Meg had already departed for the luncheon. Søren was driving her to the church where she would help set up the fellowship hall, leaving Rose, Joy, O'Dell, and the children in the house.

Rose came into the kitchen to the sound of O'Dell's voice. A rather cranky voice.

"Pray tell, Joy, why my presence is needed at a women's *fête* where they will, no doubt, serve tiny, crustless cucumber sandwiches—not to mention cake sliced so thin that a gentleman might peruse the evening paper through his serving?"

"But it is not a women's luncheon, Edmund, dearest. It is a community luncheon. Karl will attend, as will Kjell, Markus, Jon, Einar, Pastor Medford, and any number of other gentlemen. Moreover, this lunch is being held in our honor. Certainly, you see that you must come? I will be expected to introduce you to our many friends. If you refused to attend, what would that convey to them?"

O'Dell was beaten, and he knew it, but he mumbled a parting protest anyway, "I fail to see why Søren is allowed to escape the event, but I am not."

"He hardly needs an introduction to the community, dearest. Besides which, you should know that the women of RiverBend and its surrounds do not serve such faint fare as you described at their gatherings. You must think on the vast array of delectable foods you will sample. Why, the women of RiverBend are practically famous for their pies, cakes, tarts, doughnuts, salads, and *fried chicken*."

"But—fried chicken, you say?"

"Famous, indeed," Rose said from behind him. "The trick is finding opportunity to actually eat at an affair such as today's. What Joy does not mention is that the people of RiverBend, gentlemen and ladies alike, are also renowned for talking the legs off a stuffed horse."

O'Dell's defeated, woeful expression elicited a spasm of laughter from Joy and a smile from her mother.

When Joy could speak again, she ran an approving eye over Rose. "That blouse is lovely on you, Mama. Your brooch sets it off perfectly."

"Thank you, darling Joy. I declare that I recollect having a blouse very like this one years ago, but I cannot recall what became of it. My, but your dress is certainly beautiful—and the height of fashion besides. And that hat—utterly marvelous. Surely, I have not seen either before, have I?"

"No, they are new. Edmund bought the ensemble for me before we left Denver. As Edmund will be head of the Chicago Pinkerton office, we will undoubtedly receive regular dinner and reception invitations."

"Edmund has very good taste."

"Victoria Washington has very good taste," O'Dell growled. "I have a very depleted bank account."

"But the thought, Edmund," Rose chided him, "the thought behind your gift. You cared enough to give Joy a dress that would make her eyes shine, did you not? Well done."

He grinned at Rose's compliment and stood to plant a kiss on her cheek. "Thank you, Mother."

They heard Søren's little car puttering up the drive. Jon and Camille, in the farm's truck, their three children riding in the truck's bed, were not far behind. Jon parked the truck near the barn. He would be driving the three ladies to town in Søren's car, while O'Dell caught a ride with Karl and Sonja. Søren came inside with Camille and her children, while Jon turned Søren's car around in the drive.

The O'Dells' three boys and Jon and Camille's two boys and two girls bounced from foot to foot, anxious for their parents to depart and the fun to begin.

"Any special instructions?" Søren asked of Joy and Camille.

"None, as long as they are still alive and healthy when we return," Camille replied.

"Why, I believe that means exploring and hunting treasure with Captain Grandpa Søren and his band of pirate lads and lassies," Søren declared—more to the children than to Camille.

"What about us?" Matthew asked, crestfallen. "We don't have a Grandpa Søren."

"Ah, but you have an *Uncle* Søren. Trust me, he's every bit as good a pirate captain as a Grandpa Søren," Søren promised.

With many goodbyes, the ladies left the house. Jon assisted Camille and Joy (with Roseanne in her arms) into the rear seat of Søren's car, then helped Rose into the passenger seat before taking the driver's seat himself. The ladies waved to O'Dell, who would be following with Karl and Sonja shortly.

"I do hope," Joy murmured as she left off waving, "that Edmund does not find a convenient reason to miss his ride."

"He would do that?" Camille asked.

Rose turned her head a little. "I doubt it. It is my firmly held belief that Edmund's love of fried chicken will conquer any excuse to avoid the event, convenient or otherwise."

Joy laughed. "You have relieved my mind, Mama."

AS THEY DREW closer to RiverBend, the number of cars, farm trucks, and wagons joining them on the dirt road increased.

"Goodness!" Rose exclaimed, craning her neck to see ahead and behind. "In all my twenty-six years in this community, I cannot recall seeing as many conveyances on this road at the same time."

Jon grinned at her. "Where do you suppose they are going, Grandma Rose?"

Rose's lips parted slowly. "You cannot mean . . . they are all on their way to the luncheon?"

"They are," Camille called from behind Rose. "We posted the invitation in the county newspaper and received ninety-eight responses. The ladies of the community have been cooking and baking for that number all week."

Rose turned and sought Joy's eyes. "That number of attendees cannot be for us, can it?"

Joy, too, seemed shocked.

"But why?" Rose asked again, looking to Joy for an answer.

She shrugged. "I have no idea, Mama."

A few minutes later, the church came into view. And as they turned onto RiverBend's one paved street fronting the church, Rose slowly exhaled. Automobiles lined both sides of the street. Every inch of the church's grassy lot was employed for parking. Around the side of the parsonage, she spied a row of wagons and a picket line of horses chomping on freshly spread hay. Two men were directing a stream of vehicles to proceed around the block to park.

"Ninety-eight? This appears to rise above that number, Camille," Joy breathed.

"Merciful heavens," Camille responded. "I hope we have prepared enough food."

One of the men waved to Jon. "That Rose Thoresen with you, Jon?"

"I have the honor."

"Reserved parking for Mrs. Thoresen and her party over yonder," the man said, pointing to an empty spot near the fellowship hall.

Jon maneuvered the car into the prescribed slot. He had no sooner turned off the engine than a phalanx of stylishly attired ladies led by Vera Medford approached.

Rose's heart fluttered. "Joy?"

"It will be all right, Mama. I-I am sure it will be." Joy's tone rang with less certainty than her words.

The women waited for Jon to open Rose's door and hand her down from the car before descending on her.

Vera reached for Rose first and brushed a kiss across her cheek, taking the opportunity to whisper in her ear, "Chin up, my dear friend. You are the queen of this day. Just nod and be your gracious self."

Rose willed the corners of her mouth to stretch her lips wide. "Good morning," she murmured to the women waiting to receive her. Then, with dawning comprehension, she exclaimed, "Esther? Is that you? Ava? Jess? And *Edith?* Oh, my *dear*, precious girls." Rose could no longer see through the mist that clouded her eyes.

They gathered about her, laughing. Crying. Rejoicing. And Esther proclaimed, "Miss Rose, welcome back to RiverBend."

VERA AND HER troop escorted Joy and Rose into the fellowship hall and to seats of honor at the head table. Joy immediately excused herself to visit with an old friend she had spied. Rose, however, sank gratefully into her chair and stared about the packed room. The idea that all these people had come out to see her and Joy was too unexpected—and unwarranted, in Rose's view—for her to easily accept it.

A long line of tables burgeoning with food spanned the entire back wall of the hall. Rows of tables and chairs perpendicular to the back wall took up the hall's remaining space—and every chair had already been taken by happy, chattering women, a great many of whom had brought their husbands and older children.

Table space being at a premium, the men had elected to stand against the two walls the length of the room, right and left of the head table. They enjoyed (and preferred) the all-male company nearby, while they waited for the blessing—said blessing granting them leave to dig in to the bounteous spread.

Rose looked over the roomful of seated women. She sought a familiar face or anything that might ground her in the intimidating circumstances. Her eyes skipped over, then returned to an elderly lady, a lady who waggled her fingers at Rose. When Rose lifted her hand in return, the woman lit from within.

"Why, Gertrude Grünbaum," Rose whispered. "As I live and breathe." She abandoned her seat and made her way to Gertrude's table.

The old woman pushed herself to her feet. "Knew you would recognize me, Rose."

"And you vould recognize me, *too*, if Gertrude vore not so big a hat," another voice interjected.

Berta Schmidt, leaning heavily on the arm of the woman beside her, struggled to stand.

"Berta?"

"*Ja*, dat is me."

Across from Berta, a third woman stood to welcome Rose.

"And Mary Bailey? Oh, my dear, *dear* friends. What a pleasure to see you all."

"Same," Gertrude declared.

"*Ja*, same," Berta echoed. "You remember my girl, Clara?"

Berta's daughter grinned at Rose. "I am certain she does, Mama."

"Indeed, I do. How are you, Clara?"

Lemon drops. You and your precious little sister and two brothers carried my purchases from your parents' hardware store to my buggy. I paid you in lemon drops.

Rose sighed with contentment. "I am transported back in time, my friends. You hosted RiverBend's very first ladies' Bible study, Mary, but we immediately outgrew your place and moved to Gertrude's home. Why, how many Bible studies did we hold in your living room over the years, Gertrude? And are they still held at your house?"

"No, not for five years now. Got to be a bit much for me, but my daughter-in-law has taken leadership of one of them."

"One of them? You have more than one?"

"Four at last count. Three out in the county—north, east, and west of RiverBend. The other is still here in town. And twice a year, our four Bible studies meet together here in this hall for a great celebration. God's kingdom keeps expanding, you see."

Berta piped up, "*Ja*, but I still remember ven *you* teach us the Bible, Rose. Many good lessons still live in my heart."

"And we can always count on yer girls bein' part of our studies, Rose," Mary said.

"My girls?"

"Ones thet came down from Denver to us?"

"Ah. Joy calls them our 'girls from the mountain.' I am so happy to see and hear they are doing well."

"Ain't no mountain left in 'em," Mary declared with a grin. "They's all prairie now. Belong to us, they do."

"I sense a metaphor here," Rose said. "From the mountaintops to the verdant prairie? Not unlike from slavery in Egypt to the Promised Land? And do not all of us make that journey when we come to Christ?"

"Why, lands sake. I take yer point, Rose," Mary answered. 'Tis jest like you say. Say, did ya know thet Ava is our Jeremy's wife? A better woman fer him, I cain't imagine. We love her as our own."

"That Esther is sure something, too," Gertrude put in. "A husband, a young'un, a business to run, and yet she fills in whenever a Sunday school teacher is out sick or the weather keeps one from coming to town. Why, she organized most of this lunch and the cleanup afterward. Be the last to leave t'day, too, I wager. A credit to the Lord and his church, she is. Not a lick of that old 'mountain' in her. God sure can switch a person around, can't he?"

The tinkling of a spoon gently tapping a glass interrupted the many and noisy conversations. Vera stood at the lectern before the head table, and quiet descended on the hall.

"Welcome. Welcome all. What a glorious day. I have been informed that the food is ready—and from what I have seen, I believe our lovely ladies have outdone themselves. If Pastor will ask a blessing on the food and on our fellowship this afternoon, we shall begin. Jacob?

Jacob Medford lifted his voice. "Father in heaven, we lift up our voices to thank you for the bounty before us, for it comes from your hand. Please bless it, strengthen us with it, and may our fellowship this day truly be in your Son, Christ Jesus. Amen."

Vera approached Rose. "If you would care to take your seat, Rose, we have appointed ladies to prepare plates for you and Joy and bring them to you."

"How very thoughtful. Thank you," Rose answered.

Lines had already formed on both sides of the tables, the women first to serve themselves. As Vera had said, the first two women moving through the line brought the plates they had filled to Rose and Joy.

"Good afternoon, Mrs. Thoresen, Mrs. O'Dell," one young lady greeted them as she placed a plate in front of Rose. "I hope you enjoy your lunch. Which beverage would you prefer, coffee, iced tea, or lemonade?"

"Thank you. I would prefer iced tea." Rose stared at the plate of delectable fare before her. She suddenly salivated. "My, what a feast."

"It most certainly is," Joy sighed.

Behind the women who had brought their plates, another young woman appeared, carrying a tray of dessert plates on which lay an assortment of cakes, pies, puddings, cobblers, and other delicacies.

"Would you care to select a dessert, Mrs. Thoresen? Mrs. O'Dell?"

Rose chose lemon meringue pie; Joy selected a slice of triple-layered chocolate cake. They picked up their forks and smiled at each other.

"The women of RiverBend are treating us like royalty, Mama."

"I see that, Joy. And I am . . . humbled."

"Me, also." Joy forked a bite of mashed potatoes. "However, humility has not daunted my appetite. I am so glad Roseanne is sleeping right now."

The men made their way through the lines after the women, sweeping up what remained. They leaned against the walls, holding their plates while they ate. Rose could see that they were thoroughly enjoying the feast—including O'Dell, who lifted a piece of fried chicken in a salute to his wife and mother-in-law.

"I cannot take that man anywhere," Joy quipped, hiding her laughter in her napkin.

"Perhaps he is getting it out of his system because when he arrives in Chicago, he will be expected to exude solemn authority."

"You may be right, Mama."

When the meal ended, a squadron of teens—the church's youth—cleared the tables, collecting the dirty plates and cutlery, and ferrying them out the door.

"Where are they taking the dishes?" Rose asked Vera, who had settled in the chair to her left.

Vera leaned toward Rose. "To the parsonage, where they will wash and dry them. While I admire their servants' hearts, I shudder to consider the condition of my kitchen when this is over."

The years fell away as Rose and Vera smiled at each other and chuckled.

Replete, Rose sat back and sipped a fresh cup of coffee, the perfect follow-up to the pie she had sampled.

Vera nodded to Rose. "I will introduce you now. We hope you will say a few words?"

The coffee in Rose's stomach soured. "You wish me to address everyone?"

"Nothing fancy, only a thank you for the luncheon. We'll allow time afterward for a reception line, an opportunity for our guests to greet you personally."

"I see. Very well, Vera."

Rose listened as Vera spoke briefly about her being a long-time neighbor and good friend to many in and around RiverBend. She talked about the Bible studies they had started together, pointed out Mary, Gertrude, and Berta as founding members. She spoke of Joy having been born and raised in the community and the work she and Rose had pioneered in Denver. She ended with a mention of Joy's husband as being the next chief of the Chicago Pinkerton office, necessitating a cross-country move that passed by RiverBend.

"We are blessed and happy that both Rose and Joy could return to RiverBend on their way to Chicago, even if only for a brief stay. However, when news of their impending arrival began to circulate, the overwhelming response was, how can we arrange a visit with them? This luncheon seemed a perfect means of sharing them with all those who wished a moment of their time."

Joy leaned toward Rose. "Not a short visit with 'them' or a moment of 'their' time, Mama, but with *you* and *your* time. They are here to see *you*. I am but window dressing on this occasion."

Rose had turned toward Joy to gainsay her assertion, when Vera concluded, "Mrs. Thoresen has kindly consented to say hello to all of you. Will you please join me in welcoming her?"

Enthusiastic applause rang through the fellowship hall.

Joy arched her brows. "See?"

Rose made her way from the head table to the lectern, uncertain of how to begin. Vera's words rang in her ears. "Nothing fancy, only a thank you for the luncheon."

Rose smiled out into the sea of expectant faces. Meg, Camille, Sonja, Gertrude, Berta, Mary, and many others smiled back at her. Except Lucy. She sat beside Sonja, her expression carefully impassive, her eyes watchful.

I should offer only a "thank you" for this luncheon? After what this town has done for me? What this community means to me? Lord, please give me the words to express my gratitude.

Rose exhaled. "Good afternoon and thank you for this lovely feast," Rose murmured. "Joy and I are honored that all of you would come out to welcome us home with this wonderful show of friendship. We appreciate your loving hospitality, and . . ."

Rose stopped and turned inward, hearkening to a voice so dear to her, that she would tune out more than a hundred people, staring and waiting for her to continue, in order to obey the direction *he* was giving her.

Rose blinked a little, straightened, and smiled. "And I would like to tell you a little story, if I may. It is short, I promise you. Only, perhaps, a few minutes." She glanced at Vera. "May I?"

Several voices from the packed hall answered with an emphatic "yes" or "go ahead" before Vera could respond. She chuckled and nodded her agreement. "By all means. Take your liberty, Rose."

"Thank you. Well, I suppose, like many stories, this one begins with a family. A father, a mother, and three beautiful children, a boy of ten, a girl of six, and another daughter just learning to talk. They were on their way home one cold January night, almost forty-three years ago now. The roads were icy, but two reliable, sure-footed horses pulled the carriage, and their driver was as loved by this family as he was loyal and competent.

"The way home led over an old arched bridge that spanned a narrow and generally taciturn river. That night, however, the river ran high, and it was choked with ice that had broken up in a recent thaw. In fact, the unseasonable melt, followed by a cold snap, had coated the roads and the old cobblestone bridge with a layer of ice, too."

Rose paused, reminiscing. "But, you see, we were unaware of that."

The room stilled. Few in the fellowship hall knew Rose's history. The small number who did stared at their plates or their folded hands. Forced back tears.

"The horses mounted the bridge and pulled with their usual spirit. They were good horses, loved by this family. On the downward side, however, one of the horses lost his footing on the ice and fell. He could not get his legs under him. Could not get up. The other horse tried to move forward, but he only succeeded in causing the carriage to swing in an arc toward the bridge's railing. When the carriage box struck the railing, it broke through. The carriage began to slide off the edge of the bridge. Only the horses kept it from plunging immediately into the river—and only for a few scant moments. The weight of the carriage began dragging the horses in their traces after it, closer and closer to the edge. To disaster.

"The father stood inside the carriage and flung open the door. The river surged below him . . . and he saw what was unescapable. Inevitable. He did the only thing left to him that he could do. He reached for his wife and, while hanging out over the river, he flung her. Flung her from the carriage, hoping to land her as close to the rocks lining the levee as he could manage. Before he could do more, the carriage tipped over and tumbled into the river.

"The driver jumped toward the levee. He struggled to the rock-lined shore, climbed from the icy water, and survived. The woman flung upon the rocks also survived. Her husband and her children did not."

Rose moistened her trembling lips. "Perhaps six months later, that very same woman stepped onto a train headed west. She was alone, by choice, and she did not know where she was going. She only believed that the God from whom she demanded answers, the God *she did not yet know*, had spoken a word to her, had told her *to go*—not unlike what the Lord who spoke to the patriarch Abraham had told him.

"*Go*, the woman believed he had told her. *Go to a land that I will show you.*"

Rose again looked around. Not a person stirred except to swipe at their eyes.

She drew a breath. "And today, all these years later, were I a poet or were I commencing the reading of an essay, my opening sortie might ring with, 'O RiverBend, how do I love thee? Let me count the ways' . . . and you would deem those lines but poor plagiarism, even as I declare them true."

Her abrupt shift seemed to nudge her audience from their inertia, and they stirred, unhappy that Rose's tale had, without warning, "jumped the track."

But it had not.

Not really.

"It was spring 1881 when I stepped off the train in RiverBend. I was a broken woman searching for a reason to live, and I was weary of riding the train. When I stepped down from the rail car, all I sought was a day's rest before continuing my journey, a brief hiatus only.

"In the dining room of Mrs. Owen's boarding house the following morning, I encountered Meg McKennie. Meg served me breakfast. She offered me a warm welcome and her friendship. She is now Meg Thoresen, my beloved daughter-in-law, married to the son of my heart, even if he is not the son of my womb. Let me count the ways I love thee, RiverBend? *I love thee for Meg.*"

The crowd stirred. Sighed. Nodded.

"I stayed on beyond that first night, intrigued by the wild prairie all around me. Meg invited me to church. I accepted. There, not many steps from where I presently stand, I met her family—Brian, Fiona, and Meg's siblings. They took me, a perfect stranger, home with them for Sunday dinner.

"They enfolded me into their family life. They shared their faith with me. And so, after mere days in this town, I wondered how I could ever bear to leave it.

"RiverBend, let me count the ways I love thee? *I love thee for Brian and Fiona*."

Rose knew full well that Fiona was too ill to leave home. Still, she scanned the hall, missing her, searching for Fiona's flashing smile.

As her eyes roamed over the back of the room, she was surprised to notice Martha seated near the doors—and shocked to find her dear friend slumped in a chair beside Martha. Martha nodded to Rose, acknowledging with the stoic tilt of her head that Fiona's wishes, her determination to attend the luncheon, had won out over caution and good sense.

Oh, Father. My dear friend, whom you will soon call from this life, used what little strength remains in her to be here on this day? For me? How I love this godly woman! Please bless her, my Lord.

Then Fiona touched her thin fingers to her lips and lifted them toward Rose. Rose kissed her fingers and sent her love back to Fiona. Many sets of eyes followed Rose's gesture, and a murmur ran through the hall as they realized Fiona was present.

Nearly overcome, it was a minute before Rose could go on. "On my second Sunday in RiverBend, I heard the Good News of Jesus Christ—the simple and pure Gospel. The God who had summoned me from a thousand miles distant, revealed himself to me through the message Pastor Medford preached in this very church. I answered Christ's call that day.

"How do I love thee, RiverBend? *I love thee for Jacob and Vera Medford*."

Murmured "amens" punctuated Rose's declaration.

"During the week prior to my surrendering to Christ, someone had showed me an abandoned and rundown homesteader's house. The house was nestled in a hollow below its fields. A creek ran by it. I had already fallen in love with the prairie. Now I was falling in love with a little piece of it. When I bought that rundown house, I earned the everlasting scorn of some—but others, who bore no responsibility for me but who were woven into the fabric of this land, came alongside me. They taught me how to survive in this wide and wild prairie. How to make the vision blooming in my heart a reality.

"How do I love thee, RiverBend? I love this town for *Heinrik and Berta Schmidt*, who welcomed me into their mercantile and advised me on what I needed to buy to begin my life here.

"I love this town for *Jan and Søren Thoresen*, father and son, who repaired my dilapidated home so that I would not freeze to death in the coming winter. I love this town for *Amalie Thoresen*, who, I discovered, months after moving onto my homestead and quite by accident, was *not* Jan Thoresen's wife after all—"

Here Rose was interrupted by hoots of good-natured laughter and banter, and she chuckled along with them before she continued. "You see, it was Amalie who taught me how to harvest my garden and put up food for the winter. It was Amalie who taught me how to bake and can and how to make sausages, candles, and a hundred other necessities."

She looked for Amalie's children, Sigrün, Karl, and Kjell, and their children and grandchildren, as she choked out, "I love this town for Amalie, who received me as her sister long before I married Jan, and who was one of the godliest women I have ever had the great privilege to know.

"I love this town for the many kindnesses of *Robert and Mary Bailey*, for Mary who hosted the very first Bible study Vera Medford and I started in RiverBend—and oh, how it has grown."

Rose exhaled. "And I love this town more than I can say for receiving the young women Joy and I sent from Denver, the girls we had to send far away if we were to keep them out of the hands of the man who wished to destroy them. Those girls did not belong here when they arrived. They did not know our ways. And, if what I heard is true, they may have scandalized our simple community more than once. But! But you took them in anyway, and you loved them into the kingdom of God. For that, RiverBend, you have earned my undying gratitude and our Lord God's eternal approbation."

Rose did not know where all the words had come from. She had not prepared them. They had poured from her heart. "I apologize for taking so much of your time, but you see . . . although you came here today to pay your respects to my beloved daughter, Joy, and to me, it is I who wish to thank you.

"Forty-two years ago, you received me, a woman as broken as were the girls we sent from Denver. You took me in as your own. Here I found Jesus—and in him I found hope, healing, and strength.

"I was bereft of husband and children, but *here*, the Lord God restored what the locusts had eaten, what the cankerworm had devoured. Here I found a new love and a new family—a family that included all of you."

Rose lifted her chin. "Thank you, RiverBend."

The applause was thunderous. Joyful. Victorious. It went on until Rose shook her head and stepped away from the lectern.

When the applause ended, Jacob and Vera Medford stood at the front of the room, holding hands, and weeping. Jacob tried to speak. Stopped. Tried again.

"Rose has shared her heart with us, and I am grateful. I would ask for just a moment more of your time. You see, we have today an example of what can result from a single redeemed life. As she said, years ago she and Mrs. Medford began a Bible study at the home of Robert and Mary Bailey. That study grew and is now four studies throughout the county. What Mrs. Thoresen did not mention was how vital they have become to the people of this community.

"Without going to great lengths and with all the glory offered to God Almighty, if you heard the Gospel at one of our Bible studies and received Christ through that ministry, would you kindly stand?"

Rose's heart swelled as five, then fifteen, then twenty women stood.

Thirty.

Even more.

Jacob added, "And if you heard the Good News of the Savior and came to Christ through the testimony of one of these redeemed women now standing, would you please also stand?"

Husbands moved to join their wives. The scraping of chairs filled the room as children, grandchildren, aunts, uncles, brothers, and sisters pushed back from the tables. Few remained sitting.

Jacob simply bowed his head and prayed aloud. "Lord Jesus! You declared many things to your disciples the night before you suffered and died. One thing you said to them was, *Abide in me, and I in you. As the branch cannot bear fruit of itself, except it abide in the vine; no more can ye, except ye abide in me.* You also said, *Herein is my Father glorified, that ye bear much fruit; so shall ye be my disciples.*

"To you, Almighty God, be all the glory, honor, and praise. Amen."

Chapter 9

Journal Entry, October 14, 1923

Good morning, dear Lord. How I look forward to attending church this morning. I recall how vibrant and essential the worship was all the years Jan and I were members, not to mention Jacob's treatment of Scripture. Oh, yes. How I grew under his teaching!

Lord, as I begin this new season of my life, I thank you for the gift of time here in RiverBend. Time to visit with dear friends and time to remember, to rest in you. Time to consider what is ahead, to crave a fresh word from you.

Speak, Lord. I long to hear from you. Speak, and I will obey. Touch me, O God, and I will respond. I love you.

AFTER BREAKFAST, Rose, Meg, the two younger boys, and Joy, holding Roseanne, rode into town with Søren. As on the previous day, O'Dell—with the addition of young Matthew—were to catch a ride to church with Karl and Sonja as they drove past on their way toward the bridge.

Many heartfelt greetings met Rose and Joy on their way into the church. As she responded, however, Rose found her thoughts turned elsewhere.

I would like another opportunity to speak with Karl and Sonja's granddaughter, Lucy. I hope she attends church with her grandparents this morning.

She was gratified when she saw Karl and Sonja take a pew ahead of them, Lucy sandwiched between them.

If the opportunity presents itself, I will have that word with Lucy when service ends, Rose decided. *But I will not force the encounter. As my family has told me, I am here to rest, to visit with friends and family. Not to get involved in the problems of others.*

Service began, and Rose gave herself to the worship. Song after song, the congregation raised their voices as one in praise. When the hymn leader announced the last song, Rose felt something in her heart stir.

All to Jesus I surrender
All to Him I freely give
I will ever love and trust Him
In His presence daily live

I surrender all
I surrender all
All to Thee my blessed Savior
I surrender all

Rose bowed her head, the words of the hymn both challenging and convicting her. *I surrender all? Lord, no matter how many times I have declared my unconditional surrender to you, when I again sing this hymn, I find more within me to yield to you.*

She sighed. *Every surrender is but a meager whittling away at my flesh, another small chip or slice off my own will. How I fool myself into believing I have given* everything *to you . . . when, in reality, I take much of it back at the first or second opportunity.*

She listened to the third verse, rather than singing it.

All to Jesus I surrender
Make me Savior wholly thine
May Thy Holy Spirit fill me
May I know Thy power divine

I surrender all
I surrender all
All to Thee my blessed Savior
I surrender all

Yes, Savior, she prayed. *Make me wholly yours—not my own will, but yours be done in me. Fill me with your Spirit to overflowing! I long to know your divine power, to move and act under your mighty hand, covered by and moving with your Spirit. Therefore, whatever you ask of me, O God, I will do it.*

Rose was reveling in the sweet presence of the Lord, when the name *Lucy* dropped into her heart. She shook her head, but she did not draw back. *All right, Lord. Have your way in me. I* will *seek her out.*

FOLLOWING SERVICE, an impromptu line formed to greet Rose, throwing off her intention to have a private word with the girl. Many who waited in line had attended the luncheon or heard retellings of it and Rose's speech.

A grizzled farmer and his wife wrung Rose's hand while saying, "That story you told at the lunch near to broke our hearts. Hadn't heard that you had lost a family afore comin' to RiverBend. You weren't wrong, though, when you said this town is special. We arrived in 1876, we did, and our neighbors were right quick to help us get started. They invited us to church, too, a year afore Preacher Medford came to town, and this here is where we heard the Gospel. Just wanted to say we appreciate what you said yesterday."

"The Lord bless you. You are most kind," Rose replied.

As the couple moved away, Rose, out of the corner of her eye, watched Karl, Sonja, and Lucy exit a side door. She managed to catch Meg's attention and beckoned to her. When Meg crossed the church to Rose's side, Rose whispered, "Would you please ask Karl and Sonja not to leave until I have had an opportunity to speak to them?"

"Sure, and I will."

Rose reached her hand to the next couple. "Good morning."

"Yup. A good and blessed morning it is. Well, we just wanted to say how much your story touched our hearts, Mrs. Thoresen. We wish you God's best in Chicago."

Rose smiled at them both. "Thank you. Your kindness is exactly what I spoke of yesterday."

The next individual in line was a distinguished looking gent in his senior years. He wore a fine suit and possessed a full head of gray hair. He smiled with good cheer and took Rose's hand in his, covering it with his other hand, gently pressing.

"Mrs. Thoresen, my name is Theodor Warner. I was at the luncheon yesterday and did not have the opportunity to make your acquaintance at that time. However, I wanted to thank you for your inspiring message."

"You are quite welcome, Mr. Warner."

"I related to your story, you see. I lost my wife of forty-seven years two years ago come Christmas. It is difficult to pick up the pieces afterward. I know from experience how much my faith in Christ saw me through that ordeal."

He smiled again, brightly. "I hope to see you again during the remainder of your visit."

A break in the line appeared. At the same time Rose saw Karl and Sonja step back inside the church. Lucy trailed behind them. Rose excused herself to two approaching women with a "Pardon me. Please wait; I will be just a moment," and made a beeline for Lucy.

She hoped she hadn't offended the ladies waiting for her to return, but the conviction within Rose's heart urging her to speak to Lucy was too strong to ignore.

The girl, her jaw set tight, was looking out one of the church windows. At the last moment, she noticed Rose's approach and realized Rose was making her way, not to her grandparents, but to her. She shifted, foot to foot, indecisive, before she quick-stepped toward the exit.

She was not quick enough.

"Lucy. Lucy Thoresen. I would have a word with you, if you please," Rose called.

Lucy stopped, but she stared at her feet.

Rose joined her, and now that she had the girl's attention—half-hearted though it was—she began with, "Lucy, I am concerned for you."

Lucy laughed under her breath. "Well, that's rich."

Rose tamped down her irritation. "I beg your pardon?"

Lucy sneered, "The great and wonderful Rose Thoresen, concerned for little old me."

Rose looked away a moment, both to keep her frustration in check and to think before she spoke. "You are family, Lucy, my husband's great-great niece. Moreover, you are my dear friend's great-granddaughter. Yes. I am concerned for you."

"I don't want your concern."

"And yet here it is. I wish to help you."

Lucy finally looked at Rose. "You think I care? You think I'm anything like this fatuous, fixated community?"

Rose was impressed with the girl's vocabulary. She was less impressed with her attitude.

"Fatuous? Fixated? What do you mean by those descriptors?"

"They idolize you."

"They? I am sorry. Who is 'they'?"

"*They?* Don't you know how our family, our neighbors, our entire community view you? They have built you up into some kind of legend: 'The rich woman who lowered herself to get off the train in our backward town, the fashion plate who deigned to buy and live *by herself* on a run-down homestead like a common dirt farmer.' But they neglect to add, 'The woman who had all the money in the world to buy whatever she needed to fix it up.'"

Rose's eyes widened in surprise. "I hardly think—"

"Oh, there's *so* much more," Lucy spat. "Rose Thoresen, savior of fallen women! Rose Thoresen who can do no wrong! Don't you know? We should *all* model ourselves after Rose Thoresen!" Lucy mimicked a high, feminine voice, "Oh, *dear*, Lucy! We expected so much more from you. Why can't *you* be more like your Great-Great-Aunt Rose?"

Rose stilled. "Anyone who expects you to model yourself after me has forgotten that God the Father sent *Jesus* in the flesh to show us how to behave. If and *only* if my life were to reflect the life of Christ should you strive to be more like me—and, according to the abundance of 'evidence' you have carefully acquired, I surely do not measure up to that exalted status. You would do better to seek after Jesus and model your life on him and him alone."

Lucy sniffed. "Tell that to them, not me. You are, after all, *their* paragon of all things virtuous."

"Do you wish to know the truth about me, Lucy? Or do you prefer to believe lies?"

She frowned. "Lies?"

"Yes. Everything you have said about me is a lie. Oh, it is twined around half-truths, providing sufficient substance to lend credibility to the lie, but the facts are twisted and without context. Skewed."

"I do not believe you."

"I see. And are you accustomed to accusing your elder, someone of whom you personally know nothing, of propagating falsehoods? Did your parents raise you thus? More importantly, is that how the Lord bids you behave?"

"*He* says, *Thou shalt not bear false witness*." She frowned. "Do *you* heed this command?"

Shocked, Rose studied Lucy. "I find the acrimony in your address both impolite and difficult to comprehend. What *is* apparent is that you hold some kind of offense against me, an offense that, I declare to you, is based on faulty tales and misconceptions. We cannot resolve this here and now, but I do wish it resolved. Those false tales and misconceptions can only be overcome by the application of fact."

She thought for a moment. "What time do you get home from school, Lucy?"

"Why do you care?"

"Do not answer a civil question with impertinence, miss."

Lucy shrugged. "Half past three, usually."

"And you have been staying with your grandparents?"

"Yes."

Rose wanted to ask *why* but saved that question for later. "And who brings you home?"

"Either Cousin Jon or Grandpa Karl."

"That will work. Do you know my house? The house Jon and Camille lived in before they built their new one?"

"The little homestead where you enjoyed your perfect life?"

"Insolence does not suit you, Lucy Thoresen. Kindly have Jon or Karl drop you at my house after school tomorrow. I will be waiting on the front porch."

Rose turned away before Lucy could object.

ROSE KEPT TO her own thoughts on the drive home from church. She had left her encounter with Lucy somewhat discouraged. She did not expect the girl to keep their appointment, and she was still shaken by the depth of the girl's anger.

Anger toward me.

Rose mulled over Lucy's attitude. *Not toward me alone, however. Her parents also, it seems. More resentment than typically found in a teen on the cusp of adulthood.*

Rose thought, too, on Lucy's grasp of language and vocabulary. *Meg is right. The girl is quite prodigious.*

She used the remainder of the drive home to pray. *Lord, I place my confidence in you. I believe you spoke to me about Lucy. Therefore, I know your heart is to help her overcome whatever problem is vexing her heart and soul.*

Let us see you move, O God. Not by might, nor by power, but by your Spirit, O Lord of hosts.

CHAPTER 10

At exactly a quarter past three o'clock, Monday afternoon, Rose sat on the hard front steps of her old house. Beside her rested a small basket containing apple slices, a half-dozen cookies, a jar of warm, sweetened tea, and two tin cups.

Rose was waiting for Karl to bring Lucy to her . . . yet she also faced the likely possibility that Lucy would not show up.

Lord, you always lead me in paths of righteousness for your name's sake. Please bring Lucy to me that I might testify to your goodness. And, if you grant me the grace, please help me dispel the deceptions wrapped about her heart.

Twenty minutes later, she spied a trail of dust wafting from the road atop the bluff, the sign of an approaching vehicle. Either Karl would drop down from the bluff, cross the bridge, and continue toward his family's farm, or he would turn before the bridge, toward Rose, and drop Lucy to visit with her.

Rose's heart fluttered when she saw the truck slow and turn before the bridge. "Thank you, Lord."

She slowly stood, hips groaning, as Karl stopped the truck and got out. He seemed glad to see her, but he was also hesitant. Rose went to him. He bent down, and she kissed his cheek.

"It will be all right, Karl, whatever it is."

Nodding, he glanced toward Lucy. The girl opened the truck door and climbed down. Reluctantly.

"Thank you for coming, Lucy," Rose said. "I am looking forward to our visit."

Lucy shifted her schoolbooks to her other arm. "I have homework."

"You may leave your homework in the truck. I intend to have you home by dinner," Rose answered. "You can do your schoolwork then."

Lucy glared a challenge at her. Rose ignored it.

Karl studied the sky. "Almanac predicts cooler temperatures and considerable rain the rest of this week. There still a stove in that place?"

"Yes," Rose answered.

He nodded. "Thought there might be. Brought you some firewood. In case you need it."

You look tired, dear nephew. Despondent. I doubt you would have agreed to my strange request, asking Lucy to meet me here, if things were not already verging on hopeless at home.

He lifted an old bucket filled with tinder and kindling from the bed of the truck, then reached in again and hauled out an armload of wood bound with thick twine. He set the bucket and wood on a step.

"Should fend off the chill. Box of matches in the bucket. If it rains, I'll bring around the truck and fetch you both home before dinner."

"Thank you for your thoughtfulness, Karl."

"Yep." To his granddaughter he said, "You'll be all right with Aunt Rose, Lucy."

Rose thought he meant to hug the girl. It was clear that Lucy believed the same when she stepped back, avoiding his arms before he could lift them. She ducked behind Rose and waited for him to leave.

Curious.

Karl tucked his chin to his chest. "See you after a bit, Aunt Rose. Lucy."

"Thank you, Karl."

Lucy did not answer.

As the truck departed, Rose lifted her eyes to the clouds. "Shall we take the wood inside?"

Lucy shrugged. She picked up the bundle and hauled it up to the porch. Rose took up the pail of kindling and her little basket.

Lucy stepped into the house and looked around. Sniffed. "Why did you want to meet here?"

"Not the finest setting for a visit, I grant you," Rose murmured, "but it has a redeeming quality: We shall be undisturbed here. I prefer not to have an audience to my private conversations. You?"

Lucy ignored the question and asked her own. "You want me to start the fire?"

"You may wish to check for snakes first."

Lucy's eyes popped wide. "What?"

Rose laughed aloud. "I have already looked. I can assure you: no snakes—this time."

"*This time?* What does that mean?"

"I will tell you while you get the fire going."

Lucy hesitated, then—gingerly—cracked open the firebox door. Its insides were swept bare. No snakes. She expertly laid tinder, kindling, and wood. Set a match to the crumpled paper within the nest she had built. Waited as the flame caught and spread.

Rose pulled one of the chairs closer to the stove. It jiggled when she sat. "My, but this old thing is on its last legs—quite literally. I pray it does not give up the ghost while I am sitting on it."

Lucy snorted a laugh. Added wood to the fire.

"And if your opinion of this house is low today, my dear, you should have seen it when I bought it forty-two years back." Rose waggled her eyebrows, reeling in Lucy's interest. "Let me just say that I did not need to go outside to check the sky for rainclouds."

"Holes in the roof that big? Then why in the world would you buy it?"

"Maybe I'll get to that later. First, the snakes."

Lucy brought the second chair toward the fire's warmth but positioned it to the side of the stove, several feet from Rose. "I despise snakes."

"I had no experience with them to call upon when I arrived in RiverBend. None. I had never even seen a live one. Brian and Fiona came with me that first morning, after I told them I had bought this place. I was full of energy and high hopes. Had a buggy filled with cleaning supplies, yard tools, and simple household whatnot. I was under the mistaken assumption that making this house habitable was just a matter of sweeping out the cobwebs—easily done. You know Brian and Fiona, do you not?"

Lucy rolled her eyes. "Neighbors. I was *born* knowing them. But Brian is dead, in case you hadn't heard."

Rose waited until Lucy noticed the quiet. "Yes, I am aware he is gone, Lucy. He was one of my dearest friends. And Fiona is near to joining him."

Lucy wriggled, discomfited to find herself pinned under the steady gaze of Rose's sober gray eyes. "I . . . Sorry."

"Thank you." Rose exhaled. Gestured to the basket. "Would you care for a snack?"

"Okay."

Rose's eyes shifted back to Lucy.

"I mean yes. Yes, *please*."

"Thank you." Rose pulled the jar of tea and two enameled tin cups from the basket. The fire was crackling nicely now. She poured tea into the cups and set them on the stove to reheat. Handed Lucy a napkin laden with cookies and a few apple slices.

"You were telling me about the snakes?"

"Oh. Yes, of course. Brian and Fiona came with me. Fiona was going to help me clean; Brian was going to assess what repairs the house required. Fiona and I needed hot water to clean, so we were going to start a fire. Not in this stove, mind you, but in that sad, rusty old thing left here when the owners previous to me departed. Fiona lifted the lid and encountered a nest of snakes."

"A *nest* of snakes?"

"I had never heard of such a thing either, but the stove was filled with them, large and small, all venomous prairie rattlers. We did not need to see them to be certain of their kind—their rattling announced it for them. It set my skin to creeping. I confess, I wanted to run straight out of here."

"As would I," Lucy said, "but how did they get into the stove?"

"They had found their way into the firebox through the hole in the back of the stove where the pipe had fallen off. When Brian pointed that out, I was terrified they would start crawling out, onto the floor."

Lucy shuddered. "What did you do?"

Rose slowly nodded. "We burned them. Right there in the stove."

"No!" Lucy shuddered as she reached for the cups of tea. "I think the tea is hot enough now." She handed one cup to Rose. She took the other cup and sipped on it. "How did you manage it?"

"Thank you, dear. Well, we certainly did not wish to do battle with a dozen or more snakes on the floor of my house, so Brian slid the stove pipe onto the back of the stove where it belonged. Unfortunately, the fitting was loose, and the pipe fell right off—which riled up the snakes. You should have heard them rattle and slither around inside the stove. My, how angry they sounded."

Lucy had a cookie poised at her mouth, but her attention was on Rose's tale.

"I panicked and bolted. Ran out into the yard, where I tripped over a discarded length of wire. I picked it up, then showed it to Brian. We decided he would put the pipe on the back of the stove and hold it there while I wrapped the wire around it and twisted it tight."

"*Dinna ye lose yer nerve, lass. When the pipe is on, I'll be holdin' it there. The snakes canna coom out if I am holdin' it. Only be makin' the wire tight and twist the ends well. D'ye ken?*"

Lucy shook her head emphatically. "No. Not I. You could neither persuade nor bribe me to do that."

Rose lifted her shoulder. "I was frightened out of my wits—or nearly so. But it was my house. I had chosen to live here, and it was my responsibility . . . which is why, once Brian and I made certain the pipe was securely wired to the back of the stove, it was also my job to climb up on the roof and rain down scraps of paper and bits of kindling through the pipe, onto the snakes, then send burning tinder after it.

"Once the fire reached them, the snakes went wild. Even on the roof I could hear their frenzied hissing and rattling, their crazed thumping against the sides of the firebox. I came down the ladder, and the three of us listened to them burn and die."

Lucy stared at the stove's open door where the dry wood cracked and snapped. "How horrid!"

"It *was* horrid. Brian carefully added more wood through the stove lids until all the snakes were dead and reduced to ash. Fiona and I had hot water that day, eventually, and we started cleaning. Ah, what a task that was."

"But . . ."

Rose sipped her tea. "Yes?"

"But you had money—everyone says you did. Why did you buy this dump?"

"Ah. Why, indeed?"

Rose bit into a cookie and chewed slowly. *How best to explain?*

The moment dragged on without an answer.

Lucy huffed. "Well?"

It was as near a sneer as Rose had heard from the girl. Or would tolerate.

Rose lifted her eyes. Locked them on Lucy's. "Lucia Thoresen, I do not mind the question. In fact, I welcome it. But if you expect me to abide disrespect from you, then you are mistaken."

Lucy may have seen something in Rose she had not noticed before. She licked her lips. "I, um . . . I apologize."

Rose continued her stare until Lucy broke eye contact.

"Apology accepted. Now, where were we? I believe you asked why I bought *this dump*."

Without warning, Rose growled in her throat, pursed her lips, frowned, and leaned toward Lucy. "This *dump?* How *dare you*."

She huffed, sat back, and muttered, "I prefer 'this shack,' myself."

Rose watched Lucy's eyes skitter away, then back. The girl *thought* there was a chance that Rose was teasing, but she was not convinced, nor, after her recent rebuke, was she willing to risk another.

Finally, Rose waggled one eyebrow. "Got you, Miss Lucy."

Against her will, Lucy giggled. "You are joshing me."

"Good of you to notice," Rose murmured. "So. A moment ago, you made mention of my wealth. First, I was never wealthy, at least not by the standards of the truly wealthy or even my previous social circle. Did my late husband leave me adequately well off? Yes. Wealthy, no. Second, did you know that money does not make one happy?"

Lucy lifted her chin. "I should like to try it for myself before rendering an opinion."

Rose laughed. Lucy smiled back.

There you are, Rose thought, *the real Lucy. Open, sweet, and keenly intelligent.*

"You heard my story at the luncheon, Lucy. I lost my husband and children. My husband left me well provided for. I could live the remainder of my life in idle gentility, if I were careful with my assets. And, yes, money is certainly an advantage, but all the money he left me was comforting to me as were the ashes of those snakes in my stove."

She looked at Lucy. "I didn't buy this land for the house, this *dump*, as you call it. I bought it as a place where I could begin living anew and, for the first time in my life, sweat for the food I ate, work for what I wanted, and build something that mattered."

"Something that mattered?" Lucy's question was tinged with confusion. "I don't understand. Does this—" her gesture took in the house and the land. "Does all this matter? I cannot see past the ruins of yet another failed homestead. The prairie is rife with those, and I am old enough to realize that even our family farms are only one or two disastrous seasons from bankruptcy."

Rose nodded. "How did this place matter to me? Perhaps we can come back to your questions a bit later. However, since I did promise to tell you about your grandmother and namesake, Amalie, I should do so. I am sorry she died twenty-four years ago, before you were born. She would have doted on you."

"Doting? Smothering. Stifling. Interfering. Everyone in everyone else's business. *Doting* relatives I have in abundance," Lucy sniffed.

"I suppose you do. I wasn't as fortunate. When I came to RiverBend, I was in desperate need of people who would come alongside me and teach me how to manage for myself. Growing up with servants who did most everything for me, I possessed far fewer skills of necessity than do you."

"As a grown woman you knew less than I do at age fourteen? I am unconvinced, Aunt Rose. What, then, *did* you know?"

Rose sat up straight, her back away from the seatback, knees together, ankles crossed just so, her hands folded in her lap, and cast a haughty, arch look upon Lucy. "What did I know? Only the finer things in life, my dear.

"For example, I could plan and host a seven-course dinner party for twelve, chair a women's aid meeting, conduct myself in 'polite' society, with all its myriad strictures, and dress accordingly. I could also, I am sorry to confess, deliver a "cut" in the most devastating yet socially laudable manner. But I could not cook much more than an egg nor could I bake bread, tend a garden, or milk a goat."

"But you had people to do those things for you."

Rose sighed. "When 'people' do these things for you, but you cannot do them yourself, are you not a child? Wealth without effort hardly lends itself to self-respect. Why, I could not even sew except to mend a burst seam or replace a button. I could, however, turn out a perfectly embroidered pillowslip or crochet a doily—yet I am convinced that the finest doily has never fed a hungry mouth."

Lucy pulled her chair a little closer to Rose. "Well, I heard that when you came here, you had beautiful clothes, a trunk filled with them. I have listened to the older ladies talk about your attire—the height of fashion, they declared you were. Some of them can recall every stitch of an ensemble you wore to church forty years ago."

Rose watched Lucy choose her words carefully. "If your first husband left you well provided for and you can live independently, why do you wear such . . . ordinary clothes?"

Rose chuckled under her breath. "Frankly, I have been so busy these past years, I have scarcely given thought to fashion. To be candid with you, other than the annual payment I receive from Søren as my share of the crops he and Jon grow on my land, not much of my money remains."

Lucy sat up. "Why, whatever has become of it? I cannot envision you frittering away a fortune, even a small one. Did you lose it in the economic problems after the Great War?"

Rose was amazed that Lucy knew of the short-lived depression that followed the Great War or that she would, so casually, bring it into a conversation. "No, most of it was already gone by then. Your great-uncle Arnie handles my financial matters, what remains of my 'estate.' He converted what little money I had to gold five years ago. His sound actions saved that bit."

"But . . ." Lucy shot Rose a nervous glance.

"You want to ask what became of the bulk of it, do you?"

"It would be quite . . . impertinent of me."

"Yes, it would."

Rose halted Lucy's objection as it reached her lips. "Now, earlier, I told you that I settled here to build something that mattered. You wanted to know what that meant."

"Yes'm."

"I am going to ask you a question first, and I want you to think carefully about your answer. Can you do that?"

The girl huffed. "I cannot promise, but I will try."

"I like that answer, Lucy. No promise except that you will try. Here is my question. I am seventy-four years old. I have only a little of what my husband left me remaining in the bank. That, and this piece of land comprise my entire estate. When I die, how much of it will I take with me?"

Lucy sat back. She was annoyed, Rose could tell. "That is something of a trick question, isn't it?"

"Is it? Perhaps I should simplify it. Answer me this instead. When I die, what, precisely, *will* I take with me?"

Lucy rolled her eyes and quoted Scripture. "*For we brought nothing into this world, and it is certain we can carry nothing out.* First Timothy, I believe."

"That is correct, and I am heartened that your parents have taught you God's word and that you have a good grasp of truth . . . although you did call me a liar Sunday during our chat after church."

Lucy squirmed. "I may have overstepped my, um, bounds."

"Yes, and since you have admitted that you did, *I* may think I am owed another apology."

Lucy released a longsuffering sigh. "All right. I apologize, Aunt Rose. Again."

"Apology accepted. Again. Now let us revisit your earlier question. If what we build matters, why can we not take it with us? For clarity's sake, what does building something that matters look like?"

Lucy shrugged. "I suppose getting married, having a family. All that folderol into which my parents and grandparents put so much stock."

"It *can* be folderol, as you put it. I have known many married women and mothers who were dissatisfied with their lot. They did not believe that their lives mattered. What I observed in a preponderance of my high-society friends was emptiness. Purposelessness."

"Well, aren't some women made for more than just raising a family? Can we not be something else? Something greater?"

"It is my understanding from Scripture, Lucy, that God has planted eternity in our hearts. All of us, both men and women, have a longing for God, a need for him, a desire for eternity. If we realize that nothing in this life endures, we can also develop a sense of futility, that what we gain or achieve here is pointless. Our lives and our accomplishments, after all is said and done, are only temporary."

Lucy frowned. "If what we do in this life is futile, how can anyone's work and efforts matter?"

"You are nearly there, Lucy. Think it through."

Eternity, Lucy. Eternity!

Rose's head snapped up—and she realized that the light through the windows had gone out.

"The storm is nearly here," Lucy said. "We should go."

Rose could not leave without finishing her point. "The only things we can take with us into eternity are other eternal souls, Lucy. We place high value on our families because they are precious to God himself, and he charges us, above all else, to win them to Jesus and to raise them to know and follow Jesus. They, and whomever else we reach with the Good News, are the 'something that matters' in life. When I left my home back east, I was seeking answers. When I found Jesus—or, rather, he found me—I wanted to tell everyone about him. He became my 'something that matters' and has been since that day."

"If you say so," Lucy grumbled.

"I do say so."

Rose stood. "Well, I rather enjoyed our time together. Shall we meet again?"

Lucy stared at her, mildly suspicious. "Why?"

"In the first place, we never got around to talking much about your great-grandmother . . . or debunking the fictitious, idealized figure you have formed of me in your mind."

Rose shut the door to the stove's firebox and turned down the damper. She gathered up the cups and napkins and repacked the basket.

"In the second place, I would immensely enjoy the opportunity to relate some family history, including certain events that will cast me in a different light than what you have heard. Will tomorrow afternoon after school suit you?"

Rose, from the open doorway, scanned the sky.

Frowning, Lucy said, "I might have—"

"Wonderful. Have your grandpa drop you off here again after school. Oh, and ask him to bring a bit more wood? I will again supply the snacks."

When Lucy followed Rose onto the porch, she had already stepped down to the yard. She pointed south and west. Dark, boiling thunderheads reached their fingers toward them. "I outran many a thunderstorm in my day; surely we can beat this one if we try. Close that door, if you please, and let us hurry. Can you keep up with this old woman?"

Rose laughed and started off, her gait stiff, but lengthening as her legs warmed to the task. Lucy had no choice but to follow her, yet when Rose looked back, Lucy was smiling.

And gaining on her.

CHAPTER 11

As she had been on the day before, Rose was waiting when Karl's truck puttered up to her house and deposited Lucy. Her legs and hips were sore from the impromptu race to which she had challenged Lucy, but she minded the discomfort not a bit.

While Lucy dawdled by the truck, Karl gave Rose a nod and carried a bundle of wood into the house. Rose followed him inside. He took advantage of the opportunity to whisper to Rose, "We think Lucy enjoyed her visit yesterday. All she could talk about was you. And some preposterous tale about snakes in the stove."

He coughed and set down the wood when Lucy appeared in the doorway. "Enough wood to keep the chill away today."

"Thank you, Little Karl."

Rose put her hand to her mouth. "Oh, my goodness. I have not called you 'Little' Karl in decades. I do apologize."

Karl's laughter boomed in the near-empty room. "You just stripped thirty-five years off'n me, Aunt Rose."

Rose laughed with him. "Everyone called you Little Karl back then."

Lucy wanted in on the fun. "Whyever would anyone call you 'little,' Grandpa?"

He grinned. "I was named for my *far*, Lucy. My father was a big man, he was, and he was Karl before I was. Thus, I was Little Karl my entire childhood—until I was as tall as my *Onkel* Jan."

"The habits of years are hard to break," Rose added.

Lucy had lost interest. "It is cold in here." She busied herself laying the fire.

"Grandma and I will expect you by dinnertime like yesterday, Lucy," Karl said, "but if it rains, I will fetch you both."

"Okay."

"Thank you, Karl," Rose said.

Rose opened the basket and again poured warm, sweet tea from a jar into two tin cups and placed the cups on the stove to reheat.

"I was pondering last evening, what I would share with you about your great-grandmother, Amalie. As I said yesterday, I possessed none of the skills required to survive in this land, particularly back then. We had no propane for our stoves at that time. No telephones or electricity. Amalie made it her mission to teach me all she knew."

Lucy and Rose resumed their seats as though the break between yesterday and today had been but minutes.

"What things did she teach you?" Lucy asked.

"Canning, of course. We spent hours and days and weeks canning everything that grew in our gardens. Hard, hot, miserable work it was, too."

Lucy snorted. "It still is—propane or not."

"See? At fourteen, you already know how to can. Between the ordinary canning, we cooked down kettles of fruit into jams and jellies. We pickled cucumbers six different ways, chopped and canned relishes of every sort, and brined shredded cabbages for sauerkraut—not a personal favorite, by the way."

Lucy giggled. "Nor mine."

"I was embarrassed that Sigrün knew all these things and could work rings around me. And Amalie? She was one of the most disciplined, hardworking women I have ever met, but the thing I loved most about her was that she was a 'truth-talker.'"

"A 'truth-talker'? I have never heard that term."

"It means that in our friendship, she taught me more than skills. She sowed pearls of wisdom into my life that I treasure to this day. But real love, true friendship, is not always sweetness and rose petals, Lucy. Amalie was not afraid to speak truth to me when I needed to hear it. She knew how to deliver a word in due season, and she was unafraid to address issues of character when she witnessed them, to call out the flaws and weaknesses I needed to correct if I was to grow into Christian maturity."

If my marriage was to survive.

"Isn't that the opposite of minding your own business?"

"The Bible says, *Faithful are the wounds of a friend.* A true friend will hurt you to save you from yourself—and Amalie was a true friend."

Lucy studied Rose intently.

Rose's voice grew softer. "I have rarely spoken of this to anyone, because it was such a hard lesson, but I feel that you, as Amalie's great-granddaughter should know what she did for me. That is, if you are interested."

Lucy leaned forward, her elbows on her knees. "You know I am. You are just spinning this out to keep my attention, aren't you?"

"Yes and no. No, because it was one of the most difficult days in my walk with the Lord and in my marriage to Jan. It very nearly broke me."

She paused, the weight of that day still heavy. "Nearly broke us, Jan and me."

Frowning, Lucy took the cups from the stove and handed one to Rose. "If you wish to tell it, Aunt Rose, I will listen . . ."

Rose smiled. "Thank you for being considerate of my feelings. Yes, it was a difficult day, but I struggled through it to the other side, with thanks to Amalie. That is my point. Sometimes, the issues of life appear insurmountable, but with God's grace, we can reach the other side and go on from there."

Lucy nodded and raised the cup to her lips, ready for Rose to talk.

"It was spring, and Joy was about nine months old. She was teething, poor baby, and utterly miserable. It was all I could do to keep up with my chores and take care of her at the same time. Night after night, she had wakened in the night screaming. After a week of it, I was so very tired."

The details were fresh in Rose's mind—Joy's soiled bedding, the overflowing coffeepot, Joy flinging her milk everywhere yet screaming for more, the potatoes boiling over. Jan walking in on the hectic scene.

"There I stood, the kitchen a mess, breakfast late, Joy screeching and pitching a right fit, and Jan's wide eyes fixed not on the mess, but on me. When I looked down, I realized I was still wearing my nightgown. Oh, I had thrown an apron over it, but I had been out to the pump to fetch water, to the barn to do the milking, and to the yard to stake out the goats. In my nightgown."

Lucy spluttered and spat the tea in her mouth back into her cup. She tittered and laughed and rocked forward and back in her chair. "Oh! Oh, my! I cannot—this is too priceless. I wonder if my grandpa or uncles saw you."

Rose was not amused. "I am glad my tale entertains you."

Lucy reined in her laughter, but she was still aquiver with it. "I-I am sorry."

"You spend a great deal of your energy apologizing, Lucy."

Lucy sobered then. "I suppose I do. Please. I do wish you to finish telling me."

"Jan was very understanding that morning. He took Joy so I could dress, comb my hair, and fix breakfast."

Lucy's mouth puckered in disappointment. "That is it? That is all that happened?"

No, it wasn't the end. The worst was ahead.

Rose moistened her lips. "I had seeds to plant that day, and I usually brought Joy with me when I went outside. I was always so careful with her—always. Stomp down the nearby grass, as Jan had showed me. Call Baron and have him lie close to Joy, within reach of her. Bring the goats, too, and stake them near Baron, for he was guardian to us all, our protector. But I was short on sleep and weary that day."

Rose blinked slowly, the years dropping away. She could see the scene, just as it had been back then, the color and texture of the prairie grass, the dark, moist soil of the unplanted garden.

Spring. When the prairie rattlers left their dens to bask in the sun.

"I spread Joy's blanket as I always did. Put it on the edge of the garden spot. Sat her on it with her little dolly. I was focused on digging the furrows *just right*, straight as a string, and Joy was being so good. Happy to play with her baby, her gums not hurting her right then.

"I-I lost track of time. Was not paying attention—until Jan roared behind me."

Rose looked into Lucy's face, saw it crease with dread.

"I had forgotten to stomp down the grass. I had forgotten to call Baron. Had forgotten to bring the goats and stake them around Joy. *I had forgotten Joy altogether and left her unprotected.* She had crawled off her blanket into the path of a rattler. It had coiled and warned her, but she did not recognize the danger and I . . . I was preoccupied.

"Jan had promised to bring the hoe and help me with the furrows. By God's great provision, he arrived just as the snake drew back to strike."

Lucy whispered something under her breath.

"I know. I know, Lucy. I cannot sugarcoat it and call it forgetfulness or preoccupation. It was neither of those. It was neglect. *I had neglected Joy.*"

Rose shivered. "Jan struck before the snake did. He severed its head, and its blood spattered Joy, her dolly, her blanket.

"I rushed to pick her up, but Jan grabbed her up first and held her away from me. He would not let me touch her. I had never before seen him as angry as he was that day, nor did I after."

Except one time . . .

"He . . . he said things that scorched my heart. That tore my soul. My neglect had nearly killed our baby, the child God had given us to heal our grief. I had . . . I had almost killed . . . "

Rose exhaled and found she could not quite draw another breath. She tried, but her lungs would not respond, would not obey.

"Aunt Rose? Aunt Rose!" Lucy was by her side, her hands on Rose's shoulders. "Aunt Rose! Please!"

A shuddering breath racked her body. Another. Another, easier this time. Another. Rose placed her hand on Lucy's. "I . . . I will be all right. In a moment."

Rose expected Lucy to feel relieved. Instead, Lucy reacted in anger. Then she melted into tears.

"You scared me! You-you-you scared me!"

Rose stood and tottered on her feet. "Come, dear. Come." She held Lucy's face to her shoulder. "I am fine now. Just an old woman having a moment. Everything is all right."

Eventually, Lucy drew back, a little embarrassed, and they both sat back down. Lucy stared at the floor. "You . . . you might have killed Joy."

"Yes, I am aware, thank you."

"Oh. Sorry."

"Afterward, I was devastated and overcome with guilt. I was exhausted—but inside, I was filled with excuses. And Jan? I did not know him. I had never seen that man before. He would not let me have Joy, and his eyes were as cold as ice. So . . . I ran away. I ran along the creekbank and across the bridge to Amalie. She loved me. I knew she would comfort me. See the situation from my perspective."

Rose held her head in her hands. "However, things did not go the way I thought they would. Your great-grandmother, after listening to me recite my tearful tale but understanding only a few words, called Søren from the barn to translate."

I did not want to repeat my tale to Søren. I was humiliated as it was, and the poor young man had already been privy to things not of his concern, and yet . . .

"Amalie insisted that I begin again. Mortified, but certain I was not *really* at fault, and convinced that Jan had been taken over by a wicked creature, I told my story again. They nodded their understanding. Both of them were as sorry as I could have hoped for, but I also saw disappointment on their faces."

Disappointment and censure. The look in Søren's eyes was worse than Amalie's. How I hated watching his opinion of me sink.

"When Amalie sent Søren away, she sat me down at the table, that same table still in your Aunt Meg's kitchen, and opened her Bible. She handed me the English Bible Søren used, and she had me read along in English while she read aloud in Riksmål.

"*Confess your faults one to another, and pray one for another, that ye may be healed.* That was the verse she read. Confess? I did not want to confess. I had not *purposefully* left Joy unprotected. How, then, was this lapse a sin to be confessed? But she put her hand on my arm and slowly, painfully, put her own words into English.

"'You mus' da care take for Joy,' she said. 'Alla times, is big, *most* job. No 'scuse, Rose. You go. Tell God. Tell God *gud.* Tell Jan. You pray. *Helbrede*. Heal. You heal.'"

"With that, she hugged me tight and sent me home, her meaning clear in my mind."

You must take on the care of Joy, completely, fully. At all times, it is your biggest, most important work. No excuses, Rose. Go and make your confession to God—and make it a good one.

Rose lifted her head a little. Lucy's eyes were fixed on the floor, but she was nodding to herself. Agreeing with Amalie.

Rose sighed. "My city-dwelling friends would have sympathized with me. They would have scoffed at Amalie and brushed away her loving rebuke. They would have sneered, mocked her, and called her unsympathetic and harsh. After all, it was an unintentional slipup, and disaster *was* averted—yet those same acquaintances would have criticized me for choosing to live in an uncivilized wilderness where such tragedy could occur in the first place.

"I had to face a disconcerting truth about myself. You grew up on the prairie, Lucy. You grew up knowing the dangers. I did not. I had to accept that the 'rules' of the prairie do not bend to our expectations, that lack of vigilance can spell death."

Lucy said softly. "Children used to get lost in the prairie grass. They would wander into it, never to be found. We were warned continually of the dangers. I have looked after my baby sister, Adele, since she could toddle. I would *never* let anything happen to her."

Rose nodded. "Yes. The dangers and responsibilities were bred into you—but not me. On my way home from Amalie's, I began to perceive how I was using my inexperience and fatigue as excuses for not fully shouldering my responsibility for Joy's safety. I could not afford even a moment's carelessness when it came to her. She was completely and utterly dependent upon me. My responsibility. Mine. Tired or not, overburdened or not, my vigilance was required.

"Then, the Holy Spirit reminded me of Jesus' parable of the Sower and the Seed, found in the Gospel of Mark, Chapter 4. I recalled how

Jesus had to explain the parable to his disciples, and I am so glad he did. Jesus said:

"Do you not understand this parable?
How then will you understand all the parables?
The sower sows the word.
And these are the ones along the path,
where the word is sown:
when they hear, Satan immediately comes
and takes away the word
that is sown in them . . .
And others are the ones sown among thorns.
They are those who hear the word,
but the cares of the world
and the deceitfulness of riches
and the desires for other things
enter in and choke the word,
and it proves unfruitful."

Rose scrubbed at the lines of her tired face. "I am not saying I willfully sinned, Lucy, but I did need to own my carelessness. After all, the word we know as 'sin' means to trespass, but it also means *to miss the mark.*

"On that walk home, I confessed to the Lord that I had missed the mark when it came to protecting Joy. I had fallen short of my duty to her, and in doing so, I had also failed Jan. No, it had not been my intention to do so, but it did not matter that my failure was unintentional, because the dangers of the prairie—or the world, for that matter—do not lessen with our ignorance nor pause to consider our intentions."

Rose looked up to see Lucy studying her intently. "I had to admit that, amid the cares of my life and my desire for something as secondary as planting my garden, I had allowed myself to become distracted—and it is when we are distracted, careless, or thoughtless that the enemy makes his move on us or those we love.

"You see, like the rules of the prairie, the rules of the spiritual realm do not bend to our expectations, either. Satan is wicked and he does not play fair. It is no wonder, then, that Jesus cautions us often, at least a dozen times in the Gospels, to *watch* or to *watch and pray.*

"Once I had owned up to and confessed my sin, I was able to recall the remainder of Amalie's counsel."

Confess to Jan. Pray. Pray for healing.

Rose turned her face to the front door. "When I came through that door over there, Jan was rocking Joy beside the fire—in that rocker over there in the corner, sitting where you are sitting now. He lifted his eyes to me, and I witnessed his grief. I knelt by the chair and confessed that I had been at fault, that I understood the gravity of my omission.

"He wept and held me close. He, too, confessed his faults—he had allowed his fear to run roughshod over his normally self-controlled emotions, and he had used his anger to hurt me, because I had nearly hurt our dear baby. We confessed our faults, forgave each other, and received the Lord's forgiveness. Jan and I prayed together, prayed for each other.

"I came to understand that day how necessary it was to confess my faults—that is, if I intended to grow in my faith. Over time, Jan and I healed together. Grace upon grace upon grace!"

Rose again sighed. "It was a turning point for me, Lucy, a place of maturation. That terrible incident forged a determination within me that has seen me through many difficulties. The women of this land epitomize unfaltering courage, but they did not come by their courage without testing. I thank God that Amalie spoke truth to me on the day of my testing. Through her wise counsel, the Lord brought me through that troubled sea to a safe harbor."

"Is that all it takes? Sheer determination?" Lucy asked.

"Ah, I see your point. No. Sheer determination or strength of will does not result in godliness or maturity. Those who take that route find frustration and defeat. My determination that day was to surrender to the Lord and daily seek for *his* strength, his wisdom, his help. I determined to lean upon him utterly. Completely. It was the Lord who spoke these words, *My grace is sufficient for thee: for my strength is made perfect in weakness*."

Lucy did not say anything for many moments. Rose had eaten a cookie and finished her tea before Lucy spoke.

"Do these testings, as you call them, appear in unexpected ways? What I mean is . . . could my testing look different than yours?"

"Yes, I should think so."

"You said you wanted to tell me about Amalie . . . but I think you also told me these things so I would know that you are not the perfect woman all of RiverBend thinks you are."

Rose bent her head once. "That is an accurate insight, Lucy. However, I would add that I do not believe all of RiverBend thinks of me as you describe.

"Those who actually know me also know my flaws. Perhaps I opened myself to you so that *you* might take me down from that pedestal you believe our family and friends have placed me on. Only the Lord is worthy of an exalted place. Then, perchance, you will discover that your anger toward me is misplaced?"

Rose watched Lucy frown and hoped the girl was reevaluating her feelings. If so, Rose had achieved her objective.

Her first objective.

Rose had spent two afternoons with Lucy speaking only of her own life and experiences. She hoped through her openness that Lucy would grow to trust her, to become comfortable talking with her. Then, if it was the Lord's will, she might unburden herself to Rose.

This was what she had prayed for.

"Meg tells me you are an exceptional scholar. I am convinced after talking with you these few hours that you are perceptive, too. Your parents must be proud of you."

Lucy shrugged. "My teachers want me to go to college, but my parents are blind to its value. They cannot see any future for me except marriage and children and farming."

"We faced a similar quandary with Joy. She has a head for figures that outstripped her teachers. She wanted to go to business school. We dipped into my savings to let her go."

"My family has no savings to 'dip into,'" Lucy sneered.

"When will you finish your schooling here?"

"A year from this spring."

"So soon! And have you prayed about your future?"

"What would be the point?"

"Do you believe God answers prayer, Lucy?"

"I do not know. Sometimes, I suppose. But not of late."

Not of late?

Rose asked the questions she had been working up to. "Lucy, what do *you* want to do with your life? What are *your* hopes and dreams?"

"My hopes and dreams?"

"Is it your wish to go to college? If so, have you prayed for the Lord to open a door for you? What about after college? Do you wish for a husband? Children?"

In an instant, the fragile tête-à-tête between them shattered. Hardness settled on Lucy's features . . . but not before, for the most fleeting of moments, Rose thought she glimpsed something else. *Sorrow? Anguish?*

Then it was gone, replaced by anger.

She uses anger to hide her pain?

"No, Aunt Rose, I do not wish for a husband. What I wish is to go home now."

Rose blinked in confusion. "Why, Lucy. Child, have I said something to offend you?"

Lucy stood. Her words were low. Tight. Rigid with rage. "I am leaving, Aunt Rose. You may follow me, but you cannot stop me."

As if adding an exclamation mark in conclusion, thunder crashed overhead. The ongoing rumble of it shook the house, and rain pummeled the roof. Lucy was already through the door. Rose heard her run down the steps and away from the house.

She murmured softly, "Lord, please show me what is wrong."

A drip plopped from the ceiling onto the floor, followed by a thin but steady stream. She got up and slid the old washtub under it, added wood to the fire in the stove, and sat down to wait for Karl to come pick her up.

THE RAIN WAS tapering off when Rose heard the growl of Karl's truck and the slam of the truck's door. Karl stomped into the house a moment later, shedding water everywhere.

"Thank you for coming to get me, Karl." Rose stared at the stove's open door and the embers within."

"What happened? Lucy came home, soaking wet, as angry as the storm outside. I asked her what was wrong, but she did not stop. Would not answer me when I called to her. Went directly to her room."

"Will you sit a few minutes with me, Karl?

Reluctantly, he straddled the chair Lucy had vacated. Rose turned her face to him.

"Karl, why is Lucy living with you and Sonja? Why is she not living at home with her family?"

Karl exhaled. Shook his head. Wrapped his hands around the back of the chair and gripped the wood until his fingers grew white from the pressure. "We hoped the change might resolve some problems."

"Lucy being the problem?"

Karl reverted to his Norwegian roots. "*Ja.*"

"Can you describe her behavior at home?"

He dropped his head. "Defiance. Shouting . . . at Einar and Norrie, at the other children. Throwing things. Breaking things."

"Einar and Norrie were worried for the other children's safety?"

"*Ja*. And mayhap their own. One night, while everyone was sleeping, Einar woke up. He thought he'd heard something, so he went downstairs. He caught Lucy in the kitchen with Adele. Lucy had packed a rucksack with food, clothes, and some blankets. She would not answer Einar's questions, but it was obvious that she was running away—and taking Adele with her."

"Oh, dear Lord!"

"It gets worse. After he sent Lucy upstairs and put Adele back to bed, Einar could not sleep. That very same night, he heard Lucy go downstairs again. He found her trying to set fire to the kitchen.

"When he put the fire out, she told him he should send her away, that she would not stop. He called me early that morning. We came and took her."

Rose's breath hissed between her teeth. "She is so angry."

"You think we do not know this?" Karl's shout was desperate.

"But *why* is she angry, Karl? What has happened?"

"Nothing we know of. We have asked her many times. She is just . . . rebellious, I suppose. Children go through a season of rebellion, but we . . . we fear for her, for what she will do to herself or others."

"This is more than adolescent rebellion, Karl. Children do not act out in such violence without reason. How long has she been like this?"

He rubbed his chin and closed his eyes. "I think . . . maybe since last spring?"

"Six months ago. Can you tell me what has changed at home in the past six months?"

"I can think of nothing. Perhaps Einar and Norrie can remember something."

Rose nodded. "I will talk to them."

He noticed the washtub rapidly filling with water, and Rose followed his gaze up to the ceiling.

"Good gracious!"

Karl looked puzzled. "You didn't think this old roof would leak?"

"I did, and I knew what the tub was for. However, I just recalled something else."

Joy staying on with me after Jan passed. Sharing her vision with me—a house in Denver for the girls they rescued, a place for them to heal. Me, declaring I would join her in Corinth while we searched for the right house. The two of us breaking up my household, packing for my move. Taking what I needed, giving most away. But boxing up and storing the few treasures I would leave behind.

She looked up. *Storing them in the attic.*

She could not, for the life of her, remember what "treasures" she had left behind.

Whatever they are, perhaps the rain has ruined them. I will find out before I leave.

CHAPTER 12

Joy buttered a slice of toast for little Luke, who was kicking his brother. His brother, in turn was kicking the bench. "I cannot believe we are leaving Saturday. This visit has gone so quickly. Luke, stop kicking Jacob. Jacob, stop kicking the bench, please."

"It has," Meg answered. Søren nodded his agreement.

"More bacon," Matthew said.

"May I have more bacon, please," Joy admonished him.

"May I pleeeze have more bacon?"

"Matthew," his mother warned.

"Sorry—hey! Jacob kicked me!"

"Jacob and Luke," O'Dell said, "your mother asked you both to stop kicking. You will sit quietly and finish your food. If I have to speak again, you will be paddled. Do you understand?"

"Yes, Papa," Jacob said, chastened.

"Yis, Papa," Luke parroted.

Meg and Søren looked at each other and hid their smiles.

Rose was quietly eating her breakfast, oblivious to the meal's melee. Five adults and three energetic boys shared the table, but her mind was otherwise occupied.

Joy's statement finally penetrated her thoughts. "I am sorry. What did you say, Joy?"

"When, Mama?"

"A moment ago. About our visit."

"Oh. That we leave Saturday. We have only today, tomorrow and Friday left."

No, Rose objected silently. *I am not done here.*

She spoke to O'Dell. "So soon? Edmund, could we, perhaps, stay on a bit longer?"

O'Dell looked up. "As much as I would like to accommodate your request, Mother, I am expected in the office Monday morning, and we shall have just arrived in Chicago Sunday afternoon. I hope you understand that the situation is out of my control?"

"Of course," Rose murmured. She nudged her plate away, her hunger having deserted her. "Meg, do Einar and Norrie have a telephone?"

"Yis'm, they do."

"Good. I shall call them after our morning devotions."

ROSE DID NOT know Einar and Norrie all that well, but they were family, and that mattered most. They had been married three years and had a one-year-old, Lucy, when Jan passed away and Rose moved to Corinth. Still, Rose could hear Norrie's surprise on the other end of the call.

"Aunt Rose. S'good of you to call. Your speech at the luncheon is all anyone has talked about since."

"Thank you, Norrie. You are quite kind."

"Not at all. I—"

Rose spoke over her. "I should like to come visit you today, you and Einar. It is about Lucy."

"Oh."

Rose heard sorrow dripping from that single, soft syllable. She offered Norrie what comfort she could. "I have been talking with her, Norrie, and praying for her. May I come visit you today? Will Einar be available?"

"I will ask him."

"Thank you. I will await your call."

MEG DROVE ROSE to Einar and Norrie's home just after the midday meal. Their home was typical of the farmhouses in the community: a generous, open kitchen and a large living room, a second floor with many bedrooms to accommodate a growing family.

Einar and Norrie, in their mid-thirties, Rose thought, had finished their midday meal, and Norrie was about to put their youngest child, a girl, down for a nap when Rose arrived. The other children, Viktor, Henrik, and Eirik, were at school.

"Is this Adele?" Rose asked Norrie.

"Yes, our darling baby. She is three now."

The child was sweetly rounded and full of smiling mischief. She was also ready for her nap, yawning and snuggling into Norrie's neck.

Lucy said, "I have looked after my baby sister, Adele, since she could toddle. I would never *let anything happen to her." Lord, then why would Lucy try to run away and take Adele with her? Would that not put the child at risk?*

When Norrie came downstairs, she made tea for herself and Rose. Einar poured himself a mug of coffee. Einar and Norrie's manners were subdued, as if they expected Rose to deliver bad news. She noticed how Einar extended his leg as he sat and how he knuckled his thigh to massage it.

"Thank you for meeting with me," Rose began. "I hope you do not feel that I am meddling in your family's business. The fact is, I rather like Lucy, but I can see she is troubled."

Einar glanced at Norrie, who nodded. "We do not mind you, Aunt Rose, but we are concerned about gossip."

"All the more reason to get to the root of Lucy's anger and set her back onto the right track, wouldn't you agree? I will, of course, keep your family's personal affairs to myself. You may trust me on that."

"If only we understood," Norrie exclaimed. "We do not know what has become of her. One day she was our lovely, beautiful girl, so happy and sweet. The next, she was sullen, withdrawn, disobedient, and . . ."

"And a danger to Adele, to you all? I spoke with Karl."

Norrie nodded sadly. "What can we do? When it began, we talked to her. She would not answer us. When it continued, we punished her. Later, her behavior worsened."

"Is it possible that something happened to her to cause this alteration in her conduct? It would have been around six months ago, if that is when she changed."

"Yes, last spring, it was, although things worsened greatly at the end of summer. That was when we sent her to Papa and Mama's," Einar said.

"Was Lucy away from the house during that time? Did she go anywhere?"

"Only to her friends among our neighbors for an hour or two after school. And to church, of course. Naught else, I think. We are so busy during planting season and harvest."

I had seeds to plant that day, and I usually brought Joy with me when I went outside. I was focused on digging the furrows. I lost track of time. Was not paying attention.

You may not have been paying attention, either, Einar.

"Who are her friends, the ones she visits?"

"Oh, the McKennie grandchildren, the Lungrens, the Carothers. And just east of town, the Pettersens. All good, godly folk we have known for generations."

"Were others here during planting? Other than your family?"

Einar and Norrie looked at each other. Einar shrugged. "*Nei*, I do not think so."

Rose thought for a moment. "Would you show me about your farm, Einar?"

He stood with a grunt of effort. "Would be an honor, Aunt Rose."

They bundled up, and Einar took Rose around the stockyard, then over to the barn and the pens. Their farm was simple and well-ordered, nothing short of what Rose expected of Karl's son, Little Karl, whom Jan had raised like his own.

As they walked, Einar occasionally limped.

Rose paused near the chicken coops. "I see you are favoring your left leg, Einar. Have you hurt yourself?"

"*Ja*, sure, clumsy oaf that I am. Cut my thigh during the second haying, right down into the muscle, it were. A slew of stitches it took to close it up. Is healing up right fine, but I been gimping 'round since."

"I am glad it is healing, but I can understand the frustration."

"Frustration? *Ja*, that is certain. Thank you for caring—and we thank you for looking out for our girl." A glimmer of moisture appeared in his eyes. "We know you are leaving soon, Aunt Rose, but we are grateful to you for trying to help our Lucy."

Rose did not know how to answer him. Saturday loomed large before her, and her heart shouted that she would not be done in RiverBend by then, not ready to leave.

She gently touched Einar's shoulder. "I will be praying over your family and all your concerns, Einar. I trust God. I know he will answer our prayers."

JOURNAL ENTRY, OCTOBER 17, 1923

FATHER, FOR AS long as I have known you, my heart has been drawn to women and girls who were in desperate need of your grace and healing. I cannot help but feel that you brought me back to RiverBend, at this precise time, to keep Lucy's life from spiraling into ruin.

Yet, the means to help her eludes me. How glad I am that it does not elude you! You know the end from the beginning. So, I am asking, my dear Lord, that you give me guidance for the little time I have left in RiverBend. In the wonderful name of Jesus, please show me the way through this situation.

And Lord, I also bring Einar before you, asking that you fully heal his leg, and I ask that you encourage him while his leg heals. I watched Jan struggle when his knees gave out. It saddened him greatly when he could no longer work the land. If he had not steadfastly turned all his attention to discipling the young men of our community, he might have given way to despair, and despair is never your will for us.

It is you who speaks to us in your word, "But we have this treasure in earthen vessels, that the excellency of the power may be of God, and not of us. We are troubled on every side, yet not distressed; we are perplexed, but not in despair . . . that the life also of Jesus might be made manifest in our mortal flesh."

Earthen vessels, Lord. Fragile, easily broken, showing the many places you have had to mend us. I am thankful that Jan knew this passage and lived it. Because he turned to you and acquired a fresh vision for the last years of his life, he bore more fruit in his later years than in his former.

May we all do the same.

ROSE HAD DIFFICULTY dozing off and staying asleep that night. She had walked through many memories since she and the O'Dells had arrived in RiverBend. In the darkness of her bedroom, they flooded her subconscious, rousing her and keeping her awake until she was able to settle again and fall back to sleep.

As she slipped again from wakefulness to sleep, a dream took her. A peaceful meadow, a flock of sheep grazing on the lush grass. She walked among them, sometimes running her hand along a sheep's back, reveling in the thick wool, and rubbing the soothing oily residue into her fingers. The sheep did not find her presence alarming, not even the rams.

Odd that I would dream of sheep. We did not raise them, she thought in her dream. *We had goats, cows, pigs, and chickens. What do I know about sheep?*

She moved effortlessly through the flock, one with the sheep, at peace with them—until, out of the corner of her eye she caught a glimpse of something gliding into the flock. Streaks of brown, not white. Crouching lower than the backs of the sheep.

Unnoticed, unthreatening, and creeping deeper into the flock.

"No! That is a—" Rose's throat tightened and choked off her words.

She wanted to shout a warning. She opened her mouth wide, but she could not get the words to come out. She screamed it in her mind.

A wolf! A wolf is among the sheep!

Her eyes followed the creeping, slinking passage of the creature. He seemed to have a specific objective, for he passed many ewes without attacking them, instead, moving insidiously among them—lying still when one of the sheep objected, moving on when it calmed.

Then Rose saw the wolf's prey.

Deep within the flock, the ewes had opened a small patch of meadow where the lambs might frisk about while remaining within the confines of the flock. Where they could gambol and play.

Where they would be safe.

Across the meadow, on the far side of the flock, Rose saw movement—the Shepherd! He raised his staff and shouted into the wind, "*A wolf! A wolf is hunting the lambs! Save them from the wolf!*"

She woke, trembling, the words of the Shepherd ringing in her ears. "*A wolf is hunting the lambs?* What or who is this wolf, Lord? Please show me. Please show *us*, so we can save the lambs."

Rose kept awake the remainder of that night, alternately praying and listening for the Lord to speak to her, but nothing came to her.

THURSDAY, TOO, passed. She visited with Fiona a second time and helped Joy with the mountain of laundry a family of six so quickly accumulates.

While she hung wet clothes on the line, Rose prayed for Lucy and her family. When she gathered the dry garments in and began folding them, she asked the Lord to help Lucy and her family. When she retired Thursday evening, she continued to pray.

Whenever she woke during the night, she murmured her requests and ended them with, "I believe you hear me and are working, Lord. I trust you. I trust you will answer."

CHAPTER 13

On Friday morning, Rose waited until she thought it was near enough Meg and Søren's usual time to rise before she went to the kitchen and set the coffee pot to perking. When the coffee had brewed, she took a cup into her room and sat on the bed, going over her conversations with Lucy, searching for insight.

As she reviewed, she replayed telling Lucy about that fateful day, the day she had neglected Joy and only Jan's quick aim with a hoe had saved her.

I rushed to pick her up, but Jan grabbed her up first, held her away from me. He would not let me touch her. I had never before seen him as angry as he was that day, nor have I since.

Except one time . . .

"Except one time," Rose repeated.

Joy was fourteen. She had been the same age as Lucy, but tall for her age, frequently mistaken by strangers as sixteen or older. She walked to school and back, two miles each way. The community had built a new school on land adjacent to the church, and the walk was easily accomplished in decent weather. Joy usually herded Søren and Meg's older two, Markus and Colleen, and Karl and Sonja's eldest, Einar, along with her. If the weather turned wet, Jan, Søren, or Karl would take the covered carriage from Søren's barn and fetch them. If it snowed, one of them would hitch up the sleigh.

We sent Joy to school alone that morning, Rose recalled. *We were unconcerned for her safety. She had walked the route to school alone many times.*

We were troubled and caught up in that day's grievous events.

SPRING, 1897

IT WAS EARLY on a beautiful spring morning when Søren raced on horseback into their yard. He was pale and distressed. "Karl sent Einar to tell us that Amalie took ill in the kitchen and would I get the doctor. Sonja was with her and thinks Amalie had a fit of apoplexy. She cannot move. Cannot speak. I am off to fetch Dr. Nilsen."

Jan and Rose, as concerned as Søren, said they would go immediately to the farmhouse Karl had built for his bride on his father's land, farther down the creek from Søren's house. Amalie had lived with them for some time now.

"Do we send Joy to school?" Rose asked Jan. She turned to Søren. "What of Markus, Colleen, and Einar?

"Meg has taken Karl and Sonja's children to our house. We will keep the children home from school. The older ones will help her with the younger."

After seeing Joy out the door, Jan and Rose walked to Karl and Sonja's house. Unwilling to carry Amalie upstairs for fear they would worsen her condition, Karl and Sonja had laid her on a makeshift bed in their living room and were waiting for the doctor to arrive.

Rose knelt beside Amalie and took her hand. It felt lifeless to her. "Amalie. Can you hear me?"

Amalie's eyelids fluttered. Her breath rasped; she breathed out a moan. Rose sensed Amalie's confusion and agitation.

Rose bent to Amalie's ear. "Do not fret, my dear sister. Rest yourself in Jesus. Please. Trust the Savior. He is holding you right now, Amalie. Rest in him. Rest in Jesus."

Amalie calmed under Rose's words. Her breathing became less labored.

But then Sigrün arrived. She rushed to her mother's side, begging Amalie to open her eyes. When Amalie did not respond, she turned to Rose.

Rose held her as she wept. She said quietly, "Sigrün, dear Sigrün. I think Amalie can hear us but is unable to answer. She may be very afraid because she cannot move. Let us help her to rest in Jesus. Calm yourself and speak peace to her, Sigrün. Help me to soothe her heart, yes?"

Sigrün gulped and thought on what Rose had said. "You think she hears us?" she whispered.

"She may, so let us behave as if she does. We do not want her to become more agitated or fearful and thus harm herself further. We should encourage her, help her to remain calm."

"Ja, I will do that. Thank you, Aunt Rose."

Søren returned. The doctor came soon after and examined Amalie.

To the family gathered in the kitchen, he pronounced Amalie's malady a stroke. "I wish I could help her, but I cannot. She may recover some movement, perhaps some speech, or she may remain as she is.

"Right now, peace and quiet are very important lest she have another stroke."

Karl pressed the doctor. "You can do nothing for her? Nothing?"

"I am afraid not, Karl. The damage is deep within her brain, and we have no treatments to reverse the damage or keep it from progressing. Whatever movement or sensibility she regains in the next few hours will determine her fate. Sadly, the longer she remains without progress, the less we can expect for her recovery."

He allowed those words to sink in before adding, "If she does not regain consciousness in the next hours, it is a signal that the injury is too serious for her body to heal on its own. Your task will be to keep her comfortable until the end."

He struggled with his own emotions for a moment. "She is a fine woman, and I am most grievously sorry."

Sigrün, Karl, and Kjell wept together, and Søren wept with them. Amalie had been a mother to him after Elli died.

"We must send for Arnie," someone said. "For Uli, too."

Karl composed the messages. He sent them to town by the hand of a neighbor who would send them by wire to Arnie in Omaha and to Uli in the sleepy little farming town of Asher in northwest Nebraska where her husband, David, was pastoring his first church.

Jan knelt with Rose beside Amalie. He placed his hand on her and whispered over her in Riksmål. Rose did not understand what he said, only the "amen" when he finished praying. He then took it upon himself to manage the day's chores. Sigrün's husband, Harold, joined him.

Neighbors came and went, bringing food and comfort, murmuring their prayers for Amalie's recovery. Rose and Sonja served coffee and fed those who were hungry.

A neighbor offered to watch the two families' children, giving respite to Meg. She went into the living room to sit with Amalie. Rose followed and sat with her, and Meg wept in Rose's arms.

The day passed slowly. Amalie seemed no better—until late afternoon. Sigrün called for Karl and Kjell. Søren, Meg, Rose, Jan, and Sonja came, too.

Amalie had opened her eyes. She blinked and followed Sigrün's face hovering over her, then fixed on Karl's. She could not move her gaze far, only those few inches, but she seemed aware.

"She has squeezed my hand," Sigrün said, smiling through her tears. "She will get better."

Rose glanced at Jan. He sighed softly, shook his head, then raised his chin. He returned to the kitchen, and Rose followed. Jan was at the window, watching the sky.

"Rain comes," was all he said, and pointed at the spring storm bearing down from the west.

He glanced to the clock and clucked his tongue.

So did Rose. "Joy should be home by now."

"Ach! Must go, find Joy. Much rain comes."

As if in response to Jan's declaration, the clouds above the bluffs near Rose's land gave way, releasing a pummeling downpour.

We lost track of time. We were not paying attention. We were distracted—

Before Jan could pull on his coat, Rose pointed to a horse and wagon descending from the bluff, then crossing the bridge. The wagon could not outrun the storm; it clattered up the drive into the yard, bringing the pouring rain with it. Jan studied the wagon's driver and frowned. Rose went to his side and looked out. Joy was climbing down from the wagon. A young man climbed down the other side and hurried to help her, but she shied away from him.

Jan's eyes narrowed. "Who is dat man?"

"I do not know him."

Joy burst through the kitchen door. She was dripping and bedraggled but did not care. "Aunt Amalie? How is she?"

Rose beckoned Joy to her side and wrapped a towel around her shoulders. She did not answer her immediately. The young man who had brought her home stood in the doorway, also shedding water. He removed his hat and shook it out under the porch's eaves before stepping across the threshold.

Rose studied the stranger. Tall, well-built. Light brown hair and eyes. His face wore a small smile, and his eyes followed Joy to Rose. Shifted to Jan. Back to Joy. Something inside Rose made her reach her arm around Joy.

Karl and Sonja had heard the wagon and entered the kitchen. Kjell joined them.

The stranger approached Jan. "Sir, my name is Franz Mikkelmann. I am new to the neighborhood. I saw your daughter walking. The rain was almost upon her, and I offered her a ride. She told me her aunt was ill, so I brought her here."

Rose watched Jan relax a little. He extended his hand and they shook. "I denk you, Mr. Mikkelmann."

Franz's fingers worried the brim of the hat he held. "May I be so bold as to ask for a word in private, sir?"

Jan's brows drew together. Karl, Sonja, and Kjell looked at each other, then moved to the living room, closing the door behind them. Rose stayed where she was.

Franz again glanced at Joy, then back to Jan. "Sir, may I call on your daughter?"

Now it was Joy who clung to Rose. "Please, no," she whispered into Rose's bodice.

"I am not knowing you," Jan replied evenly.

"Yes, sir. As I said, I am new here. I am twenty-two. I have a job, a wagon, a horse. I work hard."

Jan shook his head. "I sorry, but Joy is not the years." He appealed to Rose.

"Joy is only fourteen, Mr. Mikkelmann."

"Fourteen!"

"Yes. She is not yet the age to receive male callers."

"*Ja*, not the age," Jan echoed.

The young man's smile slipped. "Is it because I am not like you Swedes?"

"*Nei*, she not the age," Jan repeated. He added, "Ve be Norsk, not Svede." His features had dropped into calm, kind lines. "Ve sorry, Mr. Mikkelmann. Joy not the age. Two years more."

"Two years."

"*Ja*, two years."

The man's mouth tightened. "Two years is a long time."

Jan held firm. "We denk you, bring Joy home. *Tusen Takk*." Then he nodded. "*God dag*, Mr. Mikkelmann."

Franz nodded, his jaw set. "Good day, Mr. Thoresen."

Jan watched until the young man had turned his wagon around and driven away. He rubbed his hand over the back of his neck and up into his hairline.

Rose turned to Joy. "Are you all right?"

"I suppose so, but . . ."

Jan drew near. "Vat ist?"

"That man. I have seen him before. He works the fields next to the school. For the Henrys, I believe. He. . . watches me."

"He is their hired hand?" Rose asked.

Joy nodded, her expression troubled. "I think so. I was nearly home when he stopped his wagon in the road in front of me. I told him I did not want a ride, but he insisted."

"Vhat is 'insist?'" Jan asked, a frown pulling at his brow.

"He . . . he held my arm."

"He took your arm? After you said you did not want a ride?" Rose asked.

"Y-yes. He would not let go, and I-I was afraid to pull away from him, because he held it so tightly."

Jan's expression drew down further. "I vill speak to this Franz Mikkelmann who puts his hand on my *datter*."

ROSE'S THOUGHTS returned to the present day, and her hand on her Bible stilled. *Jan left the house to give the impetuous young man a corrective lesson in the proper treatment of young women, but that was not the end of the matter. On that day, we did not know what was ahead . . . yet, I will never forget how shaken Joy was . . . after.*

Her thoughts raced on, leaping here, landing there, seeing connections, and arriving at an unwanted destination.

"Is that it, Lord? Have you shown me the answer I have been seeking?"

She knelt beside the bed and prayed. "Lord God, I empty my heart and my mind of myself and ask that you fill me with your Holy Spirit to overflowing. Grant me your wisdom and insight this day. Make my words and actions be yours, Lord, so that you might work through me. More than anything, O God, I pray for Lucy, that your truth will set her free."

She dressed quickly, combed out her hair and pinned it into place. Took her empty cup into the kitchen. Søren clattered down the stairs a minute later, just ahead of Meg. He touched the pot on the stove.

"You have already perked the coffee, Rose?" he asked.

"Yes. it should be hot still."

"Great!" He poured a cup, tipped a deep draught down his throat, then put his coat on. "See you later." He bounded out the door, headed to the barn.

"Good morn, Mama Rose." Meg yawned and reached for a coffee cup. "Joy and I were stayin' up too late last night. Chatterin' like a flock of finches, Søren said. But you be leaving on the morrow, and we will miss all of you very much."

"I hope you do not mind if I stay on a bit," Rose said.

Meg stopped, the coffee pot hovering over her empty cup. "I'm beggin' your pardon, Mama Rose?"

"I have decided that I will not be leaving with them tomorrow. I have unfinished work here. May I stay with you another week or so?"

Although confounded, Meg nodded. "Always welcome here, you are, Mama Rose. Are . . . are Joy and Edmund knowin'?"

"That I am extending my stay in RiverBend? Not yet." Rose shifted topics. "May I use your telephone?"

Meg nodded again.

Rose spoke to the community switchboard operator. A moment later, a not-quite-awake voice picked up.

"Thoresens', Norrie speaking."

"Norrie, this is Rose Thoresen calling. Good morning."

Norrie laughed uncertainly. "Any earlier and it would be 'good night,' Aunt Rose."

"Every farmer in the county is up at this hour. I knew you would be, too. However, please forgive the early interruption to your busy day."

"*Ja*, we are a-movin' here. Are you calling about Lucy?"

Rose reassured her. "Indirectly. Is Einar about?"

"*Ja*, in the barn already—*nei*, I hear him coming in."

Rose heard Norrie's faint words and Einar's muffled response. Then he was on the line.

"Einar here, Aunt Rose."

Rose dispensed with pleasantries. "I have a question for you, Einar. You said you hurt your leg during the second haying." Rose could almost hear his brows shooting upward in astonishment.

"*Ja*, sure, I did. Like I told you."

"And that was about two months ago?"

"Let's see." He mumbled to himself, counting backward. "'Twas end of July, it was, when we did the second cutting."

"And you hurt yourself then?"

"Had half the hay cut and a-dryin' in the field when I done it."

"If you were laid up, how did you manage to finish the cutting and bring it in after it dried?"

Einar was silent a moment. "Pettersens sent their hired man to help out. My boys do a fair mote of work, but they couldn't replace me and do their own chores, too."

The hair on the back of Rose's neck prickled and stood up. "A hired man, you say? For how long?"

"He helped bring in the hay and after that the wheat, along with other chores. Split his time between the Pettersens' farm and us. We couldn't rightly afford all his wages, so we fed him and fixed up a room for him in the barn."

"And he is with you still?"

"*Nei*, gone back to the Pettersens' now I'm on the mend."

"So, he helped out from the time you hurt yourself until recently. And he stayed in your barn during that time?"

Einar's answer was slow in coming. "*Ja*, that is right."

Rose persisted. "And the Pettersens. You said Lucy has friends there, that she visits with them regularly."

"That she does—or did. Used to walk home with their daughters, Emma and Hester. Stay with them after school sometimes until close to supper time."

"Used to?"

"Had them a spat, I guess."

"Around six months ago?"

Einar was silent. Rose could hear deep breathing on the other end of the line and a convulsive swallow.

"Einar?"

"W-what are you getting to, Aunt Rose? What is your meaning?"

Rose heard Lucy's voice in her head. "*I have looked after my baby sister, Adele, since she could toddle. I would* never *let anything happen to her.*"

"Einar, say and do nothing until you hear back from me. Will you promise me that?"

She again listened to Einar's breathing.

"Einar?"

"*Ja*, I am here. I . . ."

"We know nothing yet, Einar, but I am leaving directly for Karl's house. I will speak to Lucy and, God willing, I will have the truth from her."

Einar swallowed again. Hard. "And then?"

"And then we will see *Jesus*, Einar. He is the truth, and by following his leading, we will uncover what is hidden. Then we will see him do what only he can do—heal a wounded heart. Will you and Norrie pray? Will you both trust the Lord to return your precious daughter to you, whole and sound?"

Rose had heard many tragic confessions after she moved to Colorado, and she had been privy to the keening wails of grief and brokenness. Still, of all the sorrow she had witnessed over the years, the hardest to bear were the sobs of a grown man.

When Einar could finally speak, he said, "*Ja.* We will pray, Aunt Rose. We will . . . trust the Lord."

"I will call you when I have news."

Rose hung up and turned around. Meg stood silently, watching her. Joy and O'Dell had joined her.

"You heard?"

O'Dell answered. "I think we have the gist of it."

"I have work to do today, Edmund. I would ask for your support and assistance."

"I am at your service, Mother Rose."

Rose turned to Meg. "Does RiverBend have any police these days?"

"*Nay*. RiverBend is no' big enough town for police. Jeremy Bailey is bein' our constable. If we had a real crime, he would call the sheriff over in the county seat."

"Jeremy is a good man," Rose answered. "He will do."

She shifted her attention to Joy and O'Dell. "You should know that I will not be leaving with you on the train tomorrow. I will stay a week, perhaps two, in order to see this through. Do you perceive my reasoning?"

Joy nodded. "She will need help."

"Yes, and I praise Almighty God, we have the ongoing help she will need, right here in RiverBend."

"Our girls from the mountain?"

"Yes."

CHAPTER 14

Rose and O'Dell pulled on coats and hats. They left through the kitchen door and walked toward Karl and Sonja's house. It was not far, perhaps a few hundred yards. While they walked, Rose prayed silently. She had the impression O'Dell was praying, too.

When they climbed the steps to Sonja's kitchen, O'Dell knocked. Sonja answered in her apron, a wooden spoon in her hand, surprise and curiosity lifting her brow.

Apprehension swept away her curiosity when she saw their expressions. "Aunt Rose? Mr. O'Dell?"

"I must speak to Lucy, Sonja," Rose said softly.

Sonja nodded. "Come in, then. She is still upstairs, getting ready for school."

Karl came into the kitchen as Rose and O'Dell were hanging their coats and hats. "Aunt Rose?"

"I am here to see Lucy."

"I-I will be taking her to school shortly."

Rose placed her hand on Karl's arm. "This is important. She may wish . . . to miss school today."

Karl looked to Sonja. She nodded.

"Very well."

"We will wait for her in the living room, if that is all right with you?"

Rose and O'Dell stepped into the living room to wait for Lucy. Rose seated herself in one of two adjacent chairs. O'Dell did not sit.

"You will not want me present when you speak to her, will you?"

"Thank you for your insight. Not immediately, no. I assume we may need you and your particular skills . . . after."

His eyes gleamed. "I relish the opportunity."

Lucy, escorted by her grandfather, entered the living room. Lucy took one look at Rose and stiffened. "I don't want to talk to you anymore, Aunt Rose."

"Ah, but I have things to say to you, Lucy. In private. Just the two of us."

O'Dell and Karl took their cue and left, closing the door behind them.

"Come sit by me, Lucy. I believe that I have solved a puzzle—a mystery—and wish to share it with you."

Lucy flounced over to the sofa, the farthest seat from Rose. “You will make me late to school.”

“You are a clever girl. I doubt you will miss anything you did not already know. Now, let me tell you a story.”

“I have heard all the stories from you I wish to hear.”

“This one is not about me. It is about a young girl just your age.”

Lucy began to object again, but Rose halted her with lifted hand. “Tut! You will do me the courtesy of paying attention, Lucia Amalie Thoresen.”

Lucy crossed her arms and looked aside.

“The girl in my story was very bright. She came from a loving family and had a good life ahead of her. But one day, as she often did, she walked home from school with two of her young friends, sisters. She went out to their barn to help them with their chores.

“While they were there, her friends’ mother called them inside for a moment. While they were gone, the family’s hired man who worked on their farm offered to show her something, something he thought she would enjoy. He may have been a handsome young buck, and she might have been flattered by his attentions. However, that day, away from the others, the hired man made unwanted advances on her. She said *no*, and tried to get away from him, but the young man was insistent.”

Rose watched Lucy as she spoke. If anything, the girl held herself more stiffly than ever. In fact, she seemed rigid. Immobile.

“When the girl protested and threatened to scream, the young man threatened her back. Oh, it was a subtle threat, initially. An ugly warning. ‘You do not want anyone at your school to hear that you are loose with your favors, do you?’ he may have whispered. Or perhaps it was, ‘Your little friends and their parents think the world of me. Why, I am like part of the family. No one will believe you if you tell tales about me. In fact, I will say that you came on to me and I refused you. Your family will be ashamed to own you.’

“And because the girl was confused and afraid, this man took liberties with her—not too many at first, maybe a few kisses or perhaps he touched her—but she did not like it, and she knew that what he wanted of her was wrong.

“The next day when her friends asked her to come home with them again, the girl refused. When they asked her why, she blurted out that she did not like their hired man.

"Her friends, however, took umbrage with her. To them, he was like a kind uncle or elder brother, and they were offended for him. As a result, the girl and her friends quarreled. After that, she no longer went home from school with them or went to their house.

"Even though she did not have to see the hired man again, the girl grew angry. She was angry because she had lost her friends. She was angry because she felt misused—which she was. She was angry because she thought she could not tell anyone about the hired man lest her family's reputation be ruined."

Lucy stared straight ahead.

"The girl felt dirty. She felt *wrong* inside. She blamed herself and withdrew from her family. She blamed her parents for not protecting her, and when they questioned her, she argued with them. She blamed everyone except the man who had mistreated her."

Rose studied Lucy's chin. She thought it wobbled a little.

"A few months went by, and the girl's father had an accident. He cut himself at the end of a haying, and could not, by himself, bale the hay lying in the fields or stack the bales in the haymow. Then the parents of the girl's friends offered to loan him their hired man."

Lucy was visibly trembling. Rose saw it as the evidence she was looking for: She was on the right track.

"The girl and her brothers were old enough to work in the field. They had to help bring the hay in, too. And although the girl tried very hard to avoid the hired man, he sat at the family's table each noon and evening meal, sometimes staring at her. Eventually, he found a time and a place to catch her alone.

"This time, the handsome young man's advances were bolder, more insistent, and he threatened—"

"You have it all wrong!" Lucy cried out. "He isn't a nice young man; he isn't handsome! He is old and horrid and cruel!"

Rose crossed the room and sat next to Lucy.

"But the story is true, is it not, Lucy? The Pettersens' hired man has misused you, has he not?"

"Yes," Lucy cried. "Oh, Aunt Rose! I am ruined and he . . . oh! What am I to do?"

Rose gripped Lucy in her arms. She held the girl to her chest. "It is all right, child."

Lucy wept her agony into Rose's neck, and she felt the girl's hot tears soaking her collar, dribbling down her bodice.

Rose whispered over and again, "He can harm you no more. He will never touch you again—I promise you that. It is all right now."

"No," Lucy moaned, "oh no. It is not all right. He said he would hurt Adele."

I would never *let anything happen to her.*

"Lucy, is that why you tried to run away and take Adele with you?"

"Yes!" Her words became wails of terror. "My sister! My baby sister! He said if I told anyone, he would steal her away and hide her where no one would ever find her—and she would die there, all alone, all by herself, in the cold. Oh, God! Oh, God! Oh, God! Please help me!"

Lucy was like a wild animal caught in a trap, her fear and panic controlling her, overwhelming her senses. Rose shuddered under the weight of the evil poured upon her shoulders. At the same time, something about her words struck Rose as being familiar. She set the coincidence aside: Lucy had to be her focus.

"Lucy, we will not let him take Adele. Do you hear me? We will tie him up and take him all the way to the county courthouse, to the sheriff. The sheriff will lock him in a cell until his trial."

But Lucy was inconsolable, not in her right mind.

Rose lifted her voice. "Edmund? Edmund, will you come here, please?"

Immediately the door sprang open. It was all O'Dell could do to keep Karl and Sonja from rushing to Lucy.

"Karl, Sonja, please. We are most concerned for the well-being of Lucy's mind at the moment. Until she is convinced that her sister is safe, she will remain frantic. Wait, please. Wait until I have assured her that we will protect her family and catch this villain."

Karl and Sonja reluctantly withdrew, and O'Dell closed the door behind them. He pulled a footstool close to the sofa, removed his Pinkerton credentials from his suitcoat pocket, and placed them on a side table. Beside his credentials, he laid his revolver. He nodded to Rose.

"Lucy," Rose said. "This is my son-in-law, Edmund O'Dell, Joy's husband. He is a Pinkerton man. He will go to the town's constable, Mr. Bailey, and explain. They will take this horrid man into custody at once, before he can carry out his threats. Do you see?"

Lucy sniffled and turned her tear-stained face toward the items on the table. Looked at O'Dell. "How can you promise he will not take my sister?"

O'Dell nodded. "Because I will immediately send the men of your family to guard Adele and the rest of your siblings. Then the constable and I will confront this man. Please tell me the man's name, Lucy."

Lucy, sobs still catching in her throat, mumbled, "Emma and Hester said his name is Frank, but they call him Mick."

Rose frowned. Her scalp tingled.

O'Dell continued. "I will send your grandparents and Søren to your family. They will keep Adele close. At the same time, I will fetch Mr. Bailey. He and I will go to the Pettersens' farm."

"You will arrest him, that man?"

O'Dell cast a troubled glance on Rose. "It may not be quite as straightforward as that, Lucy. We need evidence that he has done the things of which you accuse him. We will need you to accompany us to the county sheriff and make a statement before him."

The air fled from Rose's lungs. "Edmund?"

"I know. It will be difficult for Lucy. You should stay close to comfort her."

Lucy whispered, "But what if the sheriff does not believe me? That man . . . h-he said he would tell everyone terrible things about me."

"We will question him first. God willing, he will admit to his underhanded deeds when we confront him."

Rose was still frowning, her thoughts racing. "Edmund?"

"Yes?"

"I need Joy. Will you send her to me?"

O'Dell picked up his credentials and revolver. "I will call her straight away. At the same time, I will send Karl, Sonja, and Søren to Einar and Norrie's farm to secure Adele. When that is done, we can plan our next move."

"Thank you."

When O'Dell left the room, Rose took Lucy's hands. "Lucy, will you answer some questions for me?"

Lucy hung her head. "Okay."

There was no easy way to say it. "Lucy, you grew up on a farm. Do you understand physical intimacy between a man and a woman?"

Rose watched her frown.

"I guess so."

"That man. He kissed you, yes?"

"Yes. It was awful. And-and-and he touched me—he wouldn't stop. Will I . . . will I have his baby?"

A spark of hope flickered to life in Rose's heart. *Is Lucy truly that innocent?* She carefully framed and posed the difficult questions she needed Lucy to answer. Within minutes, she exhaled in relief.

Thank you, Lord God, for your never-ending mercies.

"Lucy, you will not have his child. And you are not ruined."

The girl's eyes searched Rose's face. "I'm not?"

"No, dear. This cad took indecent liberties with you, yes, but that is all. And he made a mistake when he threatened your sister. That mistake took you out of his reach. You see, he does not care about Adele; to him, she was just a lever he could use to frighten you and force your compliance."

Rose tipped Lucy's chin up so she could see her eyes. "When you tried to run away, you were taking Adele to safety, weren't you?"

"Yes, ma'am," Lucy whispered. "I thought . . . I thought if I could get her away . . ."

"That you could hide her from him? Keep her safe?"

"Yes."

"But—and this is my question—what were you thinking when you tried to set your parents' house afire, Lucy?"

Rose believed she understood, but she needed to hear the answer from the girl herself. It took Lucy several minutes to frame her reply.

"When Papa found me in the kitchen with Adele and he took her back to her bed, I-I thought I had failed her. Failed her! All I could think of was that man snatching her away and putting her in a hole in the ground to die alone. I couldn't bear the thought of Adele being cold and frightened and alone. I didn't want her to be afraid, Aunt Rose. Anything was better than that."

"Anything? Even death?"

Lucy blinked back more tears. "I-I had decided to go upstairs and hold her while the house burned. She would not be alone—do you see?"

Rose stared steadily into Lucy's eyes.

"That was foolish of me, wasn't it?"

"Yes. Very."

"I-I do not know why I decided to do so. I suppose I was out of my mind with worry . . . but it was wrong of me, wasn't it? Even rash?"

"I should say so."

Lucy frowned. "My teachers say I am very prodigious."

"Intelligence means little without wisdom, Lucy. The world is replete with brilliant individuals who deny the existence of our God and who refuse his counsel. The Bible calls them fools."

"I do not wish to be thought a fool."

"You do not wish to be *thought* a fool? Should you rather wish not to *be* a fool?"

Lucy answered through gritted teeth, "I do not wish to *be* a fool, Aunt Rose."

Rose nodded. "Few of us do, Lucy, but *pride* can lead us to make foolish decisions. How quickly do you suppose all of this would have ended had you but confided in your mother the very first time that man tried to coerce you?"

"I was afraid."

"Were you not also embarrassed?"

Lucy looked down. "I suppose I was. Is that what you mean by pride?"

"Yes, it is. God's wisdom exhorts us to seek the counsel and help of those in whom we have confidence—but you refrained from doing so, and that was foolish. No matter how clever you are or how educated you become, Lucy, without God's wisdom and understanding, you will continue to make foolish choices."

Lucy blew out a long breath. "I think I understand."

"And that is a good beginning, child."

Lucy plucked at her skirt and worried the fabric between her fingers and thumb. "You said . . . you said that man, Mick, made a mistake when he threatened to take Adele?"

"Yes. You worried your parents so deeply that they sent you to stay with your grandparents, which took you straight out of that scoundrel's reach. He could no longer get at you, could he? And with you gone, he could no longer threaten you to get what he wanted, saying he would take Adele. Because your parents sent you here, he could not achieve his objective. Whatever he may say otherwise—to anyone—we will refute it."

Lucy sobbed anew, but her tears were tears of gratitude. "Thank you. Thank you, Aunt Rose."

Rose patted Lucy's hand. "I am grateful to the Lord, Lucy, for helping me understand the ordeal you were going through."

Lucy leaned her cheek onto Rose's shoulder. "Is it over, then?"

Rose thought for a moment. "Perhaps not quite. You have suffered a traumatic episode, Lucy, and although you may, at this moment, think it is over and done, sometimes the Lord Jesus needs to heal the residue of those events."

"What residue, Aunt Rose?"

Rose sighed. "Well, you may feel sadness. Or, you may experience a sense of guilt or shame, although, in this instance, you did nothing to feel guilty or ashamed of." Rose thought a moment. "Lucy, do you know what I did when I lived in Denver?"

Lucy scrubbed her eyes. "You lived in a house with women who . . . who were prostitutes."

Rose was surprised that Lucy was familiar with the word. "Yes, they had that in common. Many of them had something else in common: They did not choose to become prostitutes. Some were tricked. Others were violated by wicked men, just as you nearly were, and then forced into prostitution. A few made foolish choices that set them on a path from which they could not escape. One or two were without family or home, cast upon the street with no other means to survive than to sell themselves."

"That is awful."

"Yes, it is."

"I . . . I made a foolish decision when he asked me to come with him into the Pettersens' barn . . . by myself. I knew better than to be alone with a man."

"We have all made imprudent choices and learned hard lessons from them."

"Not you, Aunt Rose."

"Do I still occupy a place on that pedestal in your mind? Did I not tell you how I neglected Joy in my zeal to plant my garden?"

"But that was—"

"It was a foolish choice, Lucy. I was absorbed with something less important than the safety of my child. It seems a little thing, yet it could have killed her. I learned a difficult but valuable lesson that day."

"Oh. I suppose I take your point . . . now. Is that what you taught those . . . prostitutes? Not to make more foolish choices?"

"I taught them that the Lord's ways are best and how to discern the difference between wisdom and foolishness. For, as God's word tells us in Proverbs 21, *No wisdom, no understanding, no counsel can avail against the Lord.*"

"Of most importance, it was my joy and honor to share the salvation message with these young women, to love them and tell them that Jesus loves them much more than I ever could. To lead them in prayers of repentance and in prayers of healing."

"Prayers of healing?"

"Yes. Once they asked Jesus to forgive their sins, our girls asked Jesus to heal them of that residue of which I spoke—sadness, guilt, shame, brokenness. They asked Jesus to wash those things away and make them clean and whole on the inside."

Rose breathed out slowly. "When we first met, you asked what had become of the money my first husband left me. At the time, we agreed it was an impertinent question. Now, however, I want you to know what became of it. I spent a large part of it making repairs to Palmer House, the house we were given in Denver, and over the thirteen years I lived there, I paid many of the bills the house incurred.

"In my heart, though, I sowed that money as seed into the hearts of these young women. You see, Lucy, I believed that through their redemption and through their forgiven and healed lives, I would reap an eternal harvest. I will always consider it a wise investment."

"Is that . . . is that what you meant when you said you wanted to build something that mattered?"

"Ah. I think you begin to understand me at last."

Lucy twisted her fingers together. "Will Jesus forgive and heal me, too, like he did the girls at Palmer House? I-I feel terrible inside, Aunt Rose. I should not have gone into the barn with Mick by myself—and I should have told on him right away. Instead, I behaved badly at home and hurt my mama and papa very much. What if Papa hadn't found me out? I might have burned down our house and killed my whole family. Will Jesus forgive me for all those things?"

"Yes, Lucy, he will forgive and heal you. Would you like to ask him now?"

"Oh, *yes*, Aunt Rose. I would like that very much."

"Shall we kneel right here, then?"

They knelt together in front of the sofa, and Rose led Lucy in prayer. The girl's pleas for forgiveness and help were fervent, punctuated by tears of remorse. When she finished praying, they again sat on the sofa, Rose's arms about Lucy.

Lucy seemed subdued. "I believe Jesus has forgiven me, Aunt Rose, but what about everyone else? Mama and Papa? Grandpa and Grandma?"

"I would say that they long to be reconciled to you, Lucy. They love you very much and will forgive your behavior when you apologize. Moreover, when they hear about that man, they will be quick to defend you."

"Oh, I am glad! But, what about that man? When they arrest him, will our neighbors find out why?"

Rose considered Lucy's questions. "It is possible that they will, Lucy. When we make an unwise choice, we rarely see where it will take us. For a time, you may need to walk through the consequences of your actions. Keep in mind that Jesus has promised that he will never leave you, he will never forsake you. He *will* see you safely to the other side."

Lucy shuddered and leaned against Rose. "What sort of consequences will I face?"

"I am sorry to say this, but you may face, among your friends and acquaintances, those who will spread untruths about you. I caution you right now, Lucy: Gossip can be vicious. You must choose today, and each day in the days ahead, how you will respond to rumors and innuendo."

"How should I, Aunt Rose?"

Rose loved the girl's earnestness. "You must not play the victim and begin to blame others."

"What do you mean by 'play the victim?'"

"The sin of these events falls squarely upon the wicked man who sought to take advantage of you. However, you also admit to making more than one poor choice—and it was your choice that set these events in motion. You can resent the gossips and their small, petty hearts, but you cannot blame them for what you, however inadvertently, began. To blame others is to play the victim—and the problem with playing the victim is that you forget the part that *you* played.

"I will also remind you of what your great-grandmother said to me on that morning so many years ago now. *Confess your faults one to another, and pray one for another, that ye may be healed.* Do not flinch from acknowledging your flaws, Lucy. Do not give in to the temptation to blame those who point their fingers at you for the problems your choices helped along."

"But if people talk about me, how should I act?"

"Have you asked forgiveness of Christ? Have you asked for healing?"

"Yes. I prayed for those just now."

"Good. Then you can stand firm in the Lord Jesus and his forgiveness. We walk by faith in Christ's righteousness and his holiness, not our own. Even if others refuse to see you as holy, walk as Christ bids you to walk and act as he bids you to act.

"I am reminded of the passage in 1 John 3 that tells us, *Beloved, if our heart condemn us not, then have we confidence toward God.* We are to live our lives in confidence toward God."

The girl's response was glum. "This isn't going to be easy, is it, Aunt Rose?"

"Easy or hard, you will do it—and Jesus will help you."

Lucy slowly nodded. "Okay."

"Mr. O'Dell and Mr. Bailey will be here shortly. We will need to put our heads together and make a plan. While we do, I think you should go upstairs and freshen up. Wash your face. Perhaps lie down and rest."

Lucy was weak from weeping. "All right, Aunt Rose. I will."

CHAPTER 15

After Lucy excused herself, Rose remained alone in Karl and Sonja's living room . . . the living room where Amalie had lain helpless after her stroke and where she had passed away days later.

Rose dropped deep into her thoughts, rehearsing the events that led to the single most difficult episode of Joy's childhood . . .

"AUNT ROSE! Aunt Rose!" Sigrün called for Rose, her voice excited, infused with hope. Rose ran from the kitchen to Karl and Sonja's living room.

Sigrün leaned over her mother. She turned her face briefly to Rose. "Look!" Rose moved to the foot of Amalie's bed.

Amalie had opened her eyes.

"Amalie," Rose whispered. Slowly, Amalie's eyes tracked toward the sound of Rose's voice. Rose knew the very moment Amalie "found" her, not by any movement of her face, but by the peace that seemed to settle in her gaze.

"Oh, Amalie," Rose breathed. "Do not worry. We are here with you. You are not alone."

"And she can now move her hand," Sigrün said. "Come. Feel."

Rose knelt beside Sigrün and took Amalie's right hand. As soon as Amalie felt Rose's touch, her fingers closed, as if in panic. Rose tried to gently unfurl Amalie's fingers, but they resisted. Rather, they scrabbled weakly on Rose's palm, trying to grab, trying to grip. When Rose looked up, she realized that, because Amalie could not move her head, she had been unable to follow Rose with her eyes.

Rose sat on the edge of the bed, still holding Amalie's hand, and leaned over Amalie so that her face came into Amalie's narrow line of vision. The peace Rose had seen earlier returned, and Amalie's fingers within Rose's hand relaxed.

"She needs only rest," Sigrün said, rejoicing. "She will get better."

Rose did not respond to Sigrün's declaration. Instead, she said, "We should be careful not to leave Amalie alone lest she become frightened. Agitated. Someone must remain with her at all times. Holding her hand. Sitting where Amalie can see us."

"Yes, yes," Sigrün agreed. "We will take turns staying with her—but she has improved. This is a good sign. She will get better."

Rose was in the kitchen when Jan returned to Karl and Sonja's farmhouse hours later after looking for the young man who had insisted on bringing Joy home in the rain—the young man who had refused to take "no" for an answer and had grabbed Joy's arm instead.

Rose saw that Jan was subdued. Thoughtful. Distant.

"Did you find him?" she asked.

Jan nodded. "*Ja*, I find him. I tell him if touch Joy again, I break his arm. Den he will no' touch her."

Rose's mouth sagged open. "You said you would break his arm?"

Jan shrugged. He was still distant, not himself. "How Amalie?"

"A little improvement. Kjell and Lily are with her. We have not yet heard back from Uli, but Arnie will come as soon as possible."

"Gud. Dat's gud."

Joy came downstairs into the kitchen. She had been upstairs comforting her cousins. Rose knew how fond Joy was of her much younger cousins. In the same manner that Uli had been more of an older sister than a cousin to Joy, so Joy played the role of older sister to Søren and Meg's children, Markus, Colleen, and Jon and much the same toward Karl and Sonja's five children, Einar, Rune, Stig, Hilde, and Magnum.

She saw that Jan had returned from seeking out Franz Mikkelmann. "Papa?"

"Joy, come, please. We talk."

The three of them sat down at Sonja's big kitchen table, Joy across from Rose and Jan. Rose knew Jan was struggling, likely because it was difficult for him to say exactly what was in his heart using English words.

He spread his hands on the table. "Joy, must give to you father's . . . wisdom." He looked to Rose.

"Advice?"

"*Ja*, advice. Dat is good word, but also need obey."

Joy spoke. "You wish to give me a word of advice that I should obey?"

"Dat it is. Please, I tell you somet'ing, and you hear me. Dis man who bring you home? He not good. I see his heart, here." Jan pointed to his own eyes. Then he pointed to his chest. "I hear Lord, here—no trust dis man."

Joy teared up. “I did not want to go with him, Papa. H-he scared me. I was afraid he would take me somewhere else.”

Jan opened his arms. “Come, *datter*. Come to Papa.”

Joy crossed to the other bench and slid into Jan’s arms. Rose closed her eyes, thanking God for the good father Jan was to his children.

After comforting Joy, Jan motioned her to sit across from him again. “Now have advice you do.”

“Yes, Papa?”

“If man, any man, tell you do somet’ing wrong, you say *no*. Say *no* ver’ loud.” He leaned toward Joy. “If dis man say, ‘I hurt you’ or he say, ‘I hurt Mama’ or ‘I hurt friend’ if you don’t do somet’ing wrong, you say *no! I no do wrong vit you*. Den you tell Mama, tell me. All time, you tell us. You no be afraid, tell us.”

Rose smoothed Jan’s words for Joy. “Whatever it is, Joy, you can always tell us. Do not be afraid to tell us the truth.”

Joy nodded slowly. “Yes, Mama.” She looked at Jan. “Yes, Papa.”

Then she lowered her eyes. “Papa, I need to tell you something.”

Jan and Rose waited, but something chilled within Rose’s heart.

“Papa . . . this man, Franz Mikkelmann? Today is not the first day he asked to drive me home.”

Jan gripped Rose’s hand. She could feel his anxiety grow, and she asked, “Joy, what are you saying?”

“Last week . . . he stopped us—me, Marcus, Einar, and Colleen—on the way home from school. He pulled his wagon up ahead of us, just like today. He asked if we wanted a ride, but I said no, thank you. Then . . .”

“Yes? Then what?”

“He beckoned me over to him. The boys always play on the way home, so they were behind us, Colleen and me. This man, he waved me over and whispered to me. He said, ‘You should reconsider. Take me up on my offer.’ Then he said, ‘Your sister is very pretty . . . but you are much prettier. Where do you live? I will take you all home.’

“I told him no, thank you, but he answered, ‘You don’t want anything . . . bad to happen to your little sister on the way home from school, do you?’”

Rose thought her hand would break under Jan’s.

“I-I said, ‘She is my cousin, not my sister—and nothing will happen to her, because we always walk together. Always.’ He . . . then he said, ‘You never know what might happen, Miss Thoresen, so you best keep a close eye on your little cousin. You cannot know whom you can trust . . . way out here, but you can be sure that I would take good care of *you*.'"

"Joy, did you think, did it sound to you that he was threatening Colleen?"

Joy looked at her parents. "I-I could not tell, exactly. But I never took a ride from him, Mama. Even when he asked again. Three times. I know better."

Rose frowned. "If you know better, why did you not tell us all this before today, Joy?"

Joy shrugged. "He only asked. He never tried to make us—Markus and Einar might be little still, but they would fight anyone who tried to hurt Colleen or me. And I thought . . . I thought maybe the man was only being polite."

"And yet what did your heart tell you about him?" Rose demanded. "You did not trust him, did you? *Did* you?"

"N-no. But I-I also did not want him to get into trouble . . . and when we did not see him again, I forgot about it . . . until today . . . when I was alone on the road."

Joy teared up. "I am sorry, Mama."

"It is our fault you were alone, Joy, not yours. It will not happen again."

Rose drew in a deep breath. "Joy, you are made in the image and likeness of Almighty God. Your body is the sacred temple of the Holy Spirit. You are to treat it as holy, reserved only for your husband, the man you will marry. A man who is neither your father nor your lawful husband should not touch you. He should not put his hand on you without your specific permission."

Jan, who had listened carefully with growing concern, said, "And I say dis, too, datter. If man, any man make *insist* on you again, you scream, you fight—like Markus, like Einar—you fight. God giff you stronger."

"Strength," Rose supplied.

"*Ja*. Strength."

Joy's eyes widened, and Rose put her hand on her daughter's arm.

"Papa is right, Joy. In any perilous circumstances, do not be afraid to fight—and do not allow anyone to threaten you or those you love. Tell us at once, should it happen. Do you understand?"

"Yes, Mama."

Rose sat back. "It is apparent after this experience that it is no longer safe for you to walk to school alone. If your cousins are with you, you will be fine. However, from now on, if they stay home, as they did today, Papa or I will take you to school and fetch you afterward."

Jan nodded, approving of Rose's words.

OH, IF ONLY that had been the end of it, Rose thought.

She heard the *slap* of the kitchen door closing and the sound of voices, and she pulled her thoughts from the past. The living room door opened. Joy, O'Dell, and Jeremy Bailey entered.

Joy took in the room in a glance. "Mama, where is Lucy?"

"She is upstairs resting. It will be better if she does not overhear us as we make our plans."

Joy's mouth puckered in puzzlement. "You told Edmund you needed me?"

"Yes, dear." Joy, O'Dell, and Jeremy took seats, and in short, succinct sentences, Rose told Joy what she had learned from Lucy.

"We will take Lucy with us to the Pettersens'. I would like you to wait with Lucy, Joy, when we confront this man. I believe you will be a calming influence on her."

"If you think so, I am willing, Mama."

Rose turned to Jeremy Bailey. "Jeremy, you drove here in your automobile. Can it accommodate the five of us?"

"Yes, ma'am, iffin you ladies do not mind a little closeness."

"We shall tolerate it." She tapped her finger on her chin, thinking. "The Pettersen girls should recall Lucy telling them that she did not want to be around their hired man. It resulted in an argument that severed their friendship."

"We should talk to them first," O'Dell said. "Get them to speak in front of witnesses before they understand that we are accusing this man of molesting Lucy, this man whom they think of as family."

Jeremy held up his hand. "Ya-all understand thet I don't know much 'bout investigations and such? Iffin ya need a clear head and a steady gun hand, I'm yer man. And as town constable, I have the 'thority t' take a suspect into custody and run him over to the sheriff at the county courthouse."

"Those qualities make you the perfect complement for the job at hand," O'Dell assured him. "I know how to conduct an investigation but have no given authority to make an arrest. Together, we will get this done properly."

"The Pettersens' daughters will still be in school," Rose commented. "Can we pull them out to question them without causing a scene and without alerting them to our reasons?"

They thought on it for a few moments until Jeremy shifted in his chair. "My wife, Ava, knows them some and knows their teachers, too. She could do it, I s'pose."

Rose smiled. "Do you have a telephone at home?"

"Yep."

"Will you call her and ask?"

"Sure nuff, Miss Rose."

Joy showed him to the telephone in Karl and Sonja's kitchen and returned while he was making the call.

"What happens after we speak to the Pettersens' girls?"

"I have been giving it some thought," Rose said, "but it will depend upon Lucy's willingness."

She told Joy and O'Dell what she had in mind.

"It is a good plan, Mother," O'Dell said. "It is also dependent upon the Pettersens and where this man is when we arrive."

Jeremy returned. "Ava will meet us at the school in half an hour."

O'Dell repeated Rose's idea to him.

"Worth the shot," he said, "iffin Lucy's willing."

"Willing to do what?" Lucy stood in the living room doorway.

"Ah, good. We were going to wake you soon," Rose said. "Come in and sit with us. We will tell you the plan."

JEREMY DROVE O'DELL, Joy, Lucy, and Rose to the town's small school. They met Ava at the entrance.

"Miss Rose, I am so glad I could help you today."

Rose embraced her. "I have yet to have a personal word with you, Ava. You look splendid, my dear. A happy marriage and home suit you."

"Thank you, Miss Rose. Jeremy and I are quite content."

Rose took Ava's hand. "Are you able to do what we asked?"

"Yes'm. The girls know me. When I ask them to follow me, they will come. You can wait in the library, and I will bring them to you."

"Very good. Joy? I would like you to wait in the automobile with Lucy while we speak to the girls. Are you willing?"

"Yes, Mama. Lucy and I will get along fine."

Rose, O'Dell, and Jeremy followed Ava into the school. It had been built behind the church and across a field while Joy was still in attendance, but the town had added on to it after Rose moved to Denver. Inside the school's front entrance, Rose took in a welcoming foyer and, beyond that, a lengthy hallway with three classrooms on either side.

"This way, please." Ava indicated a door off the left side of the foyer. They walked into a small but comfortable library with chairs, two low tables, and several rows of bookshelves, some still empty.

"My! What an accomplishment," Rose said.

"Yes, we are quite proud of the library, although we are still growing its collection of books."

When Ava left to fetch the girls, O'Dell suggested that they arrange five of the chairs in a circle. Rose, O'Dell, and Jeremy sat in three of them.

Ava returned a handful of minutes later. She gently herded Emma and Hester into the library. Ava excused herself and closed the library door behind her.

The girls hung back for a moment when they saw Jeremy, O'Dell, and Rose waiting for them. Jeremy stood and motioned to the girls.

"Come on over, girls. We need to speak to ya."

They looked from face to face.

Rose tried to reassure them. "I am Rose Thoresen. This is my son-in-law, Mr. O'Dell. And you know Mr. Bailey. He is here as the town's constable. Would you sit down with us, please?"

"Are we in trouble?" Emma asked. She was Lucy's age or close to it. Hester looked younger by two years or more.

"Not to my knowledge," Rose replied. She glanced at O'Dell, and he took over.

"No, you are not in trouble; however, we wish to ask you a few questions. It is important that you answer them truthfully before Mr. Bailey. If you were not to tell the truth to him and it was found out later, then you would be in trouble."

The girls stilled immediately, and Rose observed Hester slip her hand inside her sister's.

"Do you understand what I have said?" O'Dell asked.

"Yessir," they answered in unison, quite anxiously.

"Very good. Now please sit down." His tone was just flat enough to convey an order rather than a request.

After they had taken their seats, he said, "I want you to think back to a conversation you had with Lucy Thoresen about six months ago. You asked her to come home with you after school, as she generally did several times a week. But on that day, she refused to come. Do you recall when this happened?"

Emma nodded. Hester seemed frozen.

"Emma, do you recall why Lucy said she did not want to come home with you?"

She huffed with indignation. "I sure do. Lucy said she didn't like our hired man, Mick. Said he gave her the willies."

"The willies?" Rose asked. "What is that, Edmund?"

"It's a slang term meaning he made her uncomfortable."

Emma continued. "Well, I told her she was plain wrong—that Mick is our friend. Right, Hester?"

Hester seemed fixated on her shoes and did not reply.

"Hester? Tell them."

The girl swiped at a tear as it dripped from her chin.

Rose squeezed her eyes closed. *Oh, Lord God . . .*

She stood. "Edmund. A word, please."

He looked from Hester to Rose and back. Rose watched his jaw clench and his mouth work. He followed Rose out into the hallway.

Closing the door behind them, Rose said, "I need to speak to Hester privately—without her sister."

"You're saying that same animal has put his hands on this little girl?"

"In all likelihood, yes."

O'Dell, fists on his hips, struggled to control his anger.

"Edmund, if you and Jeremy will sit with Emma, I will take Hester aside, behind the bookshelves, and speak to her. It should not take long."

He sighed. "Yeah. All right."

"Think of it this way, Edmund. The Lord knew that we had only Lucy's word on this man's perfidy. He will not, however, escape the testimony of *two* girls attesting to the same thing—and before this day is out, we may have a third voice."

ROSE'S PROJECTED "it should not take long" had been wrong. She and Hester sat behind a screen of bookshelves for nearly an hour—time enough for Hester to pour her heart out and for Rose to pray with her and assure her that the man they called Mick would never touch her again.

When Hester agreed, Rose called Emma to join them, and Hester, between sobs, told Emma what she had already disclosed to Rose. Rose watched as Emma's disbelief turned to concern for Hester, then outrage toward the hired man she had trusted.

"Is this why Lucy wouldn't come home with us?" she demanded.

"Yes," Rose replied, "and I hope that, when this is over, you will renew your friendship with Lucy. She has felt alone, without friends, for quite some time."

Emma hung her head. "It's my fault. I should have listened better, I should have believed her. If I had . . . then Hester would not have been afraid to tell me what Mick was doing."

"You mean *he would have been gone*," Hester said through more tears. "If we'd listened to Lucy, we could have told Mama and Papa, and they would have called Mr. Bailey, and *Mick would be gone!*"

Emma broke down. "I am sorry, Hester. I am so sorry. Please forgive me."

Rose waited a moment to say, "Girls, Mr. Bailey and the rest of us intend to remove this man from our community. We will start by speaking to your parents. Will you go with Mrs. Bailey to her home until we have sorted things out with them?"

Emma had her arms around Hester's shoulders. They both nodded.

THIRTY MINUTES LATER, Rose and O'Dell sat in the Pettersens' living room while Jeremy, from behind the curtains in the kitchen window, kept tabs on the hired man. Lucy continued to wait in Jeremy's car with Joy, but Jeremy had parked his automobile down the road, out of sight of the farmhouse, then he, Rose, and O'Dell had walked back to the Pettersens' farm.

Under the concerned eyes of Mr. and Mrs. Pettersen, Rose recounted Lucy's tale to them. They were first disbelieving, as had been Emma. Until. Until, to their dismay, Rose disclosed that Hester, too, had revealed that their hired man had molested her.

"How could this have happened?" Mrs. Pettersen said through her tears. "Why did she not confide in us?"

"He controlled her through threats," Rose replied. "It is how wicked men force the compliance of their victims. By God's grace, I can also tell you that while he took advantage of Hester, he did not actually . . . violate her."

"Does it matter? If this gets out, she will be ruined! No decent man will want to marry her!" Mr. Pettersen's voice was a shout by the end.

"It matters very much *to Hester*," Rose insisted. "She can and she *will* overcome this."

Mrs. Pettersen wept with uncontrolled grief, and Mr. Pettersen ground his teeth forward and back, but said little more.

O'Dell said, "The girls said the hired man's name was Mick."

"His nickname. His full name is Frank Mitchell."

"Okay, thanks." O'Dell wrote it down and finished disclosing their plan to arrest the man.

"You will take him to the sheriff?" Emma and Hester's father asked.

"Yes."

Mr. Pettersen looked at the floor. "What if I have other ideas?"

"I might have agreed with you a few years back," O'Dell admitted. "But my walk with the Lord Jesus is too precious to me now to sully it with acts of vengeance. I have learned . . . to trust in God's justice."

Mr. Pettersen lifted his haunted eyes to O'Dell's. "She is my little girl," he choked out.

O'Dell answered quietly, "I know. I can understand. I have a baby daughter myself." O'Dell looked to Rose for help.

Rose said softly, "As wretched as the situation is, Mr. Pettersen, we have reasons to be grateful to the Lord."

"What reasons? How can I possibly be grateful for *this?* Hester's life is ruined."

Rose's smile was tinged with sadness. "You insist that it is, but I can assure you it is not, Mr. Pettersen. She is injured, yes, but not beyond repair—and surely you are aware that I know of what I attest?"

Mrs. Pettersen's fingers were twined in her skirt, her knuckles white from gripping the fabric. She dragged her red, swollen gaze up to Rose's face. "All those soiled doves in that house up in Denver. You know how to fix this?"

Rose leaned toward the distraught woman. "I cannot 'fix' Hester, Mrs. Pettersen, but I know our blessed Savior can. I have seen him do miracles."

She placed her hands on the woman's twisted fingers and gently loosened their grip. She held Mrs. Pettersen's hands between her own.

"One of those 'soiled doves' was Ava Bailey. Her life is not destroyed, because our God intervened. The Christian people of this town took her in and showed her the Savior and his love. She believed on him, and he redeemed her life. She is now married to a godly, well-respected man—the same man who is in your kitchen right this minute, willing to help you and your family in your time of need."

Rose smiled. "We left your girls in Ava Bailey's hands. She understands what Hester is going through and can comfort her. She and Esther, because they live near you, will be able to minister to Hester and to Lucy in ways no one else in RiverBend can."

Mrs. Pettersen swallowed hard. "We were . . . we were against you sending those girls here, Mrs. Thoresen."

"Raised a stink, to be honest," her husband interjected.

"Yes, we did. We did not understand how you could associate with them or why . . . why we should try to help them. But they have . . . they have become pillars in our community. It is a continual astonishment to us. To me."

Rose's smile was wan. "I believe you will thank God for Ava and Esther in the days to come."

"Perhaps you are right, Mrs. Thoresen. Is that one of the things you said we should be grateful for?"

"Yes, it is one of them. The second is this: As I told Mr. O'Dell, if only Lucy were to accuse this man, her testimony alone would not be enough to convict him. However, combined with Hester's similar testimony, this 'Mick' does not stand a chance of escaping the consequences of his crimes."

Mr. and Mrs. Pettersen looked at each other with growing agitation, and Mr. Pettersen growled, "No. No, we do not want Hester to testify to what he did to her. It will become public knowledge—everyone will hear what he did and will talk about her."

Rose stared steadily at them both. "There may be a way we can avoid a public scandal. For the girls' sakes, we must try. That is where Lucy comes in." She turned her head toward the kitchen. "Jeremy? Do you know where that man is?"

Jeremy appeared in the doorway. "He jest went into the barn."

"He'll be mucking out the milkers' pens now," Mr. Pettersen said, referring to his dairy herd.

"How long does that usually take?" O'Dell asked.

"'Long 'bout an hour, what with shoveling out what twenty cows left behind, rinsing down thc floors, and forking clean hay into the two pens." He looked at the clock. "We bring the cows into the milking shed 'round four o'clock."

The clock read half past two.

"Shall I fetch Lucy?" O'Dell asked Rose.

"Yes. This is our best opportunity."

Minutes later, O'Dell returned with Lucy and Joy. Lucy looked from Mrs. Pettersen to Mr. Pettersen. Rose watched them slide their eyes away from the girl. She wondered if they would ostracize her. Blame her.

Lucy ventured to speak to them anyway. "Mrs. Pettersen? Mr. Pettersen? I did not know Mick would go after Hester. I am very sorry. I should . . . I should have said something. Not to Emma and Hester, but to you." Rose sighed with relief when Mrs. Pettersen stood and walked to Lucy. Took her hand.

"We are the sorry ones, Lucy. We brought that vile man onto our farm. Gave him a place to live. Will you please forgive us?"

"I-I . . . of course."

Rose said softly, "We need to put our plan in motion now, Lucy. We are asking a lot of you. Can you do it?"

She straightened her spine and lifted her chin—and Rose was unexpectedly reminded of Karl's towering presence.

Lucy looked to Rose, "*Ja*, with God's help, I can do it."

CHAPTER 16

Lucy went alone out the Pettersens' front door. At the bottom of the porch steps, she stumbled and grabbed hold of the railing. She was shaking so hard that she could scarcely make her feet do her bidding.

For a long moment, she considered running back to Jeremy Bailey's automobile and hiding in it. Then she remembered what Rose had told her on the drive from the school to the Pettersens'.

Hester. Lord, please help me do this—for Hester's sake.

The urge to flee waned. The tingling in her limbs ebbed and receded. She pressed her lips together and got herself sorted. She walked around the house and onto the worn path that led out beyond the house to the barn and the attached milking shed.

Anyone who might have been watching from the barn would think she had walked from the road onto the farm. Hopefully, their gaze would not stray to the hedgerow on the opposite side of the house.

As she got closer, Lucy heard the measured, recurring scrape of a shovel pushed over rough concrete followed by the dull, echoing *thunk* of refuse dumped onto a pile. She moved slowly into the cavernous barn and was engulfed in its shadows. The noises came from her left and led her deep inside, toward the pens where the Pettersens kept their dairy cows at night.

Within one of the pens, a man in filthy coveralls shoveled manure and soiled hay into a wheelbarrow.

Scraaaape, thunk. Scraaaape, thunk.

She stood a few yards away, waiting for him to notice her—so that he would be facing away from was going on elsewhere. When he finally did see her, he unhurriedly lowered the shovel's head to the floor and leaned his weight on its handle.

He was not the young man from the story Rose had told Lucy in order to get her to open up. *This* man was in his late forties. He owned a head of thinning brown hair; his body was lean and hard from a life of physical toil. His light brown eyes squinted through his face's creased lines and folds. Lucy thought him old, but at her young age, she deemed anyone beyond forty "old."

A smirk bloomed over the man's face, smoothing some of the creases from his brow.

"Well, lookit you, little missy."

Lucy shivered. She fought the inclination to run, screaming, far away.

The man leaned the shovel against a rail, tugged a grimy kerchief from his pocket and wiped the sweat from his face—but not the smirk. "Din't 'spect to see you 'round here again, not after the fight you had with Emma and Hester. 'Course, they told me all 'bout it. Tell me all kinda things, they do."

Leisurely like, he sauntered in her direction. At the same time, his eyes darted around the inside of the barn and toward the house, over to the milking shed, and across the pasture. Lucy knew he was making certain no one was around. No one to witness what he said. Or did.

God willing, you will be surprised . . . and undone, she thought.

"Left your folks' place in a mighty hurry last month, too, din't you? Guess they din't want you 'round no more . . . 'specially after you almost burned down their house *with them in it*."

Lucy's heart contracted.

Smiling, confident, he inched his way toward her—in no hurry, glancing toward the house, then back, shuffling his steps incrementally closer.

Lucy didn't wait for him to come within reach of her. She stepped farther to her left, putting the corner of the pen between them. Still shaking, she licked her lips. "Y-you said you'd hurt Adele. Said you'd steal her away and h-hide her in a cold, dark hole."

He laughed. "Well, I may yet, hey? All depends on you, missy. All depends on *you*. Guess I'll be over at your folks' place next week, helping your pa tear out the back porch. Rotten, it is, all the wood. Gotta rip ever bit of it out and rebuild it from scratch. A whole week. I'll have plenty of opportunities . . . with your baby sister. Sweet little thing, she is."

"Y-you're the one who is rotten!" Lucy shouted. "Rotten and filthy and despicable!"

"Now, now. Don't need to go on thata way, Lucy. Not if you and I were to come to a 'rangement. You just come with me, over to the stalls, for a few minutes. Nobody 'round, right? We'll have us some fun, hey?"

Clearly and loudly, Lucy announced, "I-I am going to tell my parents what you did to me, and-and-and they will call the constable. Y-you will go to jail for a long, long time."

If she had been anticipating a reaction from him, she had underestimated his speed and agility.

In three long strides, he rounded the corner of the pen, grasped her wrist and yanked her to him. Instinctively, Lucy opened her mouth to scream, but he wrenched her arm behind her back. Pushing her against the pen, he slapped his other hand over her mouth. Her scream melted into a groan of pain.

"Why, Lucy girl, I heard you were actin' so bad to your folks that they sent you 'way to your grandpa's house. Or was that what you were hoping they would do? Send you 'way from me? Well, who's gonna protect sweet little Adele if you're over at Grandpa and Grandma's, Lucy? Hey?

"And you best think twice 'bout talking to them, telling little lies 'bout me. They won't believe you anyways, Lucy. The Pettersens won't believe you, neither. Believe the girl who tried to burn her folks' house to the ground? Naw, they don't trust you, Lucy. And they won't believe you. 'Sides, I'm practically part of the family here."

He dragged her deeper into the shadowed interior of the barn, toward the stalls where Mr. Pettersen kept his two horses at night, all the while belittling and threatening her.

"Did you forget, Lucy? Did you forget what I promised I'd do to your precious little sister if you didn't keep coming 'round to visit Emma and Hester and meeting me right here in this barn? I promised what I would do to her if you told anyone, Lucy, and I always keep my promises."

He took his hand from her mouth to lift the rope off the broad gate across one of the stalls. He swung it open and pushed her inside.

Free of his hands, she shouted, "I know what you've been doing to Hester, too. You couldn't get at me, so you preyed on *her*—tormented *her*. Well, no matter what you do to me, I am going to tell her parents what you have been doing to her—and Hester will tell them it's true!"

As what she shouted sank in, he hesitated—but only momentarily. He shoved her against the stall's wall. Pushed his face into hers. In the dim light where shadows played, Lucy watched a fearsome, demonic aspect overtake his features.

"So you know 'bout Hester, do you? Well now, that's plumb unfortunate. Means I gotta make some decisions quick-like . . ."

His eyes stared at her, but she could tell he didn't really see her. He was thinking. Planning. When he arrived at a course of action, his eyes came back into focus and settled again on her.

Lucy could not stave off the fear jumping around in her, trying to leap out of her body and fly away. She shook so hard, she felt like she would come apart.

He laughed to himself. At her. "Well, yes'm, every cloud surely does have its silver lining, don't it? I never really took my pleasure with you, y'know, Miss Lucy. Din't want no bulging belly to ruin the good thing I got goin' on here. But I guess, since my situation has changed . . ."

Gripping her by her throat, he took a step back and held her pinned to the wall at arm's length. Lucy clawed at his hands and arms, but his muscles were lean and hard, wiry bands made strong by years of unceasing labor.

With one hand on her throat, he used his other to fish deep in one of the pockets of his coveralls. Finally, he drew out a packet of matches—and grinned. "Good. Thought I had these handy."

He tucked them back into his coveralls. "See, they'll find what's left of you when they sift the ashes of this barn. 'Course, they'll 'spect it was *you*, burned it down. They'll say, 'she tried to burn her folks' house,' and they will lay the fire at your door. But I'll have my pleasure first, if you please, afore I set you and this cursed, stinking heap alight."

Lucy's panic was full-fledged and mindless now. She fought him with all the desperation of a snared wild animal, but his hands were too strong. Too strong! Too—

The masculine voice that interrupted them was strong and self-assured. "*Ahem.* We had hoped you would threaten Lucy again, *Mick*, perhaps even incriminate yourself, but you have outstripped even our highest expectations. Thank you."

Startled, Mick spun about to face the intruder. His grip on Lucy's throat loosened just enough that, as she struggled and twisted her body, she broke free and fell onto the stall's straw-strewn floor. She scrambled on hands and knees toward the now-open stall door. Tried to get to her feet. Stumbled. Fell forward. Stood.

Ran again . . . straight into Rose's arms.

ROSE HELD TIGHT to the trembling, sobbing girl as O'Dell repeated, "We hoped you would incriminate yourself, and you've done a fine job."

Jeremy Bailey moved to O'Dell's side, a shaded lantern in his hand. Jeremy slid the shade open, and the lantern's light blazed forth. Mick had taken Lucy into the high-walled stall to contain her and hide his wicked actions, but in doing so, he had trapped himself. O'Dell and Jeremy barred Mick's only means of egress. Rose, Lucy, and Joy stood a short distance behind Jeremy and O'Dell, peering into the stall.

The lamp's illumination revealed the stall's interior and the hired man within. His eyes jinked left and right, seeking an avenue of flight, finding none. They darted past, then flicked back and settled on the revolver glinting in O'Dell's hand.

"Ah . . . yes," Rose breathed. She was the only one to notice Joy's mouth gape in astonishment.

But the man wasn't done yet. Cunning and malice played over his features. "What's this about then?" he demanded. "I found this blasted girl"—he pointed to Lucy—"trying to strike a match over the straw." He held up a book of matches to make his point. "Good thing I did, too. Know how dangerous matches are in a barn? This blame-fool girl might have burned the place down around her ears."

"No, Mick. We heard every word of *your* attack upon Lucy."

"How dare you? That is a lie. And who are you, besides?"

"Me? I'm a Pinkerton man. This here's Constable Bailey. We're here to arrest you."

The man's confidence never waffled. "Me? Step aside, Pinkerton man. If anyone is to be 'rrested, it should be that devil's imp of a child. First, she sets her folks' place afire, now this. She's a danger to this-here entire community."

O'Dell shook his head. "The four of us have been hiding outside the barn, listening to every word between you and Lucy Thoresen. We four will testify that you threatened to harm Lucy's little sister, Adele Thoresen, if Lucy did not do your bidding. And the four of us will testify that you did not deny assaulting Hester Pettersen when Lucy said she would tell Hester's parents. Rather, to prevent both Lucy and Hester from accusing you of assault, you declared that you would kill Lucy and leave her to burn after *you* set the barn alight—and we will subsequently testify that we witnessed you attack Lucy and drag her into this stall to carry out your debauched intentions."

"You can't prove nothing," Mick hissed. "They are children. No one will take the word of a child over a grown, reputable man!"

"They will most certainly take *my* word for it."

Jeremy jerked in surprise and glanced over his shoulder. Joy O'Dell, her eyes blazing, hands fisted at her side, moved into the stall's door.

Mick stared as if he could not believe what he saw. He took a step forward—and brought himself up short when O'Dell raised his revolver, but his eyes looked beyond O'Dell.

"You!" he exclaimed in wonder. "Thought I'd never see ya again."

"Yes," Joy declared. "I, Joy Thoresen, have returned to RiverBend—and I will testify that you tried and nearly succeeded in abducting me when I was fourteen years old. The same age as Lucy."

O'Dell and Jeremy were momentarily nonplussed, but O'Dell quickly brought his attention back to the man before him—and Rose was glad he had. The maniacal light that shone from the prisoner's eyes was downright disconcerting.

O'Dell was somewhat confused. "Is that right, Mick? You tried to kidnap my wife when she was a girl?"

Mick was initially astounded. "She is your wife?" Then his voice dropped and came out low and dangerous. Enraged. "*Your* wife? But for her interfering parents, she would have been *my* wife. She loved me!"

"I loved you? I give praise to God my Savior that I was never in danger of *that*," Joy retorted.

Mick's mouth worked, and his fingers twitched. "That isn't true. You did. You wanted to marry me—you even ran away with me!"

"I did not. You are delusional. *You abducted me.*"

"Joy! My love! You have it all wrong," he wheedled, "but we can fix it, yeah? We can still go away together, can't we? We can be together . . . grow old and die together."

O'Dell, slate-faced, had heard enough. He nudged Jeremy, "You have those irons at the ready, Constable?"

"Yep, I do."

Rose had been as engrossed in the scene before her as had the others, when a single phrase flashed into her mind.

It is when we are distracted . . .

Her attention flew back to Mick. She saw him ready himself to lunge and shouted a warning. "Jeremy, the lamp!"

MICK SPRANG ACROSS the stall, his fingers scrabbling to wrest the lamp from Jeremy's hands. O'Dell, immediately realizing how much danger they were all in, shoved his revolver into his pocket and joined the scuffle.

If the lamp falls from our grasp or ends up in Mick's hands, this barn will burn.

O'Dell shouted, "Bailey! Don't let go, no matter what!"

O'Dell had his fingers wrapped around the lantern's base, the reservoir that held the oil, as did Jeremy, while Mick gripped the lantern's handle. Mick seemed possessed of supernatural strength, though, and O'Dell feared some part of the lantern would come apart during the tug-o-war, dousing the dry straw with hot oil.

He did not see the kick Mick aimed at his knee until his leg buckled, and he went down. In the same instant, Mick succeeded in tearing the lantern from Jeremy's grasp, spilling and splashing oil as he did.

Mick screamed with inhuman ferocity, "Joy! We will be together forever!"

He raised the lantern high and ran forward.

"Get back!" O'Dell shouted. "All of you, get away!" He backed out of the stall while thrusting his hand into his pocket.

"*Forever!*" Mick screamed. He drew the lamp back over his head to throw it.

At Joy.

O'Dell knew he had no choice.

Two shots rang out.

Mick's face registered surprise and mild puzzlement. He collapsed onto his knees. The lantern tumbled from his limp fingers and rolled onto the straw. The straw *whooshed* into flames. Mick blinked several times before he fell facedown across the stable's threshold and into the spreading conflagration.

Rose, Lucy, and Joy fled the barn. Jeremy and O'Dell stayed to fight the fire. O'Dell spied a stack of horse blankets. He grabbed them and threw a couple to Jeremy. They unfolded the blankets and spread them over the licking flames, stomping on them. They spread blankets over and around Mick's body, too, stomping on the flames, stepping over him to fight the fire within the stall.

Fiery tongues were already licking at the stall's dry boards when Lucy and Joy appeared bearing a bucket of water each. Lucy had known where the buckets hung and where to fetch the water. O'Dell and Jeremy poured water over the flames and smoldering hot spots.

It was over. They had caught the fire in its first moments, and Lucy's quick thinking had enabled them to put it out, saving the Pettersens' barn.

Mr. Pettersen ran into the barn. He stared askance at O'Dell and Jeremy's blackened and soiled clothes and faces. "What is going on? Is everyone all right? We heard shots—and I smell smoke!"

"Fire's out, Mr. Pettersen," Jeremy said. "Ruin't some of your horse blankets stompin' out the flames and all, but that's it." He pointed to the stall and the blanket-draped body.

"Is it over?" Pettersen asked. His question was more about Mick and the danger he posed to his daughters.

"Over for you? Yes. For us? Not by a long shot," O'Dell muttered, studying the scene, committing details to memory. "We'll need to take the body to the sheriff and explain everything to him there. It's going to take some time . . . and I have a train I must catch midmorning tomorrow."

"Well, I'm thinkin' the sheriff needs t' come here, instead," Jeremy opined. "He needs t' interview the lot of us anyhoo. And iffin he can't 'commodate your schedule, I'll take down your statement m'self and deliver it to him."

Lucy, still shaking, approached O'Dell. "Is Mick dead? Truly?"

O'Dell cast a glance at the form lying prostrate under scorched, soot-stained blankets. He needed to reassure himself, as much as Lucy, and was relieved that Mick's body had not so much as twitched.

He blew out the breath he hadn't realized he'd been holding. "He is dead, Lucy. He will never threaten or harm you or anyone else ever again."

"Thank you, Mr. O'Dell. Thank you!" She fell against his chest, sobbing again, this time in relief and gratitude, then said, "Please, Mr. O'Dell. May I go home now? I want to see my Mama and Papa."

"I think they will be waiting for you with open arms, Lucy."

Jeremy called Mr. Pettersen aside. "I'm speakin' as the town constable here, Mr. Pettersen. Need you t' be leavin' the body and the scene in the stall jest as they be. Nobody's t' touch nuthin."

"Yessir. I understand. And thank you. I don't know how to thank you and Mr. O'Dell . . . and Lucy."

"You might have a talk with your girls, have 'em invite Lucy back int' your family's good graces."

"She was never out of ours. We did not understand the disagreement between our daughters and her—but we will clear it up. Lucy was very brave today. She is a heroine in our eyes."

"Won't hurt her none t' hear you say that t' her face."

The two men shook hands, and Jeremy trotted down the road to bring his automobile up to the Pettersens' house. O'Dell, Rose, Joy, and Lucy again squeezed into the car. Thankfully, the drive to Lucy's folks' house was less than a mile.

When they pulled into Einar and Norrie's long drive, the house emptied. Søren, Karl and Sonja, and Lucy's family rushed to the car for news.

Lucy ran to her parents. As O'Dell had predicted, Einar and Norrie, aware now of the circumstances around Lucy's long nightmare, opened their arms to her. Karl and Sonja joined them.

Rose, Joy, O'Dell, and Jeremy Bailey watched the tearful reunion from the drive until Søren joined them. He eyed O'Dell and Jeremy Bailey's disheveled appearance.

"What of the culprit?"

O'Dell shook his head. "Let's head back to your place, shall we? We have a mote of work ahead of us."

CHAPTER 17

Karl and Sonja stayed on at Einar and Norrie's house, and Jeremy left toward town in his car to fetch Emma and Hester home to their parents. That left Søren to drive Rose, Joy, and O'Dell home in his vehicle.

"If you do not mind, Edmund," Rose said, "I prefer to sit in the back seat with Joy."

He studied her. "As you wish, Mother."

They said little as they set out. Rose and Joy were wrapped in their own thoughts, but Joy's hand found its way into Rose's, and Rose knew of what she was thinking. Rose, too, was remembering.

O'Dell huffed and spoke into the silence. "All right. It is just us now, and I have questions."

"I know, Edmund, dearest," Joy murmured. "Mama?"

Rose sighed. It was time to disclose an event that they and their closest family members had kept to themselves for twenty-five years.

"Do you wish to tell him, Joy?"

"Someone needs to," O'Dell growled. "I'm working in the dark here and wondering why."

"Very well. I will tell you," was Joy's solemn answer. "As I have just discovered, the Pettersens' hired man is no stranger to us—to Mama and me—although we have not seen him since I was fourteen, and we had no awareness that he had returned to RiverBend."

"We knew him as Franz Mikkelmann," Rose added.

"Mikkelmann? Rhymes with 'nickel man'?" O'Dell asked.

"Yes, Franz Mikkelmann, not Frank Mitchell," Joy responded. "The first time I saw him, he was working in the field next to our school. He sometimes watched us girls during recess, but I had an odd, creeping notion that he was really watching *me*.

"At that time, I walked to and from school each day with Markus, Einar, and Colleen. One day, as we were walking home, Mr. Mikkelmann drove up on us and offered us a ride. I politely thanked him but turned him down. This happened several times.

"Then Aunt Amalie had her stroke, and I walked to school by myself that morning. On the way home after school, it began to rain. Mr. Mikkelmann suddenly appeared, again asking to take me home. He brought me home then asked Papa if he could call on me."

"He wanted to court you when you were only fourteen?" O'Dell asked, affronted.

Rose said, "It was not entirely unheard of for a country girl to marry as young as fifteen, Edmund. However, Jan and I were of the same mind to have Joy finish school before she received callers."

Joy again took up the narrative. "And I wanted to go to business school when I finished my education in RiverBend, which I did. In any event, I was quite relieved when Papa said no to Mr. Mikkelmann's request to call on me. My age aside, I think we all instinctively felt that there was something wrong with him, even if we couldn't put into words what we felt.

"Anyway, it was only after Mr. Mikkelmann met Mama and Papa and then departed that I told them how he had forced me to get in his wagon. That was when Papa went searching for him."

Søren whistled low in his throat. "Although I have heard this part, I still wouldn't have wanted to be that guy. Papa was very protective of Joy."

"From the day she was born," Rose added.

"Did you know this Mikkelmann, too?" O'Dell asked of Søren.

"No. Never met him. Never saw him except once. From a distance."

"What happened when Jan found Mikkelmann?"

Rose *hmmed.* "The only thing Jan told me when he returned was that he had given young Mr. Mikkelmann a firm warning: If he ever touched Joy again, Jan promised to break his arm. I was astonished, for Jan ordinarily exercised self-control when he was angry. He was not one to fly off the handle or hold grudges. However, I think he saw something in Franz Mikkelmann during that second encounter, something that deeply troubled him."

"Incipient madness, I should think—from what I witnessed today," O'Dell muttered.

"Yes, perhaps that is the right label. We certainly did not have to wait long for that madness to reveal itself."

"Go on, Mama. You will tell it better than I will."

Rose mulled over the details before she spoke again. "Amalie's stroke was severe, and she was dying. Jan and I knew it, but Sigrün, Karl, and Kjell . . . they could not bring themselves to accept it. When Arnie and Anna arrived from Omaha, Arnie spent but ten minutes with Amalie before he collared the doctor and demanded the truth—the truth, the doctor told him, that Sigrün, Karl, and Kjell resisted and would not hear from his lips.

"Arnie gathered his sister, brothers, and us in the kitchen. He tried to explain, to help his siblings understand that the doctor believed Amalie's condition to be 'fixed.' That she would not improve because improvements only occurred within the first day or so of a stroke—and that because Amalie was unable to swallow, to eat or drink, she would soon die.

"Sigrün, reluctantly, nodded her acceptance, but Karl and Kjell continued to deny Amalie's condition . . . for another two days.

"By then, their mother was declining rapidly. That fateful morning, Amalie no longer perceived anyone, no longer responded to voices. They knew then that she would not recover. Later that day, Amalie slipped into sleep, and that evening, she passed away."

Rose still ached as she remembered the last time she had held Amalie's hand and seen the recognition and love shining in her eyes. Soon after, Amalie's gaze changed. She took in less and less, until she closed her eyes forever.

O'Dell's question was softly spoken. "How does Amalie's death figure into this situation with Frank Mitchell?"

Rose sighed. "You will understand soon."

She continued. "During Amalie's illness, Jan, Søren, and Harold managed their own and many of Karl and Kjell's chores. They brought their young nephews alongside them, kept them focused on their usual duties but also parceled out new responsibilities to them and checked to be sure the livestock were thriving under their care.

"To make matters more difficult, it was time to plant corn and barley. Neighbors arrived to plow Karl and Kjell's fields and plant their seed. Jan oversaw it all—while you and he also sowed your own fields, Søren."

"I remember," Søren said from the driver's seat.

"Then you remember, too, when Amalie passed, how you and Jan built Amalie's coffin."

"Yeah, I do. A labor of love. An honor."

"Yes, but we were all weary with grief and labor, your father more so than the rest of us, Søren."

Rose redirected the tale again to all of her audience. "The day of Amalie's burial was particularly hectic. Families from across the county came to pay their respects. After the graveside service, we fed the crowds—Sonja, Meg, Fiona, Vera, Anna, Joy, and I.

"We held the wake at Søren and Meg's house. We cooked and baked, and our many friends brought food to help. We ferried bowls and platters out to the tables. Our friends and guests ate, then we cleared the tables for new visitors. Washed mountains of dishes again and again.

"You and your father, Søren, managed the crew of men who set up tables in the yard, directed the visitors where to put their wagons and buggies, and unhitched and cared for their teams."

Rose's voice dropped to a whisper. "I sent you home to fetch something, Joy. I can't even recall what it was."

"Clean dishtowels. And your largest platter." Joy's voice had gone flat. "'Be careful not to drop it,' you reminded me."

"Clean *dishtowels* . . ." Rose shook her head. "We were rushed off our feet . . . and I did not realize for nearly an hour that you had not returned."

The cares of this life . . . distracted us.

"I went to the kitchen window and looked across to our house, but I did not see you. I scanned from the track to the bridge, from the bridge back to Søren's farm. Nothing.

"Then . . . I began to think to myself how Amalie's death was known in RiverBend and throughout the county. How anyone and most everyone would have heard that today was her burial.

"I went in search of Jan, and when I found him, I explained that Joy hadn't returned and that I was concerned . . ."

Rose hesitated. "The look on his face shook me. Somehow, *he knew* she was in trouble. He saddled one of your horses, Søren. Instead of leading it out of the paddock onto the drive, he raced the horse across the field and jumped the fence onto the road.

"Our guests pointed at him. I . . . I said the first thing that came into my mind, that we had forgotten to put the goats out to graze. *I lied to them.* I cannot, to this day, believe that I lied, but in the heat of that moment, I did. Then I excused myself and went after him. I walked partway to our house and ran the remainder.

"When I got there and went inside, I found our home in a state of disarray. Someone had thrown things to the floor—dishes, flour, beans, sugar, books, clothes, bedding. They had stomped and trampled on our things. I found Jan in Joy's room, staring at the beautiful wedding chest he had so lovingly made for her. The lid was ripped from its hinges. Most everything in the chest was torn or scattered across the floor.

"That was where I found Jan, holding aprons and towels, trying to make sense of the mess and decide what was missing. But I knew immediately: Her quilts were gone, the ones she had made for her wedding and stored in her wedding chest. And I saw that many of her clothes were gone, too, and the valise Arnie and Anna had given her for Christmas . . .

"I cried out to him, 'Jan! That man! He has taken her! He has taken our Joy!'"

Rose's narration petered out, and she sank down into her memory of that day.

As my words reached him he roared with a terrifying rage. He pushed through the bedroom door, kicked away the debris in his path, and rushed out of our house to the waiting horse.

Never had I seen Jan thus. Never! A lust for vengeance had descended upon him, and I fell to my knees, pleading, "Oh God! Save my husband from this ungodly anger. Speak to his heart, pull him up short—knock him from his horse, if you must—but keep his hands from violence this day, my God. And save our Joy, Lord! Please."

When Joy noted Rose's preoccupation, she took up the story. "Yes, Franz Mikkelmann was waiting in our house when I walked in. He had destroyed many of our things, and I was stupefied by the disarray and waste I found. Until I saw him.

She shuddered. "He smiled and rushed to my side. His hands gripped my arms like bands of iron, and he babbled nonsense at me."

"What kind of nonsense?" O'Dell demanded.

Joy coughed to clear the knot of old fear from her throat. "Obsession. Delusion. Very like what you heard from him today. He babbled to me, 'Joy, my beloved! I have finally gotten you away from your scheming, underhanded parents. We can run away together now. Be married as soon as we are safely away and free of them. Aren't you glad to see me, Joy? Dearest, will you not give me a kiss to seal our love?'

"I remembered well Mama and Papa's words, however, and I put them to immediate use. I screamed and fought him—like they had told me. I fought him until he doubled up his fist and punched me in my stomach. I could not catch my breath, and I suppose I passed out. When I woke up, I was in the back of his rickety wagon, and he was whipping his horse, driving as fast as he could push the poor animal to go. He had tied my hands in front of me and had tossed blankets, quilts, and my valise into the wagon with me.

"I would have jumped out immediately if I could have gotten to my feet, but the wagon tossed me about as it careened around curves and over ruts and bumps. I was being bruised and pummeled, flying around in the wagon's box, and was more in danger of being thrown out than I was of hurting myself by jumping.

"At last I gathered my wits and courage, and when the wagon straightened out from a harrowing turn, I sat up—long enough to try to understand where we were—but he noticed. He reached behind him and struck me across the back of my head. Dazed, I fell back in the wagon. Then it happened.

"He had taken his eyes off the road to strike me, and the wagon ran into some obstacle—a large rock or a particularly deep rut, perhaps. With a terrific *crack*, I heard one of the wheels break. I suppose that the axle and what remained of the wheel dropped to the road and dug in, because almost immediately, the wagon flipped over. I was dumped onto the prairie sod alongside the road. Everything else that had been in the box was strewn around me. My hands were still tied, I ached all over, and it hurt to move. The box itself was in upside-down pieces in the road.

"From where I lay, I saw Mr. Mikkelmann unharnessing his horse from the wagon. The man was in a terrible state, cursing and rushing the job. I could see, too, that his horse had been injured, for blood streamed from both his rear hocks, pitiful creature, but Mikkelmann did not care.

"As soon as he had his horse unhitched, he produced a knife and cut the reins so he might ride his horse bareback, with no regard for his animal's pain or injury. I slowly got to my knees. I was determined to get away, you see, and kept as quiet as I could, hoping he would not see me until I began running.

"But he did see. He came over straightaway and yanked me to my feet. Pulled me to his horse and tried to throw me up on the horse's back. I did not cooperate, though. Each time Mikkelmann lifted me to put me up on the horse, I kicked the animal so that he moved away.

"Then I saw another horse flying toward us, and I knew it was Papa."

Joy smiled, and O'Dell, who was turned in his seat watching her, smiled back at her glowing beauty.

She added, "That awful man must have realized it was Papa, too. Well! Mikkelmann dropped me in the dirt without so much as a by-your-leave—not unlike a sack of potatoes."

Søren and O'Dell chuckled, and Rose smiled with them.

"So much for loving you forever," O'Dell quipped. "Did the cad scamper, then?"

"Did he ever. He jumped on his wounded horse and rode off across the Glendorns' pasture."

"You knew where you were at that point?" O'Dell asked.

"Oh, yes. The Glendorns' land is several miles south of our farm, and it also ran along the creek."

"Did your father follow Mikkelmann?"

"No, not right away. He was—" Joy's cheery mood crumbled a little under her reminiscence, and she sniffled. "Papa cared more about me, about my well-being, than catching that awful man. When he saw the overturned wagon, he flung himself off that horse and ran to me. He was afraid I had been injured and only wanted to get me safely away from Mikkelmann."

She sniffed again and said, "See, that was how I *knew* that the wretched, obsessed man who abducted me had never really cared a fig about *me*. I had a papa who showed me daily what love truly was. He did not have to say he loved me over and over. He lived out his love. Continually."

Joy sighed and lifted a radiant smile to O'Dell. "Papa's example taught me how to choose a *good* man."

O'Dell, usually circumspect in his displays of affection, reached behind him and took Joy's hand. "I am forever indebted to your father, my love. And I am sorry you had to endure Mikkelmann's mistreatment, my darling."

Perhaps it was the release from the day's high tension, but Rose felt a laugh burbling up in her chest, then her throat. It was happy laughter, but she slid her hands over her mouth anyway. Regardless of her efforts, her muffled snicker intruded on the tender moment between Joy and O'Dell. He quickly withdrew his hand from Joy's and growled, "What?"

Rose smirked behind her hands. "Why, not a thing, Edmund. I was . . . merely enjoying the love feast."

Embarrassed that his open display of affection had been observed, O'Dell grumbled, "Guess now I know what Jesus meant when he said, *a man's foes shall be they of his own household.*"

Rose could hold it in no longer. Her humor, along with O'Dell's chagrin, only provoked Søren to laugh aloud along with Rose—and, consequently, Joy joined them.

O'Dell, in an attempt to shift the good-natured attention away from himself, demanded of Joy, "What happened next?"

"Oh my, yes. Well, Papa untied my hands and helped me up, of course. When he was certain I was only bruised and not badly harmed, he stuffed my clothes back into my valise, then gathered the blankets and quilts. He mounted the horse and had me pass my things to him. Then he gave me his hand. I swung up behind him and took my valise from him. Thus loaded, Papa set off for home."

"When we returned to our house, Mama had already swept up the dry foods and broken china. She had replaced books and clothing and tidied all she could . . . and was sitting in our rocking chair, reading her Bible, praying, and waiting—as if nothing of note had occurred."

"Why, Joy, that is not altogether true. I was relieved and over the moon to see you both, but I had prayed, and I was resting in the Lord."

"What about Mikkelmann?" O'Dell pressed Joy.

"Guess I have to tell this part," Søren said. "We still had guests from Amalie's wake when Papa came back to our house. Quietly, he gathered the Thoresen men together—Karl, Kjell, Arnie, and me—to decide what to do about Mikkelmann. RiverBend had no constable back then. If Mikkelmann was to be caught, it was up to us.

"We saddled horses and, without a word to our guests, rode across the bridge and up onto the bluff, heading south. We started tracking Mikkelmann from where he had left the bits of his wagon and cut across the Glendorns' pasture. It was spring, and the ground was moist in some places, enabling us to find his horse's hoofprints. Joy had also told Papa that Mikkelmann's horse was bleeding, and we spotted droplets of blood here and there on the grass. We had no problem following the course he took.

"In case you did not know, Edmund, our creek runs into one of the tributaries of the Platte. Normally, it is a small river that takes a leisurely bend just outside of town, hence our town's name. That day, though, both our creek and the river were running high from spring runoff.

"We figured to catch up to him not far from where our creek fed into the river. If he wanted to cross over to the other side, he needed to do so before the creek reached the river—but the creek, by that point, was swollen, the current swift, the bed underfoot shifting. Unstable. Ideally, he should have thought to cross over as soon as he left his wagon behind."

"Perhaps he believed Joy's father was in hot pursuit."

“Whatever his reasoning, he had left it too late to make it across, and he either had to cross over or change directions—and risk us cutting him off in doing so.”

Søren shook his head. “He tried to ford the creek, and his horse had not the strength to push through the rushing water. They must have been swept apart. We saw the horse, clinging to a narrow spit of sand, slowly crawling up on it, but stranded there, for all intents and purposes.

“Papa thought Mikkelmann would have been washed away in the current, so we rode hard along the creekbank, looking for him, until the creek ran into the river. We kept going, now following the river, and finally spotted him, far downstream from us, swept along by the current, tossed about in the rapids, and being carried swiftly away. We never did catch up with him. We followed his bobbing head until we could see him no longer. Although we searched for him until night fell, we never saw him again.”

“You thought he drowned.”

“Yes. Certainly, nothing in the past twenty-five years led us to believe otherwise. Until today.”

“He came back to this county quietly and with a new name, after all those years. Hoping for what?” O’Dell mused. “To find Joy?”

Rose answered. “Perhaps. Certainly, his obsession had not died out, nor had his methods of molesting children. I wonder, were we to trace his whereabouts after leaving RiverBend the first time, if we would find a string of the same crimes.”

“No doubt in my mind,” O’Dell said. Then he frowned and asked, “Mother, when did you first suspect Lucy’s abuser was the same man who tried to kidnap Joy? What made you think it?”

“Initially, it was the way Lucy described him, how he intimated that he might spread rumors about her, then threatened to hurt her little sister—but particularly his threat against Adele seemed familiar.

“And when Lucy called him ‘Mick’? His present name, supposedly, was Frank Mitchell, a translation or transliteration of Franz Mikkelmann. But, why, if his last name was Mitchell, would he say that his nickname was Mick? It should have been ‘Mitch,’ do you see? That set a bee buzzing about in my thoughts.

“It is true that when I first heard the name Mitchell, I thought nothing of it. But as my suspicions grew, Mitchell seemed too near Mikkelmann to be a coincidence. In fact, the girls’ continued reference to him as ‘Mick’ only served to put me in mind of Mikkelmann.”

"And is that why you insisted on bringing Joy with us today?" O'Dell asked.

"Yes. As improbable as it might seem for Mitchell to turn out to be Mikkelmann, if it *were* the same villain, she and I would both recognize him—and she could testify against him to corroborate Lucy's experience."

O'Dell turned again toward Joy. "Why did you never tell me about this?"

Joy's face registered surprise. "Edmund, I suffered no long-lasting ill effects. Consequently, I have not thought on this episode in decades."

"Nor did we allow it to become common knowledge in our community," Rose added. "Jan passed off the hasty exit of five Thoresen men late in the day of Amalie's burial as a small family emergency for which he provided no details."

"Of those who went with him that day, not one of us even told his wife what had happened," Søren added.

"But what about the family who hired Mitchell? That is, Mikkelmann as they knew him?"

"They could not account for his disappearance and, when several weeks passed and he did not reemerge, they hired on another man. It was hardly the first time a hired man moved on without notice."

"But surely he left belongings behind?"

Søren glanced over at O'Dell. "Joy said he had his clothes with him in his wagon when it overturned. We assumed they were swept away in the current."

In the end, the sheriff, after listening to a confusing cornucopia of details over the telephone and hearing that O'Dell would be leaving in the morning, opted for the simplest solution: He and a deputy arrived in RiverBend hours later as dusk was covering the prairie.

By then, O'Dell had sketched a timeline of the events and those involved. With the outline before him, the Sheriff took statements from Lucy, Rose, Joy, O'Dell, Jeremy, Hester Pettersen, and Mr. and Mrs. Pettersen. The process took place in Karl and Sonja's living room and lasted well into the night.

The sheriff heard details that would have alternately enraged or sickened a less experienced policeman, but he listened with the calm, impassive mien of a seasoned law enforcement man, taking thorough notes and not interrupting except to request clarification.

When the sheriff and his deputy were ready to depart, they were in possession of Frank Mitchell's body and O'Dell's Pinkerton business card.

"Relocating from Mile High City to the Windy City, eh?" the sheriff asked. "And you'll be the Pinkerton's new chief in Chicago?"

"If I'm not fired for being tardy my first day." O'Dell smiled at the likable man. "Feel free to call me and reverse the charges if you have further questions."

"Thanks for the offer, but I think I have the gist of it—if you are certain you had no other option than to shoot this Mitchell or Mikkelmann?"

"Yes, I am certain. I am sorry to have killed him, and it was not my first objective. I would rather he have stood trial for his crimes. However, he was about to throw the lantern. As I said in my statement, several of us could have been splashed with oil and suffered terrible burns had he followed through. I think, too, we would not have been able to put out the subsequent fire. Shooting him was the only means I had of stopping him."

"But you are not unhappy to have put an end to his nefarious crimes against young ladies? And you are relieved that the young ladies will not have to testify in court?"

O'Dell exhaled. "Yes, I can admit to that."

"I appreciate your candor, Mr. O'Dell."

CHAPTER 18

Saturday morning: The O'Dell family was nearly ready to depart. Their bags and trunks were stacked outside by the pump. Søren and Jon would load them into the truck. Jon would drive the truck into town, while Søren ferried the O'Dells to the train.

Joy examined her three boys, ensuring they had done an adequate job of washing their faces. She was weary, but cheerful. A sleep-deprived O'Dell had already parted each boy's hair and run a comb through it.

"Boys," O'Dell said. "Say thank you and goodbye to your Aunt Meg and Uncle Søren. We have had a wonderful visit, haven't we?"

"Yes, sir," Matthew and Jacob answered.

The two older boys solemnly issued their thanks and said their goodbyes. They shook hands with Søren and submitted to hugs from Meg. Little Luke copied his brothers as best he could.

"Now kiss Grandma Rose goodbye. We shall see her again in less than two weeks."

When they arrived at the siding in town, O'Dell would change Rose's ticket and leave it for her to call for. Her revised departure date was a week from the upcoming Friday.

Matthew and Jacob understood that the parting was temporary. Luke did not. He crawled up into Rose's lap, clung to her neck, and howled.

"There, there, my boy," Rose crooned. "I will be along soon. Be a big boy for Grandma, will you?"

Jacob, his confidence perhaps a *little* shaken by Luke's despairing display, tugged at Rose's skirt. "You promise, Grandma? You promise to come?"

"I promise, my sweet boy."

With many more hugs and a few tears, Rose and Meg sent them on their way. O'Dell, Joy, and their family rode in Søren's automobile, with the exception of Matthew, who proudly rode by himself in the front seat of his cousin Jon's farm truck.

"Goodness, the house feels well-nigh cavernous with them gone. I shall miss them all," Meg commented. "Cup of tea, Mama Rose?"

Rose felt her fatigue right down to her bones. "Oh my, yes—and I foresee a nap in my immediate future."

They looked at each other and smiled.

THAT EVENING AFTER supper, Vera called to speak to Rose. "Rose, will you have dinner with us after church tomorrow?"

"But of course. It will be like old times."

"Please do not use the word 'old' in our conversations, dear friend. It strikes too close to the bone."

"And yet, my bones are considerably older than yours," Rose laughed in return.

They chuckled together, that perfect harmony between "old" friends. When their laughter petered out, Rose had the sense that Vera had something else on her mind.

"What is it, Vera?"

"You are always so insightful, Rose. The thing is . . . word is spreading around the community about that dreadful man and how he treated Lucy. Jacob and I have spoken to several parents who have wakened to the realization that the present generation in which their children are growing up is much changed from the one in which they were raised. They are concerned that their daughters and granddaughters need more . . ." Here Vera chuckled a little. "They need more 'straight talk' is how one father put it."

"Ah." Rose caught a glimmer of Vera's direction.

"I have approached Esther and Ava and shared this concern. They and I were wondering . . . you will be here both tomorrow and next Sunday before you leave, will you not? We thought to invite the young ladies of the community to meet in the fellowship hall later in the afternoon tomorrow. Provide cookies and punch . . . and an opportunity for us to broach the subject, to speak candidly to them and them to us. And we hoped you might . . ."

"I might offer them a bit of 'straight talk'? Is that it?"

Vera exhaled in relief. "Yes, exactly. You have such a wealth of experience to offer them and you bring God's word into everything."

"I suppose I do."

"Then you will do it? Tomorrow and next Sunday?"

"Yes, I will, but I have a few requests."

"For you? Anything."

"First, I would like Ava and Esther to consider continuing the meetings after I am gone. If an interest exists, of course. At the very least, continue meeting with Lucy and Hester to ensure that they heal well from the wounds of that man."

"And second?"

"That Lucy, Emma, and Hester attend."

Vera seemed reluctant. "We may have to cajole them."

"I will speak to their parents myself. Rather than the girls becoming topics of gossip, this meeting provides them with an opportunity to speak boldly of their own experiences and thus thwart the gossip mongers."

"Then I will leave you to it, Rose. The Lord bless your efforts."

ROSE WENT TO her room and knelt at the bed. *Lord God, what I will ask of these young girls may prove difficult. It may be difficult for Norrie and Mrs. Pettersen, too. And yet, this is their chance to lead, rather than hide. Please help me to share my heart with them . . . and please grant them the courage to stand in your grace.*

Rose returned to the kitchen and asked the operator to connect her to Einar and Norrie's line. She greeted Norrie. Then she spoke her heart to the woman.

"What happened to the Pettersens' hired man yesterday, and more importantly *why*, is circulating in our community. What he did to Lucy and Hester will soon be common knowledge. But, as you know, rumors tend to grow, to expand with unfounded details. I would use tomorrow's afternoon meeting to defuse the untruths for Lucy's sake. Will you help me, Norrie?"

Rose listened to Norrie's soft breathing on the other end as she considered Rose's proposal.

At last, she said, "*Ja*, Aunt Rose. I will speak with Lucy. Even if she chooses not to attend, I will help you. I will not hang my head in this community for the rest of my life because of that man's wickedness."

Norrie then startled Rose. "I would like to provide the baking for this meeting. May I?"

Rose's estimation of the woman jumped exponentially. "You are a woman of great courage, Norrie Thoresen. Einar chose well, and I am right proud of you."

She could almost hear the woman's smile across the lines. "Thank you, Aunt Rose. I . . . I treasure your words."

With Norrie's acceptance, Rose's second call was easier. In fact, Mrs. Pettersen jumped at the hope Rose held out to her. "You are saying it is an opportunity to regain our footing in the community? To save our daughters' reputations and future prospects?"

"That is precisely what I am saying. Lucy and Hester need not wallow in shame or guilt. They should lift their chins and walk without fear—and they should start immediately."

"Well, if Norrie can do it, surely I can, too. And if we show a little courage, mayhap our girls will take their cue from us."

"Norrie is baking cookies tonight," Rose mentioned, keeping her tone casual, "for tomorrow's meeting."

"*Ach!* Is she now? Well, I cannot allow her to bear all the responsibility, can I? I will do the same."

"Excellent, Mrs. Pettersen."

"I would be honored if you called me Greta, Mrs. Thoresen."

"The honor is mine, Greta. And please call me Rose. I look forward to seeing you tomorrow in church."

After Rose returned the receiver to its cradle, she smiled and whispered, "Lord, it seems that you found it needful to prove to me, once again, the truth of Romans 11:29. Its truth is as valid and compelling as the rest of your word: *For the gifts and calling of God are without repentance*. You called me to this ministry, a ministry I did not ask for. Then you gifted me for this work, anointing me to do it. You have not changed your mind, about either the gift or the calling."

She laughed low in her throat. "So. I may have left Palmer House behind, but your calling on my life has not left *me*. Very well, Lord. Have your way. For as long as you give me strength, I shall keep doing what you place before me, bearing fruit for you even unto my old age."

CHAPTER 19

Rose closed her eyes to join in the last hymn, sung after Jacob had finished his message and given the altar call. She felt the stress and all her weariness of the past week flow away as she sang.

What a friend we have in Jesus
All our sins and griefs to bear
What a privilege to carry
Everything to God in prayer

Oh, what peace we often forfeit
Oh, what needless pain we bear
All because we do not carry
Everything to God in prayer

She murmured quietly, "Lord Jesus, thank you for bearing our griefs as well as our sins. Where would I be had you not taken my sorrows on yourself? I am forever grateful."

She glanced with fondness to her right: Meg, Søren, Jon and Camille's three children, then Jon and Camille themselves. Ahead of them, Colleen, Feor, and their girls. She looked to her left: Markus, Delores, their four daughters and one son—Nils.

Nils, his right leg bouncing lightly against the pew, his attention anywhere but on the hymn, noticed her looking. He grinned.

She grinned back.

He crossed his eyes and wiggled his ears.

Rose slapped her gloved hand to her mouth to choke back a laugh, while Delores, with longsuffering patience, tugged her son's ear to her mouth, and whispered a rebuke.

Sigrün and Harold and their four. Karl and Sonja. Einar, Norrie, and their brood. Kjell, Lily, and four more little Thoresens, sprouting up before their eyes.

This church is filled with Thoresens, Rose realized. *Ah, Jan. You would be bursting with pride to see how our family and your brother's family have grown. Grown in numbers. Grown in Jesus.*

THE HYMN ENDED, and Jacob asked Vera to make an announcement before he offered the benediction. Vera rose and faced the congregation. Generations of beloved friends waited expectantly on her.

"Most of you have likely heard the news regarding the Pettersens' hired man."

Nods and serious expressions affirmed her statement.

"Our community has weathered a storm, and by God's grace, we will be stronger and wiser in the future. It is concerning wisdom that I believe the Lord has spoken to me. Our job as parents and grandparents, as much as lies within our power, is to protect and defend our children . . . particularly our daughters.

"We may, however, have left one avenue of defense undone. We should instruct our girls to recognize danger and teach them to be unafraid to speak out when they are in peril. But how to do so and with what words is often difficult to teach.

"To that end, I would like to invite the young ladies of our church and community to gather this afternoon for cookies, punch, and pearls of wisdom. Those pearls will be dispensed by our own Rose Thoresen. She will also field questions.

"As the topic will be of a sensitive nature, we recommend that parents judge for themselves if their daughters are mature enough to take part in such a conversation. And, certainly, all mothers are invited to attend with their daughters.

"We shall gather at three o'clock in the fellowship hall. I understand that Greta Pettersen spent last evening baking two batches of her blue-ribbon apple walnut cookies and that Norrie Thoresen will contribute her widely loved oatmeal raisin bars. We hope to see a good turnout. Thank you."

Meg leaned toward Rose. "You are eating Sunday dinner with Pastor and Mrs. Medford. I will drive into town and join you at the meeting, then take you back home, Mama Rose."

"Thank you, Meg."

As had happened on her first Sunday in RiverBend, a line formed to greet Rose after service. She smiled, murmured pleasantries and encouragement, and left no hand unshaken. The line was nearly gone when a well-dressed couple approached Rose, a girl of about twelve with them.

"Mrs. Thoresen, we met last Sunday. I'm Theo Warner."

"Yes, we did, Mr. Warner. A pleasure to see you again." She turned her attention to the woman with him.

"This is my daughter, Patricia, and my granddaughter, Alice."

"I am pleased to meet you, Patricia, and you, Alice."

"Likewise, Mrs. Thoresen," Patricia responded. "Alice and I will attend your meeting this afternoon. We are looking forward to it."

"Thank you, Patricia."

"Mrs. Thoresen, if you have no plans as yet, we would be honored to have you take Sunday dinner with us."

"Oh, how lovely of you. Sadly, I do have a previous engagement."

"Perhaps another time?"

Rose chuckled. "I would be delighted. However, I will be taking the train a week from this coming Friday."

"Then it must be next Sunday if we are to have you before then. Are you free that day?" Patricia asked.

"Yes. Thank you most kindly.

THAT AFTERNOON, Rose looked about the fellowship hall with delighted satisfaction. A good turnout? Just shy of three dozen girls and mothers in the fellowship hall that afternoon were making quick work of the goodies. Latecomers were spared the crumbs when Esther produced two plates of sugar cookies.

"I baked them just in case," she murmured.

Rose still found Esther's domestic skills and her simple attire and hairstyle incongruous with the few memories she had of the woman. Shortly after Jan died, Joy had returned to her lodge in Corinth, and Rose had accompanied her. She joined her efforts to Joy's with the objective of freeing the women held captive in Corinth's two houses of ill-repute. Not many days later, the men who ran those houses burned Joy's lodge to the ground. Their attack had been swift and merciless.

I had hardly begun to consider Corinth Mountain Lodge my home before it was gone, Rose realized.

However devastating the loss was, much good had come from it. O'Dell returned from Denver with a phalanx of US Marshals eager to arrest the men (and one woman) who had forced young, unsuspecting girls into a life of slavery, thus releasing the unwilling prostitutes of both houses.

But Rose had been shocked to discover that not *all* of them had been unwilling.

She remembered well her open-mouthed chagrin, her utter amazement when a quite young Esther, tossing her beautiful head, had proclaimed, "We are whores—and good ones. We will rent our own place in Denver, decorate it tastefully, and take care of each other. We intend to make excellent money and never allow abuse from our customers. No man will ever mistreat us again. No, this time, *we'll* be in control."

Esther had served as spokesperson for three other girls, Molly, Jess, and Ava—the same Ava who was now Mrs. Jeremy Bailey. They had left Corinth for Denver, rented their own house, and were succeeding in their twisted aspirations. Esther had even asked additional women to join them in their "business endeavor."

Enter Cal Judd, owner of Denver's notorious *Silver Spurs Bawdy Hall.*

He had insinuated himself into Esther's affections. Then he had taken over their business and their lives.

O'Dell and Marshal Pounder had freed the women from Judd's control—but not from Judd's sworn declaration that he would punish them . . . Esther in particular.

We sent six girls away from Denver. Sent them to RiverBend to hide them from Judd, Rose recalled.

Three had moved on to new lives and good employment in other towns. Jess married a widowed farmer with children who lived at some distance from town. Esther and Ava had remained in RiverBend and, under Vera Medford and Fiona McKennie's loving tutelage, had surrendered their lives to Jesus. Slowly—and with frequent missteps—they had forged a place for themselves in the community.

Rose marveled at Esther and Ava's transformation. *Lord God! What wonders you have wrought.*

Two rows of chairs were arranged in a semicircle. Ava, Esther, and Norrie quickly added another row to accommodate the thirty-some girls and mothers.

Vera placed Rose in a seat facing the semicircle. She opened the meeting with a prayer. "Lord God, we ask you to be present in all we do and say today. Please bless this meeting, we ask in Jesus' name. Amen."

"Amen," was the response—and close to three dozen sets of eyes turned on Rose. Waited for her to speak.

Rose felt a familiar stirring within her. *Holy Spirit, I thank you for your grace and insight this day. Come stir us and have your way. Please heal us, mold us into one heart, and equip us to love and serve the Lord, our God.*

She smiled. "Good afternoon, ladies—and yes, my greeting includes all of you younger women. Thank you for joining us women of, shall we say, a more mature age?"

She was rewarded with the low, breathy laughter she had hoped for.

"Today we gather simply as women, as sisters in Christ, with no other distinctions. Scripture tells us that we are one body in Christ and as such, we do not harm each other, the other parts of that body. Rather, with great love and care, we labor to lift each other up. Scripture calls this 'mutual edification,' meaning that we are to help build in every woman an *edifice*, a strong house, a fortified tower, able to withstand the storms of life.

"The storms of life? Yes. Life in this fallen, sinful world is often difficult, unfair, and even tragic. May I ask of you ladies, who here has suffered tragedy? Who can recall a hardship, one that very nearly shipwrecked you? Will you raise your hand if you can admit to such a time?"

The girls and their mothers slid furtive glances at their neighbors. A hand went up. Another. Then many were in the air—some high, others cautiously at half-mast. Generally, the younger girls had not raised their hands, although they watched Lucy lift hers.

Most of these youngsters are not yet old enough to have experienced such sorrow, Rose thought. *I am sorry, Lucy, that someone wounded you at a young age.*

Rose said, "Thank you. You affirm what I said: Life is often difficult, unfair, and even tragic. Would anyone wish to share, briefly, an instance of suffering they have endured?"

All hands descended and stayed down. Until one slowly lifted.

"Yes? Will you stand? I apologize, but I do not know your name, madam."

The woman, thin, worn, perhaps in her thirties, with a shy daughter seated on either side of her, said with quiet dignity, "M' name is Bekkah Wheeler, Mrs. Thoresen, and these here are m' daughters, Catherine and Marie."

Rose noted that the woman and her daughters wore simple dresses made from the same bolt of inexpensive fabric. Their garments, however, were spotless and carefully pressed.

She is poor, but she is proud. Lord God, please bless her.

"You are welcome here, Bekkah. Welcome, Catherine and Marie."

Bekkah nodded. "Thank ye."

She took a moment to gather herself. "See, ya asked iffin anyone would talk 'bout a hard time. A sufferin' time. Sumpthin thet 'most shipwrecked us? Well, my Bill died two years back. We ain't got no kin anywheres I know of, so 'tis jest us—me and m' girls."

"I am very sorry for your loss," Rose murmured. "Did Mr. Wheeler pass suddenly, or did he take ill before?"

"Was in the prime o' life, he was, and had jest brought in the harvest," Bekkah answered. "Fell dead in ourn barn, he did."

Her voice dropped a little. "The grief was s' hard, thought I would die. And I couldn't see no way t' keep body and soul together with no one to farm ourn land and pay the mortgage. Thought what Bill had harvested would rot away, too. Then neighbor menfolk, three o' 'em, shows up and tells us they'd take all ourn corn and wheat t' market, even the ten head o' beef we'd raised and fed out, and they would write me a receipt to prove what they had taken.

"Two weeks later, they shows up agin and gives us ever bit o' the cash money from our harvest—more'n enough to keep us through till spring. Not only that, they brung their teams and plowed under all Bill's fields and brung us a load o' wood fer the winter."

Tears began to drip from Bekkah's cheeks. "'We'll be back in the spring t' plant yer crops,' they says t' me, 'and t' bring the harvest in when it comes.' Two years now they done this fer us. I always thank 'em, I do, and bake 'em each a pie. Thing is, they's all Christian men, always say 'God bless you,' but t' my thinkin', they have saved ourn lives. I have hope fer m' girls' future now, I do."

"I am so glad, Bekkah," Rose whispered.

"Yes'm. Thank ye kindly. Well, I might not be a God-fearin' woman, and we ain't church-goin' neither, but when one o' their wives come t' me after our noon meal t'day and tells me 'bout this-here meetin', that its fer teachin' young girls how t' pretect themselves, I figger we should come. See, I love m' girls more'n life itself."

She looked steadily at Rose. "Don' know 'bout no 'sisters in Christ' nor buildin' no strong 'ederfices' like you said. Don' have no women friends, come t' think on it. But I figger what ourn neighbor men done fer us is enough like what ya meant by buildin' up, that this'd be a good time t' thank 'em, 'cause without 'em, I'd a been that wrecked woman you spoke on."

Bekkah sat down to a solemn hush.

"Thank you, Bekkah," Rose said softly. "You are exactly right. A loveless neighbor may have ignored you. A godless neighbor may have tried to take advantage of your situation. But true Christian neighbors understand that we do not tear each other down. We build up—and that is precisely what I mean for us as women. When difficulties knock one of us down, we help them stand again."

Rose thought for a moment. "I wish to ask all of you another question. And may I have your eyes on me as I ask it?"

Every girl and woman met her gaze.

"My question is this: Am I better than you? More valuable than you? Please be honest and tell me."

Some heads moved slowly side to side, one or two up and down. Mostly, though, Rose observed confusion.

"Let me answer the question for you, using the Holy Bible as our infallible source. Scripture tells us in Genesis 1:27, *So God created man in his own image, in the image of God created he him; male and female created he them.*

"Every human, whether man or woman, is created in the holy image of God. To be made in God's image and likeness is a great and powerful honor. It signifies that God views *people* as the most special part of his creation. The most valuable. Do you see? *You* are special. *You* are created in God's image. Before him, we are of inestimable worth, *each of us*.

"How do we know we are valuable? Because God the Father paid a great and terrible price for us. He sacrificed his only begotten Son to redeem us from our sins. That is precisely *how valuable* each one of us is.

"Recognizing that we are special and valuable to God, is important. Acknowledging that our sisters are just as special and valuable to God as we are, is equally important. The Lord tells us so in Matthew 22:37-40.

Jesus said unto him,
Thou shalt love the Lord thy God
with all thy heart, and with all thy soul,
and with all thy mind.
This is the first and great commandment.
And the second is like unto it,
Thou shalt love thy neighbour as thyself.
On these two commandments
hang all the law and the prophets.

"We are all neighbors here, commanded to love each other in the same way we love ourselves. If I were to think of another woman—a woman whom God loves—as less than I am, if I were to believe myself better than another woman whom God loves, I would be sinning against the Lord himself.

"The answer to my question is no. No, I am no better and no more important than you. Conversely, you are no better and no more important than I am."

She smiled. "I ask you to turn to the woman on your left. Look her in the eye, and tell her, 'God Almighty sent Jesus to redeem you because you are valuable to him.'"

She waited for the timid whispers to finish. "Now look to the woman on your right. Tell her, 'I am not worth more than you. You are as important to God Almighty as I am.'"

The voices were more than whispers this time, as the truths sank deeper into hungry hearts.

"Dear sisters of mine, we cannot tear down another woman in the false hope that it will improve our own standing. We do not gossip or spread falsehoods about those whom God loves. We care for them. We heal them. We help them to stand. We follow the admonition found in Philippians 2:

"*Do nothing from selfish ambition or conceit,*
but in humility count others
more significant than yourselves,
and
"*Let each of you look not only to his own interests,*
but also to the interests of others."

She looked from face to face. "Do you hear what I am saying? Do you perceive how it relates to what has happened in our community recently?"

They did.

With murmured "amens" and more than a few tears of conviction, they signified that they received Rose's strong word of exhortation. She waited until they were ready to go on before she spoke again.

"Very good, my dear friends. Now, let us go on. For I wish to discuss two small but powerful words, two words we all possess, two words given to us by God himself, two words by which we determine the course of our lives.

"Those two words are *yes* and *no*.

"Jesus tells us in Matthew 5:37, *But let your communication be, Yea, yea and nay, nay.* Quite literally, this means, 'let your yes mean yes, and your no mean no.'

"God has given every individual a free will, the ability to choose between right or wrong. He allows each of us to decide when to say yes or when to say no.

"While we are children, living under our mother and father's authority, God charges our parents to raise us with the knowledge of his commands. Our parents are to *train* us to choose right, so that, when we are grown, we know *how* to choose right."

Rose said slowly, "God has given each of us this awesome power and responsibility so that we might say yes to him and no to temptation. Those words are echoed in Joshua's command to the people of Israel: *Choose you this day whom ye will serve.*

"We have come together this afternoon, because a man who lived among us—a man who was trusted—attempted to abuse two of our beloved daughters. This man threatened to harm someone these girls loved. By his threats, he endeavored to silence them. What does it look like when a man tries to stifle or silence a young woman? My husband and I counseled our daughter, Joy, when she was fourteen years of age—when she was similarly threatened."

Rose's announcement sent a wave of murmurs through the meeting.

"Yes, our daughter suffered an experience quite similar to the one Lucy and Hester suffered. Young ladies, I speak to each of you as we did to our daughter, using the same instructions we gave to her: You are made in the image and likeness of Almighty God. Your body is sacred. It is holy, reserved only for your husband, the man you will marry.

"A man who is neither your father nor your lawful husband is not to touch you. He is not to put his hands on you. He is not to grab, pull, push, or *ever* hit you. These admonitions also apply to family members and trusted friends of your family. A true and godly gentleman will never disrespect your purity. *He will keep his hands to himself.*

"Furthermore, not all who claim the name of Christ are his. Young ladies, exercise wisdom and discretion; avoid any situation where you might find yourself completely alone with a man. Mothers, I caution you: Do not disbelieve your daughter if she confides in you that a trusted friend or family member has touched or threatened her."

Rose watched the older women as she spoke. They grew subdued, some nodding to themselves.

"Please listen well, young ones: Learn to say no *at once* when it is warranted. If a man invites you to come apart from all others, say no. If a man places his hand on you, tell him no and push his hand away. Say no, loudly and definitively, and leave his presence forthwith.

"However, if he does not honor your refusal, if he does not allow you to leave, if he continues his advances, I give you the same instruction Jan and I gave our daughter: Scream and fight. *Kick*, *hit*, and *scratch*, if needed."

Rose's audience of girls sat in stunned silence. Their mothers moved uneasily in their seats. Lucy Thoresen cautiously lifted her hand.

"Yes, Lucy?"

Lucy sat beside Norrie on the back row where the end of the semicircle was not far from Rose. Lucy got slowly to her feet and turned a little so that she faced Rose and most of the women.

"I see now that I had an opportunity to say no the first time . . . the first time that man approached me. He *said* he wanted to show me something in the barn. I could have called Emma to go with me, but . . . but I was curious. I suppose I was also a bit afraid. Afraid to say no, because he was older than me. A grown up. And . . . and later, it was too late. He would not listen."

She twisted a damp hankie in her hands. "Aunt Rose, how do we learn to say no . . . and mean it?"

As soon as she asked, Lucy sat down. She bent her shoulders and head far forward and studied her shoes so that she would not have to watch those around her stare at her.

Rose nodded. She thought and prayed a moment. Nodded again. Then something against the wall to her right caught her eye. She got up and walked to the small spinet piano, placed her hand on it. Stroked its lovely cherry wood. The veneer had cracked; it was no longer glossy and clear. The piano was old, but well used.

"Vera, is this . . . ?"

Vera, at the very back, stood. "Yes, Rose. That is your piano. You gave it to the church when you moved to Denver."

"Oh, my. I . . . I had it shipped here the year I arrived in RiverBend. It was 1881, I believe. It was brand new . . . back then."

"It has been lovingly played many, many times. Thank you again for giving it to us."

"Yes. You are most welcome . . ." Her voice petered out.

She was losing her audience. They fidgeted. A low buzz of whispers began and grew—until Rose's knuckles rapped the top of the piano, recalling them to her.

"Lucy asked an important question. *How do we learn to say no and mean it?*" She scanned the women. Her gaze settled. "Hester Pettersen, would you be so kind as to come here to me?"

A startled and confused Hester shot from her seat and danced from foot to foot. She appeared more inclined to bolt from the room than to walk to Rose. Greta Pettersen whispered to her and patted her hand. Hester swallowed and, with tripping steps, went to Rose.

"Hester, would you please sit down and play us a hymn?"

"What?" Hester reddened. Her head twisted toward her mother. Titters ran through the watching women.

Rose smiled and repeated, "Would you please sit down and play us a hymn?"

"But . . . I am sorry, Mrs. Thoresen, but I don't know how."

"Suppose I showed you. Taught you. Could you then?"

"N-no, I don't think so."

"I see. What would you need to do if you intended to play a hymn as I asked?"

Hester stared at Rose, her brows lifting, comprehension dawning on her child's face. "I-I would need to practice. A lot."

"That is right. You would need to practice." She enfolded Hester in a warm hug, then released her. "You may go now, darling girl. Thank you very much."

The women clapped for Hester. She grinned, bobbed a little curtsy, and fled to her seat. Rose returned to the women who now watched her carefully. She looked directly at Lucy.

"Lucy, to answer your question, you will need to practice your no."

"Oh. But . . ."

"But how?" Rose spoke to them all. "Find yourself a private place. In your prayer closet when you are alone in the house. In the pasture. Down on a creek bank. Out on the prairie. Anywhere you might be free to speak your mind. Say it aloud: *no*. Taste the word and what it means."

She held up her hand to forestall the questions furrowing many foreheads. "Yes, of course, God does not grant anyone a license to be disrespectful or uncharitable of heart, so let us, initially, discuss the ordinary, commonplace circumstances an adult woman may face.

"Since everyday requests require a courteous, respectful response, first, learn to say 'no' civilly: 'No, thank you,' 'No, but thank you for asking,' 'No, I am sorry, but I cannot,' or 'No, not at this time.'

"Next, let us address situations in which a young lady would say no to an adult. She might reply with, 'I would need to ask my parents' permission to do that,' or 'No, I am not allowed to do that.'

"Young ladies, shall we try it? May I suggest that you close your eyes and say aloud, 'No, I am not allowed to do that.' Perhaps you will need to say it more than once. Go ahead now."

She heard low murmurs as the girls repeated the phrase.

Rose nodded. "Very good. In addition, whether young or adult, we will on occasion be asked to do something we believe the Lord does not wish us to do. We may also be asked to agree with something we cannot, in good conscience, agree with. We may feel pressured to say yes to a request, when we mean to say no.

"You should realize that some people dislike it when others deny them or disagree with them. They may ask you, 'Why not?' and demand an explanation. You are not required to justify your response or provide a reason. Remember to let your yes mean yes and your no mean no. Repeat yourself to that person, 'No. I must respectfully decline.'

"And you young ladies should understand that I do not mean for you to say no to your mother or father or to an individual in authority over you, unless—*unless*—what they ask of you verges on sin or compromise. In those occasions, say no, withdraw quickly, and if it is someone trying to draw you into sin or danger, seek a trusted adult such as Pastor or Mrs. Medford immediately."

She let her words settle a moment.

"But of course, we are not here this afternoon to address ordinary circumstances. We are here to teach our girls how to protect themselves. Young ladies, when faced with temptation or danger, use a *strong* no: 'No, I will not.' Out in the pasture, where you are practicing, say it aloud, '*No*. No, I will not.'"

The anointing of the Spirit poured out upon Rose in that moment. She paced along the semicircle, staring into each face as she passed. "Shout it if you must while practicing. Say, '*No, devil!* I choose God, not sin!' Say, '*No!* Do not touch me,' or '*No!* Take your hands off of me!' Say it again and again, until *no* becomes wholly yours, until speaking no to temptation or danger becomes second nature, until you do not hesitate to speak it in time of need."

She returned to her chair but did not sit. "But in your private, alone place, say *yes* to God. Whatever he asks of you, say yes. Train yourselves to answer him aloud, to respond to him quickly, to do what he says when he says it, to do exactly as he says."

She smiled, then chuckled. "What serious expressions I see. Yes, perhaps I have given you overly much in one sitting, so that is all I have this afternoon. Please prayerfully consider my advice. If it agrees with Scripture, I encourage you to put it into action.

"We shall meet again next Sunday at the same time. Shall we close now in prayer and then enjoy a time of fellowship? Let us keep it brief, however. Our nights are growing longer, our evenings descending more quickly, and I do not wish anyone to travel home in the dark."

AS ROSE HAD intimated, the period of fellowship did not last long, for many of the women had come in from their farms. Still, Rose observed Hester and Lucy become the recipients of many hugs and what she hoped were words of encouragement. She had also seen Ava during her message taking copious notes. She was still seated, scribbling in a notebook.

Then she recalled Bekkah and her two daughters. *They do not know you yet, Lord, but I sense a hunger in Bekkah. Please bring her into your glorious kingdom.*

She need not have worried. Bekkah and her girls stood off to the side in deep conversation with Vera and Esther. Bekkah, an arm around each daughter, smiled shyly and nodded.

I see love and healing all around me, Lord. How I thank you.

Rose sighed with contentment. *Yes. Thank you, Lord.*

MEG AND ROSE drove out of town as the sun slowly kissed the horizon. They rode in the quiet of those who are comfortable in each other's company. About halfway home, as the last gleam of daylight plunged below the prairie behind them and disappeared, Meg switched on the automobile's headlamps.

She said, "I'm not believin' I have ever heard anyone preachin' the way you do, Mama Rose."

Rose, who was beginning to nod off, jerked awake. "Hmm? What is that you say, Meg?"

"When you are a-teachin' the Scriptures, you bring them down to us, down to where we be livin'."

She shook her head. "Find an alone place and practice sayin' no to sin and yes to God? Aye, and I never thought on it like that."

"Was it too much, Meg?" Rose asked.

"Too much? Nay, just right, I'm thinkin'. For although m' heart be longin' for you to be speakin' on and on, I fancy m' head couldna hold even a wee dram more."

They were coming up on Brian and Fiona's homestead. As they drew near the road that turned off toward their house, Rose felt a craving rise in her.

"Meg. Meg, please turn. I would dearly love to see Fiona before we go home. Just a moment's visit, I promise."

"Nay a problem, Mama Rose."

She maneuvered the little car up the road and into the McKennies' yard. Martha's husband, Robert, opened the door.

"Miss Rose! Meg! Aye, and won't Martha be that glad to see you. Come. Come in."

Moments later, Martha showed Rose to Fiona's room. "She's bein' in and out, Miss Rose, and in terrible pain. Have a care for her. 'Tis easy to be makin' it worse."

Rose crept into the room and sat on the edge of Fiona's bed, careful not to disturb her friend. She first thought Fiona to be sleeping, but then she opened her eyes. As she recognized Rose, a drowsy smile touched her face.

"S' ye coome t' tuck me in, eh?"

"Aye," Rose answered in Fiona's brogue. "And be layin' a wee kiss g'night on ye, too."

"And right glad o' it I am."

Fiona's hand fumbled for Rose's. As their fingers touched, Rose flinched. She stared down at their joined hands. Rose's hand was wrinkled but pink with health. Fiona's hand had no meat to it. It consisted of pale, dry skin over bones that were altogether too prominent.

When Rose looked up, she realized Fiona had been watching her.

"'Twon't be long now," Fiona whispered. "Soon, I'm thinkin'."

Rose could not speak.

"Told ye afore. 'Twill be glorious on thet day."

"Yes."

"Need I put ye in remembrance o' what ye promised?" Fiona asked.

"No."

"Be sayin' it for me, then, eh?"

"I-I will rejoice for you, Fiona."

"And I will be holdin' ye t' it, m' dear friend."

CHAPTER 20

Rose wakened on Monday as weary as she had been when she retired the night before. "I am tired, Lord. Seems the stress and all the activities of the past two weeks have taken a toll."

She sat up slowly. Put her feet on the floor. As she began to dress, her short conversation with Meg on the way home from the women's meeting came back to her.

While she pulled on her stockings and boots, she prayed, going carefully over every word she had shared at the meeting, hoping she had not crossed any bounds of Scripture . . . or propriety. At the same time, she had to acknowledge she may have overstepped, that elements of what she had taught might have come across as forward, even mildly revolutionary, to this simple, conservative community.

I may hear from Vera that my "straight talk" was a bit too forthright, even for her. It is because I have spent the past thirteen years with young ladies whose hearts were in tatters, whose sensibilities were blunted, and whose souls and minds needed no-nonsense, practical instruction. Not soft, winsome platitudes that cannot be applied to everyday problems.

I suppose I have grown accustomed to delivering the straight-forward teaching of God's word—but I have seen the power of the Gospel shatter bondages and mend brokenness. It is too late in life to change my methods.

Rose sighed. "Ah, well. I spoke only what I believed you spoke, Holy Spirit. If I strayed from your wisdom, will you please mend the fences I crashed into? Thank you."

She combed, braided, and pinned up her hair. Washed her face in the basin beside the dresser. Finally presentable, she made her way to the kitchen and dropped onto a bench at the table.

"Good morn, Mama Rose," Meg called with quiet consideration. "'Tis worn out, I am afeared you are—and no thanks to us."

"Then pour your kindness into a cup for me, darling Meg, for I am in dire need of it."

Meg chuckled and brought Rose her coffee. She sat across from her. "We will be askin' naught of you this day, Mama Rose. Will you be restin' instead? Please?"

Rose brought her face close to her cup and inhaled. Nodded. Put the cup to her lips and drew in her first sip. "I will wake up and feel right soon."

Meg's head snapped around. "Feel right soon? Are you feelin' poorly?"

"I have a little headache. It will not last."

Meg opened her oven door, and a heady scent reached Rose. "My, that smells wonderful. What are you baking, Meg?"

"Muffins. Applesauce, cinnamon, nutmeg, raisins, bits of walnuts. They are just done. May I be bringin' you one?"

"Aye, you may be bringing me two!" Rose laughed. "Goodness, I am as hungry as a horse."

"An, why is't, I ask you?" Meg said. "Is't you were bein' too tired last evenin' to eat supper?"

Rose frowned. "Was I?"

Meg chuckled to herself as she set a steaming muffin on a small plate before Rose. She slid a dish of butter and a jar of preserves toward her. "Aye, that you were. You went to your room to freshen up and were niver a-comin' back. I peeped through the doorway, I did, and you were already abed and fast asleep. Tuckered, I'd say."

Rose blinked several times. "Merciful heavens. I have no memory of doing so."

"Rest t'day, Mama Rose."

"Well. I suppose."

AN HOUR LATER, Meg rang the bell hanging above the back steps, summoning Søren from the barn to breakfast. Rose had not budged from the table while Meg simmered sausages, fried potatoes, and scrambled eggs to round out the muffins.

When Søren joined them at the table, Rose tucked in to her breakfast with an appetite that surprised her. As they finished eating, Meg stood to clear the table. Rose started to get up, but Meg waved her off.

"*Nay*, Mama Rose. I be needin' no help this morn."

"Well, if you are certain."

"Aye, that I am."

A good thing you are, Rose thought. *I have no more energy than I did when I woke.*

"Shall I be bringin' you a fresh cup of coffee for our Bible time, Mama Rose? Søren?"

"Yes, please." Søren reached for their family Bible.

Under her breath, Rose prayed, "Lord? I seem too tired to even answer Meg."

Rest. You will help her soon.

Soon? Rose slowly lowered her fork.

The telephone on the wall jangled.

Rose's heart clenched within her. *Fiona.*

Meg picked up the phone's earpiece. "Hello?"

On the other end an agitated voice spoke rapidly.

"I will come." Meg hung up.

She turned to Rose and Søren. Her words shook. "'Twas Martha. Says Mam won't wake up."

ROSE STOOD BEHIND Meg in the doorway to Fiona's room. Fiona lay curled on her side, eyes closed, her breathing slow but even.

"Have you called the doctor?" Meg asked Martha.

"Yes. He will be here before evening."

"So long a wait?

Martha took Meg's hand. "He can do nothing more for her, Meg."

They moved further into the room, allowing Rose to cross the threshold. Meg and Martha watched Fiona, uncertain of what they should do.

"If I may offer a suggestion?" Rose whispered.

The sisters turned to her. "Please."

"I assisted the nurse who tended Joy's first husband, Grant, near the end of his struggle. Her name was Tabitha. She turned Grant regularly, but she also sat him up with pillows behind his head. It helped him to breathe easier. Perhaps we could sit Fiona against her pillows? Then . . . we can better assess her condition."

"Yes," Martha replied. She seemed glad to have something to do and someone to tell her. "Meg, be helpin' me?"

They turned Fiona's wasted body onto her back while Rose piled up the pillows to support her. Meg and Martha pulled the covers up under her arms. They gently extended Fiona's arms on either side.

"You ken she is breathin' easier, Martha?" Meg asked.

"*Nay*. I canna tell."

Meg bent to her mother. "Mam? Mam, can you hear me? Mam, please wake up."

When Fiona did not answer and her eyes did not flicker, Meg turned to Rose. "Why will she not wake?"

Martha and Meg looked to Rose for an answer.

Rose recalled the Voice that had spoken to her earlier. *You will help her soon.*

"May I have your leave to reach under the covers and feel Fiona's legs, Martha?"

"A'course, if you are needin' to."

Meg nodded her agreement. She lifted the thick covers over Fiona's legs. Rose lowered herself until she knelt beside the bed. She slid her hand under the covers and across the mattress until she encountered the fabric of Fiona's nightgown.

Even through the gown, Fiona's thighs felt cool to the touch. Rose moved her hand down to Fiona's knees, then shins, then feet. The farther down Fiona's legs Rose felt, the cooler they were.

Fiona's feet were stone cold.

With Meg's help, Rose struggled up from her knees.

"Wist?" Martha asked.

Rose beckoned to Martha and Meg and stepped from the room. She closed the door behind them, then slipped Martha's fingers in hers, and Meg's in her other.

"Martha. Meg . . . your mother is dying. She will likely not wake again—but neither will she suffer."

THROUGHOUT THE remainder of the morning and into the afternoon, Fiona declined. Called by Martha's husband, Robert, Fiona's family came. Darra, Rory, and Sean arrived, bringing with them their wives and children—Fiona's grandchildren, including Connor and Esther. Søren came, then Meg and Søren's children and grandchildren, until the house was bursting with family. By twos and threes, they gathered around Fiona's bed to pray for her and say their goodbyes.

Fiona did not stir.

As the sun began to sink, Meg, Martha, and Rose sat beside Fiona's bed. Rose lifted her hands to her face and massaged her forehead. The headache from that morning had not left her. If anything, it was worse.

Perhaps an hour later, Fiona's breathing slowed. They heard it catch and stop. Resume. Catch again.

A small exhale . . .

Meg leaned over Fiona. "Mam? *Mam!*"

She turned to Rose. “Mama Rose?”

“Safe. Safe in the arms of Jesus,” Rose whispered.

Oh, Fiona! I am so glad we stopped to see you last evening. How grateful I am to have seen your smile, to have kissed your cheek one last time. Thank you, Holy Spirit, for putting it in my heart to stop. Yes, I am grateful.

Martha rushed from the room. Meg sank down on the chair, put her face in her hands, and burst into tears. Rose held her and wept with her.

I promised I would rejoice for you, Fiona, my dear friend, and I will honor my promise.

But not today. Today I can only mourn.

THEY BURIED FIONA on Wednesday, but Rose was unable to attend.

She had awakened Tuesday morning with a sore throat, a cough, and a dripping nose. Denying her symptoms, she dressed and stated her intention to help Meg and Martha with the preparations for Fiona’s wake.

They thanked her but would only allow her to sit in Fiona’s kitchen, nursing a cup of tea and watching.

“I am not sick,” Rose protested. “I have, at worst, a tiny cold. Nothing serious.”

Martha put her hands on her hips. “Aye, and we’ll be thankin’ you to be sharin’ your ‘not sick’ elsewhere— no’ in m’ home by touchin’ nor breathin’ on the food.”

“Fiona is my friend. I want to help,” Rose insisted. “Please give me something to do. That cup of tea with honey did the trick. I am *fine* now.”

But she was not.

An hour later, Meg felt her forehead. “*Ach!* Mama Rose, ’tis fevered you are.”

Søren put his foot down. “I am taking you home to bed.”

Rose opened her mouth, then shut it. She was too sick to argue with him.

When Søren and Meg left for Fiona’s burial Wednesday morning, Rose was tossing on her bed, shaking and achingly cold, her fever higher than the day before. When the service was over, Søren drove back to check on Rose. He telephoned the doctor, then telephoned Meg and said he would be staying with Rose. The doctor left a bottle of aspirin with Søren and instructions to give Rose one every four hours until the fever broke.

"I believe it is only a cold," he told Søren, "but we mustn't let it sink into her chest if we can help it."

ON SATURDAY, after spending nearly four days abed, Rose got up, bathed, and dressed. The fever had left her yesterday, and hour by hour, she was regaining her strength. All that remained of her cold was a persistent cough.

Midmorning, she insisted on seeing Fiona's grave.

"Only a brief visit, Søren."

"I don't think it wise yet."

"Please. Will you take me?"

"No."

"Then I shall walk. It is not that far."

Søren glowered at her. "*Fine.* I will take you."

Meg added mittens and a thick woolen scarf to Rose's coat and hat against the cold, blustery day, and Søren, still testy, brought the car around to the back door.

Like the Thoresens, the McKennies had their own little cemetery on their land. Brian and Fiona's graves were side by side, the only two occupants of the family plot.

Meg wept softly on one side of Rose. Søren, on the other side, kept a protective arm wrapped about Rose's shoulders as an added bit of warmth. However, it was not her recent illness that made Rose's knees weak.

She stared with sorrow at the newly turned soil. *Ah, Fiona, my friend. I think the welcome you received in heaven far outshined any poor, paltry sendoff we could devise. Nevertheless, I would have been here to honor you, had my silly body not let me down that day.*

She lifted her eyes to the far vistas of the prairie before her . . . and stared back into the years gone by. She heard Fiona's voice, as clear and as cheerful as the day they met.

"*Sure and 'tis proud we are t' meet ye, Miss Rose; 'tis been hearin' all about ye since Meg coom home last night, and too glad she was of bein' your guest yest'day. We're thankin' ye for your kindness, and would ye be honorin' us by takin' supper wi' us today after service?*"

Oh, Fiona.

That was when she stumbled. Just a little.

Søren caught her easily. "Are you all right, Rose? Shall we return home now?"

"A moment longer, if you please."

She glanced down again. *Lord, it does seem that I have spent more time of late in graveyards talking to those I love than I have otherwise—and I confess, I do not care for the trend, however common it may prove at my age.*

She wheezed out a silent laugh, then stared out at the open prairie around her until Søren spoke. "The wind is sharpening, Rose. Please. Let me get you home before you take a chill."

Home.

"Yes. Thank you."

The outing had taken its toll. Rose was exhausted. Depleted. Without argument, she did whatever Søren and Meg asked of her. She spent that afternoon in their living room, seated before an enormous fire. Meg bundled her up, heated a brick on the stove, wrapped it in a thick towel, and placed it on her chest. While the brick's warmth penetrated to Rose's lungs, Meg brewed a pot of steaming tea, swathed it in a cozy, and set it beside her.

Søren and Meg are so good to me. And, although Joy and my precious grandchildren are not here with us, for some reason this house feels more like home than Palmer House did. Surely more like home than the house Edmund has leased for his family in Chicago will feel initially.

She pondered the 'why' of it. *Strange that I should feel an attachment to this house. I have never lived here, after all.* She studied the cluster of photographs hanging on the wall, away from the stove, photographs that included a wedding portrait of Jan and Elli; another of Jan, Elli, Søren, and Kristen; one of Karl, Amalie, and their children, minus Uli, who had not been born at the time; yet another of Jan and Rose with Joy as a toddler.

Whenever Rose looked up, Jan's familiar face greeted her.

Ah, perhaps that is why. And you poured your love into this home, my darling, did you not?

She stared and stared at the image, waiting for those eyes to twinkle, for that mouth to curve into a gentle smile. But it did not.

She sighed. *Goodness. You were far younger in that photograph than I am now. What would you think if you saw me at this age? Would you still call me 'your' Rose? I hope so.*

She nodded off, woke, sipped on honeyed tea to soothe her throat, and prayed.

SHE STIRRED WHEN a soft whisper asked, "Mama Rose? Are you awake?"

"Yes, Meg."

"Einar has brought Lucy to see you."

Rose perked up. "Oh? I would like that."

Lucy tiptoed into the living room and sat in a chair across from Rose. The silence was awkward between them, although Rose sensed a difference in the girl.

"Are you glad to be at home again, child?"

Lucy nodded. "Yes'm."

"How are things?"

Lucy smiled to herself. "Good."

"Only good?"

"Better than good, I think. Mama and Papa are happy. They smile a lot."

"And your baby sister?"

"Adele is over the moon that I am back, and I am grateful she is safe."

"What else?"

"Emma, Hester, and I are friends again." She snorted. "My brothers are as awful as ever."

"So, things are *normal*, yes?"

Lucy giggled a little. "Yes'm. For me, too. I can sleep at night."

"Praise God Almighty for his goodness," Rose murmured.

Lucy tipped her head a little. "Do you know, I think I *do* praise him more than before. But . . ."

"Hmm?"

"Don't you deserve some credit? You know," and she rolled her eyes, "the way you kept after me."

"*Someone* had to keep after you." Rose laced her reply with just enough acerbic sarcasm to draw a smile from the girl.

"Well, I thought . . . I thought I should thank you for all you did, so . . . so I baked you a pie, like that lady talked about at the meeting? She baked pies for the men who helped her after her husband died. I hope it is all right that I baked one for you?"

Rose sniffed. "A pie. Indeed? Baked it yourself, you say?"

"Yes'm. All by myself."

"Hmm. By yourself. Well, I do not know . . . What kind is it? I am rather particular, you know, little missy."

Lucy muttered under her breath, "Oh, *yes*. I know."

"What was that?"

"Cherry and rhubarb, ma'am—but canned, not fresh. Um, sorry."

Rose chuckled. "Canned is fine, Lucy. It *is* past season for cherries and rhubarb. I shall ask Meg to cut me a great slice of it after dinner. Goodness. Quite makes my mouth water to think on it. Thank you, child."

Lucy sighed with relief. "You were joshing me again, weren't you? You are very clever at putting me on." She hesitated. "And you are not going to die, are you?"

"Die? Not today—God willing. But who filled your head with such nonsense?"

"No one, just . . . just when Grandma Sonja called Mama and told her you had a fever, Mama seemed really upset, and she had us pray for you three mornings in a row. Then she said you were better, but I was still worried."

"Why, Lucy Thoresen. You sound as if you might love this old woman."

She replied, shyness creeping into her voice, "You *are* my Great-Grandmother Amalie's best friend as well as my grandfather's step aunt and I . . . I suppose I have learned to love you."

Rose squeezed Lucy's hand. "And I you, my dear girl."

Lucy, pleased, brushed a kiss across Rose's forehead and departed.

Rose smiled. Chuckled to herself. She slept again, woke, drank tea, read from her Bible, and prayed.

CHAPTER 21

Søren and Meg had waited on Rose hand and foot. They had pampered and fussed over her, had insisted that she rest. By Sunday morning, however, Rose had had quite enough.

"You have taken excellent care of me, especially you, sweet Meg, even while you are grieving the loss of your dear mother. How deeply grateful I am to you both.

"That said, the meeting this afternoon is too important for me to miss it, and I declare that I am fit enough to conduct this meeting. So, please. Do not discourage me from attending worship this morning. I must go and receive strength from the Lord for this day's work."

"We are only concerned for your health, Rose," Søren said.

"I know, Søren, but if the Lord has called me to this, he will sustain me, will he not?"

Meg slid her gaze to Søren and nodded. He blew out a breath, then acquiesced.

"Very well, Rose."

"Church an' the meetin', aye," Meg added. "But, if I be rememberin' correctly, you have an invitation to Sunday dinner today, too? From Patricia Warner Babcock?"

"Oh, dear. I had completely forgotten."

"I will telephone and offer your regrets, Mama Rose."

"I do need to eat," Rose protested.

Søren shook his head. "What you need is to conserve your strength for the meeting."

"Perhaps a nap tis bein' in order this afternoon," Meg supplied.

"But—"

Søren interrupted Rose with, "Mrs. Babcock will understand."

Rose sighed. "Very well, Søren, and thank you for your loving care. You are a good man."

"And you, I think, may have absorbed my papa's obstinacy."

"Why, thank you again, dear. I shall take that as a compliment."

Søren snorted.

ROSE DID NOT croak along with the congregational singing lest she strain her voice, but she let the worship wash over her and soak into her soul. Every song touched her, drew her closer to that heavenly throne. When the last song began, her heart shouted for joy within her.

How awesome you are, O Lord God, King of the Universe! That you would, on my last Sunday in RiverBend, choose the first song I ever heard in this church . . . so many years ago now.

There is a fountain filled with blood,
Drawn from Immanuel's veins
And sinners plunged beneath that flood,
Lose all their guilty stains.

Tears stung Rose's eyes.

Lose all their guilty stains,
Lose all their guilty stains,
And sinners plunged beneath that flood,
Lose all their guilty stains.

The congregation sang the second verse and chorus louder. They lifted their worship higher. In fervor. In grateful praise.

The dying thief rejoiced to see
That fountain in his day;
And there may I, though vile as he,
Wash all my sins away:

Wash all my sins away,
Wash all my sins away,
And there may I, though vile as he,
Wash all my sins away.

Overcome, Rose sank down onto the pew. *Oh, dear Lord, how I thank you! Thank you for your gift of salvation. Thank you for this life you have given me. Let me honor you with all I have left, even if it is little, even if it is not long. I love you and long to serve you.*

NEAR THE END of service, Vera announced the second meeting "for young ladies and their mothers" at three o'clock that afternoon. When she finished, Jacob asked the congregation to keep the McKennie family in prayer as they grieved their loss. Then he dismissed the congregation.

Søren suggested that Rose stay inside where it was warm until the crowd dispersed. He would bring his car up to the door to fetch her. Meg remained with Rose as those around them filed into the center aisle.

Rose overheard excited murmurs and bits of conversation as the congregation shuffled toward the rear doors. *Interest in our meetings has grown*, she thought.

The church did not immediately empty out, however. A number of girls and their mothers wished for a moment with Rose. They lined up in the empty pew ahead of Rose and Meg, reaching across the pew's bench and back to shake her hand and thank her for the previous Sunday afternoon's meeting. Both daughters and mothers had something to say to Rose.

A mother: "Thank you for speaking plainly to us last Sunday, Mrs. Thoresen. Plain talk is good. We hope to hear more this afternoon."

A young girl: "Mrs. Thoresen? I-I told my mama and papa . . . about my cousin. I was afraid to tell them until I heard you talk last week. I feel ever so much better. Like a heavy rock has lifted off my chest. Thank you."

A second mother: "Thank you for teaching me how to answer with a civil no. See, I would get angry trying to say no before. I know now that I don't need to."

A daughter: "I told Lucy I was sorry about what happened to her. She was very happy, and we are going to be friends now. I-I don't have many friends, but I like her a lot. She is brave."

Another mother: "Want t' thank you fer carin' 'bout our girls, ma'am. We been havin' some real good talks since last Sunday."

Yet another mother: "Mrs. Thoresen, I have been saying yes to God all week, and I feel much closer to him for it. Have to say, though, that my young'uns b'lieve I have lost my mind because I have taken to muttering to myself—so they think."

Rose and the woman chuckled together, their shoulders shaking. Even Meg, beside Rose, laughed.

"The Lord bless you," Rose murmured, "and I thank you for a much appreciated hearty laugh."

Then she was face to face with Patricia Babcock and her father. Young Alice hovered in the background.

Patricia took Rose's hand. "We were so very concerned to hear you have been ill, Mrs. Thoresen."

"Thank you. Yes, I caught a bad cold. Quite took me down for most of the week. I do apologize, however, for reneging on our dinner engagement today," Rose murmured. "As it is, I had to coerce my son and daughter-in-law into allowing me to come to service this morning. They insist that I take a nap after dinner today so that I have energy for the meeting this afternoon."

Theo Warner shook Rose's hand, concern marking his features. "I agree with your son and his wife. Please recover soon." He hesitated, "You will still be leaving us this coming Friday?"

"That is my plan, yes."

He slowly shook his head. "We wish you were staying longer. Have a blessed afternoon, Mrs. Thoresen."

When Søren returned to walk Rose and Meg to the car, Rose was greeting the last in line.

"I am grateful to you, Mrs. Thoresen," the girl said. "I-I feel that I can talk to my mother about anything now."

"God bless you, child," Rose murmured. "I realize how hard growing up can be. The Lord will help you to stay close to him and to your mother, if you keep on the way you have begun. You may not perceive it now, but I believe your mother has a wealth of wisdom to share with you."

"Thank you, ma'am. I will keep that in mind."

On the drive home, Meg shook her head. "'Twas God a-workin' in this community last Sunday, Mama Rose. Here I was a-thinkin' that perhaps you had spoken over their heads."

"I had the same fear, Meg."

"Did you?"

"Yes. But now that I see how the Lord has ministered to these young women and their mothers, I am encouraged. We will have another good meeting in a few hours."

"Are you prepared for it?"

"I have had much time this week to sit, study God's word, and pray. I think I am ready. Where I am weak, I trust and believe the Lord will be strong."

"Amen," Meg said.

"Amen," Søren echoed her.

THAT AFTERNOON, the attendees of the previous meeting were joined by an additional nine girls and mothers. Norrie and Greta had again overseen the refreshments. This time they arranged for plenty of cookies and punch to meet the added demand.

The all-female conversation in the fellowship hall gladdened Rose's heart. She heard excitement, laughter, and playful banter, and she sensed loving, joyful freedom behind it.

How good and how pleasant it is, Lord God, she prayed silently. *How good and how pleasant . . . when your children get along.*

As Rose settled into her chair, she found that the semicircle had edged closer to her. A lot closer.

Why, I could reach to my right or left and touch these young ladies waiting with such expectation to receive from you, Lord. And she prayed, *I lean upon you, Lord. Fill my mouth, O God, with your Spirit of wisdom and power.*

Vera opened the meeting in prayer. Rose nodded her thanks.

Then she leaned forward and said softly, as a conspirator might, "This afternoon, I wish to talk about marriage . . . and physical intimacy."

One could have heard the proverbial pin drop.

Rose glanced around the room and observed the whites of rounded eyes. *More wide-eyed wonder here than a paddock full of new calves,* she laughed to herself.

She lifted one brow. "Let me recite the words our Heavenly Father spoke in the book of Genesis.

"*Therefore shall a man*
leave his father and his mother,
and shall cleave unto his wife:
and they shall be one flesh.

"*They shall be one flesh.* Our Creator had a purpose for shaping the bodies of husbands and wives so that they fit together. And he who created us had a reason for placing within us a desire for such intimacy. Why? Because he wished for marriage, the joining of a man and a woman, to be singular and exceptional. Precious. Sacred. You see, God intended physical intimacy to be the 'glue' that binds a husband and a wife together. It is a bond never to be broken except by death.

"That bond between husband and wife is to be a unique experience, one that generates respect and deep trust. It is also the baring of two hearts and souls to only each other. *In the entire world,* only the two of them share such affection and familiarity. I like to think of the intimacy of marriage as a sacred space.

"This sacred space is for you and your husband only, a holy canopy under which the two of you may lie down together. The bond of marriage intimacy is a priceless gift from God. It is not to be spoken of with others; you are not to invite others into it. This is why purity before marriage is so essential."

Rose looked from face to face. "The marriage union extends beyond the marriage bed. When a man and a woman are faithfully bound to each other, every comforting embrace, every special look and smile, and *every tender kiss* takes on that special, sacred bond."

Some of the girls giggled when Rose drew out the words, "every tender kiss."

"Oh? Are you surprised that an old woman such as I can speak of tender kisses? Oh my, yes. Why, I could tell you stories of the tender kisses my beloved husband, Jan, placed upon my brow, my cheeks, and my lips while we were married—"

The titters became pronounced laughter, and Rose broke off, smiling and laughing with the girls and their mothers.

"See? Even an old woman can hold to cherished memories of a good and godly marriage. But I will go no further because the rest is sacred, do you see? Only for me and my husband."

She continued. "Let us be frank at this juncture. I admit to having painted a rosy picture of marriage, for even a godly marriage can be difficult and challenging. Last Sunday I said that life was hard, that we will face many storms, and that is true. However, within a good marriage—a godly marriage—a husband and wife will face those storms together, and they will overcome them together.

"I say 'a godly marriage,' because when our Heavenly Father is Lord over a husband and wife, it is no longer with just human strength that they fight battles and face hardship. The Lord is with them, twined within their marriage, uniting them and adding his strength to theirs. Scripture tells us plainly, *a threefold cord is not quickly broken*."

Rose folded her hands and sought the eyes of the young women in the meeting. "I speak now to all of our young women, those who are not yet married. Your choice of husband is important. No, it is *critical*, critical to your physical, emotional, and spiritual well-being. Critical to the children you will bear."

She had their attention, and she pressed her advantage. "Young ladies, have you received Christ as your Savior? Have you proclaimed before all that he is the Lord and Master of your life? Have you given yourself wholly to him? Have you declared this publicly?"

She looked around. "Have you?"

Several girls nodded. Some, instead, shifted their gaze aside.

"Please look at me. Pay close attention to what I am about to say."

Every eye turned to Rose. "*Do not* marry a man who has not surrendered and committed his entire being to Christ."

She waited. No one moved. Not a sound disturbed the silence in that room until Rose spoke again.

"Young ladies, the Lord God commands you not to yoke yourselves to an unbeliever. *For what fellowship hath righteousness with unrighteousness? and what communion hath light with darkness? And what concord hath Christ with Belial? or what part hath he that believeth with an infidel?*

"Young ladies, your bodies are the temples of the living God, and he has said to you, *I will dwell in them, and walk in them; and I will be their God, and they shall be my people.* You must come apart from ungodly gentlemen callers. You must separate yourself from potential spouses who do not honor Christ Jesus as you do, from any man who will not be a godly leader of the home or a godly example to your children.

"It is your duty to probe the commitment of a prospective suitor, to ask him to articulate his faith in Christ *and to demonstrate it.* Do not satisfy yourself with a glib answer. Look into his life—not for a day, a week, or a month, but for the years he has walked with Christ. You do not want to marry a new or infant Christian, one who is not ready to lead a family. You want a man with a godly reputation, a man who has grown into mature faith."

She again scanned the faces hanging on her words. "Has God made himself clear in this matter?"

A murmured yes rustled through the room.

"Good. But perhaps I should rephrase what I have said and provide a warning to those of you who are struggling to accept this word. If you are not yet married, it is not too late to right your situation.

"*This is my warning*: You know the Lord's will concerning marriage. If you allow your feelings for a man to overrule the Lord's command, please understand that you have chosen the sin of idolatry."

Rose heard a startled gasp and a sob, but she did not turn toward it.

Instead, she whispered within herself, *O Holy God! Bring your conviction where it is needed, "For godly sorrow worketh repentance not to be repented of," a turning to God that not one woman here today will later regret. Have your way, your full and complete will, in these young lives.*

She continued, "Dear ones, among us this afternoon are those who have not yet committed themselves to Christ. If this is you, if you have not yet trusted Jesus for your salvation, I have wonderful news for you. You may, this very day, be born again. Right now, if you lift your hand, we will come and pray with you to surrender your life to the Savior."

Rose heard weeping. She saw Bekkah's hand shoot into the air. Her daughters, too, responded. And there, a young woman lifted her hand. And another.

The sweet Spirit of Holiness descended upon the room. Those who knew the Lord slipped from their chairs to their knees in prayer.

Vera, Meg, Esther, Ava, and other mature women went to those who had raised their hands. They knelt with them and led them in prayers of repentance and surrender.

Rose bowed her head. *I thank you, Lord, for the great and awesome privilege of serving you.*

CHAPTER 22

Rose woke in the morning thinking, *My time in RiverBend is almost done. I leave on Friday. I cannot waste a minute of the time I have left.* She dressed and did her hair quickly.

Meg and Søren had been up for some time. Meg was kneading bread dough when Rose reached for the coffee pot.

"Good morn, Mama Rose. Feeling rested?"

Rose hugged Meg's waist. "Good morning, Meg. Yes, I am feeling well. I do believe I am on the far side of that nasty cold, thank the Lord."

Rose walked to the window to sip her coffee and check the weather. She glanced at the thermometer fastened just outside the window. It already read 51 degrees.

Meg spoke from the counter where she worked the dough. "Warmer this morn. Tis hopin' for a bit of Indian summer, we are."

"I will be glad of it. Perhaps I will walk over to my old house again this afternoon. But first? What can I help with?"

Rose and Meg, working in contented companionship, shaped a half-dozen loaves and put them in pans to rise. Then Rose set herself to peeling apples for a pie while Meg started breakfast.

Meg said softly, "'Tis comfortin' havin' you with us, Mama Rose."

"I miss her, too, Meg," Rose whispered, "but I know your loss is greater than mine. I know it is hard."

"Aye. 'Tis a sharpish pain in my heart that does not pass. When I am forgettin' for a bit, and remember again, 'tis like losing her anew. Over and over."

Rose dried her hands and went to Meg's side. "I am so sorry, Meg."

Meg laid her cheek on Rose's shoulder and sobbed.

"There, there, child," Rose crooned. "Lean on me. I will mingle my tears with yours. We will weep together, dear Meg."

"I am being ever so glad you are here," Meg said through her tears. "Such a terrible lonely I feel."

"I understand, Meg. I know. I am glad I am here, too."

Meg sniffled and wiped her eyes on her apron. "And I am reminded to thank you for asking to stop and visit Mam last Sunday, after the meetin'. 'Twas the last time Mam and I spoke. Oh, what if we had not turned in at their road?"

Rose grew thoughtful. "It had to have been the prompting of the Holy Spirit, Meg. I had taken no thought of Fiona before or during the meeting. Only when we came close to her house did I feel the sudden urge to see her."

She looked at Meg. "What did she say to you, Meg?"

Meg smiled wistfully. "That she was proud of me. That she loved me and mine. That Jesus was a-callin' her."

Rose shook her head and sighed. "We cannot ignore his call, can we? If he calls us to go, we go. If he calls us to stay, we stay. *For I am in a strait betwixt two, having a desire to depart, and to be with Christ; which is far better: Nevertheless to abide in the flesh is more needful for you.*"

Meg stared into Rose's face. "Many of us still be needin' you, Mama Rose. Fair to frightened out of ourn wits we were when you took sick. We canna be losin' you, too."

Rose tried to smile. "I thank you for the love you have poured on me. I know that it is not my time. Not yet. I . . . I have much more to do."

THE DAY WARMED nicely. Rose helped Meg clean up following the noon meal, then made the pie she had peeled apples for. Afterward, Rose put on her coat and set out for her house. She carried the same basket with her, having dutifully packed, in addition to a jar of warm tea, a blanket Meg insisted she take with her. She took her time, pausing often, not because she was tired and recovering from a cold, but because she wanted to take in and savor every bit of the scenes around her.

I want to capture this day, this moment, and hold it fast in my memories, for I may never come this way again . . . except in my heart.

Rose stopped on the bridge and studied her house from afar. *What happy times we shared, Jan and I. And I would not trade what we had for anything, even though from the beginning we both knew I would outlive him.*

She reached the house, climbed the steps, and found the inside of the house cooler than the outside. Instead of kindling a fire in Amalie's old stove, Rose chose to sit outside where she could enjoy the view.

She dragged the old rocker from its corner, wiped it down with her hankie, and maneuvered its complaining bones through the front door, onto the porch.

"Much better. Now my tea—and the blanket, lest Meg demand to know if I used it when I did not."

She lowered herself onto the rocker, pulled the blanket over her knees, poured tea into her tin cup, and lifted the cup to her lips. "Perfect, Lord. I have all afternoon to commit this panorama to memory."

She finished the tea, set the cup on the porch, stretched a little, then pushed the rocker forward and back at a nice, sedate pace.

Craaaack. Rose stopped the chair's motion, but something below her groaned, and she felt an ominous wobble on the chair's right side.

"Well, of course it is broken. No one would have abandoned a perfectly fine chair." She sniffed. "Perhaps if I sit completely still, I will not end up kissing the porch with my backside."

She did sit still. Her eyes roamed hungrily down the slope to the creek, across to the fields Jan and Søren had plowed and planted together, to the prairie in the distance. . . to . . .

A TRUCK DOOR slammed, and Rose jerked upright. Then she heard giggling.

"You were sleeping," a man's familiar voice said. "I'm right sorry we awakened you. Should have telephoned you this morning at Søren and Meg's to ask if we could come."

Rose rubbed her eyes. "Hmm?"

Einar appeared in her bleary vision. "Are you all right. Aunt Rose?"

Rose laughed softly. "What time is it?"

"Quarter to four."

"Gracious sakes! I have been asleep for hours."

"Well, I apologize again," he jerked a thumb toward his truck, "but this gaggle of giggling girls pleaded for me to drive them over to Meg and Søren's—to see you. When we were coming down the incline, Lucy said she saw you over here and pointed you out, so we came here instead."

Einar pulled off his hat, scratched his head. Frowned at the house. "Didn't realize this old heap was still standing."

"That is what *some* people are beginning to say about me."

Rose's tart response set the girls to tittering again, and they inched toward the porch. Einar flushed but did not reply.

Rose took stock of her visitors: Emma. Hester. Lucy. And Lucy's new friend. The girl who, after church, said Lucy was brave.

Lucy plunked down on the step closest to Rose. "Aunt Rose? I told Emma and Hester how we played at being homesteaders inside your old house. Made a fire and drank tea together while you told me stories about when you first lived here.

"Then we told Trudy—pardon me, Aunt Rose, this is my new friend, Trudy—and we . . . well, we were going to ask if you would invite all of us inside to do the same."

Lucy looked up at Rose with a hopeful expression. "I brought the cookies this time?"

"Is that a question, little missy?"

Lucy ducked her head and grinned. Rose grinned back.

"You may leave them with me, Einar."

"Are you sure? When should I come back for them?"

"Am I sure when you should come back for them? You haven't *said* when you are returning, therefore, I doubt that I have the ability or foresight to ascertain when that will be."

Lucy covered her mouth and snickered into her hand.

Rose's lips twitched.

Einar blinked, then slowly dragged on his hat. He wagged his head side to side in ponderous disapproval. "Oh, I see how it is now, *Aunt* Rose. You're no better than they are! In fact, I'm beginning to believe that you deserve these young hooligans."

"Why, yes, I believe I do," Rose said airily, rising to her feet. "Leave them with me, and they will shortly out-hooligan the worst hooligans on record in this county. Come, girls. We have a fire to start. And cookies to gobble."

Rose would have sailed regally through the front door at that point—except that the old rocking chair, having audibly cracked under her weight earlier (giving warning of its imminent expiration), chose at the moment she stood up to let loose the broken leg from under the seat. The other leg on that side having previously gone missing, the chair listed severely to starboard . . . and fell over into a splintered heap.

Rose waved her hand. "Pick up those dead, dry bones and bring them along, girls. We shall set a sacrificial fire, confer proper honors upon the remains, and burn them up—after we have checked the stove for snakes."

CHAPTER 23

Rose slept late Tuesday morning. Even with an added hour of sleep, she felt tired. *Goodness, I could count on one hand the instances I have overslept in the past decade.*

As she yawned over her coffee, her thoughts wandered, falling into prayer. *My body may be weary, Lord, but I am beyond grateful for what you have done for Lucy and for her family.*

She smiled into her cup. *Today, if Meg can get away, I will treat her to lunch at Esther's little café in town.*

Halfway through Rose's second cup, Meg opened the back door and walked inside, her apron cradling fresh eggs. "Good morn, Mama Rose. Are you rested?"

At the same moment, Rose remembered the boxes she and Joy had stored in the attic of her house. "Oh!"

"Eh?"

Rose laughed. "I am sorry, but at the very instant you said good morning, I recalled something I should do while I am here."

Meg began transferring the eggs to a thick towel on the countertop. She would rinse and dry them before storing them in the cellar. "May I help?"

"I believe I will need Søren and a ladder for this task. I stored a few boxes in the attic of my house before I moved to Corinth with Joy. I would ask him to bring them down for me to sort through. If I can finish by noon, I wondered if you might care to have lunch with me in town?"

"Aye, that I would! Sech a treat. We can be askin' Søren at breakfast if he would fetch the boxes down for you."

DIRECTLY FOLLOWING breakfast and devotions, Meg and Rose donned coats and boots to walk to Rose's house across the creek. Søren stayed behind and finished a few tasks, then loaded a folding ladder, some tools, and some firewood into the farm truck.

Rose and Meg had a fire going in the stove when he arrived. They helped him carry in the tools and firewood while he toted the ladder up the steps and into the house.

He glanced around, his eyes lighting on the old stove. "Why, that is my mother's stove, isn't it? Sure brings back lots of memories."

Rose smiled at Meg. Meg smiled back and said, "Aye, the one she was bringin' with her from Norway. It should be protected, shouldn't it? Taken care of. I will be askin' 'round in the family. 'Tis hopin' someone will see the value in it."

Søren thought briefly. "We don't really have a place for it ourselves."

"I was thinking . . ." Rose said quietly. "That stove was as much Amalie's as Elli's."

"She did cook on it for more than a decade," Søren agreed, "until Karl finished his house and she moved in with him and Sonja."

"As Amalie's namesake, Lucy may be willing to care for it. She has her own memories attached to it now, memories that, I hope, will grow more precious as she matures. And Karl might wish to help her restore it."

"I like that idea," Søren said. "I think Karl will, too."

He again looked around the empty house. "I remember before you and Papa married, before he built on the bedrooms, it was just this space here. Was it Thanksgiving evening? It felt like half the county was invited, and we were packed into your house like sardines. You and Mrs. Medford served dessert and punch, and then Mrs. Medford played your piano."

His gaze seemed focused far away. "I have never since felt the presence of God as I did that evening while we sang and worshipped together."

"Oh." Rose's heart squeezed and, unbidden, tears stung her eyes. "Yes. I remember, too."

"And I," Meg sniffed. "'Twas a blessed, holy night. It grieves me heart sometimes that we canna go back. And we have lost s'many loved ones since then."

Søren swept his sleeve across his eyes. "We can only go forward, forging on . . . until we meet them again in heaven."

Forging on, Rose repeated to herself.

Søren exhaled. "Let's get those boxes down for you, shall we?"

"Yes, please."

Søren unfolded the ladder. He climbed up to the trapdoor and pushed the hinged door up and over. When his eyes had adjusted to the dark, he said, "I see two boxes in a corner. I'll fetch them."

To the accompaniment of poofs of dust sifting down from the trapdoor, Rose and Meg heard him carefully make his way across the old and unreliable attic floor and drag the boxes toward the trapdoor.

Amid a veritable shower of dust and dirt, Søren climbed back onto the ladder, reached up and grabbed the first box, and handed it to Meg. She set it on the floor and received the second one. She placed it on the floor, too.

Although the boxes were filthy, the lids were tacked on tight, and Rose saw no evidence of water damage. She and Meg wiped down the boxes with rags and moved them closer to the stove, away from the tailings of dust and grime.

"Let me pry these open for you," Søren said.

As he did, Meg asked, "Would you be likin' me to stay while you open these, Mama Rose?"

"Thank you, Meg, but I believe I will be fine. I will walk home afterward and change my dress for our outing."

After they left, Rose placed a box on one of the rickety kitchen chairs. She sat down on the other chair and pulled the first toward her until the chairs faced each other, the box before her. She lifted the lid and carefully folded back the brown paper that lined the box.

The box contained memorabilia from Joy's childhood, and Rose sighed with contentment. One by one, she took the items in her hands and studied them.

Joy's earliest doll, a stuffed fabric caricature sporting thin strips of fabric for hair and with eyes, nose, and mouth Rose had stitched onto its face. Rose had even knitted the doll yellow shoes, adding straps that Joy could button to fasten the shoes onto "Molly's" stuffed feet.

How Joy loved this doll.

The doll's pretty dress had been one of Joy's baby dresses.

"I cut that dress down to size after I scorched a hole the size of my hand in it," Rose muttered. "No, Jan, I was never very good at ironing."

Joy's favorite blanket was next, a small quilt Rose had made for her and faced with a yard of velvet saved from an old skirt. A tiny pillow to match. Both blanket and pillow were rubbed bare in spots.

She would lay on this blanket and stroke its softness while she fell asleep. So often did she do this that she wore the velvet right down to the nub.

Beneath the blanket and pillow was a pull toy, a fancy train Jan had carved for Joy's second Christmas. She was walking and running by then and delighted in drawing the engine and its two cars and caboose behind her in a route that often began at Jan's chair, skirted the perimeter of the living room, into the kitchen, around the table, and back.

The engine made a soft but satisfying *clack* with each rotation of its wheels. Joy loved the sound, copying it under her breath as she pulled the train.

The last item in the box was a cloth sack nestled into a bottom corner. Rose removed it, undid its drawstring, and pulled out Joy's first pair of "dress" shoes. The shiny black patent leather had dried and was cracked and peeling, but Rose only saw them as they were the first time Joy wore them.

She closed her eyes and let the vivid scene play in her mind—Jan in his best suit, standing in the doorway of the church. Joy clutching his finger while trotting proudly up the aisle with him. Joy stopping every few steps to bend over and study the shiny black shoes on her feet. So excited to see her big brother Søren, already seated in the pew. Climbing onto his lap to display her new shoes, asking if he liked them.

Søren's face lit with the same pleasure Joy exuded. He whispered to Joy, "They are *bee-u-tee-ful*, Joy, and you are the prettiest little sister ever."

Happiness bubbled up in Rose's heart, and she laughed aloud. *Lord, thank you. Thank you for these precious, precious keepsakes!*

A moment later, she added, *Yes, Meg, it grieves me as it does you that we can never go back to those times, so I must take what Søren said to heart. We can only go forward. We must forge on. "I must work the works of him that sent me, while it is day: the night cometh, when no man can work." I will continue to do what God has called me to . . . until we all meet again in heaven.*

She sighed, smiled, and carefully repacked the box.

I wish I had remembered about these boxes before Joy and Edmund left. No matter. I will bring Joy's things along with me when I leave for Chicago—and I care not at what cost.

She moved the box to the floor and lifted the second box onto her makeshift table. The box was half as deep as the first, and another box, made from pasteboard, rested within, taking up half the space. She lifted it out, knowing already what was in it. When she unfastened the lid, the contents within were no surprise.

The photograph of her and James on their wedding. Rose peered deeply at herself. *Who was this girl? I do not recognize her*. She looked just as deeply at James. *I do not know you either, James. It has been too long.*

She spotted a framed picture of herself and James with Jeffrey and Glory, taken before Clara was born. No photograph of Clara had been taken before she died.

We had planned to have a photographer in when she had her next birthday, but . . .

Beneath was an even older photograph of her mother and father, a little girl at her mother's side and a smaller boy on her father's knee.

Tom, my little brother. I will see you again, too.

The other things in the pasteboard box were small toys and trinkets special to her children, pictures they had drawn or painted with water-colors, and a favorite book she had read to them at bedtime. She shook her head, put their things back into the box, fastened its lid, and wondered what to do with the box and its contents.

There is no one left alive who remembers James or our children except me. No one who could take my children's things out and look at them and recall with love who had owned them so many years ago.

She reopened the box, removed the photographs, and set them aside to take with her. Then, one piece at a time, she fed the remaining bits into the stove: the toys and trinkets, the little art projects, the book.

As she did, she prayed, *O Lord God, they have been with you for forty-two years now, this family I lost. You healed my wounds of grief by your love and your many blessings. When I see Jeffrey, Glory, and Clara again, it will be a day of rejoicing in your presence. But until then . . .*

Last of all, she tore the pasteboard apart and fed it to the fire, then opened the first box and placed the photographs she had saved atop Joy's childhood things.

I will give the photographs to Joy; perhaps she will want the picture of her brother and sister, although she never knew them.

Tucked into the other side of the box was one of Jan's favorite shirts. The fabric was a soft woolen flannel in blues and blacks.

I never told him, but the blue in this shirt matched the rich hue of his eyes. Blue, the color of the sky—the color of my world. I loved seeing him in this shirt. She tried to pick up the shirt, only to realize she had wrapped some-thing in it. Her fingers traced the edges of a book, perhaps two books. With both hands on the bundle, she pulled it out, and placed it on her lap.

Jan's scent reached out to her from the shirt's folds, shocking her as it slammed into her senses.

"Oh! Oh, my love!" Rose sobbed. She held the bundle to her face and breathed him in.

When she stopped shaking, she set the bundle back in her lap and unfolded the worn, supple fabric. What she uncovered were Jan's Bibles, one in Riksmål and one in English. His scent clung to the covers and pages of them, and Rose pressed them to her heart.

"Thank you, Lord. Thank you for this unexpected gift."

The edge of a sheet of paper slipped from the pages of the Riksmål Bible. Rose gently tugged it free and unfolded it.

A letter.

In Jan's careful script, she read the salutation: *Min kjære Elli.*

She knew the meaning of those words, what they said.

"My dearest, my darling Elli," Rose repeated aloud.

She found it hard to breathe.

Then she chastened herself for her reaction. *This letter was not intended for you, Rose. It was private—from Jan to Elli. And it is, no doubt, old—from long before you knew him, back when you loved James and were married to him. There is no justification for this petty . . .*

Petty what? Was it jealousy?

"Stop it. I will give the letter to Søren. No doubt, he will cherish it."

She intended to fold it up right then, but an itching in her heart wanted to know *when* Jan had written it.

Her eyes sought the date in the upper right-hand corner.

June 1882.

Rose's heart thudded in her throat. *Not before Elli passed away. Not years before I arrived in RiverBend. Not before we fell in love . . . but in June.*

A month before we married.

She scanned the letter. It was not long, only a few paragraphs. She could make no sense of it other than the date and salutation.

June 1882. *My darling Elli.*

Rose refolded the letter and, with slow, unflinching resolve, placed it inside the back cover of Jan's Riksmål Bible.

It is Søren's now.

Telling herself to let it go and determining to distract herself, she paged through the Bible. In many of the margins, Jan's careful hand had added notes and cross references. She could not read those, either.

She opened his English Bible and saw the same thing—copious notes, in English, not Riksmål. Her paging stopped at Proverbs 31; her fingers traced verse 10.

Who can find a virtuous woman?
for her price is far above rubies.

There, in the margin, were the words, "Twice blessed."

See? she told herself. *He had a life before he met me, just as I had a life before I met him. Marriage is until "death do we part." He loved Elli until she passed away. She died long before he loved me.*

But the letter's date and salutation were already burned into her heart: June 1882. *My darling Elli.*

She shook herself again. *These Bibles are treasures Søren should have—they are part of Jan's legacy to him and to his descendants. Søren will pass them down to Markus, and Markus will leave them to his son, Nils, and Nils to his son after him.*

She couldn't hold back a slow smile. *Another Søren to honor his grandpa, according to our Nils.*

She rewrapped the Bibles in Jan's shirt and placed them atop the first box. She did not need the smaller box and left it by the stove. She closed the stove's damper, picked up the first box and Jan's Bibles, and set off for Søren and Meg's house.

She was puffing when she finally arrived, and her arms ached from carrying the load, but she had made it.

"Mama Rose! I could have come to fetch you in the car," Meg protested.

"No matter. I am here now." Rose set the Bibles on the kitchen table and unwrapped them, then took the box and Jan's shirt to her room. When she came out, Meg was fixing Søren's lunch.

"I'll be ready to go as soon as I am done here, Mama Rose."

"Oh, yes. Let me clean up a bit." She returned to her room, changed into a fresh dress, and recombed and pinned her hair.

When she returned to the kitchen, Søren was sitting at the table, going through one of the Bibles.

"You found Papa's Bibles? They were in one of the boxes?"

"Yes, wrapped in one of his favorite shirts. I have been looking through them, his Bibles, I mean. The margins are filled with his notes. I thought that you should have them."

"Rose, thank you. I-I am most grateful to have them."

Rose cleared the knot from her throat. "Søren, I also found a letter in one of them, the Riksmål Bible. It is from Jan to your mother. It is between the last page and the back cover."

Søren slowly opened the book. He found the letter where she said it would be, and unfolded it, scanned the first lines, then looked up to Rose.

"I don't understand. It was written long after Mama died. Ten years after."

Rose nodded. As hard as she tried, the letter's date stuck like a burr to her. "I saw that."

Søren seemed to suddenly realize Rose's distress. He looked again at the letter. "June 1882. You and Papa married . . ."

"The next month," Rose murmured, "a few weeks after this letter was written."

Meg looked from Søren to Rose. Concerned, she turned back to Søren. Søren was still poring over the letter. He glanced up, frustrated. "My Riksmål has suffered over the years. I understand it and sometimes speak it, but I rarely read it. I'm making a hash of this, but I'll work my way through it yet."

Rose just nodded.

Jan? Did you not love me as much as you said you did? Were you still longing for Elli on the cusp of our wedding?

She wanted to run and hide the pain growing under her breastbone—but run where? The room she slept in was not really hers, and its walls would not conceal the grief welling in her heart.

Oh, Jan. Was I but a poor substitute for Elli?

At the same time, everything within her denied that possibility.

No. How can I believe this of you? You were a faithful, dedicated, self-sacrificing husband. I saw your love in your eyes, in your smile, in your touch, in our fellowship with our God—for twenty-seven years.

Meg's face reflected her distress for Rose. "May I fix you a cup of tea, Mama Rose?"

"Thank you. That would be . . . helpful."

Søren grabbed his Bible from the end of the table and pulled a sheet of paper from it. He began writing on it, referring to the letter, then writing further. At one point, he crossed out what he had written and scribbled something else. Finally, he silently read what he had written and nodded his approval.

Søren seemed subdued. A little emotional. "I think I have the translation now. I will read it in English."

Rose did not want to hear it. "I will be in my room when you are ready to leave, Meg."

Søren shook his head. Gently placed his hand on Rose's. "Please don't go, Rose. I think . . . I think you should hear this."

Rose pulled her fingers from his and wrapped them around her cup of tea. Stared down at it.

I should want to hear Jan profess his love for Elli? her peevish flesh sniffed.

Then her spirit spoke a chastening to her. *If you were sixty years younger, Rose Thoresen, I would call you a petulant twit. Now, stop being a silly ninny.*

Søren cleared his throat and read aloud.

My darling Elli,

You have been gone now for ten years. Ten years. It is hard to believe. While we were married, I loved you with all my heart. You were *my heart, Elli, but then our Lord took you home.*

I grieved for a long time after you left. I was a whole man no more, dear one, because I believed you had taken my heart to heaven with you. I struggled even to be a good father to our son and a good example to Karl's sons until our Lord, in his love, dealt with me. He asked me to be a father to the fatherless, to take to myself young men who needed a godly example. It was difficult, putting away my sorrow that I might ease the pain and burdens of others. It was difficult, but it was good. Slowly, I began to live again.

Then our great God, in his wisdom, sent someone to me. Her name is Rose. She is not a Viking queen as you were, in fact, she is slight of stature. However, I have watched her blossom on this prairie, and her faith in God and her courage are splendid. I tell you this, because my heart has begun to beat again. Yes, she has brought it back to life.

Elli, I will see you in heaven, and Rose will see the husband she has lost. I do not know how relationships will work then, but Scripture tells us that in God's great kingdom, the only marriage will be that of his bride, the church, with the Lamb, our Savior Jesus. And he has promised to wipe away all of our tears.

Until then,

Jan

Rose sobbed into her hands. She could not help it.

Oh, Jan. I am sorry. How utterly foolish of me.

Distraction.

Yes, Lord. I allowed myself to be confounded when I should have known better. I am sorry.

Søren knelt by Rose and wrapped his arms around her. "I don't know if I have ever properly told you how important to this family you are, Rose. You were the piece that perfectly filled the hole in my father's heart. You brought my papa back to life—for all of us."

Rose clung to Søren and wept on his shoulder. Meg, too, wrapped her arms around Rose.

"I still miss him," Rose confessed. "Every day, I miss him—and I often long to be here, to be home. Sometimes . . . sometimes I cannot bear it, being away from here, from the prairie."

"We know. We feel your loss," Søren whispered, "but, in every way, you have made us so very proud, and we will always love you. If . . . if you ever wanted to come back to RiverBend, Meg and I would be honored for you to live with us."

Rose was overcome by their generosity. "I-I cherish your invitation, Søren . . . and I thank you, but . . ."

Meg finished Rose's thought. "But you are havin' Joy and your grandsons and wee baby Roseanne to love and care for."

"Yes. That is it. Perhaps, someday, it will be time for me to come back, but for the foreseeable future, I must go to Joy and Edmund and help them raise their children."

Søren kissed her cheek. "We understand, Mama."

Rose lifted her face and stared at Søren. "Søren? You just called me Mama. You have always called me Rose."

Søren nodded, slowly. "Is it all right that I do?"

"But . . . but your mother, Elli . . ."

"Has been gone to heaven since I was a youngster, a boy barely in his teens. I had Aunt Amalie as I grew to adulthood, and she was wonderful, but no one can replace a mother . . . only, sadly, I can hardly remember Mama now. And then, when I was in my early twenties, Papa married *you*. You never tried to mother me. You understood that I was a man and did not need to be mothered, but that did not prevent you from being a true friend to me. And you have remained so through the years since.

"Rose, I am in my sixties now, a grandfather many times over. Yet, whether you or I realized it, you grew a place in my heart. You were my father's faithful wife, the mother of my sister, Joy. *You* have been my mama for a long time."

Tears stood in Søren's eyes. "Please. Let me call you Mama. Let me be your son."

"Oh, Søren! *Yes*. Yes, you are my dear son. Yes."

THE TIME BEING too late for Rose and Meg to go to town for lunch, they passed the remainder of the day at a slow, gentle tempo until late afternoon. Rose retired to her room and sorted her clothes, aware she needed to wash a few items before she packed them.

Through her closed bedroom door, she heard an unaccustomed sound. It took her a moment to recognize it as a knock on the front door.

Not the kitchen door, but the living room door.

No one uses that entrance, Rose thought. *Mercy. I suppose I had forgotten it was there.*

Stranger still was the expression on Meg's face when she called at Rose's bedroom door and Rose opened to her.

"Why, Meg. What is it?"

"You . . . you be havin' a caller, Mama Rose." Meg's brows were arched so high, Rose wondered if they might disappear into her hairline.

"I have a caller?"

"Yis'm. Waiting on you in the living room."

"Who is it, Meg?"

But Meg, shaking her head, withdrew to the kitchen.

Rose walked slowly into the living room with no idea of who would be waiting for her.

She was astonished to find that it was Theo Warner. He stood beside the stove, studying the wall of family photos. When he turned, Rose saw what he held in one arm. A pot of flowers—lilies—and she caught the heady scent of them. Under the other arm she spied a large box of chocolates.

Rose felt her face heat.

He noticed her embarrassment. "Mrs. Thoresen, please forgive me for not asking your permission to call first. I . . . that is, you are leaving Friday, and I could not allow you to go away without first speaking my heart to you."

Good heavens!

Rose's tongue was stuck. She had to swallow twice before she could speak. While she worked to moisten her mouth, she studied the man. His thick salt-and-pepper hair was freshly trimmed and brushed, his shoes gleamed with polish, his fine suit was pressed, the tie at the throat of his *perfectly* starched shirt was *perfectly* tied.

And he is, she thought, *at least ten years younger than I am.*

Finally, she croaked, "I beg your pardon?"

"May we sit?"

"Oh. Certainly. I apologize for my lack of hospitality."

"It is I who should apologize. I did not telephone ahead to ask if I might call on you. I simply had to see you today."

He placed the pot of lilies and chocolates on the table between them. "I should back up a few weeks. You see, we moved to the area after you left, so when you returned and the community seemed in an uproar to fête you, I determined to see you for myself. When you gave that speech at the luncheon, I was struck by your qualities—your godly manner, your knowledge of Scripture, your family's good name and reputation. I thought you had everything I was searching for in a woman. A wife."

Rose began to shake her head, but he said quietly, "As much as I regret the acknowledgment, I know you are not for me, Mrs. Thoresen. While you might have what I am seeking in a mate, you are not seeking at all. You have a daughter and grandchildren waiting for you in Chicago. Your life is full and fixed."

Rose nodded. "Yes."

"That being said, I want you to know how very highly my daughter, Patricia, esteems you—something of an accomplishment in itself—and that she and I are in agreement: You are a remarkable woman. I had hoped, if you came to dinner on Sunday, that we might get to know one another better, that I might show you what I could offer you, and if all went well, approach you with the possibility of pursuing my suit. However, I have given up on that."

Rose's relief was palpable, and he tipped his head toward her and chuckled.

"At my age, Mrs. Thoresen, I can't afford to waste any time."

"Ah," Rose murmured.

She relaxed further. *Whatever this is, I need no longer fear him going down on one knee. Merciful heavens, I have not the stamina to witness that.*

"Well, in preparation for dinner on Sunday, I telephoned Columbus and ordered the flowers from a hothouse and the candies from a chocolatier. Had them sent by train. They came in on Saturday, and when you were unable to come to dinner, I hated to waste them."

"I am still terribly sorry to have cancelled at the last minute, Mr. Warner."

He waved away Rose's apology. "Please call me Theo. Everyone does. And don't worry about the cancellation. When we saw you Sunday morning, it was apparent that you weren't tip-top. You did have the afternoon meeting ahead of you, too."

He hesitated. "I suppose that is the real reason I called on you today. To thank you for that meeting."

"To thank me?"

"Yes, to thank you. My daughter, Mrs. Thoresen, has always professed her church membership, but she has never professed Christ. She and Alice came home from that meeting changed. Patricia said she finally understood salvation. Said she had avoided it, gone around it, and tried to earn it. She told me, 'Daddy, this afternoon, I gave my life to Jesus. I finally know *him.*' For that, Mrs. Thoresen, you have earned my undying gratitude."

Theo drew out his handkerchief and dabbed at his eyes. "I decided to pay you this call and bring you these flowers and chocolates anyway. To thank you. *To honor you.* You have done our community a great service with these meetings. I am, personally, indebted to you and I . . . I hope you will consider me a friend."

Rose hardly knew what to say, but the fragrance from the potted lilies called to her. She lifted the pot and raised a glossy bloom to her nose.

"A friend, yes. And the lilies smell heavenly. Thank you . . . Theo."

CHAPTER 24

Rose woke on Wednesday morning with a song in her heart. *These few weeks have been precious and full, Lord. And you have been present and active in all of them. Thank you. And thank you for this new day.*

She sat on the edge of her bed and gently stretched. She stood and stretched a little more.

Why, I believe I am strong again. Fully recovered from that nasty cold. Thank you for restoring my health, Lord God . . . for I have things to do this day.

She dressed and went in search of her morning coffee.

"Top o' the morn, Mama," Meg called to her.

"Aye, and a grrrand one 'tis bein'," Rose tossed back.

"Why, what do me ears be hearing? 'Tis a foine Irish lilt you have, Miss Rose O'Thoresen."

Rose laughed and piled it on even thicker. "Lairned frrrooom the best, I'm thinkin'."

Meg grinned. Rose reached her arms around Meg, and they hugged.

"Oh, Mama. What a joy 'tis, havin' you here w' us."

"It is pure pleasure for me, Meg. You know that."

"Ist the day ahead filled w' plans?"

"No, my day is free. This morning, I thought I would help you clean."

Meg, with a smile curving her lips, said, "We were to be havin' lunch in town yesterday, but got a wee bit sidetracked. Would t'day be workin' for you?"

"My, yes. That would be lovely. Yes, indeed."

"My treat, then."

"No, if you recall, *I* invited *you*."

"*Nay*, 'tis bein' *my* honor," Meg insisted.

When nothing Rose said could change Meg's mind, she gave up. Or did she?

While Meg went out to the chicken coops to collect eggs, Rose finished her coffee. When Meg returned, Rose was hard at work cleaning the living room. By the time Meg rang the bell for breakfast, Rose had swept the living room carpets, walls, and curtains, dust mopped the floor and baseboards, and polished the furniture.

After breakfast and devotions, Meg made Søren's lunch and began early preparations for dinner. Rose turned her attention to cleaning out the living room's wood stove, scooping out its ashes then wiping down and blacking the stove's exterior. She stepped away to regard the shine on the stove.

She was pleased with the results. "It has been a few years since I have cleaned a stove, but I have not lost the knack."

Rose looked to her bedroom next, sweeping the walls and curtains, dust mopping the floor, and polishing the furniture, after which she washed the kitchen windows, wiped down the table and benches, and swept the floor, working around Meg as she finished preparing Søren's lunch, placing it on the back of the propane stove, and covering it with a clean tea towel.

Meg laughed at Rose's cheerful spate of energy. "Mama Rose, 'tis makin' me head spin you are."

"I am working up an appetite, Meg, so that I might treat us to dessert after lunch."

Meg snorted. "You shall do no sech thing. I will be payin' and that is that." She then chuckled. "But I grant you respect for the tryin'."

AN HOUR LATER, Rose and Meg left for town. They had fixed their hair for a second time that day, donned fresh dresses, and were in fine humor.

"'Tis early we are for the noon meal. Shall we be payin' a visit to Esther and Ava's shop?"

The little café, the only place to eat in town since Mrs. Owen's boardinghouse had closed a decade past, was two doors down from Esther and Ava's shop.

"I would like that, Meg."

A bell on the shop door tinkled pleasantly, and Esther stood as they entered.

"Why, Miss Rose and Meg! What a welcome surprise."

When a toddler with shimmering gold hair ran out from behind Esther and halted, studying Meg and Rose with large blue eyes, Rose was the one surprised.

"Hello. Who have we here?"

"Our son, Brian. He is a year and three months now. We came to the house the evening Fiona passed, but I think you had too much on your mind to take in all the family that had gathered there." She touched the top of the boy's head. "Brian, Love, will you say hello?"

Little Brian grasped hold of Esther's skirts, but stared without fear at Rose and Meg.

"'Lo," he whispered.

Rose clapped her hands. "And you have named him for his grandfather? Wonderful. Fiona must have been so pleased."

At that, Brian wobbled over to Rose, still staring at her with interest. She bent down and took his little hand. "I am pleased to make your acquaintance, young Brian McKennie."

He grinned, then succumbed to a fit of shyness and flew back to his mother's skirts.

Rose smiled. "How precious he is."

Meg said to Esther, "'Tis comin' to town for lunch we are, and Mama Rose hast no' seen your shop."

"I would enjoy showing you our latest acquisitions, Miss Rose. Will you come see what I have in your size?"

"Oh, my. I apologize, but I am afraid I cannot afford to purchase anything today—even though I realize how sorely in need of a new wardrobe I am."

"Perhaps we can prepare you to shop in Chicago—not that anything we have in our humble business could compare to the stores in that great city. However, I could show you what you might wish to look for when you are ready to buy something new."

"Well, all right. Yes. That *would* be helpful. I confess to being terribly out of vogue these days."

Esther seemed to have figured Rose's size merely by looking her up and down. She lifted a skirt and matching jacket from one of the round racks in the shop.

"I think this would be lovely on you, Miss Rose. Come stand in front of the mirror while I hold them up to you."

Rose watched as her brown pinstriped skirt disappeared behind a forest-green one. A pleat of spring-green plaid peeped from the skirt. Bisque-colored piping trimmed the pleat, and spring-green buttons followed the line of piping.

"Hold the skirt just there, if you please, Miss Rose."

Esther then held the matching jacket before Rose. It, too, was forest green with piping in bisque and cuffs of matching spring-green plaid.

She pronounced her judgment. "Stunning, Miss Rose. Perfectly suited to your coloring, too."

The image in the mirror dazzled Rose. "It . . . it is not too young for me, do you think?"

"Not at all." Esther reached into the rack and pulled out another garment. Held it up to the jacket. "This blouse, a shade lighter than the piping, and set with the exact same buttons as the skirt and jacket, completes the look."

Meg stood behind Rose and gazed into the mirror. "Aye, Mama. 'Tis glorious on you."

"I-I will certainly bear it in mind when I next go shopping," Rose whispered. She did not move, however. In fact, she found herself wanting the ensemble. Badly.

But I have only pocket change with me, nor do I have much remaining in my savings. Ah well. All to thee, my precious Savior. I surrender all.

She smiled into the mirror, again content with what she already had. "Thank you, Esther. I perceive how your shop has succeeded so well here." She turned to Meg. "Is it time for lunch now?"

Esther glanced at a clock behind the counter. "Ten past noon. Yes, the café is open now. I believe Connor is serving roast pheasant today."

Rose blinked. "Connor?"

Esther's gentle laugh was as pleasant as the tinkling bell over the door. "You did not know? We own the café, too, Connor and I. He manages it and does the cooking, often providing wild game for the menu—turkey, pheasant, duck, goose. Whatever is in season. Connor's niece, Kayleigh, does the serving."

"You are a born businesswoman, Esther."

Rose was recalling the young blond with midnight blue eyes who had tossed her beautiful head and declined to move to Denver with Rose and Joy—and had then pilfered every object of value from Corinth's two houses of ill-repute in order to stock her own high-class brothel in Denver.

"God has blessed the work of our hands, Miss Rose . . . now that our hands belong to him."

When Esther smiled, Rose realized that the woman knew *exactly* what Rose had been remembering.

She smiled back, took Esther's hands in hers, and gently pressed them. "He certainly has. I am beyond proud of you, Esther. To God be the glory."

"Amen. To him be all the glory," Esther whispered.

THEY RETURNED TO the house after a long, leisurely lunch. Connor had plied them with every delicacy he had on hand: tender roast pheasant seasoned with fresh sage, braised potatoes and turnips, piping hot dinner rolls, followed by coffee and cake with buttercream frosting.

"I will no' be eating supper this evenin'," Meg groaned on the drive home.

"Nor I," Rose agreed. "My, but Connor is a good cook."

She thought for a moment. "Did you truly think the ensemble Esther showed me was appropriate for a woman my age?"

"Eh? Aye, that I did. Esther can be makin' no mistakes when it comes to fashion."

Lord, I am certain you will help me refresh my wardrobe when it is time. All to thee, my precious Savior. I surrender all.

Meg changed her clothes, put on a clean apron, and started a pie for the evening meal—a pie intended only for Søren. Neither Meg nor Rose would be touching it.

Rose, too, changed out of her nice clothes, donning one of her simple housedresses. She replaced her good brown shoes with her boots. When she had buttoned them up her ankles, she was ready.

She took in the time, nearly half past three o'clock. "I am going to walk off some of my lunch, then I will be across the creek, Meg, should you need me. I shall be back before dark."

She stepped off the porch and bypassed Meg's garden, then began the climb through the apple orchard, up the slope to the family cemetery. She took her time, stopping twice to ease the stitch in her side.

I will not hurry. No need.

When she opened the wrought iron gate, she was less out of breath for taking her time than on her previous visit. Slowly, she walked around the plot of ground set aside for the family. Near the back there was still plenty of open space.

She nodded to herself, then returned to the front and sat down on the bench. Stared fondly at the headstones before her. Karl. Amalie. Elli. Jan. Kristen.

Back to Elli.

I know you do not hear me, Elli, but I want to say that you have a fine son. I am blessed to have him in my life. Honored to call him son, too.

She shifted her eyes to Jan's stone, then got up, surprised at how her hips complained.

You did clean half of Meg's house this morning, Rose Thoresen. When was the last time you did such strenuous work?

She chuckled as she edged toward Jan's grave. "I suppose I may have overdone it a bit."

Sighing, she touched the name on the stone. Traced the letters with her fingers: *Jan Arvid Thoresen.*

"I will see you again, Jan, before the throne of our great and holy God. It won't be terribly long now. Oh, what a day that will be!"

Her back straight, Rose closed the gate behind her and walked carefully down the slope. When she reached the bottom, she kept walking until she had crossed the bridge, until she reached her little house.

She did not go inside, choosing instead to sit on the porch steps and see with the eyes of her memories.

Joy was six, I think, when we allowed her to ride Prince by herself. She would climb the porch, with Prince waiting patiently in my flowerbeds, stomping down whatever tried to grow there. Then she would climb over the railing and throw herself onto Prince's bare back. Dear, gentle Prince.

Joy knew the limits her papa had placed on their sojourns, and she did not stray from them. Up and down the creekbank they would go together, just wandering, not racing. That is, unless I had called her to dinner, and she was late.

Prince was often her companion during the long, hot days of summer. When the creek was low, they would wade together in its cool waters, passing those idyllic afternoons together.

Rose heard Joy's girlish voice echoing on the breeze, "*Mama! Come wade in the creek with us!*"

I often did, too, she recalled, *putting off my chores, choosing to spend time with my daughter instead.*

Rose glanced up and saw movement on the road coming off the bluff. Someone walking this way. She shaded her eyes. After a moment, the movement resolved.

It was a girl.

Momentarily, Rose was confused. "Joy?"

From a distance, the girl saw Rose sitting on the porch steps and waved. Then she ran, stretching her long legs, laughing as she raced down the hill toward the bridge.

"Silly woman. It is Lucy."

Rose's heart gladdened when she recognized her great-grandniece. *I have left something undone. How good of her to remind me before I leave.*

"My dear girl. Did you walk all the way from home?"

"Yes. Papa could not bring me, so I came under my own steam."

"But, did you come all this way just to see me?"

Lucy grinned. "It isn't terribly far . . . and you're worth it."

Rose put her arm around Lucy's shoulder and squeezed. "That is the nicest thing anyone has said to me all day, my dear."

"Well, you are going away, day after tomorrow, and I just . . . I just wanted one more of our little homestead talks. That is, if . . . if you don't mind?"

"Mind? Not at all. I was thinking of you anyway."

"You were? Truly?"

"Truly. And I have something to give you. That is, if you would care to have it. Afterward, after I show you, do not let me forget that I also have a few questions for you."

"I will remind you," Lucy said. "What is it you want to give me?"

She looked expectant, so Rose offered her hand. "If you will help me up, I will show you."

They walked into Rose's house and immediately took their seats in the two old rickety chairs, as comfortable with each other as with old, cozy slippers.

"Have I told you about this stove, Lucy?"

"You mean about the snakes?"

"No, no. The snakes were in my old stove, not this one. This stove, actually, has a wonderful provenance."

"Provenance?"

"At last! A word you do not know," Rose teased Lucy. "Provenance means history of ownership. You see, this little beauty belonged first to Søren's mother, Elli. She brought it with her all the way from Norway to America. It was a gift from her parents."

Rose dropped momentarily into her own thoughts. "I wonder if her mother and father knew it would be the last time they would ever see their daughter?"

She shook her head. "Søren was fourteen when his mother died. Elli, Karl, and Kristen died in the same year, leaving Jan a widower and Amalie a widow. Amalie then cooked on this stove until Little Karl—I mean your grandfather—had grown up, built his own house, and Amalie had moved into it with him.

"Later, Meg and Søren bought a larger propane stove and gave this one to Jon and Camille. That is how it came to be here."

Lucy looked from Rose to the stove and back and wrinkled her nose. "Little beauty?"

Rose smiled, "I confess that it has seen better days, but when I first saw it, it *was* beautiful. The enamel was clean and bright without any chips, all the tiles on the doors were intact, so colorful and pretty. I loved this stove."

Lucy glanced at it again and frowned. "If you say so."

"Well, when I arrived here a few weeks back, imagine my surprise to find Elli and Amalie's pretty little stove here. I reminded Meg that it had come on the ship from Norway to America, that it is part of this family's history. I suggested that we find someone in the family to take it in hand. Restore it to its previous condition."

Lucy again frowned. Her eyes on the stove this time were considering. "Could it be? Fixed up, I mean."

"I think your grandfather would think so."

Lucy looked at Rose. "Why do you think that?"

"Because he grew up watching his mother cook on it . . . and because I would like to give you this stove, Lucy. I would like you to consider restoring it and keeping it for the family."

Lucy, for the first time in Rose's acquaintance, was at a loss for words. "I . . ."

She now stared at Rose. "Are you saying it is yours to give?"

Rose nodded. "Legally, because it belonged to Elli, I suppose it passed to Søren, and he gave it to Jon. However, since Jon left it here in my house to rust away, I asked Søren if I could give it to you. He said yes."

"He said yes?"

Rose again nodded. "I believe your grandfather would help you with the restoration. It would be something the two of you could do together."

Lucy said nothing. Then she was in Rose's arms. Weeping. "Thank you, Aunt Rose. Thank you. I . . . it will always be mine?"

"Yes, Lucy."

"It will remind me of *you*, Aunt Rose."

"Yes, dear girl. It will hold your memories—your *good* memories—of this year. Long after I am gone."

"Yes," Lucy sniffled. "Good memories."

Pride of ownership is a powerful thing.

Lucy slid her eyes toward the stove. Still sniffling, she got up and studied it with new eyes. "I know a lady who makes tiles. I wonder if she would make some like these for us."

"A good place to start. You may use this house as long as you like while you work on the restoration."

Lucy turned to her. "Thank you, Aunt Rose. This means a lot to me."

"Good. I am glad."

"Oh. And you said not to let you forget the questions you wanted to ask me.

"Ah, yes. Thank you. Perhaps you might sit down again? You see, I was thinking last night how you tried to take Adele away from your home to keep her safe from . . . that man."

Lucy plunked down on the chair and nodded. "I don't know where I would have taken her, actually. And now, looking back on it, it is hard to remember what I was thinking." She shrugged her shoulders while shaking her head. "Most of it is all a muddle in there, in my head."

"I understand. I think . . . I think it not unusual to go through a difficult, distressing experience and feel that way."

"Muddled, you mean? Like a ball of string all knotted and twisted up together?"

"Yes, like that exactly."

"So . . . I shouldn't be worried that I cannot remember everything right?"

"Perhaps, in a little while, your thoughts will untangle all by themselves or as you talk about them with someone you can trust, say, Ava or Esther. You may feel a bit of anxiety as you talk or as your memories come clear, but if you are patient with yourself, and tell the Lord that you trust him, I do believe he will steer you through it. Do not rush. Trust him to help you."

Lucy exhaled. "That is a relief to hear. I mean, I am relieved every day that *he* is gone, that Papa and Mama understand and have forgiven me my horrible behavior, but sometimes . . . sometimes I am scared to go in thc barn by myself. My head knows he cannot be there, but I get all jiggly inside and can't quite breathe."

"That is the anxiety I mentioned, Lucy.

"I don't like it."

"No, I do not expect you do. Tell me, Lucy, did you pray when that man threatened you? Did you call out to the Lord for help?"

"Yes. That is, at first I did. After a while, I stopped because . . . he wasn't answering me." She looked up, guilt written across her face. "Is it wrong to say that?"

"Is it wrong to say he wasn't answering you?"

"Yes."

"Tell me something first."

"Okay."

"Did he, eventually, answer your prayers?"

Lucy's brows lifted. "Ohhh."

"Hmm?"

"But . . . well, I mean, when everyone was talking about you and Joy coming for a visit, I didn't want you to come. I got pretty angry about it."

"With me? For no real reason?"

Lucy sighed and stared down. "Yeah."

She sighed again. "I mean, yes, Aunt Rose. I . . . I *am* sorry, you know."

"Of course I know. Water under the bridge. We are talking about how God answered your prayers—in the time and manner of his choosing. So, Lucia Amalie Thoresen, would you like to hear something amazing?"

Lucy, her guilty expression unchanged, nodded. "Yes, Aunt Rose."

"Do you recall the first Sunday the O'Dells and I were in town? That morning when you and I spoke after church."

"Yes'm."

"We sang a song during the service. *I Surrender All.*

Lucy mumbled under her breath.

"What was that?"

Another heavy sigh. "I said, I despise that song."

Rose laughed aloud. "Oh my, yes. I know what you mean."

"You do?"

"Certainly. When we sing that song, the Lord asks us to surrender everything, yes? But we cannot even *list* what 'everything' means let alone surrender it. Why, I have sung that hymn hundreds of times through the years, and each and every time I do, I am convicted of something else I have not yet given over to him. Also, it is not uncommon for that 'thing' to be something I didn't even realize was in me."

"You? But . . . I don't understand."

"Let me tell you something, Lucy Thoresen. Not one of us knows his or her heart. The Bible tells us *the heart is deceitful above all things, and desperately wicked: who can know it?* That is a rhetorical question, of course. We do not know our own heart. Only God does.

"Our heart—that is our will, emotions, desires, feelings, thoughts, and so on—our heart *hides* things from us. It hides how ugly we are inside until Jesus saves us and begins to clean us up. And just to be clear? That cleaning-up process is not a one-time event. It takes the Holy Spirit a lifetime to sanctify us wholly, body, soul, and spirit, prompting us to work out our salvation one inch of crucified flesh at a time.

"This is why, Lucy, whenever that hymn asks us to 'surrender all,' we are to respond. We are to respond and give over to him *all that we know to give him*. Yes, we yield the specific things of which he convicts us, but we also yield our entire being—trusting that whatever is hiding within our flesh is included in the 'all' that we give him. Step by step, surrender by surrender, he changes us. Does that make sense, dear?"

Lucy said slowly, "I think that being a Christian is a very hard thing."

Rose took Lucy's chin in her hand and turned the girl's eyes to her own. "*Life* is hard, Lucy Thoresen. Growing up is hard. Taking responsibility for our lives is hard. Getting married and raising a family is hard. Being a Christian is also hard, but just try doing all those other things without Jesus? Now, *that* is truly hard. Hear me, Lucy: Following Jesus is the *best* most hard thing you will ever do, and *it is worth it*. Count the cost now, child. Whatever he asks of you, it is worth it, I promise you."

When Lucy remained quiet, Rose said to her, "I brought up that hymn for a purpose. While I was singing it, the Lord asked me yet again to surrender all to him, but on that day, I did not feel the necessity of it. You see, my family thought I needed a rest. A vacation they call it. 'You have been working too hard,' they told me. 'Have fun. Relax.'

"Well, let me tell you, my flesh thought that was an excellent idea—except that was not at all what *Jesus* wished of me. When I realized that he, during that hymn, was asking something particular of me, I finally said, 'Yes, Lord. I will surrender to you. Whatever you ask of me, I will do it.'"

Lucy was watching her. Studying her. "What did he ask of you, Aunt Rose?"

Rose became even more serious. "He said one word to me." She drew a breath. "He said . . . *Lucy*."

Lucy began to tremble. "H-he did? He said my name to you? Are you sure?"

"Yes, dear."

"He . . . *God* told you my name? You aren't joshing me? Having me on again?"

Rose shook her head. "No. I would not make light of such a divine assignment. After church that day, I sent Joy to ask Karl and Sonja to come back inside. Then, I cornered you. I dared you to come meet me here, in this house. And over the past few weeks, the Lord has been faithful to show us, by his Spirit, what was going on.

"What I am saying is that *he heard you*, Lucy. The Lord heard your prayers, and he mustered the forces necessary to deliver you—and others—from the control of that wicked man."

Rose folded her hands in her lap. "So, what do you think about that song now?"

Lucy licked her lips. "You said following Jesus is the best most hard thing I would ever do. But you said it is worth it."

"I did. It is."

Lucy chewed her lip. Drew in a breath and blew it out. "Okay. I'll do it. That 'surrender all' thing."

Rose felt her heart leap for joy, and she smiled. "Good girl. Shall we pray? I . . . think I can manage to kneel down on these bare boards if I try."

Lucy touched Rose's arm. "I will help you up, Aunt Rose . . . after we have finished."

CHAPTER 25

Rose sat at Meg's kitchen table, joined by Meg, Vera, Esther, and Ava. They sipped tea and enjoyed Meg's freshly made peach cobbler, but they relished their fellowship even more.

It was Rose's last day in RiverBend.

She heaved a sigh. *What better way could I spend this day? Thank you, Lord, for such loving, godly friends.*

Vera slid her gaze around the table, a twinkle in her eyes. "Through the various members of our congregation, I often have occasion to hear the heartbeat of this community." A smile tugged at her mouth. "I liken it to the drums of restless natives talking across the jungle or smoke signals sent from mountaintop to mountaintop."

Esther pursed her lips. "Sooo, what you are saying is that the county's gossip train stops regularly at your house?"

Rose's mouth dropped open—just as Vera, Esther, Meg, and Ava cut up.

Vera, laughing so heartily that her eyes watered, finally replied, "Some cars on that train have made our home a regular destination on their route. Truly, I have been obliged to ask our worst gossipmongers to join me in prayer over the salacious stories they persist on bringing to me. I have found it an effective means of curtailing malicious talk: Bring your slander to my house, and you will end up on your knees."

The five women laughed and laughed. Wiping her eyes, Ava added, "Well, after that train leaves your station, it frequently rolls into our shop. But you were saying?"

"Ah, yes. What I have heard—from five individuals now—is that our community is positively rife with broken engagements and the severance of ongoing courtships. The 'blame' for this phenomenon, if one is to ascribe blame for it, has been repeatedly and decidedly laid at your feet, Rose Thoresen."

Rose was astounded. "What? Me? How am I responsible for broken engagements?"

Ava nodded. "Quite so. It seems that the seeds you sowed last Sunday afternoon fell upon fertile ground, took root, sprang up, and bore the fruit of sundry earnest conversations . . . or might we term them *inquisitions?*"

Esther took Ava's drawing a breath as leave to interject her own information. "Put plainly, our young ladies are demanding that their fiancés or gentlemen callers articulate their spiritual convictions—and the young ladies who have found lack in those convictions have placed their engagements 'on hold' or called them off altogether. Why, I heard—"

"For shame, Esther." Ava interrupted. "*I* was speaking."

Esther and Ava laughed at each other, and Esther said for Rose's benefit, "This is what ensues when two women share a business. We talk over each other—"

"And finish the other's sentences," Ava added.

"Yes, precisely. Why—"

Vera held out her hand in that universal signal for "halt." "Perhaps *I* should finish what I began?"

She said to Rose, "What we have heard is that the young Christian ladies of our community have arrived at a general consensus. They have decided that they will no longer receive a gentleman caller whose Christian life is not demonstrably evident and long-lived."

Vera tried to keep a straight face as she added, "Why, we have even heard that that certain disreputable young gents of the county have considered pooling their cash resources to commission the printing of wanted posters—posters with your likeness on them."

"Merciful heavens," Rose breathed.

"Isn't it wonderful?" Vera grinned. "Our younger sisters are scrutinizing *their own* walks with the Lord—and, I must say, some of them need to, for they themselves have been lacking in purity of heart and body. The three of us have received visits from their earnest young ranks asking what they can do to turn around, to renew their walk with the Lord and grow in their faith."

"As a result," Ava put in, "We are forming a young ladies' Bible study and Helps Committee—"

"Which I will lead temporarily," Esther interrupted, "until we raise up leadership within the committee itself. Ava and I have a burden to train the next generation of women to see needs in our community and step in to meet them without waiting on the married women. You know, needs such as caring for the children of new mothers or cleaning house for those who are sick, organizing used clothing drives, and—"

Ava smoothly slipped in, "and volunteering to assist in our church's Sunday School classes for children, even undertaking to teach the lessons."

"Oh my, but this is all *wonderful*," Rose exclaimed.

"Tell that to the rebuffed young men nursing their recent rejections." Ava said it lightheartedly, but her words held a note of gravity.

"I expect that is where we shall come in," Meg said.

Rose turned to her. "Oh?"

"Søren and I talked it over last evening . . . after Pastor Medford telephoned and explained precisely what Vera, Ava, and Esther have been saying. Do you remember the weekly meetings Jan used to hold?"

"Most certainly. I garnered many means of teaching the word by listening to Jan share Scripture with the boys and young men who ate with us once a week and stayed to study the word together."

"Well, Søren decided last night to take up his father's mantle. Yes, he acknowledges that he has waited far too long to do so, but now it is time to begin what he has, up until the present, put off. He will follow the pattern his father used: Invite the single men of the neighborhood to sup with us, then adjourn to our living room to open the Bible and learn from it."

"Oh, Meg!" Rose was near to tears.

"I know. 'Tis quite *beyond* wonderful. An answer to my prayers."

The five women looked around the table at each other. Without a word, they joined hands.

Vera prayed, "Lord, you have opened up heaven and poured out your Spirit upon this community. We give you *great* praise from our humble hearts. We put our hands to the plow to do your work, declaring that what has begun is *your* doing, and it is marvelous in our eyes.

"Please lead us and guide us as we teach and counsel these young men and women in your ways. To you be all the praise and glory and honor, in heaven and on earth. These things we pray in the holy and mighty name of your Son, Jesus, our Savior. Amen.

Four voices echoed, "Amen."

After a moment's reflection, Vera said, "I suppose we should say farewells to you now, Rose. You did ask that none of us accompany you to the station tomorrow to see you off, and we will honor your request."

"This is better, I think," Rose murmured.

They got up from the table. Esther and Ava took turns hugging Rose. Then she gathered them in her arms and whispered to them both,

"I am so proud of the godly women you have become."

Esther whispered back, "We're a far cry from the high-dollar whores who turned down your offer to move to Denver and, instead, declared that they would go their own way."

"Yes, a far cry. It only proves that God's grace can travel any distance and reach any heart."

She held them tighter. "Tell this community about Jesus, Esther. *Tell them*, Ava. And bind up the wounds of the brokenhearted—our Lucy and our Hester."

Esther sobbed, "We will. We promise."

"Yes, we promise, Miss Rose," Ava said.

She kissed them both on their cheeks. "The Lord bless and keep you."

Vera then embraced Rose and they stayed locked in that embrace until Vera asked, her voice choked with emotion, "Will you ever come back to us, Rose? Come back to RiverBend?"

Rose smiled through her tears. "Yes, I believe I will. Someday . . . God willing."

CHAPTER 26

Rose was packed. Her trunk, her two suitcases, and the sturdy box holding Joy's childhood memorabilia were ready. Her valise and handbag waited on the bed. She checked her hair in the mirror and frowned. But only for an instant.

Then she laughed at her reflection. "When did you get so old, Rose Thoresen? Why, look at that gray hair and all those wrinkles. And what is that cackling I hear?"

She smiled into the mirror. "And when did you decide to become *spunky* old Aunt Rose, the one who relishes teasing the youngsters of the family? Where has *that* woman been hiding all these years?"

She stared more critically. "Hmm. Could these creases be laugh lines in disguise rather than wrinkles? Yes, I declare it so! From here forward, you are *laugh lines.* The Lord has given me a merry heart, and I will not be afraid for my face to demonstrate my joy."

She pinned a cameo brooch to her neckline and patted her hair a last time. "Goodness, I have been away from the responsibilities of Palmer House near on to four weeks, and now I scarcely recognize who I am."

She cocked her head. "But I do believe I like this different Rose. I shall endeavor to know her better."

A knock at the door interrupted her.

"Come in."

Meg opened the door and peered around it. "Are you needing any help, Mama?"

"Thank you, dear Meg, but I believe I am ready." Rose glanced around the room. "I hope I have tidied up enough. You and Søren will have your room back tonight—I am certain you have missed it. You have my great thanks for your selflessness, for saving me from climbing those stairs."

Meg stepped over the threshold into the room. "Sure, and if I am bein' truthful, Mama, 'tis with gladness I would be givin' up this room for good if it meant havin' you here with us always. As would Søren."

"Be careful what you ask for, Meg."

"Aye. That I am, Mama."

SØREN AND JON loaded Rose's trunk, suitcases, and the box of memorabilia into the farm's truck, then Jon headed into town ahead of them.

"Are you ready, Mama?" Søren asked.

Rose wandered around the kitchen, touching the table, running her fingertips across the lovely rosemåling that adorned the shelves. "I suppose I am. No—wait a moment, if you please."

She walked into the living room and stared at the array of photographs across the wall, then at Jan's face. She touched the glass over his lips. *Thank you, my love, for making me part of your family.*

With her heart composed, she returned to the kitchen. "I am ready now."

"And I will be with you both shortly," Meg promised.

Søren and Rose left by the back door, and Søren helped Rose into his automobile's front seat. He went around to the driver's side and started the engine.

MEG GLANCED THROUGH the window, then picked up the telephone's receiver and spoke to the switchboard operator. "Sure, and we are a-comin'."

"I will pass the word, Mrs. Thoresen."

Meg hung up and went out the door and down the steps to the car.

ACROSS THE BRIDGE Søren drove, gunning the engine for the climb up the bluff. Rose pressed her face to the window, keeping sight of her little house until it disappeared from view. Unbidden, tears dripped from her cheeks. She lifted a handkerchief to her eyes but found it unequal to the task of stemming her anguish.

Wordlessly, Meg handed Rose her own clean hankie.

Rose was still wiping her eyes as they drew abreast of Brian and Fiona's house, now Martha and Robert's house and land. She let the hand holding the hankie drop into her lap and stared.

"But . . . what is that?"

Martha and her husband stood at the end of their drive near the road's edge. With them were their children and grandchildren. They saw the car coming toward them and began to wave. Søren lowered his window and slowed the automobile. Martha and Robert's family waved and blew kisses through the window as the car passed.

"Goodbye!"

"We love you!"

"Safe travels!"

Rose lifted the hankie to them all and waved it their way. Søren sped up and continued toward town.

She sat back. "Oh my. How utterly precious. Do thank them for me, Meg, please?"

"Aye, that I will."

Soon Søren turned onto the road that led into town. They approached the church and parsonage.

"Look, Mama," Søren said softly.

Jacob and Vera waved to them from the edge of the road where it fronted the church's lot. And from the field behind the church, RiverBend's school children streamed toward the road. Two girls already stood along the roadside, holding a sheet of butcher paper between them.

Rose gaped. "Why . . . is that Hester and Emma? And *their parents?*"

"Hmm. I think it is, and everyone in their class," Meg murmured.

Emma and Hester held up the paper. On it, a sign had been painted in large watercolor letters.

GOODBYE, MRS. THORESEN
COME BACK TO US SOON,
ROSE OF RIVERBEND

Søren, grinning like a kid, again slowed and rolled down his window. Rose leaned over him to wave Meg's hankie and smile, but her eyes were overflowing.

"We love you, Mrs. Thoresen!" Emma and Hester shouted together.

Their classmates waved enthusiastically, too. She recognized a number of them as being grandchildren to Søren and Meg, Karl and Sonja, and Fiona and Brian.

"Goodness. Are all of RiverBend's children related to each other?"

"The McKennies and Thoresens are bein' like the stars in the sky and the sand on the seashore," Meg replied with a straight face.

Minutes later, they rolled into the town proper, and there, on the sidewalk to their right waited Esther, Connor, and little Brian along with Ava and her daughters—joined by other shopkeepers and customers, all waving and shouting their goodbyes.

"But I don't understand," Rose whispered. "All this fuss . . ."

"You made everyone promise not to say goodbye at the train. We keep our promises."

"Lord have mercy on me," Rose breathed.

"His mercies endure forever," Søren replied, grinning.

They arrived shortly at RiverBend's simple "station," the siding where both passengers and freight were loaded onto the train. Jon and Jeremy had already unloaded Rose's luggage from the truck and were loading it onto the baggage car under the supervision of the conductor.

Søren again helped Rose from the car. He collected her coat, handbag, and valise.

"Is this everything, Mama?"

"Yes, dear Søren."

As requested, no one else came to see Rose off . . . except Lucy, Einar, and Norrie. Einar carried a wide pasteboard box under his arm.

"The train leaves in five minutes, Mama. You will need to make these goodbyes quick."

"I know. Spare me one minute, please."

"Aunt Rose," Lucy said softly.

"Lucy, dear girl. I hate messy goodbyes."

"I know. Meg told me . . . but, I wanted to say thank you. Thank you for all you did to help me. And Hester. All of us."

She fumbled her words a little. "I have something for you."

"From us," Einar said. "A token of our deep gratitude."

Einar handed Lucy the box. She handed the box to Rose. "Will you open it now? I want to know that you are pleased by it."

Søren shuffled his feet. "Mama?"

"One more minute, Son."

Meg held the box while Rose slipped off the lid. She gently unfolded the layers of tissue paper. She saw . . . forest-green fabric, spring-green plaid, and a line of bright green buttons.

"Oh, Lucy. And Einar, Norrie, what have you done? This is too much. I—"

"You will take it, Aunt Rose, and you will wear it, and you *will* enjoy it," Einar demanded. "You saved our Lucy—please, *take the dress!*"

"I . . . Yes. All right. Thank you. It is so beautiful." She looked around, and her eyes landed on Meg. "You. You planned this. You and Esther, you—"

"No, Aunt Rose," Lucy said, pride shining through her declaration. "*I* planned it. It was *my* idea for Meg to take you to Esther and Ava's shop and for Esther to show you the dress."

She laughed. "They were all my coconspirators. Of course, you will also need a new hat, a smart one, picked especially for this dress. I mean, that old felt thing you are wearing? It won't do for a stylish ensemble like this one."

Rose stared down her nose at Lucy. She pursed her lips and frowned.

Lucy deflated under Rose's inspection. She began to fidget and appear uncertain.

Rose sniffed. "*Lucy Thoresen.*" Frost coated her words.

The girl *thought* there was a chance that Rose was teasing her, but she was not completely convinced. Her voice was small and meek when she answered, "Yes, Aunt Rose?"

A tiny smile cracked Rose's stern demeanor. "Well done. *Very well done*, indeed, Lucy."

Lucy huffed and exclaimed, "Again. You did it again!"

Rose clasped Lucy in her arms. "I tease those I love, Lucy girl. And you are *very* loved."

Lucy sobbed within Rose's embrace, "Oh, Aunt Rose! How I love you, too."

"Aaaaall aboard! "Aaaaall aboard!"

Søren couldn't take any more. "Mama, you will miss your train if you do not get on right this minute."

"There are worse fates, Son," Rose laughed.

Søren grabbed Rose's coat, her handbag, and the dress box, and bundled Rose onto the train. He saw her into a seat then raced down the aisle and down the steps as the train shivered, jerked, and began to roll forward.

Rose stood at the window, staring out. She kissed her fingers to those watching her.

"Goodbye, my loved ones. Goodbye."

CHAPTER 27

Hours later, Rose's train stopped in Omaha where she changed over to an express line. Her train arrived in Chicago late that evening. A conductor on the station platform offered Rose his hand.

"May I be of assistance, madam?" He took her valise and the large pasteboard box and helped her navigate the steps.

Rose was a mite wobbly when her feet reached the platform, but she was standing on her own.

He released her hand and gave her back her belongings. "You have a good night, madam."

"Thank you for your kindness, sir."

He smiled and sketched a bow. "It was my pleasure."

He walked away leaving Rose on her own, where she was quickly enveloped in the cacophony of Dearborn Station (or Polk Street Depot as some called it). A crowd of passengers pushed through the train shed, moving toward the terminal, so many individuals, each one in a hurry to reach his or her destination.

Rose walked slowly forward, the dress box acting like a sail. She was unable to resist the rushing current of passengers sweeping her toward the terminal. *Dear me. I hope Joy and Edmund can find me in all this confusion.*

"Grandma!"

Rose halted and sought the source of the shout. *There.* She lifted her hand and waved. She shivered with excitement. *My babies.*

Edmund bulled his way toward her until he reached her side, and Rose, a smile wreathing her entire being, dumped the box and her valise in his arms. "Dear Edmund. Do please take these."

"Dear Mother," he grinned, drawing her away from the onrushing crowd, "I am so glad to see you. We have missed you terribly."

Was that moisture glimmering in his eyes?

Then she was surrounded by her grandsons, who clasped her legs and hung on her skirts, hugging her with all their small strength.

"Gramma! Gramma! Gramma!" Little Luke, his arms lifted for Rose to pick him up, melted into tears.

"Oh, my dear Luke. Don't cry, sweetheart. Grandma is here now."

"Up! Up!" he insisted—but Rose hesitated to lift the hefty little man on her own.

Edmund scooped Luke up in one arm and handed him to Rose. He promptly wrapped his chubby arms around her neck and planted a sloppy kiss on her cheek.

"See? Here I am, sweet Luke. I am so happy to see you all again."

Edmund took Luke back and motioned to Matthew and Jacob. "Boys, let your mother have a go now. Come stand by me, please."

The boys released Rose, and she saw her daughter, holding baby Roseanne, waiting her turn.

"Oh, my beautiful Joy! It is wonderful to see you, to be here with all of you." Rose embraced Joy, the baby sandwiched between them.

THE FOLLOWING DAY, after her first night in her new bedroom, Rose unpacked and arranged her clothes and belongings and listened for hours to her grandsons recount their recent adventures.

Later, when dinner was finished and when the children were tucked into their beds, the adults at last had time and opportunity to talk. Joy, O'Dell, and Rose sat together in the O'Dells' modest living room, sharing a cup of tea before retiring for the night.

"Did you find Pinkerton's Chicago office to your liking?" Rose asked O'Dell.

His dark eyes gleamed. "Quite to my satisfaction, Mother. Thank you for asking. I see opportunity for improvements in this city's Pinkerton presence, but it is enough for now that I and my agents are getting acquainted, that I am learning their particular skills and methods, and that work abounds for us at this present time."

Joy and O'Dell had many questions for Rose, too, regarding the nearly two weeks she remained behind in RiverBend after they departed.

"Were you able to help Lucy and Hester, Mama?"

"Oh yes. The Lord moved on their behalf, and I left them in good hands and good spirits. I have much to share with you. Quite wonderful things, in fact."

She began with Vera's call that Saturday evening, after the O'Dells had caught their train. She repeated how Vera had asked her to meet with the community's young women and their mothers. She shared what the Lord had done at that first meeting.

"It was a promising beginning, but I was terribly tired the next morning. Sadly, that was when Martha called us to say Fiona would not wake up."

"Fiona?" Joy whispered.

Rose nodded. "She passed away that evening without regaining consciousness. For that reason alone, I am glad that I stayed behind in RiverBend. Meg and I had stopped for a short visit the evening before, on our way home from the meeting.

"I can only describe it as one of those instances when the Holy Spirit prompts you to do something, and you discover why afterward. Had we not stopped, neither Meg nor I would have had opportunity to say goodbye to Fiona before she passed."

Rose smiled and did not mention the cold and fever she suffered for the remainder of the week. "However, our God had further purposes for keeping me in RiverBend after you left."

"Oh, yes? We are anxious to hear what happened."

"Well, the second meeting, the following Sunday afternoon, was more profound than the first.

"The Spirit of the Lord moved upon those young ladies in such a powerful manner, that I believe the face of that generation of RiverBend's community will be changed forever. I am convinced we will hear of many, *many* lives turned to Christ for his glory as a result.

"I heard just this past Thursday that Esther and Ava will be conducting Bible studies with these young women and growing a Helps committee strictly for the younger, unmarried women to manage and maintain. They will learn, under the tutelage of older women, to look for needs in the community and reach out in service to the Lord."

She bent her head, happy, and yet tears sparkled in her eyes. "And Joy? Your brother Søren is taking up your father's ministry."

"Søren? He will be calling the single men of the community to disciple them?"

"Yes. He and Meg will invite them to eat with them weekly. Afterward, Søren will lead the young men in prayer and study in God's word."

O'Dell shook his head. "Wow."

Joy sighed. "Oh, Mama. How marvelous!"

"Yes. I . . . I admit to being sorry to leave at such a juncture, for my heart was already fully invested in these young ladies."

Rose finished her tea and announced, "I remain weary from the train ride and the activity of the past days. I should retire now."

She stood up. "Good night, dear Edmund. Good night, my darling daughter."

Joy slowly set down her cup. "Mama?"

Rose glanced down. "Yes, Joy?"

"Are you . . . are you sorry you have moved to Chicago with us?"

Rose was surprised. She looked at Joy's question and turned it over in her mind. "No, dear. I am happy to be here with you and your family. I love you all dearly. Why, how could I leave my grandchildren? Or, for that matter, you and Edmund? You need my help, and I need your love and support. This is my place, Joy. Right here. For now."

"For now? Do you . . . do you consider leaving us . . . later?"

Again, Rose studied Joy's question, and she suddenly realized O'Dell was studying *her*, a grimace of pain hovering on his lips.

"No, Joy. I will not leave you and Edmund. Not, at the very least, for the foreseeable future. Perhaps . . . perhaps *much* later, when the children are older, I might return to RiverBend.

"Søren and Meg have made me understand that I would be welcome in their home, and I confess . . . that I should like to see the prairie again . . . before . . ."

Joy's voice cracked, "But Mama, we—"

"We should entrust our futures to the Lord, should we not? As I gave my life to him a long time ago, both my present and my future belong to him. Whatever his plans, I live in the assurance that they will glorify him. *For it is God which worketh in us both to will and to do of his good pleasure.* We should leave our worries and concerns in his capable hands, yes?"

O'Dell cleared his throat. "Yes. In his hands."

"Thank you, Edmund."

Rose bent over and placed a kiss on Joy's forehead. "Perhaps I can help you finish unpacking your trunks tomorrow."

"Thank you, Mama. You are such a blessing to us."

"Good night, then. I will see you in the morning. I cannot wait to hug all my grandchildren again and see what the Lord has in store for us."

She smiled. "What a wonderful day tomorrow will be!"

EPILOGUE

SPRING 1935

A rioting host of pink-and-white blossoms burst from the gnarled, straggling branches of the old apple orchard. And, from among the blooms, the tender, greening tips of unfurling leaves peered out, each one seeking the sun and its warmth. In every tree the ancient, cyclical battle played out—the glorious splendor of spring overcoming the barrenness of age and winter.

Those gathered within the sheltering bower of those trees recognized a further truth, an eternal one: Spring was nature's portrait of Christ's promised victory—resurrection life triumphing over death and decay.

A mound of freshly turned earth marked the tidy and unpretentious grave. The stone was already laid. The engraver, who had known Rose for more than half a century, had devoted sixteen continuous hours to its completion . . . so it would be ready on this day.

Joy and Edmund O'Dell waited beside the grave. Their three sons, young men each reaching for adulthood with both hands, waited solemnly with them. Joy and O'Dell's daughter, a tender bud herself, clung to her mother's hand. Søren and Meg stood across from them. Lucy Thoresen, now Lucy Gunderson, clutched her husband's arm and wept. Others gathered outside the wrought iron fence—every Thoresen in the county and many friends besides.

When it was time, Joy addressed those assembled around the little cemetery, "Last year, when Mama told us she was returning to RiverBend, we understood why she wished to go. She had spoken openly of the possibility over the years. She longed to return to her prairie home, to live out her last days near this very place where we are now gathered."

Joy drew in a composing breath. "We did not wish her to leave us, of course. We tried, at first, to keep her to ourselves. Quite selfishly, we hoped to talk her out of it, all the while couching our advice in terms of *her* good and not our own. The Lord knows how earnestly *we did try* . . . but we were wrong to hold her to us. After decades of giving herself to the needs of her family and friends, we realized her return to the prairie was what *she* needed.

"Following our last attempt to persuade her to stay with us, she only smiled and said, 'Now, dearest Joy and Edmund, please listen to me. I am leaving two weeks from tomorrow. I hope we can share some special times together before I go.'"

Joy laughed just a little. "I must tell you, if you did not already know this about my mother, that there was no changing Rose Thoresen's mind once it was made up. She was always gracious, but in her obedience to God she was also as immovable as a mountain."

A small, dark-haired woman replied in a gentle lilt, "Aye, we were a-knowin' thet about Rose," and a low murmur of agreement rippled across the crowd.

Joy smiled at Breona and her husband, Pastor Isaac Carmichael, then at those behind them. Her expression brightened as she acknowledged Sarah and Bryan Croft, Billy and Marit, Olive, and many of those who had lived at Palmer House, both past and present.

The woman standing beside Breona—she, her husband, and her children of Chinese ancestry—also answered Joy. "Rose's love and care drew many of us to Jesus, but it was her strength of will *in God* that saw us through to wholeness and maturity in him."

Joy smiled. "Just so, Mei-Xing, just so. Once she had heard from the Lord, nothing could deter her from answering his call. I saw this in her while I was growing up. Many of you saw it in her later, in Denver, when we established Palmer House, and as it grew and thrived.

"That is why, when she told us she believed the Lord had released her to return to RiverBend, we became convinced that we had no choice but to give her back . . . back to the prairie she loved."

Her gaze shifted to the stone at the head of the grave. "And thus, we are here today, saying goodbye . . . but not forever."

ROSE
Blake Brownlee Thoresen
1849–1935
Beloved Wife, Mother,
and Friend to Many
—I know that my Redeemer lives—

Joy wiped tears from her eyes, then turned and faced the family and friends who surrounded her, many of them the fruit of Rose's labor. "Thank you all for coming today. Some of you have traveled many miles to be here with us to celebrate Mama's homegoing."

She dabbed at her eyes. "Tabitha, I believe have something you wish to say?"

"Yes, Joy. Thank you." Tabitha joined by her daughter, Sally, now a young woman engaged to be married, faced their fellow mourners.

Tabitha lifted her chin and said, "I last spoke to Rose twelve years ago, the evening before she departed Denver. We knew the likelihood of meeting again on this earth was small, but I could not bear the thought. My final words to her were, 'Until we meet again?'

"I will never forget her answer. Rose smiled at me and said, 'On that great and glorious day, when we meet before the throne of grace. Until then, Tabitha.'"

Tabitha nodded to her daughter, and Sally placed a single pink rose bud on the grave's damp earth.

"For you, Grandma Rose," Sally whispered. "When you were leaving, you bid me remember, '*Grandma Rose loves you. I always will, even while I am away.*' Thank you. I have never forgotten. I know you love me still."

Tabitha caressed Sally's tear-stained cheek, looked a last time at the grave, then turned her gaze to the cloudless sky.

"On that great and glorious day, when we meet before the throne of grace. Until then, Rose."

THE END

Thank you, my dear and wonderful readers, for walking with me on the amazing journey that is *A Prairie Heritage*. I love and appreciate each of you.

To God be the glory, now and forever. Amen.

—VIKKI

About the Author

Vikki Kestell's passion for people and their stories is evident in her readers' affection for her characters and unusual plotlines. Two often-repeated sentiments are, "I feel like I know these people," and, "I'm right there, in the book, experiencing what the characters experience."

Vikki holds a PhD in organizational learning and instructional technologies. She left a career of twenty-plus years in government, academia, and corporate life to pursue writing full time. "Writing is the best job ever," she admits, "and the most demanding." Vikki and her husband, Conrad Smith, make their home in Albuquerque, New Mexico.

To stay abreast of new book releases, sign up for Vikki's newsletter on her website, **http://www.vikkikestell.com**, find her on Facebook at **http://www.facebook.com/TheWritingOfVikkiKestell**, or follow her on BookBub, **https://www.bookbub.com/authors/vikki-kestell**.

www.faith-filledfiction.com | www.vikkikestell.com

Made in the USA
Las Vegas, NV
13 September 2021